KEEPER OF SCALES

KEEPER OF SCALES

BOOK ONE OF THE TRIANID

ANNE MOLLOVA

ROSE LEAF PRESS

Keeper of Scales

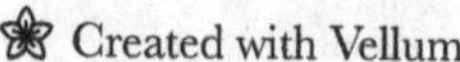 Created with Vellum

For Mom and Dad,
who taught me to believe in faeries.

ALSO BY ANNE MOLLOVA

Slayer of Monsters

Seer of Strands

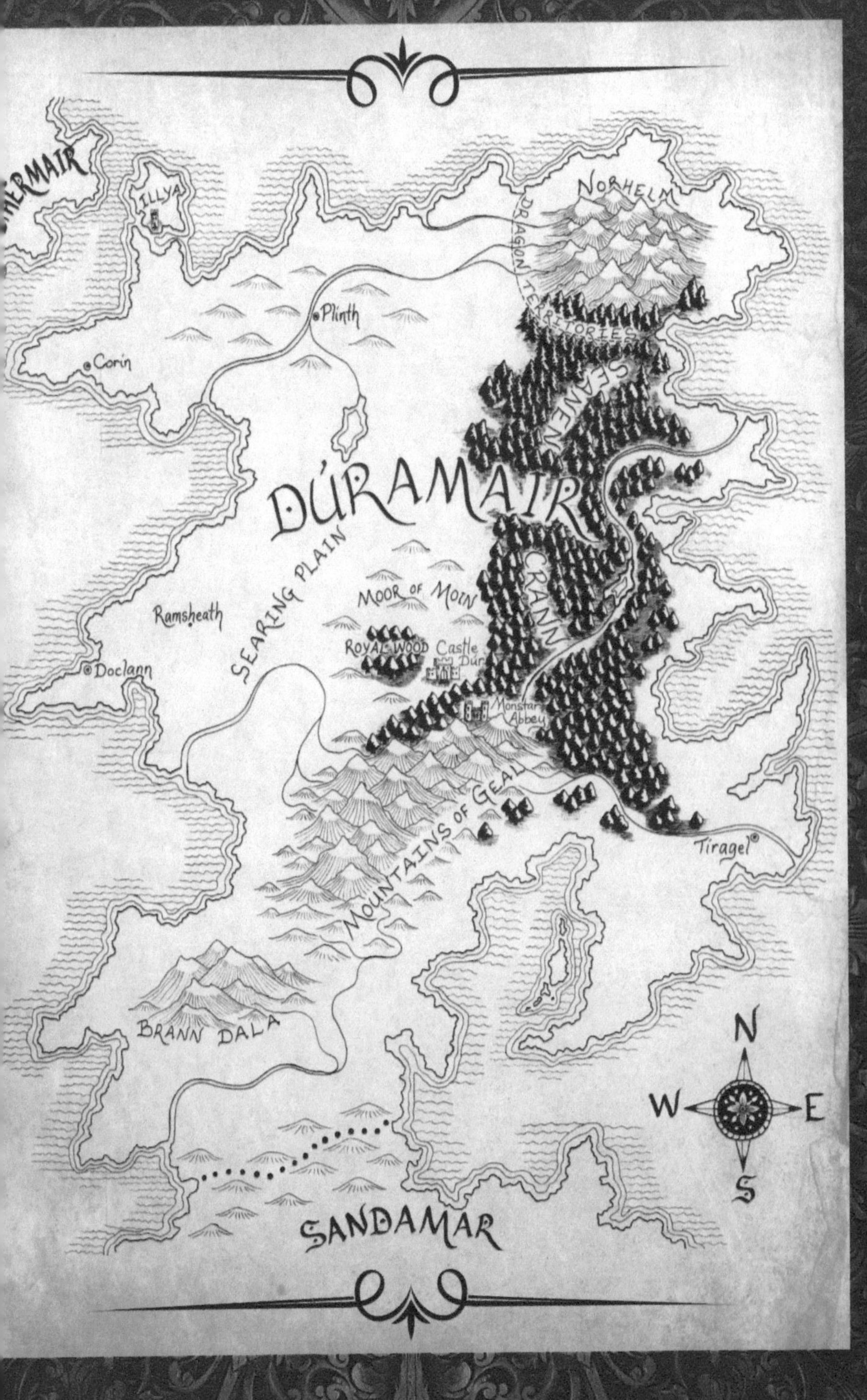
NERMAIR
NORHELM
ILLYA
DRAGON TERRITORIES
Plinth
NENNES
Corin
DÚRAMAIR
SEARING PLAIN
MOOR OF MOIN
Ramsheath
CRANN
ROYAL WOOD Castle
Dúr
Doclann
Monstar
Abbey
MOUNTAINS OF GEAL
Tiragel
BRANN DALA
SANDAMAR
N
W E
S

KEEPER OF SCALES

I

THE ROYAL WOOD

Alyen had vowed never to enter the Royal Wood again. It was a promise she'd made herself too many times to count, and one that had, yet again, proved too hard to keep.

She slid off her horse in the dim forest light, heart fluttering in her chest, breath coming quick. Keeping her eyes cast downward, she tied Lusa's reins to a low-hanging branch, then removed her shoes and stockings and stowed them in her saddlebag, bare feet sinking into the cool, spongy moss. She paused to take a steadying breath, then turned, blinking, to let her eyes adjust to the half-light.

Gradually the trees came into focus. The vague, familiar tingle in the air brushed against her skin, sending shivers up her arms. It would start at any moment. It always did. Each time, she waited less. Now, it started almost immediately.

There!

And again!

In her periphery, tiny shapes darted and flashed in the trees, the ferns, and in midair. Excitement danced with fear in her gut, her heart beating faster beneath her ribs.

She walked softly, slipping between the looming trees, skirting around bushes and boulders. The forest scents of moss, pine, and fern filled her as she followed a familiar path of dappled sunlight and fallen leaves. The flickers and flashes continued, seeming to move with her, whether following her path or leading her, she couldn't say.

At last, the forest thinned to reveal the Ancient Oak. Alyen placed her hands on the immense trunk and leaned against it, feeling the steady current of life running beneath the rough bark. She sank down to curl up between two enormous roots and relaxed her gaze on the forest around her.

The flickering had grown strong over the past months. And it was always strongest here, near the Ancient Oak, the heart of the forest. *What are they?* she wondered. Faeries? Elves? Some other elemental group she didn't know the name of? The pulse of the forest thrummed through her body, excitement blooming in her chest as she watched the dancing shapes. For a stolen space of time, Alyen allowed herself to bask in the joy, the rightness, the *belonging* she always felt in the forbidden Royal Wood.

But eventually, as it always did, dread began to creep unbidden from her belly up her spine. Her breath grew shallow, and her heart seemed to constrict, as the one thought she could never entirely banish echoed through her mind.

The fact that the flickering appeared to *her* was not good news.

A chill wind rustled through the autumn woods and Alyen shivered. Suddenly she wanted to leave. She rose and retraced her steps, trying to ignore the flickers that continued to flash in the trees. Her throat was dry; she glanced toward the stream, just visible to her right. But she pursed her lips and pressed on. She'd grown up hearing the rumors of faerie magic that would ensnare any who drank from the trickling brook, leaving them to wander the forest, forever lost to the faeries and the mist. As a girl, Alyen had never quite believed it, but now…

I need to stop coming here, she thought for the hundredth time, fingers fumbling to untie Lusa's reins. *It's only getting worse. There's a reason this forest is forbidden.*

She swung a leg over Lusa's back and threw a final glance into the forest depths. Flickers winked at her everywhere, so thick her vision almost wavered. Face set and grim, Alyen turned her back on the Royal Wood and kicked Lusa to a run across the moor.

The sun had burned away the haze of early morning by the time she rode into the courtyard of Castle Dúr. Garret was waiting, and Alyen handed him her reins as he helped her down from the saddle. He patted Lusa's side affectionately, the old angry scars on his hands shiny and tight.

"Did you have a nice ride?" he asked with a sparkle in his eye.

Alyen hitched a smile on her face, determined not to glance toward the lingering flickers. Not only were they appearing more quickly in the forest, it was also taking them longer to fade once she left. Sometimes they didn't completely disappear for days.

"I did—Lusa rode well. Give her an extra carrot for me, will you?"

"Of course, Your Highness." Garret nodded in a curt bow. "Though may I add that she hardly seems winded at all considering how long you were gone? Were you perhaps … detained?" He glanced pointedly toward the tops of Alyen's feet—dirt-stained and hastily shoved back into her shoes without her stockings.

He suspects. Alyen's stomach flipped. *Figures—he was the one who told me faeries could be seen in the Royal Wood to begin with.*

"Not at all," she countered. "She must simply be a marvelously strong horse. Any news this morning?"

Garret nodded, his face suddenly grim. "Rowenna arrived while you were out."

Alyen frowned as she followed Garret through the wide stable doors, the comforting smell of horses, hay, and earth not quite able to banish the foreboding she felt at Garret's expression. She'd never seen him look upset at the arrival of his sister. "Rowenna? She's back from the search? Did she find an apprentice, then?"

Garret shook his head. "There's other news from the north. I'm sure they'll be wanting you to hear all about it inside."

"In that case, I'd better go change. Best not to keep everyone waiting."

Garret glanced up at Alyen as he scooped grain into Lusa's trough. "Good luck, cailínna."

Cailínna. It was the nickname Garret had used since she was very young, but only when they were out of earshot. In old Dúramairian, it meant "small girl." Somehow, hearing it usually managed to lift the weight of learning to rule a kingdom from her shoulders, if only for a moment. But her nerves were wound too tightly today. She forced a smile to match the one Garret offered and patted Lusa in farewell, trying to ignore the flickers coming from a corner of the stall.

Her smile faded once she turned away. *Rowenna still hasn't found an apprentice. But if there's bad news waiting inside, I surely can't say anything now.*

If Rowenna didn't find an apprentice soon, Alyen would have to confess the secret she'd been keeping so long. And it would be devastating.

Unable to silence the worried chatter of her thoughts, she hurried across the courtyard, unaware of Garret's assessing gaze on her back as she entered the doors of Castle Dúr.

Alyen glanced nervously at the hourglass as she pulled her arms out of her riding gown. She hadn't realized how long she'd been gone until she saw Cook Nellie sliding tiny bowls of midmorning faerie food out the kitchen windows as she entered the castle. Her parents knew she often went for a morning ride, but if she returned too late there would be questions—questions she didn't want to answer. She shoved her feet into a pair of shoes not stained by the forest floor and hurried out her door.

She had almost reached her destination when a voice made her skid to a halt.

"I trust, Your Highness, that if you were planning on completely skipping your tutoring today, you would have done me the courtesy of letting me know?"

Alyen closed her eyes momentarily, cursing under her

breath. She turned and retraced her steps until she reached the doorway to the study where Professor Glibb sat, glowering over the spectacles perched on his ink-smeared nose. His face looked even more sour than usual.

"My apologies, Professor," Alyen said in her best attempt at a regretful but even tone. "It seems I'm needed by the king and queen this morning. I'll reschedule with you for another time, if you're agreeable."

Professor Glibb sniffed. "It seems I have no choice. Though the quality of your most recent lettering indicates that you may want to make your studies a higher priority."

Alyen nodded and practically fled down the corridor.

She stopped outside a private audience chamber that glowed from the hearth and the autumn light streaming through tall windows. Her parents were already seated in large armchairs across from the woman accepting a steaming mug from a servant. Alyen waited for the servant to leave, then curtsied.

"Mother, Father. Welcome, Rowenna," she said, willing her voice not to sound breathless.

"Hello, Alyen." Rowenna's voice was warm. "It's good to see you again."

"Alyen," Queen Réanna said, her beautiful smile thinner than usual. "Join us."

King Stephan squeezed Alyen's hand lightly in greeting as she sat beside him in the remaining armchair. His face looked worried.

"I hear there's news from the north?" Alyen said before anyone could ask about her day.

"There is." Her father let out a long breath. "Rowenna's just told us that Castle Illya went up in flames."

Alyen paused for a heartbeat, then looked to Rowenna. "Truly? It burned?"

"It did." Rowenna's voice was grave.

"So, Mother Brenwyn's vision has come true. So soon."

A log in the fire crackled and a flurry of movement flashed in the rising flames. Alyen flinched and hastily looked away, only to find that Rowenna's gaze had sharpened as it fixed on her. She swallowed and closed her eyes. *Focus, Alyen. You're a ruler—you've been trained for this. Ignore the flickers, and deal with the issue at hand.* She opened her eyes. "What happened?"

"According to reports," Queen Réanna supplied, "the fire is out. The castle still stands, but it remains surrounded by an unnatural plume of black smoke that doesn't disperse or change with the wind."

Alyen's heart sank. "Dark magic?"

"It looks that way," Rowenna confirmed.

"Did anyone see anything else?" Alyen asked, hoping desperately for a less ominous explanation than the one that seemed apparent. "It's an abandoned castle, after all. Any chance the Nethermairians are just trying to find an empty place to experiment?"

Rowenna and her parents exchanged dark glances and her father cleared his throat. "There are rumors of a black-robed woman sailing alone to the island from our shore several days prior, but no one can confirm this, and no one has seen her since."

Curses. Alyen sat back in her chair. *Dark magic—and from our own kingdom.* She found herself wishing she hadn't picked this day to visit the Royal Wood. The flickering coming from the flames in the hearth was terribly distracting, and the air itself seemed to shimmer, particularly around Rowenna. With effort, she forced herself not to glance around the room, steadying her gaze on their guest.

"I'm assuming Morten knows. Did he have any insight?"

Rowenna shook her head. "He knows, yes, but no more than we do. Even the Slayer of Monsters can't wage battle against a hidden enemy, and we really have no way to figure out what's beneath that cloud of smoke, monster or otherwise."

"But there hasn't been a monster in Dúramair for centuries. *Dark magic* hasn't been in Dúramair for centuries, so how would anyone have learned it?"

"That," Rowenna said, gazing at Alyen over her mug, "is a very good question."

Alyen's stomach gave an anxious squirm. More and more over the past year, her parents had been letting her handle conflicts and matters of state while they watched and guided from the sidelines—absent enough to give Alyen a real chance to practice ruling, present enough so the Dúramairians and dignitaries felt that the king and queen were still in charge. But Dúramair was a peaceful kingdom. Problems and conflicts were mostly small. This unknown threat was not. And it wasn't lost on Alyen that everyone was watching how she would handle the situation, not knowing about the secrets she was carrying, or the flashes and flickers that kept distracting her from every corner of the room. She swallowed in an attempt to calm her nerves. *Breathe, Alyen. You can do this. You just need time to clear your head and think.*

Alyen rose from her chair and strode to gaze out the window. Movement flashed through the tree branches, and Alyen's head turned sharply to follow it before she could think to stop. She tried to disguise the movement by turning back to the room and swallowed as she saw the expression on Rowenna's face. Her eyes had narrowed, and she was looking at Alyen with something close to undisguised suspicion. Alyen felt her nerves quiver but drew a breath and steadied her voice.

"Rowenna, we owe you thanks for bringing us this news. I realize it means you had to interrupt your search for an apprentice. Have no candidates been found yet?"

Rowenna's face was unreadable as she shook her head. "No, not a single one. I never expected it to take so long."

Alyen's father ran a hand across his brow. "This business with Illya couldn't have come at a worse time. Dark magic threatening from the north, and we're one apprentice short of ensuring the continuation of the Trianid."

Alyen felt a chill as her father's meaning sank in. If one of the Trianid should fall with no apprentice and their knowledge lost ... Alyen's stomach clenched again, and she harnessed all her will to press down on the panic that threatened to rise in her throat. "Do you think it could really come to that?"

Rowenna raised one eyebrow. "*I* certainly hope not. But the fact remains that the position of Keeper of Scales is vulnerable. Morten's been training Aaron for nearly a decade, and thank the saints, Mother Brenwyn found Lirianna this spring. But I've been searching now for over a year, and I haven't found a single person with the Sight." Her eyes bored into Alyen's. "*Not one.*"

Alyen's stomach plummeted and for a moment she thought she might be sick. She turned back to the window, breathing through her mouth. Behind her the conversation continued, but she only half heard. Flickers were coming now from all directions—the water pitcher, the fire, the air in front of the hearth, the trees outside. *I'm going to have to say something. I can't keep it a secret anymore.* She exhaled a shaky breath.

"Alyen? Are you feeling all right?" The conversation had stopped, and everyone was looking at her.

"No, actually. I—" Alyen shook her head, unable to force out the words she feared she must say.

"Alyen," Rowenna's voice was direct if not unkind. "What is it you need to tell us?"

Alyen met Rowenna's gaze and saw the knowing in the other woman's eyes. She swallowed. "I think … I think I have the Sight."

The silence that followed was profound.

"W—What?" Alyen's mother was the first to speak.

Alyen merely nodded, her eyes fixed on a spot on the floor.

"How long has this been going on?" asked Rowenna.

"Since spring," Alyen said quietly, acutely aware that she was admitting to months of secrecy despite the full knowledge that Rowenna had been scouring the kingdom, searching for anyone with the Sight. "I—I've been sneaking out to the Royal Wood and it's always stronger there. But it's happening in the castle now, too, and more today than ever. I think it's because you're here." She lifted her eyes to Rowenna's, waiting for the angry words she was sure would come. But Rowenna merely held Alyen's gaze, her eyes thoughtful.

"I suppose I can't blame you for your silence. In your position I may have done the same. Can you describe for me what you see now?"

Alyen's eyes darted around the room. "Something's in the hearth, the trees out the window are constantly flickering, there's something hovering in that corner, and the air's full of motion. Particularly near you."

Rowenna's eyebrows lifted as she took a deep breath, one hand absently fingering the flashing stone of the brooch on her shawl. "Well. This is … unprecedented."

"Unprecedented?"

"Yes. The Keeper of Scales has never before come from the royal line."

"It's true then?" King Stephan asked. "Alyen has the Sight?"

"It appears so," Rowenna said, sounding as if she couldn't quite believe it herself. "But she hasn't fully broken through yet."

"What do you mean, 'broken through?' Is it different for you?" Alyen asked.

Rowenna's expression softened as she looked back at Alyen. "The reason you see flickering, Alyen, is because the elemental world hasn't fully opened to you yet. Right now, it's like you're trying to see into a room through a frosted window —all you're getting are flashes of movement and light. That's how the Sight always starts, and then it either fades away or continues to grow until you finally 'break through' and see the elemental world in its entirety. When that happens, you won't see flickering anymore. The elementals you see will look normal, just like anything else."

"So, I might not actually be your apprentice? It might go away?" Alyen wasn't sure if the pang in her chest was relief or disappointment.

Rowenna pursed her mouth. "I suppose it might. But I have to say, it's usually only young children who catch glimpses of the elemental world without actually possessing the Sight. Very few ever experience it at your age—that's how we know someone might be a candidate for Keeper."

The room was silent again. Alyen resisted the urge to cringe or fidget. *This is supposed to be a good thing. When one of the Trianid finds an apprentice, it's supposed to be a celebration.* But Rowenna was frowning in thought and Alyen's parents looked like they were in a state of shock.

Finally, King Stephan spoke. "How do you suggest we proceed, Rowenna?"

Rowenna took a slow sip from her mug before replying. "For a start, I think we should keep this news as quiet as possible. As we are all well aware, Alyen is first in line to the throne with no siblings. I believe the next in line is a cousin, is that correct?"

Queen Réanna cleared her throat. "Yes. My sister's son, Merrith. I think he's twelve or thirteen now."

"So, an heir does exist and from the same lineage," said Rowenna, "but it would be unexpected for Dúramairians and, I'm sure, for him. And any hint of instability is not what we need circulating when dark magic is threatening at the same time. The situation isn't ideal, but as Alyen is also the only candidate to be found for Keeper, the apprenticeship is a possibility I think we need to consider. It will be difficult for her Sight to mature here in the castle without attracting attention to it, so with your permission, I'd like to take her to Monstar Abbey, where she'll be safe under Mother Brenwyn's care. We can say she's there to further her studies or to develop her relations with the Trianid—at least until her Sight fully opens. When it does and she makes her choice, then we can decide how to proceed from there."

"My choice?" Alyen asked quickly. "So—I do get to choose?"

Rowenna met Alyen's eyes. "Of course you do. It's always a choice. A Keeper forced into the position would be useless."

A wave of relief washed over Alyen and she almost didn't hear as her parents continued to discuss the logistics of the move to Monstar. *I can choose*, she thought. *I can say no. I can still be the princess, and no one will have to worry about training an unprepared heir for the throne.*

Or I could say yes…

"Then it's decided," King Stephan was saying as Alyen's thoughts returned to the conversation. "Rowenna and Alyen will leave for Monstar in three days' time. I shall organize an escort tomorrow." The words sounded thick in his throat.

"And I'll arrange for Alyen's things to be packed," Queen Réanna said, a tremble in her voice.

Everyone stood and Alyen's parents reached out to her. Tears stung at her eyes as she felt their arms circle around her. They weren't angry. She didn't have to carry the secret anymore. She didn't have to solve the problem alone.

When they broke their embrace, Alyen took the moment to search her parents' faces, hoping to see reassurance. But her relief disappeared as her heart sank. *They're devastated*, she realized. *And worried. And now the choice rests on me.*

2
POWER

Atop the black tower of Castle Illya a woman stood, her robes rippling in the breeze as she gazed at the sea. Above her, the dark plume of smoke hovered, tethered to the tower by the circle of symbols she'd spent days etching into the stone floor. Triumph warred with uncertainty in her heart. She'd achieved the impossible—but now what?

From the depths of the smoke a voice whispered the name of the woman who'd woken it.

"Ylvain … Ylvain … Ylvain …"

Ylvain's face flinched as a stab of fear sliced her chest.

She hadn't intended on raising him.

Years she'd spent searching out lost records of the dark arts in Dúramair. And many more years again, isolated and alone, she'd pored over those records—teaching herself, growing her power, honing her skills. She'd etched the circle, harnessed the power, spoken the words—merely to practice. But her power had grown more than she'd known, and she'd been swept up in it, intoxicated by its thrill and pull.

And it had worked.

"*Ylvain …*"

The voice had called to her often, but she wasn't foolish enough to reply. Once ensnared, an evil spirit could escape only by tricking its summoner into releasing it.

And this was no ordinary spirit.

Ylvain exhaled slowly and continued to contemplate the ocean waves that slowly devoured a blood-red sun.

"You don't have a plan, do you?"

Ylvain started and spun to stare at the smoke that rose from her summoning circle. The voice had never uttered a word other than her name until now. She stood tense and wary, eyeing the smoke that undulated before her.

"If you did, you would have spoken to me long ago. No one would dare raise a child of darkness merely to stare at it silently for days. Tell me, Ylvain, was my rebirth an accident?"

The accuracy of the whispered words rankled Ylvain, but she kept her face blank and her lips pressed tightly together. The smoke seemed to swirl with impatience.

"Come now, Ylvain. You are wise to be cautious, but don't insult yourself with stupidity. If you possess the knowledge to raise and hold *me*, then you are impressively educated in the ancient arts. You know that I can do nothing to you without your consent, nor can I escape this circle without your order. And if your power is great enough to have achieved *this*, you are certainly no coward. Surely you are not too frightened merely to speak to me, your servant?"

A silent pause, then the whisper, softly caressing.

"I can help you. I wish only to help the woman who broke my prison. A woman with the power to rule the world."

Ylvain's posture straightened. *Tricks*, she told herself firmly. *He's trying to seduce me with promises of power. I must not be fooled. But perhaps there's something to be gained from speaking with him.*

"Rule the world?" she asked in a voice she forced to be steady. "And how would I do that? I have no royal lineage, no army—even you couldn't hand me the world at my bidding."

The voice purred in reply. "All true. I cannot give you the world. But I can give you an army. An army stronger and more powerful than all the kingdoms combined could defeat. And with that army, you can *take* the world."

"What army is this, that cannot be defeated?" Ylvain's lips were white, her breath quick.

"One we shall give birth to together, you and me. That is, if your power is sufficient to the task."

"What do you mean? I've raised you, haven't I? Doesn't that prove my power sufficient?"

"Perhaps. But there are many kinds of power all stemming from different places, different desires. Yours must be of the right variety for this plan to work. Sadly, I suspect it is not."

Ylvain's eyes narrowed. "Tell me."

The smoke billowed. From within came a sinister orange glow that reflected in the darkness of Ylvain's eyes. "Your power must come from ambition—a merciless disregard for anything but yourself and your own power. It must be cold, calculating, and ruthless. But I know humans well, Ylvain. Sentiments of such purity are rare and at best transient in your kind."

Ylvain's mouth twisted, and she spoke between clenched

teeth. "Believe me, Dark One, my heart is filled with ambition aplenty."

"True. But if I am correct, your power is fueled by hatred, your hatred from rage, your rage from pain, and your pain from love. With love at your core, you can never rise to your full potential. With love comes mercy, loyalty, forgiveness. Love will make you weak." The voice spat the words as if they burned.

Ylvain drew a sharp breath and took a step backward to think. She was on dangerous ground. He was baiting her, but she was still in control.

"You are bound to do as I command," Ylvain said. "And I forbid you to lie to me."

"As you say."

"Is there a way to determine the quality of my power?"

"There is."

"What is it?"

"You must let me into your heart."

Ylvain sneered. "If you think I am so foolish as to release you anywhere near me—"

"I said nothing of release," the voice interrupted. "I said only that I must be allowed a glimpse into your heart. You would maintain control and I would remain bound."

"You are speaking the truth?"

"You have commanded me not to lie, and so I cannot."

Ylvain turned her back to the smoke and strode to the battlements. She studied the waves and inhaled the salty heaviness of the air as her mind repeated the exchange over and over, searching for Any loophole, any falsehood, any crack in the wall of her control. She could find none.

Ylvain returned to the summoning circle and chose her

words carefully. "I command you to enter my heart solely to determine the quality and source of my powers. You will tell me truthfully what you find. And you will leave me completely at my slightest command."

"As you wish," the voice whispered.

"Then begin."

A tendril of smoke snaked down from the plume hovering above the black tower. It hesitated before Ylvain's chest, then surged forward and melted into the front of her robes. Ylvain's head snapped back, her eyes wide as the smoke rushed into her heart, her lungs, her limbs. She felt it twine around her spine and race through her blood as it sought every crevasse in her being and filled it with a power that was clean and cold, terrifying and wondrous. She gasped in fear and pleasure, then asked in a thick voice, "What do you see?"

The whispered words filled Ylvain's ears and echoed in her mind. "It is as I thought. You possess ambition and a promising talent, but your heart is filled with the pain of loss and betrayal. Both are worthless, and both will break you."

Ylvain gritted her teeth against the disappointment and rage that filled her. It was time to end this. She had been foolish to go so far.

"But there may still be a way …"

Ylvain bit down on the command she'd been about to utter. Somewhere in her mind, her own voice shouted at her to abandon her pursuit and banish from within what was best left alone to begin with. But the power vibrating through her body was intoxicating. She cringed, thinking of the emptiness she would feel when it was over. If only to delay that moment, she spoke again.

"How can it be done?"

"You will not like it."

"Tell me!"

There was a pause, then: "You must release me. I must be your master and you, my pupil. I can transform your anger, teach you a colder hate, fill you with a power that can conquer the world and make you its queen. Bow before me, Ylvain, and I shall raise you to greater heights than you have ever dreamed of."

Ylvain said nothing, her breath coming fast.

"I warned that you would not like it. Perhaps it would be best to banish me. You have power enough to amuse yourself if you do not wish to rise further."

"What do you mean? My powers can grow no more?"

"Not without guidance."

"Do not lie to me!"

"As I said, I cannot."

Ylvain stood trembling, her fingers straying to the hilt of the knife she kept strapped to her side.

"Come, Ylvain," the voice cajoled. "Be the courageous woman I know you can be. Join with me, and together we can take everything you've ever wanted and more."

Ylvain's eyes squeezed tight for a moment. Then her hand whipped upward and her blade flashed as she smashed it downward onto the stones at her feet. Metal screeched against rock and a long gash sliced through the runes of the summoning circle.

A hiss of triumph sounded as the smoke billowed free and encircled Ylvain. Slowly her eyes darkened, filled by a shadow the world had long since forgotten.

3
MONSTAR ABBEY

It had taken a full day to cross the Moor of Moin. By the time dusk was falling, they had reached the edge of the forest of Sheanen Crann, the canopy ablaze with color as the last rays of the setting sun lit the autumn leaves afire. They stopped to make camp under the shelter of the trees, Garret and the two guards setting up tents and seeing to the horses, while Rowenna saw to the food and the fire.

Alyen was sore, chilly, and irritated that she'd been left to ride alone all day, mostly ignored by Garret and Rowenna. She'd assumed the Keeper would want to talk about her Sight, the apprenticeship—perhaps attempt to sway her decision one way or the other. Instead Rowenna had barely spoken to her since she'd admitted to her Sight, leaving Alyen feeling lost, adrift, and alone with the fate of the kingdom resting on a single decision she had no idea how to make.

She dismounted Lusa and settled onto a rock, pulling her cloak tight against her body as the evening air grew colder.

It was comforting to feel the forest around her, but not enough to lift her mood, particularly as the flickering was getting worse again. She shook her head in frustration, willing the flashing to stop as she blinked forcefully into the trees.

Suddenly Rowenna was beside her holding out a leather flask. "Here, drink some of this. It will help."

Alyen took the proffered flask and sniffed at its contents. A strong but pleasant aroma of spices, herbs, and something distinctly alcoholic filled her nose. Alyen raised a questioning eyebrow in Rowenna's direction. The Keeper smiled.

"That's right, it's made from wine. The alcohol is all cooked out, so it won't make you drunk, but the soothing effects are still in place. It will help you relax while you wait to break through. If you try too hard, it won't happen."

Alyen sipped at the flask. Delicious warmth spread through her body, seeping from her stomach out to her fingers and toes. She exhaled, feeling her shoulders relax.

"Better?" Rowenna asked.

Alyen nodded and met the woman's eyes, trying not to betray the anger she felt at being all but ignored for several days. "I have some questions," she ventured.

Rowenna's smile was understanding. "I know. But there's really nothing that can be done until you break through, and honestly, too much information will just complicate that process. It's best if I give you some space."

Alyen swallowed her disappointment and nodded. Rowenna squeezed her arm. "I know it's hard to wait. And you've had to leave your home as well. Just try to relax and give it time. Drink more of that," she said, pointing to the flask, "but not too much. It's a potent brew."

She retreated to the campfire, leaving Alyen to the trees and her flask.

In the morning, a misty drizzle was falling, which quickly turned to a light but steady rain that pattered down on the leaves about camp. Alyen mounted with the others and rode sullenly through the damp forest, listening to the dripping of rain on fallen leaves.

Suddenly another noise perked her ears: hoofbeats—but not from their horses, and not from the path. Alyen peered into the forest and tensed. Something dark was moving, half hidden in the trees, keeping apace with the caravan.

Alyen turned sharply in her saddle and pitched her voice low. "Rowenna? We're being followed."

Rowenna glanced toward the forest and urged her horse forward until she rode next to Alyen. "I know. Not to worry; we're expecting him."

The road curved and suddenly Alyen saw a rider, dressed in the black robes of Sandamar, sitting motionless atop a black stallion as he watched the caravan pass from between the trees, his face like stone. Alyen shuddered involuntarily.

"Who is that?"

"That," Rowenna replied as she nodded to the rider, "is Nah'dar, an assassin of the Bahari tribe. He's keeping an eye on you."

Alyen gaped. "You have an assassin tracking me?"

"Not just any assassin. The very best assassin. And he's not tracking you. He's your bodyguard."

"A bodyguard? Is that really necessary? I thought Monstar was supposed to be safe."

"It is." Rowenna looked at Alyen, her eyes serious. "But we're taking no chances. You know better than most the implications of the fire at Illya. If there *is* danger afoot in Dúramair, the Trianid's apprentices—and the kingdom's heir—must be protected."

Alyen glanced back into the trees, but the rider was gone.

Rowenna noticed her troubled expression and added, "Don't worry about Nah'dar. As long as you're in no danger, you won't even know he's there."

Alyen nodded but doubted she would be able to forget that an assassin was watching her.

By noon they had arrived. Monstar Abbey loomed above, an enormous stone fortress on a cliff overlooking the rolling hills of Sheanen Crann and backed by the craggy peaks of the Mountains of Geal. Alyen had seen it before on visits with her father, but its magnificence rising out of the trees never failed to steal her breath.

They were greeted in the courtyard by three young novices who took the riding party's horses, and a fourth who indicated that Garret, Rowenna, and Alyen should follow her inside. They entered the abbey's great wooden doors, and Alyen felt the familiar sensation of being struck by a wall of color. Tapestries of all sizes, shapes, and hues covered what seemed to be every inch of the abbey walls. The scenes were incredible. Some showed battles; others showed saints, stories, or fairytales, all in amazing detail. Many Alyen recognized as myths or bits of history; others she didn't know at all.

The records of Dúramair—and ages of visions woven by the Seer of Strands, Alyen thought, glancing around. *I wonder if there's a tapestry somewhere of Illya burning.*

But there was no time to look or admire. Instead, they passed through the entrance quickly, following the novice down a corridor to the left.

The room they entered at the end of the hall was simple and elegant. Unlike the hall they'd just passed through, the chamber's walls were white and sparsely decorated, arching up into an equally unadorned domed ceiling. A row of large windows gave the room plenty of light, and the stone floors were covered in a thick rug finely woven in reds, blues, and greens.

A woman rose from the wooden desk in the center of the room as they entered, her smile warm and inviting.

"Alyen," the woman said as she came around the desk to take Alyen's hands in her own. "Welcome to Monstar."

"Mother Brenwyn," Alyen said nodding. "Thank you for your hospitality."

"Your fingers are like ice. Have a seat and I'll get you some tea."

Alyen shrugged off her damp cloak and handed it to the novice. Mother Brenwyn had turned to embrace Rowenna and Garret, and Alyen watched as the abbess instructed the novice to show the guards to Alyen's room so they could unload her things. She was a small woman, perhaps only reaching Alyen's nose, and as she spoke, a beautiful stone pendant on a thin silver chain flashed against the deep midnight blue of her robes and wimple.

The door closed behind the novice as Alyen, Rowenna, and Garret sat on cushioned wooden chairs, and Mother Brenwyn placed cups of hot herbal tea that smelled of lemon and chamomile in their hands.

"How was your journey, Alyen?" she asked, sitting across from them holding her own cup of tea.

"Smooth enough," Alyen replied, unable to think of anything better to say. "A bit wet today," she added.

"Well, it is a blessing for you to be here, safely among us. Unfortunately, Lirianna, my apprentice, is visiting her home in Tiragel right now so she's not here to meet you. But once she's back, I'm sure you'll make wonderful friends."

She speaks as though I'm staying forever. Unexpectedly, her nose began to smart, and the corners of her eyes prickled dangerously, so she just nodded and hid her face in her teacup. Mother Brenwyn kindly spared her any more discourse, and instead spoke lightly with Garret and Rowenna about news from the castle while Alyen concentrated on drinking her tea.

After a time, however, the tea was gone, Alyen's things had been unloaded, and it was time for Garret to leave. Mother Brenwyn gave Alyen a knowing look and turned to Rowenna.

"Come, Rowenna. I'll show you to your room. We have much to catch up on."

The door closed, and they were alone. Alyen didn't move. When Garret finally spoke, it was gently, his voice filled with enough sympathy to make Alyen's lip tremble.

"The castle won't be the same without you, cailínna."

Alyen tried to sniff away the sting in her nose, but a tear escaped her eye and rolled down her cheek. She dashed it away with the back of her hand, annoyed with herself for crying.

"Ah, don't take it so hard," Garret soothed. "Nothing in this life lasts forever—and once your Sight comes through, the choice will be yours to make."

Alyen looked up at him. "You knew, didn't you? You knew I was sneaking off to the Royal Wood. And you knew I had the Sight?"

Garret tilted his head in a one-shouldered shrug. "I

suspected, is all. You pick up a few things being the brother to the Keeper of Scales."

Alyen nodded, determined not to think that she might never visit Garret in the stables again to beg a riding lesson or listen to stories on a rainy afternoon. "What would you do, Garret? What would you do in my place?"

Garret huffed the air out his nose and shook his head. "I don't begin to know, cailínna. But whichever choice you make, it'll be the right one."

He stood to leave, looking down at Alyen with half a smile. Alyen rose and embraced him tightly.

"Goodbye, Garret. And thank you—for everything."

"Goodbye, cailínna," Garret whispered after a few moments, gently dislodging himself from her grasp. He gave her one more reassuring nod, then the door closed behind him, and he was gone.

Alyen awoke in her new room the next morning having slept poorly. She rose from her bed and took a large swallow of Rowenna's brew, trying to let her eyes relax despite the flickering outside her window. Her gaze rested on the heaps of crates and belongings scattered throughout her room, left untouched where the guards had set them. Unpacking would mean she was staying, and that wasn't a decision she'd made yet. Alyen threw on the same dress she'd worn the day before, took another swig, and went in search of breakfast.

When she entered the dining hall, she glanced around halfheartedly, disappointed but unsurprised to find that Rowenna was nowhere to be seen. Alyen ate her breakfast of porridge, yogurt, and fruit alone in the far corner of the hall and was just swallowing the last of her tea when a plump and freckled nun crossed the room toward her, smiling brightly.

"Princess Alyen? I'm Sister Agatha—I manage the upkeep of the abbey. Mother Brenwyn's asked me to give you a tour if you're finished …?"

Alyen managed a polite smile and followed Sister Agatha out of the dining hall. As they approached the abbey's entrance, the nun stopped, a small frown on her face.

"I know you've been here before. How much of the abbey have you seen already? I won't waste your time showing you what you already know."

Alyen blinked, realizing she had no idea how she was expected to spend her day, other than unpacking, which she was avoiding anyway. "It's been a long time since my last visit," she said. "Why don't you just give me the whole tour?"

This seemed to please Sister Agatha, and she set off briskly, chattering and pointing happily as Alyen trailed behind her.

The abbey was vast, and the constant array of tapestries on every wall amounted to an impressive display of color. They passed first through the chapel, its altar adorned beautifully with candles and autumn flowers.

"There are dozens of abbeys and monasteries dedicated to the saints," Sister Agatha was saying, "but Monstar's the only place in Dúramair dedicated solely to Béathan, the One. Then again, I suppose you knew that already …"

Sister Agatha's commentary continued without pause as they turned a corner into the infirmary, conveniently located just down the hall from the medicine rooms, where older sisters supervised novices in drying, powdering, distilling, and brewing the many plants from the gardens into tinctures, creams, and salves. Near the dormitories, Sister Agatha showed Alyen the bathing rooms filled with curtained-off, tiled cubicles, each containing a deep stone bathtub, soaps, oils, and pumps for cold and warm water. Next, they wandered down to the kitchens, which reminded Alyen so much of the kitchens at Castle Dúr that she almost glanced about for Cook Nellie, plump, flushed, dusted with flour, and always ready to sneak Alyen a treat.

After puffing up several flights of curving stone staircases, Sister Agatha pushed open a wooden door to a suite of connected rooms filled with dozens of looms, each strung in brilliantly colored yarns. Portrayals of plants, animals, knights, ladies, dragons, and all manner of magical creatures stood in various stages of completion on each large, wooden frame. The rooms hummed with the clacking of shuttles racing back and forth, and the talk and laughter of nuns at work.

Sister Agatha led her through the rooms, pausing here and there to admire her sisters' progress. They reached the end of the suite, and Sister Agatha paused before a door that stood shut with a single eye carved into its wood, as if it were designed to survey the activity in the room. She placed her hand on the door almost reverently, but made no move to push it open.

"This is Mother Brenwyn's private workroom. It's the only room in the abbey that no one, save her apprentice, may enter without her direct order or permission."

Without further comment, Sister Agatha led the way back out of the weaving rooms. "Now the last thing to show you inside is the library," she said as they halted before a tall doorway of dark wood. She pushed it open, the hinges squealing noisily.

The library was old and impressive. The shelves lining the walls were perhaps ten or fifteen feet high, with an occasional rickety-looking ladder attached with wheels to a track running around the perimeter. Above the shelves, the walls continued up to a high ceiling, and like almost every other wall in the abbey, were covered in tapestries. The rest of the room was a labyrinth of bookcases, most of which were taller than Alyen, and archways at the far end of the room led to what appeared to be more rooms of more shelves. Alyen's eyebrows rose; it certainly rivaled the library at Castle Dúr.

"As you can see, it's one of the largest collections in Dúramair," Sister Agatha chirped into the cavernous space as Alyen gazed around hungrily. "Feel free to borrow whatever you'd like. Now follow me out to the gardens."

The gardens were nearly as extensive as the abbey itself, covering most of Monstar's grounds in fragrant tiered beds of herbs, vegetables, and medicinal plants. Apple trees bordered the garden laden with ripe fruit ready for the autumn harvest, and the morning sunlight hitting the dew made the entire landscape sparkle.

But Alyen had no time to admire. As she approached the first rows bordering the vast plot, her vision began wavering and flickering so intensely that she lurched, stumbled, and was forced to grab hold of the low stone wall at the garden's edge for balance. Dizziness swept over her, and she felt a moment of alarm at her body's sudden rebellion.

As if through a tunnel, Alyen heard Sister Agatha's concerned voice asking if she was all right. She lifted her head with a vague notion to answer, but vertigo seized her again.

Squinting through the blinding flashes, she saw Rowenna exiting the abbey, her gaze focused intently on Alyen. She was saying something, her lips moving, but Alyen couldn't make out the words. She reached an arm out to Rowenna, then staggered and plopped down in the dirt beside the round, leafy heads of cabbage plants. The flashing in her vision surged, making her head feel as though it would split, and she winced against the pain.

Alyen put out a hand to steady herself and her fingers grazed the crisp green cabbage leaves. In an instant, the cabbage seemed to transform. What had been a harmless bundle of greens a moment before now stared back at her as a grinning, crinkly face, the cabbage leaves forming its wrinkled features and squinting eyes. Alyen stared as the leaves shivered, making the cabbage face appear to giggle, one leaf rising to cover the smiling mouth. Something in Alyen's head exploded. She saw stars against the pale sky as she fell backward onto the soil, before the world went dark.

4

BINDING

A lyen stood in a forest, tall trees towering around her as mist curled about their roots and her ankles. All was strangely still except for the churning fog, but Alyen sensed that hundreds of invisible eyes watched her from rock and tree and fern. The mist before her billowed, and from it stepped a figure.

"Rowenna?"

"Yes," the Keeper said, smiling.

"Where am I?" Alyen asked, looking at the strange and silent forest about her.

"You're dreaming," came Rowenna's reply. "So, in a sense, you are neither here nor there. Nowhere, but also everywhere and anywhere."

This made no sense to Alyen, so she turned to her more immediate question. "What—what happened? In the garden … there was a cabbage …"

Rowenna clasped one of Alyen's hands in both her own. Her grasp felt warm and solid and real.

"Here's what you must do now, Alyen. Leave this dream and wake up. When you do, go outside the abbey into the garden once more. I'll be waiting for you there, and we can talk about what happens next."

"How do I wake up?"

"You simply open your eyes ..." Rowenna released Alyen's hand and stepped back as the mist began to close around her and the forest faded to black.

Alyen woke up to find herself back in bed in her room in the abbey. Night had fallen, but someone had left a candle by her bed. The flame cast dancing shadows across the walls.

The garden. Her dream remained fresh and vivid in her mind. *I must get out to the garden.*

Alyen raised herself on one elbow to reach for the candle and froze. In the center of the flame, a tiny figure danced. So small it could easily be missed, the creature seemed to be made of fire herself. Flaming hair swirled around her graceful limbs as she licked about the candle wick. The flame darted and swayed in accordance with the dancer's every movement, her image wavering in and out of sight, making it almost impossible to tell where the fire ended, and she began. For a breathless moment, Alyen watched as the figure swirled and spun in the firelight before it disappeared in a sudden flash and a shower of tiny sparks.

The candle flame now stood still and innocent in the darkened room. Alyen realized she had been holding her breath.

She emptied her lungs, noticing that her head felt completely clear and focused, her senses heightened, her heart welling with excitement. She snatched up the candle, shoved her feet into her slippers, and stole quietly into the abbey halls in her nightgown, without pausing to wonder how she had come to be wearing it.

Alyen's steps slowed as she reached the arched doorway leading to the gardens. Taking a deep breath, she pushed open the great oak slabs and stepped outside into the moonlight.

Alyen's jaw dropped as she took in the sight that met her eyes. Every bed, every row, every inch of the garden was teeming with small beings. Tiny human forms with shimmering wings no thicker than spider silk flitted through the air, darting from one place to the next. Stout, sturdy little creatures with wrinkled, weathered faces trundled along between rows of beets and potatoes. Lithe and limber sprites clad all in leafy green ran along the tree branches, leaping from limb to limb. And in the water of the spring that gurgled up from the earth, silvery figures with fish tails in place of legs leapt and dove, flashing in the starlight.

At the edge of the spring sat Rowenna, smiling at Alyen's astonishment. She patted a stone beside her and Alyen settled onto it, still unable to tear her gaze away from the scene around her. The beings were so many and so varied, she felt she could stare for hours and still not see each kind of sprite or gnome that scampered throughout the garden. Alyen had never before been speechless—in fact she'd been trained how not to be. But for once in her life, all words escaped her. She could only stare.

"What are these?" she finally asked, pointing at the tiny,

silvery elementals that dove and splashed in the water of the spring, their tails flashing in the night.

"Those are undines, the elementals of water. They care for the rivers, streams, ponds, lakes, and all the creatures who live within them."

"And which ones are faeries?" Alyen asked, looking around.

Rowenna shook her head. "None, actually. Faeries are the nobility of the elementals and seeing them is rare. But the gardens at Monstar have always been a popular place for all manner of elementals—the Balance here is strong—so you're getting a good show."

"It's better than good. It's incredible …" Alyen's voice trailed off, and Rowenna studied her face intently.

"I sense you're conflicted."

Alyen tore her eyes away from the elementals around her to look at the Keeper squarely. "Shouldn't I be?"

Rowenna smiled. "I suppose it's only natural. After all, you're likely the first potential Keeper in history who might not automatically see this as a far better life than the one you would otherwise live."

"It makes the choosing hard." Alyen looked back at the garden, dismay clouding her excitement.

"I expect you have questions," Rowenna said gently. "I'm here to answer whatever you need to ask before choosing."

Alyen looked at Rowenna again, hoping her expression didn't look too mistrusting. Rowenna chuckled.

"I know, I'm hardly an objective informant and, to be frank, having a royal candidate for Keeper caught me off guard as well. But you have my word: I'll answer your questions truthfully and openly without trying to persuade you one way or the other. I honestly just want to help."

Alyen nodded and took a considering breath. After a pause to gather her thoughts, she looked up. "So, if I agree to the apprenticeship, what happens next?"

"Well, if you wish to be my apprentice, we will perform a binding ritual. You should know that once the ritual has been completed, there's no turning back. The binding between Keeper and apprentice is permanent and can be broken only by death."

"And then?"

"Then we train. And after several years, when we know that you're ready, the Ceremony of Three takes place, which will make you the Keeper, Aaron the Slayer, and Lirianna the Seer."

Alyen suddenly flinched as something brushed past her ear. She turned to find a cluster of sprites riding on the backs of moths, tiny golden lanterns held aloft to light the way.

"Those are sylphs," Rowenna said, following her gaze. "The spirits of the air. They're adventurous, flighty, fickle. They seem delicate, but don't be fooled—they can change in an instant, like the gentlest breeze that suddenly becomes a raging storm."

The cavorting sylphs disappeared into the trees, and once again Alyen felt her heart swell with the excitement of her new world.

"How would we train? Would I live with you?"

"I think not," Rowenna said, and Alyen noticed her eyes looked troubled. "I'll be dealing with Illya, and I feel it would be too risky for an apprentice to be with me, not knowing yet what we may be facing."

"Aaron's with Morten, though. He's still an apprentice."

"True," Rowenna conceded, "but Aaron has been Morten's apprentice now for what—eight or nine years? He's already quite advanced in his training."

An unpleasant squirming that felt something close to envy rose in Alyen's chest. Irritated at herself, she shoved the feeling down and forced herself to focus on the conversation.

"Then what will we do?"

"You'll stay here at Monstar, and we'll train at night while you sleep."

"What? How?"

"The same way we spoke tonight in the dreamworld after you fainted. You won't have to do anything but fall asleep each night as you normally do, and I'll be waiting to meet you for a lesson."

"But I don't always remember my dreams."

"You'll remember these," Rowenna assured her. "They won't be like normal dreams; it will feel almost exactly like the waking world."

"What exactly will I be learning? Things about sylphs and undines and all the rest?"

"Yes, in part. You'll learn all the varieties of elementals, their purposes and characteristics, and how to speak and work with them. But the Keeper, as you know, is also a healer, acting as a bridge between the elementals and the gifts they give to the world, so you'll undergo a thorough training in herbology and the use of plants and stones for healing."

"And what about during the day at Monstar?"

"You'll need to practice what I teach you at night in terms of gathering and preparing medicines, and you'll need to spend time with the elementals. Sometimes you'll be able to do this here in the gardens, but more often you'll need to go down into the forest—hence the presence of Nah'dar. And when you aren't doing any of that, I want you to go to the library and keep up your studies. Soak up as much knowledge as you can about whatever sparks your interest—you never know what bit of wisdom will come in handy one day."

Rowenna paused as if she wanted to say something but was unsure how. Finally, she said, "I, myself, have never regretted choosing this life, but I do feel I should warn you, Alyen. The Keeper's path isn't an easy one. It's not all magic and faeries in the forest. Much of what you learn will be wondrous and exciting, but some of it will also touch on the shadowed side of our world. A Keeper must keep the Balance with the light *and* the dark. It's a path that at times requires hardship—and sacrifice."

Alyen raised her eyebrows at these words. "I thought you weren't going to try to convince me to go back home."

Rowenna shook her head. "I'm not. But I *am* trying to prepare you. You've lived your whole life expecting to be a queen, and you would be a good one. The Keeper's path is also noble and respected—but in a much different way. This role would require you to develop a different frame of mind, and I don't think it would be fair to ask you to make that kind of choice without giving you the fullest possible picture."

Alyen looked down, letting Rowenna's words sink in. The tiny dancer had reappeared in the candle she'd placed on the rock next to her.

"The little ones that dance in the fire—what are they?"

"The fire spirits are called salamandars. Don't underestimate them because they're small. Like all elementals, their power multiplies infinitely when several join forces. Just as the sylphs can turn the wind to a raging gale, so the undines can make a flood, the salamandars a forest fire, and the gnomes a chasm in the earth at your feet. The elementals exist to uphold and foster life, but at times the line between creation and destruction is thin."

Alyen paused, still watching the salamandar, then asked, "If I choose to return to Castle Dúr, will I still see the elementals?"

"That's a good question, and honestly, I'm not entirely sure of the answer," Rowenna replied. "It's possible that you would keep your gift throughout your life—it's rare, but it has happened. Unfortunately, it's more likely that over time the elemental world would fade and perhaps disappear to your eyes altogether."

Alyen felt a pang at Rowenna's words. She pursed her lips. "How long do I have to decide?"

"Given the state of things, not long at all. But you can only choose once. Whatever you choose, you won't be able to change your mind later."

Alyen's voice was soft. "And if I choose to return to my old life?"

Rowenna shrugged with half a smile. "Then destiny will make other arrangements."

Alyen took a breath and willed herself to think rationally. She'd been born to rule. If there really were dark times coming, she would have to face them whether she was Queen or Keeper. Did it really matter which? Both jobs were ultimately about keeping her kingdom prosperous and safe. She would be a good queen. Maybe even a great one. But as Keeper she would also have the elementals. She would see magic and power that no one else could. And she would always be a close advisor to the throne, so her rulership training wouldn't necessarily be wasted. But what if she chose the apprenticeship, and was unhappy with it later?

Alyen shook her head. Thinking wasn't getting her anywhere. She closed her eyes and pictured returning to Castle Dúr, knowing that the elementals would likely fade away and that she'd always wonder what her life would have been if she'd chosen differently. A heaviness settled over her heart.

She imagined saying yes, knowing the future was a mystery. Her heart rose.

So that's it, then, she thought, feeling her indecision turning slowly to steely resolve. *I've already made my choice—I just don't want to admit it. I can wait a couple days, but it'll just delay the inevitable* … She straightened and looked Rowenna in the eye.

"My answer is yes. I want to be your apprentice and the next Keeper."

"Are you sure, Alyen?" Rowenna asked, her face serious. "You can take more time to think. You must be very sure."

Alyen paused only a moment, the memories of Castle Dúr burning like a fire in her chest. She willed her eyes to stay dry and her voice steady. "I'm sure."

Rowenna's eyes were warm and shining. "Then stand with me," she said quietly, rising from her seat on the spring.

Alyen stood as Rowenna reached into a basket that had been sitting by her feet and pulled out several small candles. One by one, she lit them from Alyen's candle and placed them on the boulders in a circle around the spring. Alyen glimpsed salamandars flashing in the ring of flames. *She prepared that basket before I chose. She suspected I would say yes tonight.*

A familiar whispering sounded. Above Alyen, dozens of

tree elves scurried along the dark branches of the fruit trees as sylphs wove in and out, rustling the shadowy leaves. Trundling slowly, backs hunched under heavy packs of gemstones, a gathering of elementals with faces as craggy as the rocks themselves formed by the boulders at the base of the spring. *Those must be gnomes,* Alyen thought. She shivered as a growing tingle of magic gathered in the air.

Rowenna turned and straightened to address the gardens and the elementals who had gathered. Moonlight accented the silver shining in her hair and she was suddenly as regal as any queen. The elementals drew closer. Rowenna gestured Alyen near, and as she drew up alongside, she suddenly found herself nervous.

"Do I have to do anything?" she whispered, making an effort not to rub the goosebumps rising on her arms.

"No," Rowenna replied calmly. "Just hold out your hands."

Rowenna enclosed Alyen's pale hands in the warmth of her own. Silence fell suddenly in the gardens. Rowenna's voice, though not loud, rang in the stillness.

"Hear me, spirits of the trees, fire, earth, air, and seas. The future Keeper have I found; a new apprentice not yet bound to me and to our common task. I have a simple boon to ask, that on our binding you will place the seal and blessing of your race."

Alyen listened, transfixed by Rowenna's flowing words. It wasn't poetry, not exactly, but the words rolled like spoken music through the gardens. With each syllable, Alyen could feel the air intensify as more and more elementals flocked to the sound of her voice. A rustle of anticipation shivered through the trees as Rowenna continued.

"First the gnomes who toil the earth, bless our binding at its birth."

The gnomes who had gathered near the boulders moved forward to form a circle around the human pair. As one, they began to stomp gently on the ground in a slow rhythm, and though not one gnome's height reached Alyen's kneecap, she could feel tremors from the center of the earth vibrate in time with their dance. The rhythm shook through the soles of her feet, through her bones and down her arms, to her hands still resting in Rowenna's grasp.

"Sylphs, good spirits of the air, I ask you to bless the bond we share."

A breeze suddenly stirred, and with a rustle of leaves, the sylphs swooped down and began to dart in and out of Alyen's and Rowenna's outstretched arms, weaving a knot of rushing wind around their clasped hands. Alyen's eyes widened as she felt her breath take on a new rhythm, the air rushing in and out of her lungs stronger and deeper than ever before.

"Undines of the sea and spring, your blessing to our binding bring."

Flashing silver and blue, the undines sprang into the air from the spring. As Alyen tilted her head up to watch, they wove through the space above her; tiny drops of water splashed her face, each sphere sparkling in the moonlight. As the raindrops fell on her hands, Alyen felt cool ripples pass up her arms, trickling through her chest and down her spine and legs.

"Last, salamandars' flaming spark, seal our binding with your mark."

Alyen looked to the burning candles circling the spring as the salamandars rose from the flames as one. They joined together in a swirling sphere of fire that hovered, glowing red and orange before it suddenly flashed into motion, tracing a fiery arc that burned white-hot against the dark sky. Alyen's breath caught as the fireball engulfed her hands. She instinctively tried to pull away, but Rowenna tightened her grip. Alyen gasped as she felt not the expected burn of skin, but a hot current that flashed through her blood, racing like lightning from her hands, through her limbs, and igniting a fire in her chest.

Rowenna's voice rose above the rush of wind, the crackle of flame, the patter of the raindrops, and the rumble of the earth as she addressed the clearing, crackling with magic, one final time.

"May all here present witness be! Alyen of Dúr is bound to me and from this night all nature hails the future Keeper of the Scales!"

Alyen shut her eyes amidst a roar of wind and leaves, fire and thunder. The ground shook and the trees groaned as they swayed.

Then all was silent.

Alyen stood shivering in the moonlit garden that was once again calm. The elementals trundled, scampered, and flitted as if nothing had happened. Rowenna released Alyen's hands and circled her arms around her new apprentice in a steadying embrace.

"Well done, Alyen," Rowenna whispered in her ear. "And welcome to the Trianid."

5
MEMORIES

It was a black night with no moon and dark clouds that hid the starlight. Tiny waves slapped restlessly against the obsidian shore, and an uneasy stillness hung in the air as if the wind didn't know whether it dared to blow.

Ylvain stood before a brazier, orange flames setting the edges of her face aglow, sharp and beautiful in the darkness. Opposite her the smoke billowed, visible against the starless sky only by the faint glow within.

"Are you ready?" the whisper sounded over the crackling of the fire.

"What must I do?"

"You must yield to me completely. I will enter your mind and search the memories of your past, banishing each seed of pain, every source of anger, every spark of love."

"I'll forget my past?"

"You will not forget, but you will never again feel pain or betrayal. Only love can make you feel these things, and I will eliminate love from your heart forever. All that will be left is power. Clean. Cold. And wondrous."

Ylvain's hooded eyes rested on the flames, and she felt her blood tingle through her limbs. His power had never fully left her, not since the night she had released him. She craved it, ached for it to fill her again, welcomed the numbness and clarity her new power would bring.

For deep within, she knew she was tired. Tired of anger. Weary from pain. Exhausted by rage.

She was ready to be rid of love.

Unbidden, memories bloomed in her mind. Her village of Ramsheath and the house where she grew up. She and Rowenna picking flowers in the fields. Laughing at the sylphs they saw tumbling in the breeze. Singing songs by the brook as they watched undines splash in the shallows. Sitting close, heads together by the fire, drowsy as they watched salamandars dance in the darkness.

Are you sure? her own voice asked from somewhere within. *Not all the memories are bad. Not all are etched with sorrow. There was good as well. Do you want to lose that, too?*

The smoke shifted restlessly on the other side of the brazier. Ylvain could feel his impatience and a drop of fear spread cold through her belly.

Licking her lips, she gathered the memories up and shoved them down, far down to the hidden place her own voice called from. She continued to push down, burying them so deep they could never be found or seen again—not by him, not even by her.

They were as good as lost. And her voice with them.

Ylvain raised her eyes. "I am ready."

The orange glow flickered with satisfaction in the heart of

the smoke, then two tendrils snaked their way to hover, one before her forehead, the other before her breast. For a moment all was still, then again, the smoky arms surged forward, entering her mind and heart, filling her once more with the thrill of darkness and power.

Suddenly images were flashing through her mind. She was young, in Ramsheath. Rowenna stood beside her. Sylvan, the Keeper, was addressing them both before the village. She was stealing a pitying glance at Rowenna. Yes, they both had the Sight, but Ylvain knew herself as the stronger candidate. Rowenna had never been ambitious, never thought of what could be done with her gift, never considered how high she could rise … Yet it was not Ylvain's name that came from Sylvan's lips. There was Rowenna smiling her acceptance as Ylvain shrank, humiliated, into the shadows. Ylvain felt her heart contract, felt it snarl at her friend's image, felt the familiar mix of jealousy and hate.

"The first betrayal," the voice hissed. "Feel the anger you have carried, Ylvain. Let it grow, let it burn—pour it into your heart and mind. And give it to me."

Ylvain stood, eyes closed, fists clenched, and did as the voice commanded. Her anger burst forth, flaring hot in its freedom. The smoke swirled within her, surrounded the flame, and suddenly the anger was gone. In its place was nothing but cool indifference.

Ylvain exhaled slowly through her mouth and lowered her head, opening her eyes. Her mind felt sharp and clear; her body thrummed with energy.

"Do you feel the difference, Ylvain? Do you feel how your power grows as your care vanishes?"

Ylvain's mouth curled into a slow smile and from her throat came a low chuckle.

"We continue," the voice said, and once again, her mind was filled with images.

She was still in Ramsheath, relegated to the life of a village wench, withering with jealousy as Rowenna bloomed under Sylvan's tutelage. Rowenna was a fool, thinking their friendship was unchanged. But naiveté had its uses. It took little urging to convince Rowenna to share all the newfound knowledge of her apprenticeship with her dearest friend. Bitterness coursing through her, Ylvain watched as her younger self grew more powerful in secret, fueled by anger and knowing that, no matter how skilled she became, it was all for naught.

But magic was not the only path to power. She was beautiful, quick-witted, resourceful. Soon a string of suiters formed—perhaps there would be hope for an advantageous match. But the first proposal proved a disaster. A boy with no ambition, a family that would keep her in the shadows forever, and, according to the village, a perfect choice. Without an excuse, refusing would make her seem too proud, and others may be dissuaded from making offers of their own. Her ambitions would die, and she would end her days a peasant in Ramsheath.

It had been clever, the way she'd handled it. The way she'd batted her eyes, feigned sappy declarations of love, then sobbed with false heartbreak after she'd used the salamandars to humiliate the boy. He was ostracized as a fool and left Ramsheath soon after.

Then Ylvain's heart clenched as Rowenna flashed before her mind's eyes once more. Rowenna, who suspected what she'd done. Rowenna, whose eyes now held caution and mistrust when they looked at her. Rowenna, who told Sylvan her suspicions and confessed to Ylvain's secret education.

"The second betrayal," the voice whispered in her ears.

Anger flashed white hot through Ylvain's blood once again. Her teeth grated together as she gathered it, longing for freedom from it, waiting for the smoke to dissolve it into nothingness.

Release came like cool water in her veins. She flexed her fingers, savoring the new strength coursing through her. The memories resumed.

Sylvan was speaking with her—inane words of caution and responsibility meant only to limit, to stunt her power in its youth. He left with Rowenna to continue her apprenticeship elsewhere and at last she was free from the constant reminder of her once-friend's shadow.

Then up swam the image of the mayor's son. The man was an idiot, but he would take his father's place one day. Marriage would come with a respected title and the promise of travel. Flashes of their wedding flickered past: the guests, the revelry, the smile she wore to hide her scorn of it all. She would stomach the pageantry if it meant securing a position of influence. All that was left was for her to produce an heir.

Suddenly the smoke writhed within her. Memories were flashing with a brightness that made her cry out in pain: her belly was swollen, she could feel the child moving within—a new, small life. For the first time since childhood, she felt a sense of purpose—and perhaps something akin to happiness. Not even Rowenna's return to Ramsheath as the new Keeper could dampen her spirits for long.

Ylvain knew the memories that were coming and shrank

from them, but the smoke wrenched her back to the blazing images. She saw the night, the terrible night she woke, pain seizing her belly and blood between her legs. She knew it was beyond the skills of the village midwife, and in a desperate panic she went to Rowenna.

She saw Rowenna working through the night. And she saw the sun rising as she lay in bed, childless.

Despair and rage consumed her. Not only had she lost her child, she had also likely lost her position. There would be talk. They would say the mayor's son should put her aside. They would say she was barren. They would say it was her fault.

"But it was not your fault," the voice hissed. "It was Rowenna's. Surely the finest healer in the kingdom, with all the elements at her disposal, could have prevented such a thing. She didn't try hard enough. Perhaps she failed you on purpose. The third betrayal."

Ylvain was shaking. The pain and the anger had grown to such a height within, she felt her body would soon be unable to contain it. This was the heart of her hatred for the woman who once had been her friend. Rowenna had taken everything from her—vocation, knowledge, position, marriage. Even her child, her tiny child. Ylvain raised her face to the dark sky and uttered a wail that sounded more animal than human. As she keened, the smoke surged through her; it swirled and slashed and clenched her heart in a grip as tight as any fist.

And it was gone.

Mid-cry, Ylvain's voice cut off and silence surrounded the black tower. The smoke swirled once more within her. It paused, hesitating somewhere near the place she had pushed her memories down, out of sight, out of reach. Then the smoke melted out of her robes and returned to swirl slowly across the brazier.

Ylvain raised her hands and massaged her chest curiously. She felt hollow, as though she no longer possessed a heart, yet she felt the steady beat under her palm. Her blood pulsed, filled with a power eager to be tested.

She strode forward and drew the knife from her waist. The blade flashed against her palm, and she held her clenched fist over the brazier as blood slowly dripped into the flames. Her eyes rested on the fire, watching the tiny salamandars swirling within. Then she began to speak, her voice low, commanding, and terrible as blood continued to hiss on the embers. The salamandars' dance changed. The flames became agitated and fitful and Ylvain's voice rose. Abruptly, the fire changed from glowing orange to a sickly green. The salamandars within were shriveled, ragged, and sinister; their eyes as black as dead coals.

Ylvain drew her hand back slowly, gazing wide-eyed at the altered flames. Then she threw her head back and laughed, her terrible exultation echoing over the stillness of the uneasy sea.

6

LIRIANNA

lyen woke to a new world. Sylphs flitted about her room and through the corridors, undines flashed in the water she splashed on her face in the lavatory, and looking out the windows, she could see tree elves clad in fiery colors to match the autumn leaves of the forest scampering amid the branches.

Before she left her room, Alyen rummaged through one of her crates until she found a bit of parchment, a pot of ink, and a slightly rumpled but functional quill. Her parents would, of course, be notified of her decision, but Alyen wanted them to hear it from her first. She sat at her desk, dipped the feather in the ink, and wrote:

Dear Mother and Father,
I am well here at Monstar. I wanted you to know that my Sight
has broken through, and I have accepted the apprenticeship. I hope

*my choice meets with your approval—it was difficult to make. But
in the end, I think it's what's best for Dúramair.*

Alyen hesitated, her quill hovering over the glistening
inked words. She felt the urge to add an apology but decided
against it. Instead, her thoughts turned toward the cousin,
Merrith, who would now be called upon to inherit the throne.
Her throne. Likely no time would be wasted in bringing him to
the castle to start his own training. Her heart twisted—she
hadn't counted on how hard it would be to imagine another in
her place. *The choice was mine to make*, she told herself. *And I think
I chose well.* She gritted her teeth, then pressed her quill to the
parchment once more.

> *I wish you both well, and I miss you very much. Please give*
> *Merrith my best regards when he arrives.*
> *With all my love,*
> *Alyen*

Slowly, she put down the quill. She leaned forward to blow
on the ink and smiled as two tiny sylphs flitted over to help by
fluttering their wings at the page, sending a gentle breeze. As
soon as the ink was dry, Alyen rolled up the letter, tied it with a
bit of string, and carried it with her as she went downstairs for
breakfast.

Rowenna was in the entrance hall, fastening her cloak.

"You're leaving?" Alyen asked.

Rowenna nodded. "I want to get to Castle Dúr quickly.
Your parents and I have much to discuss—and then there's
Illya." She smiled wryly.

Alyen held out her letter. "Would you mind giving this to them? Before you tell them I'm your apprentice?"

"Of course," Rowenna said, understanding. She tucked the letter into her cloak, then embraced Alyen. "No need for goodbyes," she said brightly. "I'll be waiting for you tonight for your first lesson."

Half an hour later, Alyen stood in her doorway once again, taking in the daunting mountain of mess that still sat untouched in the middle of her floor. It was time to unpack. She tied her hair back in a knot and began prying lids off crates.

She was half-buried in packing straw and random belongings, hands covered in scrapes from the rough wood, when she opened a crate to find it stuffed full of her dresses. Alyen paused, then pulled them all out and lay them on her bed. She stood back and studied them, hands on her hips.

They were beautiful. Too beautiful. Each one was made of fine silks and linens with embroidered skirts that swept the floor. Even her riding dress that she'd always worn to the Royal Wood was elegant and already showing signs of wear from her brief excursions in the forest.

They were perfect clothes for a princess. None of them were suitable for spending her days in the gardens or the forest.

Alyen turned and rummaged through her belongings until she found her mostly unused sewing box. She took out a pair of scissors and grimly approached the line of dresses. She could at least shorten them—or perhaps split the skirts down the middle and resew them into something more functional. She selected one of the older gowns—violet with tiny, embroidered flowers—and spread it out on the barest spot of floor she could find. Her heart gave a lurch at what she was about to do, but she shoved the feeling aside and raised the scissors. Then, just as she was about to cut into the fabric, a shout startled her into dropping the scissors completely.

"*Stop!* What in the name of Béathan are you doing?"

Alyen twisted around to see a girl standing in the doorway, looking as horrified as if she'd just walked in on someone setting fire to the abbey.

"*Saints,* you scared me," Alyen breathed, covering her heart.

"Sorry," the girl replied. "It's just—you can't do that. You can't."

Alyen tottered to her feet, overturning a stack of books, and nearly smashing an extra ink pot. "Lirianna, I'm guessing?"

The girl flashed a grin and held out her hand displaying something hidden among the folds of a woven napkin. "I was bringing you a tart. They're supposed to be for dinner, but I snuck one out of the kitchens. Am I … am I supposed to curtsy or anything? I've never actually been around a royal before."

Alyen blinked. "Cur—no! No, I'm … not really a princess anymore."

The words felt awkward coming out of her mouth. Lirianna paused as she gave Alyen a considering look. "That was brave of you," she finally said. "It must have been a hard choice."

Alyen shrugged, unsure of what to say.

Lirianna looked around at the mess and raised an eyebrow. "It doesn't look like you've had much time to unpack yet."

"Well, I was trying to. I got distracted trying to figure out how to make myself apprentice clothes." Alyen gestured vaguely at the gown on the floor.

Lirianna shook her head and took a step into the room. "I can't allow you to destroy your dresses. They're probably the most beautiful garments in the kingdom. The weaving rooms are full of cloth—you can take whatever you want and make something new."

"Oh—yes! That's a better idea. I'll do that," Alyen said, trying not to sound like someone who had never sewn a sock let alone a whole dress.

Lirianna suddenly smiled. "Would you like some help? Mother Brenwyn gave me the day off so we can get to know each other. We could set up your room, and later we can go to the weaving rooms and design something."

"That would be fantastic," Alyen exhaled in sincere gratitude. "I think I'm just making the mess worse."

Lirianna set down the tart and reached to tie back her own flaming curly hair. "I think it will look better once we get all the crates out of the way ... oh!"

Lirianna stopped short. Her face took on a strange expression as she stared at a tapestry hanging on the wall over the bookshelf—the only decoration the room had contained. It depicted a girl kneeling in a forest next to a gleaming sword, and she was surrounded by tiny golden lights.

"What?" Alyen asked.

"The tapestry," Lirianna replied. "I wondered where it ended up."

"You've seen it before?"

"Of course I have. I made it."

"*You* made this tapestry?"

"Yes," Lirianna was looking thoughtful. "It was the first

one I wove when Mother Brenwyn started teaching me how to weave a foresight vision."

"Then—then this is a vision you had of the future?"

"Well, I hope it is. I can't become Seer until one of my foresight tapestries comes to pass."

"But how will you know when it does? Do you know who the girl is?"

Lirianna was looking back and forth from the tapestry to Alyen. "I didn't know when I wove it," she admitted. "But I think I do now."

Alyen raised an eyebrow. "You mean …"

Lirianna nodded. "Yes. I think it's you. It hasn't happened yet, has it?"

"I don't think so. I mean, I've been in the forest, but never with a sword. And nothing ever happened with little lights around me like that."

Lirianna nodded. "Good. It's a true foresight, then. If it happens—*when* it happens—you have to tell me."

Within an hour, Alyen felt she had known Lirianna her whole life. They worked all morning, their talk and laughter echoing in the corridors, and by midday Alyen's room was completely transformed. All the crates had been removed, and the room did seem much more spacious without them towering in the center of the floor. Her rescued dresses had all been hung neatly in the wardrobe by Lirianna, and Alyen had organized her desk and filled the trunk with her things. The bookshelf was full, and her warm, goose-feather winter quilt hung neatly over the foot of the bed. Alyen smiled as she surveyed the result of their work; it wasn't as luxurious as her room in Castle Dúr, but it was clean, comfortable, and even cozy.

The afternoon was spent in the weaving rooms. Upon entering, Lirianna grabbed a piece of parchment and a quill, her hands making quick, deft stokes across the page.

"What do you think of this?" she asked after a few moments, offering Alyen her sketch.

Alyen studied the drawing. It was almost like a simple dress, but it had two legs instead of a skirt, each with a pocket on the hip. "It's perfect. Really perfect," she said, impressed.

They turned their attention to the shelves that held Monstar's stock of finely woven cloth in every shade and fiber imaginable. There were several bolts of silk the girls stroked and admired—pale creams and the lightest shades of lavender and sage—but Alyen reluctantly admitted that earthy tones and a sturdy fiber might be most practical given the amount of time she would need to spend in the forest. In the end, they settled on a rust red, a soft brown, and, despite Alyen's protests that three new garments were far too much work, a vibrant sapphire blue.

"It matches your eyes perfectly," Lirianna insisted, plopping the bolt deftly on top of the other two. "Besides, what's life without a little fun?" She pulled out a measuring cord and began winding it around Alyen's waist, effectively ending the debate.

By the end of the day, Alyen's new garments had been patterned and cut, and, to Alyen's relief, Lirianna had generously offered to help with the sewing the following day. After sharing a dinner of roasted meats, vegetables and, indeed, raspberry tarts, Lirianna rose to go to evening services. "Are you coming?"

"I'll come tomorrow," Alyen promised. "I have to do something in the library."

They agreed to meet at the library in an hour. Lirianna joined the nuns filtering into the chapel, and Alyen headed up the stairs.

The library was quiet, the sun slanting through the windowpanes in dusty golden shafts as it sank toward the horizon. Preparing her room had been necessary and she'd loved Lirianna's company, but Alyen had been itching to start exploring the library since she'd seen it the day before. She walked slowly through the maze of shelves, her fingertips lightly brushing the silent tomes. There were many she was drawn to: faerie stories, books on healing tinctures and poison antidotes, and an ancient field guide to garden sprites with tattered pages and dried leather binding that cracked at the spine. Suddenly she stopped as her hand landed on one title that made her heart leap. *The Legend of Thor Lynn* was embossed in gold lettering down the spine. Alyen pulled the book off the shelf and studied the cover, which showed a warrior wielding a flashing sword. It wasn't an especially long book, and Alyen guessed it would only take her a day or two to finish it. She found an armchair, curled into it cross-legged, and opened to the first page.

A shiver tingled down her spine as she read words that were familiar and foreboding.

"Let all be warned! A time shall come
Two suns shall set to leave but one ..."

Alyen's mind flashed to the stables at Castle Dúr as her eyes traced the words of the prophecy she barely remembered. Garret had taught it to her and Aaron on the day she'd met the future Slayer. She thought of Garret, how she would miss visiting him in the stables and listening to his stories. She thought rather longer of Aaron. She hadn't seen him in at least a year. Where was he now? What would he think when he found out she would be the next Keeper?

Alyen shook her head, turned the page, and began the first chapter. Soon she was completely engrossed and almost didn't hear Lirianna call her name from the library's entrance. She gave a start and sprang out of the chair, taking the book with her.

Lirianna was waiting at the door and smiled as Alyen came into view. She glanced down at the book in Alyen's hand.

"Were you reading? Is it good?"

"It's fabulous!" Alyen replied. "It's just the legend of Thor Lynn that everyone knows, but it's a more detailed version than I've ever heard." Alyen handed the book to Lirianna, who took it almost gingerly.

"It looks nice," Lirianna said without opening the cover.

"You can read it after me if you like," Alyen offered. "I should be done with it in a couple days."

"Yes. Maybe. It's just that … I'm not very …" She sighed, resigned. "You're going to think I'm stupid."

Alyen hesitated, not wanting to offend her new friend, but finally asked, "Lirianna, can you read?"

Lirianna looked up from the book. "Well, I *can*. I'm just really slow. Tiragel is bard country, you know, and everyone puts a lot more value on memorization and learning by rote than reading. Mother Brenwyn told me to practice and said she would help, but she hasn't had time lately and—"

"I can help you if you like," Alyen broke in.

Lirianna scanned the shelf-lined walls longingly. "Could you really? You wouldn't mind?"

"Of course not! We can start now if you like."

Lirianna looked back at the book and stroked the leather cover, admiring the fine binding. She looked out the windows at the evening sky and grabbed a lamp from a nearby table.

"Come on," she said, her eyes suddenly excited. "I know a good place we can go."

They left the library and Lirianna led the way through twisting corridors and up a spiral stairway Alyen had not seen before. At the top, a door opened to the outside, revealing a narrow walkway across the top of the battlements. Lirianna continued down the walkway until they reached an enormous stone basin sitting atop the abbey wall, with a short wooden ladder leading up to it. Lirianna hitched up her blue novice robes, climbed up the ladder, scrambled into the basin, then leaned over the edge to peer down at Alyen.

"Come up," she said. "It's a fantastic view."

Alyen scaled the wooden rungs and hoisted herself into the shallow dip of the basin. She straightened to look out over the abbey wall and gasped at the sight that met her eyes. Sheanen Crann stretched for miles beneath them, and the sinking sun set the trees ablaze with the reds, golds, and yellows of their autumn splendor. Alyen could see the Moor of Moin stretching beyond the forest to the west, and she imagined Castle Dúr nestled somewhere in the vast stretch of grassland. Far, far away, at the north horizon, the purple shadow of mountains jutted upward, reaching for a slivered moon that hung in the sky. Flitting about on wings as fine and transparent as a dragonfly's, sylphs darted in and out of sight, and Alyen could swear she saw them flinging sparkling dust into the air to color the sky in sunset hues.

Lirianna smiled at Alyen's face. "I told you it was pretty."

"I wish you could see all of it, though," Alyen replied, and described the sylphs.

"Really? You can see them right now? Where?"

Alyen smiled as a breeze played gently through Lirianna's fiery hair. "There's a couple near your face right now. I think they like your hair." She laughed as Lirianna raised a hand, then froze in place.

"I won't squash them, will I?"

Alyen shook her head. "They're too quick for you. Besides, I think they're like the air—you can feel it and touch it, but you can't hold onto it. It just moves around you."

"It's a wonderful gift, Alyen," Lirianna sighed. "I wish I could see them."

"And I wish I could see the future," Alyen said, smiling wryly.

Lirianna looked down at the book still clutched in her hands and opened it to the first page. Her eyes scanned the prophecy. She looked at Alyen, who nodded encouragingly. Taking a deep breath, Lirianna began to read aloud slowly, frowning in concentration as her finger traced her progress from word to word.

> *"Let all be warned! A time will come*
> *Two suns shall set to leave but one.*
> *When shifting scales foretell our doom*
> *And from below a darkness looms.*

> *Our only hope in darkest night*
> *To turn our world back to the light*
> *Shall lie with one who seeks to win*
> *The weapon of the knight Thor Lynn.*
>
> *Oh, Second Slayer, ye tread a path*
> *Of villains' snare and monsters' wrath,*
> *Past riddles and spells of magic laid*
> *Alone ye cannot claim the blade.*
>
> *Yet let none crave this hero's lot*
> *Though fame be prized, and glory sought,*
> *For if on you the fate should fall*
> *Remember this: death changes all."*

Lirianna reached the end of the prophecy and looked up at Alyen, satisfaction in her eyes.

"It was perfect," Alyen confirmed.

"It's a beautiful rhyme." Lirianna traced the flowing letters once more with her fingers. "I grew up hearing the stories of Thor Lynn, of course, but I never heard this."

"Really? I wonder how Garret knew it. Then again, Garret knows more stories than anyone. Even the bards."

"Who?"

"Garret. My father's Master of Horse. He taught Aaron and me the legend of Thor Lynn and the prophecy years ago, when we got caught in the stables in a thunderstorm."

Lirianna's eyes sparked with interest. "So, you've already met Aaron? What's he like?"

"Aaron? He's—well, he's nice. I don't really know him that well." Something had started squirming in Alyen's stomach.

Lirianna was watching her intently, and Alyen was reminded strongly of Mother Brenwyn's gaze that always seemed to see more than what met the eye.

"Yes, but what's he *like?*" she repeated. "If you've known him for years you must have some idea of his character."

"Well …" Alyen cleared her throat. "He's easygoing and laughs a lot, but he takes his training very seriously. He's always courteous, but he gets bored with formalities and prefers to be outside."

"And he's a good warrior?"

"I don't know, I've never seen him fight. Although I suppose he must be if he's going to be the next Slayer."

"And his looks?" Lirianna inquired.

Alyen's stomach gave an extra squirm. "He's tall, with dark blond hair and hazel eyes. And he's really well built—from all the training, you know," she added.

"Sounds like you know quite a bit about him for not knowing him well at all."

The squirming thing in Alyen's stomach fluttered, and Lirianna smirked.

7

THE BALANCE

It took Alyen longer than usual to fall asleep that night. She felt a strange but wonderful warmth in her chest after the day spent with Lirianna, and her limbs were tingling with the anticipation of her first lesson with Rowenna. After tossing and turning for an hour or more, she finally forced herself to lie still, breathe deeply, and at last she found herself stepping out of the mist into the dreamworld.

She was standing beside a cottage in the same forest clearing she'd dreamt of before, and Rowenna was waiting for her.

"Alyen," Rowenna said, smiling. "How was your day? Are you settling into Monstar?"

Alyen nodded. "It was lovely. Lirianna helped me unpack."

"Good, you've met. Feel free to spend some extra time together over the next few days. The bonds between members of the Trianid run deep, and it's important you have time to connect."

"Those bonds," Alyen asked. "Is that the warmth in my chest when Lirianna and I are together?"

Rowenna nodded. "Exactly. It's a feeling unique to members of the Trianid—like friendship, but much stronger. Now if you're ready, we'll begin with tonight's lesson."

Alyen didn't object, so Rowenna headed into the trees, gesturing for Alyen to follow.

"As you well know," Rowenna began as she walked, "the primary function of the Trianid is to maintain the Balance in our kingdom. Your upbringing has likely given you a better idea of what that means than most, but still, it's very important to be clear on this point at the beginning as it's the foundation of everything we do."

"The Balance is what governs our way of life in Dúramair," Alyen supplied. "It's the idea that everything must live together in harmony to ensure the greatest possible health and prosperity for all."

Rowenna was nodding. "Very close, but not quite there. What you've described is the philosophy we've developed to aid us in *keeping* the Balance. But the Balance itself isn't just an idea *about* everything; it *is* everything," she explained as they walked. "Without it, nothing can exist. The Balance is every tree, every rock, every bird or fish, dragon or garden sprite. We ourselves are part of it. Imagine a golden tapestry composed of millions of threads that all weave together to form the earth and everything in it. Every strand in the fabric represents a living being, be it mouse or mountain, and all the threads interweave in beautiful, intricate patterns to form the stories of our world. That's the Balance."

Rowenna stopped walking. They had reached another clearing much like the one they'd just left, but older, and wrapped in the kind of forest stillness only found where humans seldom tread. They seated themselves side by side on a large boulder, and Rowenna continued.

"In order to keep the Balance, each one of us—the Keeper, the Slayer, and the Seer—must be vigilant to ensure that our efforts remain pure and unbiased. The Seer, for example, must watch that personal opinions or desires do not affect her interpretations of her visions. This is what the Seers have come to call Purity of Sight. The Slayer, on the other hand, must always remember that, though he is trained in combat to the highest degree, his duty is a peaceful one. Violence is rarely if ever needed anymore, and he must equally guard against the temptation to use his skills as a means of intimidation. This law is known as Integrity of Might."

"And our law?" Alyen asked.

"Our law is called Sanctity of Life. It is perhaps the most difficult of the three to grasp, so I shall try to explain clearly."

Rowenna thought for a moment as she stared up at the forest canopy. Finally, she lowered her gaze back to Alyen, her eyes intent. "It's important—very important—never to forget the limits of our own knowledge. We are tasked with keeping humanity in harmony with nature; however, the workings of the natural world are vast, and we can see only a fraction of the great tapestry of the Balance from where we sit on our one single thread. The greater design is hidden from us. But because of our role as Keeper and the power that comes with it, a mistake made from ignorance or arrogance could be disastrous. Do you understand how this is so?"

Alyen nodded uncertainly, unsure if she did completely understand.

Rowenna pressed on, her tone grave. "The greatest and most arrogant mistake that can be made is to think we possess the wisdom to judge the worth of another living being—to think we understand another's purpose in the weaving of the Balance and can determine whether or not that purpose is worthy of life. It's confusing, I know, so consider this example. Look over at that bush across the clearing."

Alyen followed Rowenna's gaze to a shrub growing in the shade of the trees. Its dark leaves did not stir in the stillness of the forest, and purple flowers the shape of Monstar's chapel bells dipped their heads delicately in the mist. From each branch hung a cluster of plump black berries that enticed Alyen's eye with their glossy sheen.

Rowenna's voice was soft. "That plant is called deadly nightshade. It's incredibly poisonous—even just one or two of the berries can kill you. And it's not just the berries—every part of the deadly nightshade is poisonous, from the roots to the leaves. Not only does it kill, those who find themselves the victims of deadly nightshade suffer greatly before their deaths; aside from the pain and sickness it causes, horrific and terrifying visions plague victims as the poison gradually takes over the mind. So why, if the deadly nightshade is so horribly dangerous, has it been allowed to exist at all? Why not just eradicate it, kill each plant that's found until it's wiped from the face of the earth, or at least from any place people might come into contact with it? Would this not be a service to humanity? So much suffering avoided, so many curious, unsuspecting children saved from early death?"

Alyen remained silent, knowing Rowenna wasn't finished.

"You see, Alyen, while everyone knows of the dangers I have described, there is another side to the deadly nightshade that most people are unaware of. Although it's risky, a wise and well-trained healer can at times use the nightshade as a healing agent, for the plant also possesses unique powers when the right amount is used in the correct manner. For instance, in severe cases, when a body shakes from an illness and is unable to stop, nightshade will relax the muscles and help the body to lie still. When added to a healing salve and applied to the chest, nightshade will help to ease pain and discomfort around the heart. And ironically, it has even been known to act as an antidote in cases of poisoning from certain mushrooms. Should these gifts, the best this living plant has to offer, be lost to us and the world simply because we fear the consequences of our own ignorance?

"But there is also another reason to protect the deadly nightshade—one perhaps only you and I can fully appreciate. Look closely down by the roots of the plant ..."

Alyen squinted through the haze and, after a moment, noticed a small sprite crouching at the base of the shrub, her arms entwined gently around the fleshy stalk. Clad all in the nightshade's dark green leaves, with one of the purple bell flowers atop her head for a hat, the sprite stared intently at Alyen with eyes that shone, round and black as the berries hanging from the branches above. The sprite and Alyen regarded each other silently; she sensed the elemental was shy and untrusting as it stroked the nightshade protectively with slender fingers.

"Each and every growing thing on the earth has a guardian," Rowenna said, her voice now gentle. "These are the garden sprites, the tree elves, the nyads—there are as many varieties as there are species of plant. The one you see there is the caretaker of this nightshade plant. Its well-being is the sole purpose of her entire life. She is a part of it, it is a part of her, and she loves it more than any other thing in the world. If her nightshade were to be killed before its natural time, her grief would be unbearable. She would mourn for her nightshade as her life slowly faded, and eventually she, too, would die."

Alyen watched as the nightshade's guardian probed tenderly around the roots of her plant, loosening the soil where it had become packed and patting it more firmly where support was needed.

"Tell me, Alyen: is our peace of mind of greater worth than the life of this little one? I think not. And now do you see how easy it is for us, so often ignorant, to cause great harm with an action that would seem to us of little consequence? And how each of these seemingly small actions can tip the cosmic scales, causing tears in the fabric of the Balance?

"This then, is the meaning of Sanctity of Life: We honor each being's equal right to existence. We vow to never knowingly end the life of another prematurely, acknowledging that only nature itself can know when any single thread of the Balance should be cut. Now I'm not talking about instances which *are* part of the natural order—we must, after all, harvest plants and animals in order to eat, or cut trees to warm ourselves and build shelter. Do you understand the difference?"

Alyen nodded.

"If Sanctity of Life is broken by a Keeper," Rowenna said intently, "the results can be devastating. Trust in the Keeper by the elemental world will be shattered, and, for a while at least, the elementals will refuse to appear or assist the Keeper in maintaining the Balance. It is very difficult to regain that trust once it's broken and in the worst cases, the elementals may abandon the Keeper forever."

Alyen frowned. Thoughts of Illya burning, of dark magic, and of the assassin guarding her in the forest were flashing through her mind, and an uncomfortable scenario was unfolding in her head. "Rowenna, what if you're being attacked? We're allowed to defend ourselves, aren't we?"

"Of course."

"And, if your opponent should die …?"

Rowenna's face was impassive as she considered her answer. "Keep in mind, Alyen, that one may always aim to wound rather than kill. If there is no other way to save yourself, or if an accident occurs, then so be it. But to intentionally kill another, it must truly be a very last resort—the elementals will know if it was not."

Alyen paused, not wanting to seem contradictory. "It seems to me," she said slowly, "that the lines of this law are quite blurry. Especially in the case of dark or dangerous times."

Rowenna nodded, her face serious. "You're right. We could come up with countless scenarios that would seem to demand an exception to the rule—many of which may be quite valid. For now, just remember that this is the law that enables us to retain the trust of the elementals, and so we must follow it as closely as we can. And we shall pray to Béathan and all the saints that destiny does not bring us alongside one of those blurry lines."

Rowenna stood and motioned for Alyen to follow her back the way they'd come. Alyen glanced back once at the nightshade as she rose, and the plant's elemental followed her with dark eyes as she left the clearing.

They walked in silence until they had nearly reached the cottage once more. Alyen wasn't sure her mentor had approved of her questions, but when Rowenna stopped at an evergreen bush, her tone was light once more.

"There's one more thing I want to teach you before we end for tonight. Ideally, I would wait to teach you this until you'd had more time to settle, but all things considered, we may want to focus on training you faster than usual."

"How long does it usually take to train a Keeper?"

"It depends on the Keeper," Rowenna said as she examined the bush, peering between the dense branches. "It generally takes several years to develop healing skills and build a thorough knowledge of plants and herbs, but most Keepers start out with at least some familiarity with the plants. You, however, being raised in a castle—"

"I do know some things," Alyen broke in quickly. Rowenna turned to her with raised eyebrows and Alyen flushed, realizing how childish she'd sounded. "My tutor, Professor Glibb," she explained more calmly. "Whenever he wanted me to practice penmanship, he would assign pages from a botanical treatise for me to copy. I think he figured the subject would be boring to a princess so I wouldn't be distracted by the content, but I thought it was interesting. Fascinating, actually. I memorized most of it. As a result, I'm afraid Professor Glibb might have a lower opinion of my handwriting than it really deserves."

Rowenna nodded thoughtfully. "Well, that's welcome news, then. I'll take whatever time we can save, and we shall hope that Professor Glibb's treatise and your memory are accurate. In any case, to answer your question, the main point is that you cannot be initiated fully as Keeper of Scales until you gain the trust and approval of Faer Dinnán."

"Faer Dinnán, the faerie king?" asked Alyen, remembering the name from stories she'd heard as a child.

"The very one."

"Faer Dinnán is real?"

"Quite real. But unlike the other elementals, Faer Dinnán can appear to any human at any time, not just the Keeper of Scales. He can also keep himself hidden from whoever he wants—including the Keeper of Scales."

"And I'm going to meet him?"

"I certainly hope so."

Excitement surged through Alyen's veins. Faer Dinnán, who feasted with his court beneath the trees on Midsummer night! The spirit who married a mortal maid and made her his Faerie Queen! The one who was reputed to steal children away into his enchanted forest kingdom ... Alyen's thoughts stopped short. She had never believed the faerie stories to be true—not completely at least—but suppose they were?

"Rowenna," she asked, "you've met Faer Dinnán, haven't you?"

"Of course," Rowenna said, straightening from the ground where she had been feeling around the roots of the bush. She held out her wrist to Alyen. Emblazoned on her skin was an imprint of a single green leaf. "This is the sign of Faer Dinnán. When he trusts you enough to bear his mark, we know you are ready to be Keeper."

"Is Faer Dinnán ... is he good?" Alyen asked awkwardly, not sure how to put her thoughts to words.

Rowenna studied Alyen's face before replying. "Is this bush good?"

"I—I don't know."

"You don't know because it's neither good nor bad. It simply is, as all of nature is. The same is true of Faer Dinnán. But it is important to remember that he doesn't follow the same moral code as humans do."

"What do you mean?"

"I mean that he doesn't reason the same way we do. He doesn't necessarily consider the same things to be right or wrong as we do. To us, he can seem unpredictable."

Before Alyen could reply, Rowenna called her attention to the slender green branches of the bush she had apparently finished examining.

"It's almost winter, which is not the ideal time to begin your apprenticeship. You won't be able to do much outdoors when everything is covered in snow. But what you need to begin to learn right away is how to work with the elementals as partners and allies in healing, starting with how to communicate with them and, through them, with the natural world that lends us its healing powers. Now, this bush here—do you recognize it?"

"It's a juniper bush," Alyen replied promptly. "Its berries and oil can be used to cure a number of ailments."

"Exactly right," Rowenna looked pleased. "I'll show you how to extract the oil later, but first we must collect the berries. There are more of them earlier in the fall, but there are still a few left on this bush."

Alyen reached out her hand toward a small cluster of somewhat shriveled, dusty, blue berries still clinging to the juniper's branches, but Rowenna stayed her hand.

"Wait, Alyen. The first rule of gathering is to ask before taking."

"Ask?"

"Yes, always ask," Rowenna confirmed. "Consider this: juniper is a well-known remedy, and any village healer can easily pick a basket of berries and make a basic medicine. But remedies from the Keeper of Scales are usually significantly more effective. Do you know why?"

Alyen shook her head.

"Because we know how to partner with the elementals and enlist their help. You saw how carefully the guardian of the deadly nightshade tended her charge. Do you think she would have taken kindly to a part of it being ripped off without a thought? But if you ask a nyad or sprite for permission to take a part of their precious plant, explaining the need and expressing your gratitude, they will likely want to help you. Then, instead of leaving with something you have—from the elemental's perspective—taken by force, it becomes a gift given freely from nature. The elemental will imbue it with good intent before relinquishing it, greatly increasing its healing effect. All because you showed respect for nature and asked before taking."

Alyen eyed the berry cluster. "And so, I just ... ask? It's that simple?"

"Yes," Rowenna replied. "But you have to ask in a way that will get the elemental's attention. You have to learn their language."

Alyen's heart sank. At Castle Dúr she had spent countless hours with tutors poring over long lists of foreign words, learning the languages of neighboring kingdoms. Although she had eventually developed passable skills, she found the memorization and constant repetition a tedious business. Rowenna saw Alyen's face fall and laughed.

"Not to worry, Alyen. There are no new words to learn. You just need to develop a different way of speaking the words you already use. Do you remember how I spoke during your binding ceremony?"

Alyen nodded. "It sounded like poetry, or like a spell. Am I going to learn spells?"

Rowenna smiled. "There's no such thing as spells. At least not ones that work. Spells came about from people trying to emulate the Keeper of Scales, hoping that if they said the right words in just the right way, they would somehow receive elemental aid. It's a little sad, really, since so many put their hopes in spells and charms to relieve the suffering of loved ones when they have no other source of help.

"But your first guess—poetry—was actually quite close," Rowenna continued. "Nature, you see, has a rhythm: waves lap, seasons turn, flames dance, leaves rustle in the wind, the moon waxes and wanes. Because of this rhythm surging through the earth, the thing elementals love above all is music. So, the more musical you can make your words, the more the elementals will give you their attention. We call it 'singing speech,' and the better you're able to speak it, the more elemental magic you'll be able to gather to yourself."

"So, I have to speak in poetry all the time?"

"It doesn't have to be perfect, and you'll get better and better with practice," Rowenna assured. "But the more you can incorporate rhythm, meter, and rhyme into your speech, the more musical it will sound and the more effective it will be. So, let's practice with the berries. I'll call the juniper sprite, then you ask permission to gather."

Rowenna leaned toward the juniper bush, her hands on her knees, and spoke softly into the branches. "Will you who tends this evergreen come out to where you can be seen?"

A moment passed when nothing happened, and Alyen wondered if Rowenna's request had been denied. But then, peeking from between the branches, a small face appeared, the same dusty blue of the juniper berries and crowned with a wreath of the bush's branches. Dark brown eyes peered up at Rowenna, then noticing Alyen, flicked back and forth between the two. Rowenna smiled at the sprite and gestured to Alyen. "Alyen, the Keeper after me, has a wish to ask of thee."

Rowenna signaled Alyen's turn to speak. But Alyen hadn't been able to think of what to say. She was too distracted by the way the air had started to tingle as soon as the sprite appeared. Trying to ignore the way the empty space around her head seemed to crackle, she stared back into the sprite's expectant brown eyes, trying desperately to think of something that rhymed with "berries" or "juniper" or "bush" or any two words that rhymed at all for that matter. But her mind was blank, and the tingling had grown to a distracting degree. She looked to Rowenna for help.

"Try to relax," her mentor whispered. "The rhythm is already here all around us—let it guide your words."

Alyen closed her eyes and took a breath, willing her mind to grow quiet and still. She thought only of the breeze, the forest, and the gentle lilt of Rowenna's words. Slowly she opened her eyes to meet the gaze of the sprite once more. In a halting voice that wasn't nearly as elegant as she'd hoped it would be, she said, "May I take your berries ... please ... to bring relief to those who sneeze?"

The moment it was out, Alyen realized how stupid it

sounded. Reddening slightly, she looked sheepishly at Rowenna, who suppressed a grin but nodded toward the juniper bush. Turning back, Alyen found that the sprite, glittering eyes still fixed upon her, had grasped the branch bearing the berry cluster and was bending it in Alyen's direction. Alyen looked again to Rowenna, who nodded. Very slowly, Alyen reached out her hand and plucked the cluster off the branch. The sprite's blue face flashed a grin, and as quickly as it had appeared, it disappeared into the thick branches of the bush and the tingling in the air vanished.

Rowenna leaned toward the juniper once more and said softly, "Many thanks I give to you for your gift of berries blue."

She straightened and turned to Alyen. "It's always important to say thank you afterward as well. Even if you can't see them, they can still hear you."

"I was horrible, wasn't I?"

"No. A bit crude, perhaps, and juniper isn't actually an effective remedy for a cold. But for a first attempt, it was very well done."

"I was distracted by the tingling. What was that?"

"The magic of the sprite," Rowenna replied. "Whenever you ask an elemental for assistance, if it's willing to listen and help, it will send its magic out toward you. Eventually you will learn to harness the magic and direct it to a specific purpose, but it takes time to build the stamina to control such power. You saw how distracting the magic of only one small juniper sprite can be; can you imagine how overwhelming it would be for you to try to ask several elementals at once for help right now? You must be careful not to push yourself to attempt too much too soon. An overload of magic on one who isn't ready can backfire and have devastating effects."

"What kind of effects?"

"Extreme exhaustion. Illness. A breaking of the mind. In the most extreme cases, it's even possible to be killed from trying to control too much magic. But not to worry. We'll build your abilities gradually and safely."

"So even though there are no spells, there's still magic?" Alyen asked hopefully.

"Of course there's magic," Rowenna replied, turning to walk to the cottage. "Magic is everywhere, all around us, all the time. That's what makes it so hard for us to see."

Arriving at the cottage door, Rowenna held out her hand for the juniper berries and Alyen placed them in her palm.

"I think that's enough for tonight. Tomorrow I'll show you how to dry these. During the day, go down into the forest where you won't be distracted and practice talking with the elementals. Gather things if you can. Don't worry about specific plants or remedies for now—just work on the singing speech. Do you have any questions?"

Alyen shook her head and Rowenna smiled as the mist began to rise. "In that case, I'll see you tomorrow night. Sleep well, Alyen."

The mist swirled and the dreamworld went black.

8

FIRST MAGIC

"What's wrong?" Alyen asked a frowning Lirianna in the dining hall the following morning.

"I'm not sure," Lirianna replied as she pushed eggs across her plate. "I started working on a new tapestry last night—a foresight tapestry."

"Is something bad coming?"

"I think so. Mother Brenwyn has me looking northwest to Illya, but all I see is darkness. It's not normal nighttime darkness, though. It's very … unsettling."

Alyen frowned. "Why's she making *you* look there? Can't she see it herself?"

"No, that's what's so worrisome. She knows something's going on, but somehow her Sight's been blocked. That's why she asked me to start the tapestry, to see if I could help."

Alyen took in the tired lines on her friend's face and tried to sound more optimistic than she felt. "I'm sure whatever's happening at Illya, it's no match for the Trianid."

"Dark magic's been gone for centuries, Alyen. How could the Trianid know how to fight it?"

Alyen couldn't think of a reply, and the two friends spent the remainder of breakfast lost in their own troubled thoughts.

An hour later, Alyen saddled Lusa and started down the narrow path into Sheanen Crann. She could have gone on foot, but Lusa would enjoy the walk and Alyen enjoyed the company of her horse. Once they entered the forest at the bottom of the cliff, Alyen gave Lusa the reins for a time, and sat back in her saddle to enjoy the solitude, the crisp autumn air, memories of sneaking to the Royal Wood, and the sight of tree elves painting orange and yellow over the last remaining tinges of green on the canopy of leaves above.

Eventually, Alyen tethered Lusa to a tree not far off the path. She peered between the trunks looking for Nah'dar, her supposed bodyguard, but if he was there, he wasn't showing himself. The feeling that she was likely being watched was uncomfortable, but with Lirianna's worrying reminder of Illya still lingering in her mind, the thought of a nearby warrior on her side was not entirely unwelcome.

Alyen seated herself on the trunk of a fallen tree and surveyed her surroundings. Rowenna had told her just to practice the singing speech, but she wanted to gather something—to prove that she could learn quickly. She began to take a mental inventory of the plants around her, sending silent thanks to Professor Glibb.

Mint—good for colds and congestion. Burdock—useful for ailments of the skin. More juniper, but I've already gathered that. I want to try something different.

She was preparing to stand and search elsewhere when a dainty bush caught her eye, half hidden in the shade of a large evergreen. Slender branches, a few faded bell-shaped flowers, and a shriveled cluster of dark round berries waved gently in the breeze. *Deadly nightshade. Perfect.*

Alyen walked over to the bush, trying to think of a rhyme to call the nightshade's elemental into view, only to find when she reached the branches that the sprite was already there, intently watching Alyen approach. It looked just as the other had with its large dark eyes and bell-shaped hat, but Alyen noticed that its garments looked a bit faded and limp, just as the bush did with winter on the way.

Alyen hesitated, unsure of how to proceed since she already had the elemental's attention. Would it be rude just to come out and ask without any introduction? The sprite leaped up to a branch extending out toward Alyen and perched, eyes still fixed on her, obviously waiting to see what she would say. Alyen felt the air begin to tingle around her and realized that the sprite's magic was already gathering in the air between them. She swallowed once, trying not to let the sensation distract her, and focused her mind on her words.

"Sprite, who tends each leaf and twig ... will you let me have a sprig?"

The tingling grew stronger as the nightshade sprite considered Alyen carefully, its head cocked to one side. It made no move to offer up any part of its plant. *Perhaps I need to explain more,* thought Alyen, and though her head was starting to spin, she concentrated on remembering everything Rowenna had told her the nightshade was used for. She took a breath and tried again.

"I ask because I want to make ... a ... calming cream for limbs that shake."

It wasn't a wonderful rhyme, but it was all she could

manage. Magic crackled in the air and the pressure around her head began to blur her vision. She clenched her fists, blinking, then saw, as though in slow motion, the sprite reach above its head, pluck three leaves from the branch above it, and offer them in an outstretched hand. Alyen's trembling fingers closed around the leaves and in the same instant she felt an electric jolt that drove her to her knees with a gasp. Suddenly the air was still, her vision clear, and the sprite was gone.

Alyen sat on the soft ground, panting, not trusting her shaking knees to hold her. She stared down at the three leaves in her hand. Dimly, she realized one of them was resting against a small cut on her finger, still unhealed from her unpacking the day before. Rowenna's words rang in her head: *Every part of the deadly nightshade is poisonous, from the roots to the leaves.* With a start, she dropped the leaves in her lap, snatched her hand back and inspected it for any sign that the poison may have penetrated her skin. It looked normal. She was trembling slightly—but that could have been from the exertion of bracing herself against the nightshade sprite's magic. *I'm probably fine,* she reasoned, giving herself a moment to breathe. *I'll just be more careful next time.*

She gathered up the edges of her cloak and pinched the leaves between two fingers, shielding herself from the poison with the thick wool fabric. She suddenly realized that she had not thanked the nightshade sprite, and, looking quickly up to the bush, said, "Sprite, if you can hear me still, my thanks to you for your good will." She didn't see the sprite, but the nightshade branches shivered slightly.

Exhausted, but feeling her head beginning to clear, Alyen smiled in triumph, got to her feet, and stumbled back to Lusa.

"You gathered deadly nightshade?" Rowenna leaned forward in surprise.

"Yes," Alyen replied.

"And you didn't faint?"

"No. Should I have?"

"Well, no, but I wouldn't have been surprised if you had. I'm very impressed. Deadly nightshade is a powerful plant and not the type of magic I would expect anyone to be able to handle on a first attempt."

"If I had poisoned myself with it, I would know by now, right?"

Rowenna's eyebrows rose. "Do you have a reason to think you were poisoned?"

Alyen's face flushed. "I don't think so. There was just this cut on my finger …"

Rowenna took Alyen's hand and peered intently at the cut. Then she met Alyen's eyes. "Yes, you would know by now, so I'm sure you're fine. But don't push yourself too far too fast, Alyen. We cannot afford to be taking risks."

Alyen nodded.

"Incidentally, what did you do with the nightshade?"

"I didn't know what to do with it so it's sitting on the desk in my room."

Rowenna nodded. "Tomorrow ask for a small, dark jar in the medicine room at Monstar. Give the leaves a few days to dry out and then bottle them up. Just be careful not to touch them too much."

Alyen returned to the dried juniper berries she was

funneling into jars. "Why was it so much harder for me to gather the nightshade than the juniper?"

The table between them was covered with jars filled with various dried leaves, sticks, bark, roots, berries, oils, and the occasional crushed mineral. On the hearth near the fire, the lid on a small black pot began to rattle. Rowenna rose and, opening the pot, slowly stirred in tiny pinches of a mixture of crushed leaves.

"Each plant has a unique energy that corresponds with its properties," Rowenna explained. "No single plant is necessarily more powerful than another, but the energies of some are much more intense for us to interact with. Juniper's energy is fairly tame, so it was a good choice to start off with. Deadly nightshade, on the other hand, is one of the most difficult to approach."

Alyen screwed a lid tightly onto her jar of berries. "I don't understand. If no plant is more powerful, why does the energy have a stronger effect?"

"Think of it this way," Rowenna replied, straightening from the hearth and coming back to the table. "What happens to a human if they stand in water?"

Alyen paused. "Not much. They might get cold feet or wrinkly skin."

"And how long could they stay there?"

"As long as they wanted, I guess."

"Now, how long could a human stand in a fire with no ill effects?"

Alyen shook her head, understanding. "They can't."

"Correct. It's not that fire is any stronger than water per se, but we interact with each differently. And it's exactly the same with the plants. Nightshade isn't *stronger* than juniper, but at this point in your training, it should be much more difficult to come in contact with the energy of the nightshade than that of the juniper."

"But it gets easier?"

"It does. Your mind will strengthen quickly—quite quickly, it would seem, in your case. In fact, much of the apprentice-ship is actually about ensuring that your conscience keeps pace with your abilities."

"This is where Sanctity of Life comes in, isn't it? The mind might not take into account wisdom that seems illogical on the surface?"

Rowenna's expression was approving. "Exactly correct. If your mind takes over, it can easily corrupt you with its desire for power and control, and magic seized with this intent can lead only to disaster. I fear this is the trap Ylvain has—"

Alyen looked up, realizing from the look on her mentor's face that Rowenna had said more than intended. "Who's Ylvain?"

For a split second, Rowenna hesitated. Then she resumed her perusal of several jars on a high shelf. "Ylvain was my childhood friend."

"And she's … a magician?"

"Honestly, I don't know. I haven't seen her in a very long time." Rowenna's expression was impassive.

Alyen's eyes narrowed, her mind calculating. "Is Ylvain part of what's going on at Illya?"

"We really don't have enough information to know for sure what's happening at Illya, Alyen."

"But there were reports of a robed woman sailing to Illya just before the fire. Are you suspecting it was Ylvain?"

Rowenna looked sharply at Alyen. "As I said, I don't know. Right now, the robed woman is just a rumor."

"But if there's a dark magician in Dúramair—"

"If there is, the Trianid will handle it," Rowenna said firmly, and held up her hand as Alyen opened her mouth to protest. "We need to focus on your training, Alyen, so that's enough about Illya for tonight. Now, are you done with the berries? If so, you can start jarring this ointment; it should be done boiling. And while you work, I want to talk about ginger—juice from the root is wonderful for infections of the ear, and with winter on the way, it's one of the handier plants to be familiar with."

Rowenna turned to take the pot from the hearth and Alyen knew she would get no further by pressing for answers. She turned to the empty jars on the table, listening to Rowenna lecture on ginger. But half her mind was elsewhere.

Rowenna was being evasive. And Alyen knew that when people were evasive it meant one of three things: they were guilty of something, protecting someone, or keeping secrets. *So, which is it?* she wondered as she screwed the lids onto full jars of ointment. *Or is it more than one?*

9

SEEDS OF DARKNESS

"We have done it, Ylvain, my queen." The familiar whisper curled around Ylvain's ears, sending a shudder down her spine. "We have given birth to the army that will lay the world at our feet."

Ylvain's hood hid the cold darkness in her eyes as she surveyed the shore beneath the tower. Barely visible in the gloom, tiny forms squirmed and writhed over the obsidian rocks. It had taken magic more powerful and more evil than she had known to exist. Ylvain had known well what she had raised. Still, the cruelty and darkness of the whispering smoke as they had worked their sorcery had come as a shock. It had shaken her. But it had worked.

"When we have taken Castle Dúr, what then?"

"Whatever you wish, my queen. My revenge will be satisfied with the fall of Dúramair—the order of the remaining kingdoms matters little to me."

"And how long must we wait until we strike?"

"Patience," the whisper purred. "It will take time for our fledgling army to mature. I will infuse myself into them tonight; my darkness shall run through their veins as they grow and come to know you as their queen. And as we wait, you will use our combined power to sow the seeds of darkness throughout the hidden places of Dúramair, thus tipping the scales of nature's Balance to our cause."

The smoke billowed and moved toward the edge of the tower. It paused there, the orange glow at its heart flickering. The whisper came almost like an afterthought. "There will be one other task you must complete before we make for Castle Dúr."

Dread filled Ylvain's heart at the words, though she could not say why. "And what is this task?"

"I think you know. Is it not wise to eliminate all who would pose a threat before claiming our prize?"

Something hidden away was squirming inside Ylvain. She cocked her head to the side, as if to hear a nearly imperceptible voice on the wind. At the edge of the tower, the glow within the smoke flashed in anger.

"It is a small request, Ylvain, and one that would not pose a problem if your power and ambition are pure. Why do you hesitate? If you have hidden something from me, none will save you from my wrath!"

Ylvain raised her eyes to the smoke, forcing her face calm and her voice steady. "No, Master. It shall be as you wish. Shall I make the arrangements now?"

There was a pause as the roiling smoke stilled and the flashing orange faded back to the dull glow from within. "Not yet. When the time comes to act, I will summon you."

The smoke rolled over the battlements and trickled down

the side of the tower. Ylvain watched as it disappeared, melting into the darkness. Gradually her heartbeat slowed, and her shallow breath deepened. The sun set, and she was left alone with a sensation deep within that twisted and writhed like the dark things on the shore below.

IO
MIDWINTER

S now fell thick over the grounds of Monstar in the dim afternoon light. Alyen watched from the library window as large flakes floated past, carried softly downward in the arms of sylphs and undines. Midwinter was fast approaching and, for the first time, Alyen would not be at Castle Dúr for the feast.

Though Alyen tried not to think such lonely thoughts, her mind was filled with images of the castle decked in greenery and holly, hearths blazing, servants bustling to-and-fro, and waves of delicious aromas wafting through the halls, hinting at the feast Nellie had been planning for weeks. She thought of her father, too; of the way his face took on a special glow on feasting days and how his booming laugh would ring through the castle. How her mother, always serene and lovely, would look even more radiant in her holiday garments and jewels. Alyen shook herself and turned away from the window, banishing the thoughts to the back of her mind. There would be many more Midwinters, she told herself, and many more feasts in the halls of Castle Dúr. But this year she would spend the holiday at Monstar. Rowenna, Morten, and Aaron were all coming to celebrate.

It would be the first time all six of them would gather and, despite her homesickness, Alyen was excited at the prospect of everyone being together. It would also be the first time Alyen would see Rowenna in the waking world since her apprenticeship began and, though her nightly lessons felt as substantial as anything during the day, it was still difficult for Alyen to think of the dreamworld as real.

And she would get to see Aaron.

Seeing the light dim, Alyen lit an oil lamp and paused to watch the salamandar dancing in the flame. That had been one adjustment she hadn't anticipated—getting used to seeing elementals all around her, all the time. Not that she didn't love seeing them, because she did. But she hadn't counted on the fact that never again would she feel *alone*. Sylphs were always flitting or drifting in the breezes, salamandars danced in every hearth and candle flame, and it had been an awkward moment in the lavatory the first time Alyen realized that the bath she was about to sink into—naked—was filled with flashing undines. Rationally, she knew that she herself had changed, not the world around her, and that the elementals had been there all along. But it was still hard not to hurry through changing out of her nightgown each morning.

Alyen wandered through the library, squinting at the small labels attached below each row of books as she conducted her weekly search for interesting reading material. By the time she had reached the back wall, the stack of books cradled in her arms was getting heavy. She was just turning to leave when a faded label beneath the topmost corner shelf caught her eye. She couldn't make out the writing from the floor, but the books standing silently on the shelf looked thick and ancient with dark, cracked leather bindings. Feeling a twinge of curiosity, Alyen shifted her load to one arm and with the other grasped the rungs of the ladder conveniently resting alongside the shelf in question.

She climbed slowly upward, her progress made awkward by the teetering stack of books on her arm. As she drew nearer, she saw that the shelf was coated in cobwebs—the small section had been neglected for some time. Alyen reached the top and, squinting at the faded writing, made out the words "Dark Works." She frowned and squinted her eyes, trying to make out the faded titles on the aged leather. *Dark Creatures, The Science of Torture, Dormant Monsters.* Alyen inhaled sharply. She'd thought all texts on the dark arts had been destroyed ages ago. What were these books, and why did the abbey keep them? Half horrified and half fascinated, Alyen read on, her hand stretched toward the foreboding titles. *I should just climb back down and leave these alone*, she thought. *Obviously, that's what everyone else has done.*

Suddenly her gaze fell on the spine of a book that made her eyes stop. Alyen frowned and realized she could make no sense of the words forming the title: *Aetatis a Daemonisai.* A shiver ran down the length of her spine. She licked her dry lips and tried to reread the words, but again she could make nothing of them. Curiosity rose in her chest as she grasped the cover and pulled the book off the shelf to lie open on top of the stack she carried. Her eyes scanned the page, repulsed and eager at the same time.

She couldn't read a word.

The text was written in a language she couldn't begin to recognize. It resembled nothing even close to any of the languages of any kingdom she'd studied. Alyen flipped through several pages, but the words were utterly foreign to her. Reluctantly, she closed the book and placed it back on the shelf.

"Alyen?"

Mesmerized as she was, any interruption would have given Alyen a substantial fright. But as she was growing accustomed to living exclusively in the company of women, the sound of a man's voice calling her name startled her so greatly that she flew backward from the top of the ladder, limbs flailing in a vain attempt to avoid the inevitable plummet to the floor.

Alyen landed in a heap of books and legs. Before she had a chance to right herself, Aaron was at her side.

"I'm so sorry, Alyen!" he exclaimed. "Oh, that must hurt."

"What must hurt?" Alyen asked vaguely, not yet clear on which direction was up and which was down. Aaron touched her cheek and drew back his hand to show her a trace of blood on his finger.

"You have a cut on your cheek. Is there an infirmary here? You should have it looked at."

"It's on the other side of the abbey."

"Let me take you," Aaron offered. "Can you stand? Walk?"

Aaron raised Alyen to her feet. *Saints,* his arms were strong. Alyen's legs wobbled slightly as she stood, and she wasn't sure the fall had anything to do with it.

"I'm fine," she assured the future Slayer, now beginning to feel flustered and strangely pleased. "Really, I can get to the infirmary myself."

"Nonsense, I'm coming with."

At the infirmary, Sister Rutha steered Alyen to sit on a low table, where she dabbed at Alyen's face and smeared salve on the cut. Aaron sat on a chair near the door. Alyen found herself uncharacteristically shy and at a loss for words. She was grateful for the distraction of Sister Rutha's ministrations, but too soon the nurse finished her work and left the pair alone. Alyen gulped in the awkward silence.

"This seems to happen to us quite a bit," Aaron said finally.

"What does?"

"You. Falling."

Alyen frowned.

"Don't you remember the first day we met?" Aaron asked, his hazel eyes uncertain.

Alyen groaned. "You're right. The tree!"

"Yes, the one you *fell out of*." He tried and failed to suppress a grin.

"You mean the one *you* made me climb?" Alyen raised one eyebrow.

"I didn't make you do anything! You wanted to."

"You said it would be safe!"

"It was a big tree, Alyen. How could it be safe?"

"You said you would catch me if I fell."

"I—well, yes, I did say that. But I couldn't reach you. Good thing Garret was there to do it."

Alyen was laughing now. "It's lucky he saw us."

"I'll never forget his face. I thought he was going to beat us."

"Garret never would have gotten away with beating the princess!"

"Maybe not, but *I'm* not a princess."

"Garret would never beat anyone," Alyen said firmly.

"I know," Aaron replied, grinning. Another pause stretched between them. Alyen absently pressed her fingers beneath the cut on her cheek, checking for soreness.

"Are you sure you're all right?" Aaron asked. "I *am* sorry."

Alyen dropped her hand. "Really, I'm fine." She wished he would stop apologizing. "I was just surprised. I didn't know you were coming."

"Well, I thought I would come early for Midwinter," Aaron said, searching Alyen's face. "I haven't met Lirianna yet, and Morten said we should all spend some time together. I was glad when I found out you were Rowenna's apprentice. Is it all right that I came?"

"Of course!" Alyen said quickly. "I'm glad you're here. You'll like Lirianna—she's wonderful."

As if on cue, Lirianna suddenly flew into the infirmary, cheeks flushed.

"Alyen! What happened? The whole abbey is talking about you being attacked by a man in the library, which obviously can't be—" she halted abruptly upon seeing Aaron. Both her eyebrows shot upward.

Alyen stifled a grin. "Lirianna, this is Aaron."

"You attacked Alyen?" Lirianna said incredulously. Aaron's face flushed as he tried to protest.

Alyen laughed in earnest and slid off the edge of her table. "He didn't attack me; I just fell off the library ladder."

"It was my fault, though," Aaron insisted, a grin breaking across his face. "I scared her. By *accident*."

A glow was spreading throughout Alyen's chest. It was strong and deep, spreading into her stomach and flushing her face as she looked at Aaron laughing with Lirianna. *It's the bonds of the Trianid, like Rowenna said. That's all it is,* she told herself, knowing even as she thought the words, that she didn't believe them.

"Alyen, they're here! I just saw them ride into the courtyard." Lirianna and Aaron were already dressed in winter cloaks, eyes bright with excitement. Alyen grinned, grabbed her own cloak from its peg on the wall and pulled it on as she ran after her friends through the dormitory corridors.

They burst through Monstar's heavy wooden front doors, their breath rising in puffs of steam in the crisp, snowy mountain air. Mother Brenwyn had arrived just ahead of them and was half running, half sliding across the icy ground toward the stables, wimple fluttering behind her like a flag. Morten was already swinging down from a powerful gray steed, the steel pommel of his sword flashing at his waist. Rowenna's cream-colored mare stood beside him, but Alyen couldn't see its rider.

Morten caught sight of Mother Brenwyn careening toward him, no longer fully in control of her progress across the slick courtyard. His hearty laugh echoed against the quiet stones of the abbey as he swept the tiny woman up in a bear hug.

"Brenwyn," he said, fondly, "you haven't changed a bit."

Alyen thought she could say the same for Morten, who looked exactly as she remembered him from his visits to Castle Dúr. Perhaps a few more strands of silver mixed with his long brown hair, but the smile, the laugh, and the twinkling eyes were all the same.

"Brenwyn! Alyen!" a familiar voice called, and Alyen turned to see Rowenna emerge from the stables. For several moments the courtyard was a confusion of greetings, hugs, slips on the ice, and shouts of "Joyous Midwinter!" until the horses were finally stabled and the six retreated into the abbey.

That evening and late into the night, they sat in Mother Brenwyn's study sipping mulled wine and passing around a bowl of roasted chestnuts. Aaron and Morten told of their travels to Brann Dala in the Southlands for the phoenix hatching, and how they had run into a drunken centaur who claimed the planets had told him that Aaron would soon go bald. Rowenna and Alyen, with the help of the salamandars, put on a fire show, making ribbons of red and green flames dance in the hearth while burning sparks whizzed through the room.

As the night grew later and the fire began to dim, Morten stretched out his legs contentedly and said, "I've heard you come from Tiragel, Lirianna. Did you train as a bard at all?"

"I did learn to play the harp. But I'm nothing like the real bards," Lirianna said.

"She's being modest," Mother Brenwyn said. "Lirianna plays and sings beautifully."

"Will you give us a song, then?" Morten asked.

Lirianna reached for her harp leaning against the wall and

pulled a tuning key out of her pocket. "Which would you like?"

"I shall leave that to you." Morten gestured gallantly, and the stone in his armband flashed in the glow from the fire.

"'Thor Lynn' is traditional for Midwinter," Lirianna suggested. "I know a version that's not a song exactly, but it's how the story is told in Tiragel each year."

"Well, the bards of Tiragel are famed throughout the world," Rowenna said. "If you've learned it from them, we're in for a treat."

Nothing could be heard but the faint crackling of the fire as Lirianna closed her eyes, holding her hands still on the strings of her harp. She breathed in and slowly her fingers began to move, conjuring a world long lost to the shadows of time. Then, over the rippling of the strings, Lirianna's voice spoke out softly.

"Long ago, in a time remembered only as legend, our ancestors lived in grave fear of magical creatures, thinking them no different than the monsters of darkness that also plagued our land. For generations the Slayers of Dúramair led the kingdom's warriors to slay these beings by the thousands—monster, dragon, centaur, phoenix, and gryphon alike—and the land began to suffer for it."

Lirianna's fingers began to move more quickly, her harp speaking of urgency and danger.

"In retaliation," she continued, her voice growing stronger, "the dragons of Norhelm, led by the dragon king, Nimrath, made a plan to strike back and annihilate all humans throughout the Northlands. As the attacks began, the people flew into a panic, and sent urgent pleas for help to the Slayer,

Thor Lynn, although everyone knew that one human would never stand a chance in a battle against the dragons.

"But Thor Lynn was unlike any Slayer before him. He was the greatest warrior ever to wield a sword, yet he had no thirst for blood, and a more noble or moral man you would never find. No one knows where he came from or how he came to be the Slayer of Monsters, but he alone understood that the magical creatures were not the same as the monsters those bearing his title were charged to kill.

"So even though it meant certain defeat for him, Thor Lynn approached King Nimrath and challenged him to a duel to the death. The bargain was, if Thor Lynn won and slew Nimrath, the dragons would agree to end the attacks on the humans. If Thor Lynn lost and was himself slain by Nimrath, then there would be no other to stand between the dragons and the destruction of humanity."

Lirianna's face tensed in concentration as her hands ripped clashing chords from her harp, the music and her voice both terrible and beautiful.

"On a day when lightning and thunder tore at the sky and rain poured down in a torrent, the battle between King Nimrath and the Slayer Thor Lynn began. Nimrath was an enormous dragon—the size of three barns—with fearsome teeth, razor claws, and deadly spikes at the end of his tail; Thor Lynn wielded his great sword, Scala, which had never yet seen defeat in battle. They met on a mountain cliff with lightning striking all around, and with a mighty roar from each, they lunged at each other, and the fight began.

"For three days and three nights the battle raged, neither opponent stopping for food, drink, or rest. So great was the skill of Thor Lynn, that several times he gained the upper hand and could have moved in to vanquish the dragon king. But always at the last minute he backed down, and the battle continued. As the days wore on, Nimrath realized that Thor Lynn did not intend to slay him at all, and this show of mercy began to soften the dragon king's heart toward his enemy. At last, on the third day, Thor Lynn dropped his sword and fell, exhausted, to the ground, ready to meet his death."

Lirianna struck a mighty chord that rang through the room until it faded slowly into the stillness of the night. When her fingers began to move once more, her notes rang with hope as her voice took on a tone of wonder.

"But Nimrath did not strike him down. Instead, he declared the battle a draw, and so great was his respect for Thor Lynn, he did something no dragon had ever done before or since. Nimrath took up Thor Lynn's sword from where it lay among the rocks and with its blade, he sliced into his chest, leaving a gaping wound that would not kill him, but let his blood run free. He cupped a small pool of his own blood in his claws, and breathed fire onto it until it became a solid jewel. He took the ruby and placed it into Scala's hilt, giving the sword such power that whoever wielded the blade in battle could not know defeat."

Lirianna's fingers slowed until only a few sparse chords grounded her voice as she spoke the end of the tale.

"After the battle, Thor Lynn and Nimrath wrote the Dragon Treaties and worked toward peace between human and magical races. Though it took many years, and both Thor Lynn and Nimrath were long dead by the time it was fully achieved, peace was eventually accomplished. And so, each year in the darkness of Midwinter, we remember the Slayer

Thor Lynn, who taught us to value kindness and life over blood and death."

There was a pause, and Alyen thought Lirianna had finished when her fingers moved suddenly to the upper strings of her harp, plucking a soft melody that held mystery and a question.

"And what of Scala, Thor Lynn's great sword?" Lirianna asked the silence. And though her voice was soft once more, her strings carried it to each corner of the room.

"With Scala, Thor Lynn at last rid Dúramair of the dark creatures that had been the true enemy of our kingdom. Yet, when Thor Lynn died an old man, the next young Slayer decided with the dragons that the sword should not be entrusted to any other. They could not risk a blade of such power falling into the wrong hands. So, Scala was buried with Thor Lynn in a great stone tomb in the mountains where he had fought Nimrath. From that day until this, none have passed the tests set to protect the tomb and the blade that lies within.

"But the legend says that one day, in the kingdom's direst hour, when the Balance once again lies on the brink of destruction, the one who is meant to take up the blade of Thor Lynn will come to claim it. This hero, the Second Slayer, will save Dúramair and restore the Balance, completing the work Thor Lynn began so long ago.

"May he never be needed. May the light hold strong."

Lirianna's final note faded to silence and for a long moment no one moved. Finally, Morten spoke in a hushed voice.

"You'd have made a mighty bard, Lirianna."

Lirianna smiled quietly. "It's a beautiful tale. I hope I did it justice."

"You did it more than justice," Rowenna said quietly, glancing at Mother Brenwyn and Morten. "You brought Thor Lynn to life."

As Lirianna turned to put down her harp, a look passed between the three mentors that made Alyen realize there was more to Lirianna's performance than a beautiful story masterfully told. And it was just as clear that they had no intention of sharing it with their apprentices.

Rowenna wasn't the only one keeping secrets.

II

EAVESDROPPING

After breakfast the following morning, Morten and Aaron insisted on training in the courtyard for a few hours, so Lirianna and Mother Brenwyn retreated to the weaving rooms and Alyen took Rowenna to her room to show her the bottles of dried herbs she had prepared. She was pleased to have time alone with her mentor, but she was also hoping to uncover the reason for the odd glances following Lirianna's performance of "Thor Lynn" the night before.

Rowenna studied Alyen's work while Alyen stood to the side, surveying the row of jars on her shelf with pride. The first jar contained the deadly nightshade she had first collected in the forest, followed by jars of juniper berries, valerian root, and rosehips. She had even managed to gather the roots of licorice and marshmallow, as well as a few lingering marigold blossoms, before the season's first real frost set in.

"This is fine work," Rowenna said, carefully replacing the lid on the deadly nightshade. "I was worried you wouldn't have a chance to make any progress before winter set in, but you've learned more quickly than I expected. Have you been keeping up your studies?"

Alyen nodded. "I keep a running stack of books to read in the library."

"Good. I'd like to see what you've picked. Will you show me?"

Alyen led Rowenna into the library and showed her the growing pile of books she had collected on a small desk. *The Legend of Thor Lynn* was still resting on top, and Rowenna picked it up to finger the pages.

"*Thor Lynn*," she said. "Have you read it yet?"

Alyen's heart leapt, thrilled that she wouldn't have to contrive a way to bring up the topic. "Yes. Twice, actually. Lirianna wanted to practice her reading, so we read it together."

Rowenna looked up from studying the cover. "Why this one?"

Alyen shrugged, certain that Rowenna would be more forthcoming if she didn't feel pushed. "I don't know. It's always been one of my favorite stories, ever since Garret told it to Aaron and me years ago."

Rowenna turned to the page that showed the prophecy, carefully penned in a spidery script. "Do you still remember the prophecy by heart?"

"Maybe, I—how did you know I knew it by heart?"

"Garret told me," Rowenna said, closing the book and handing it back to Alyen.

"Why would he bother telling you about it? Why is Thor Lynn so important?" Alyen pressed, unable to stop herself.

"No reason," Rowenna replied, and she steered the

conversation to one of the other books. Only the smallest catch in her voice alerted Alyen that her mentor was trying too hard to sound casual.

Later that night the six reconvened in Mother Brenwyn's study, sharing a private dinner. Alyen pushed the food around her plate trying to think of a way to discover what their mentors were concealing. She wouldn't be able to trick any of them into letting information slip, especially not with all three of them together. And asking Rowenna bluntly about Thor Lynn hadn't worked. Perhaps if she brought up the other topic Rowenna had been evasive about, the rest would follow? Surely Lirianna and Aaron would back her up if their curiosity was sparked as well.

"Has anything been discovered about Illya yet?"

From the sudden silence and the five stares in her direction, Alyen had the impression that she'd inadvertently cut someone off mid-sentence. But apologizing would give them an excuse to ignore her question. So, she said nothing, her face expectant, and was relieved to see that Lirianna and Aaron were nodding as well.

The three mentors looked at each other and after a moment Mother Brenwyn shrugged. "We were planning on telling them everything soon, anyway."

Morten looked to Rowenna. "It's all right with me. But it's your story, so your decision."

Rowenna's face was resigned—almost sad. Finally, she inhaled deeply and lowered her mug to the table. "Very well. We believe that Illya is currently inhabited by my childhood friend, Ylvain ..."

For the next half an hour, Rowenna relayed the tale of a girl who was beautiful, ambitious, cunning—a girl who had possessed the gift of elemental Sight but had not been chosen as Keeper. How Rowenna had thought to preserve their friendship by teaching Ylvain in secret. How a boy, heartsick with love, had proposed to Ylvain, and of the fire that had maimed him, leaving him rejected and in disgrace.

Guilt and regret filled Rowenna's eyes as she told how she had confessed her fears to Silvan, her mentor—fears that Ylvain had set the fire using the knowledge that Rowenna herself had given her. She told how she'd left Ramsheath with Silvan, cutting off Ylvain's source of knowledge. And she told how once she'd returned she'd been unable to save Ylvain's child.

The room was still when Rowenna finished speaking, the only sound being the crackle of wood in the fire. Aaron was the first to speak.

"But where's Ylvain been all this time? How could she just vanish for decades?"

Rowenna shrugged. "That's the big question, isn't it? Not long after she lost the baby, her barn caught fire and she disappeared. Most in the village assumed she died in the fire, but I suspect she started it herself to fake her own death and escape what had become an unbearable life. I thought she would start over somewhere else under a different name, and I honestly never expected to hear of her again."

"But there have been troubling signs over the past year," Morten said, his face uncharacteristically grave. "First Brenwyn's tapestry of Castle Illya burning, which has now come to pass. The centaurs tell of ill omens in the planets. Rowenna's even seen a darkling in the Northlands."

"What's a darkling?" asked Alyen.

"An elemental that's turned to serving evil," Rowenna

said. "It's very difficult to convince an elemental to turn its back on the natural order of things, and it's a sign of powerful dark magic."

"And you think it's Ylvain," Aaron said.

"It's almost certainly Ylvain," Rowenna said. "I can feel her presence in the magic. What we don't know is if it's *only* Ylvain. After all, it would have been extremely difficult for her to find information on dark magic to begin with, let alone teach them to herself, and at a high level at that. Almost certainly, someone—or something—is helping her."

Mother Brenwyn was shaking her head. "Ever since Castle Illya burned, my Sight's been blocked from the entire area. Nothing I've tried has worked. Illya is too remote and exposed to spy on undetected in person, and without a vision to guide us, we can only guess blindly at what she's up to or who else may be involved."

"And that's why you've had me weaving Illya," Lirianna said, understanding. "But I've been working on it for weeks now, and I haven't seen anything either."

Mother Brenwyn smiled ruefully. "It hasn't worked *yet*. But maybe having more details now will help."

"Alyen, you can help, too," Rowenna said. "You can be on guard for anything out of the ordinary you come across in your training, especially in the forest. If you see anything unusual, anything odd, anything that seems out of place or out of character—you must tell us at once."

"And what can I do?" Aaron asked.

It lasted only a moment, but Alyen saw it all. A heavy pause filled the room with silence. Rowenna and Mother Brenwyn were looking intently at Morten who studied his apprentice seriously. Finally, he spoke. "Aaron, you know that in times of peace our task is to maintain balance with the realm of magical creatures and that battle should rarely, if ever, be necessary. What you may not know is that I've pushed you harder than most apprentices to hone your combat skills so that if and when the time comes, you'll be prepared to live up to your title as Slayer."

Alyen felt a shiver at Morten's words. The tension waned, but it didn't fully dissipate and Alyen caught the glance that passed between Rowenna and Mother Brenwyn. Morten shifted in his chair. "The truth is, we don't have much time. Soon we'll need to confront Ylvain, whether or not we know her plans, or it may be too late."

"Too late for what?" Aaron asked.

"Too late for light to win," Morten replied.

"But light has to win," Lirianna insisted. "It always wins."

"Yes," Rowenna agreed with a tired smile. "So far, it always has."

By the time they stopped talking, full night had fallen. As they sat finishing their mulled wine, Lirianna stretched and said, "I think I'll turn in early tonight. Can I take anyone's dishes on my way out?" As Alyen handed over her plate, Lirianna caught her eye and gave her a hard stare with a nearly imperceptible jerk of her head toward the door. From the suddenly closed expression on Aaron's face, Alyen guessed Lirianna had done the same to him.

"I think I'll go, too," Alyen said.

"I'll help you with the trays," said Aaron. "See you all in the morning."

They closed the study door behind them and headed toward the kitchens.

"What was that about?" Aaron asked Lirianna once they had turned the corner.

"I figured we need to talk on our own," Lirianna said quietly over her shoulder as she marched down the corridors.

"What do you mean?" Aaron asked.

"I mean that obviously they aren't telling us everything."

"What? How do you ..."

"Shh!" Lirianna hissed. "Just wait until we get to the kitchens."

The sprawling kitchens were dark when they entered, the only light coming from the embers in the hearth below a massive black kettle filled with a simmering broth for the following day. The dull red glow of the coals glinted off pots and pans hanging from hooks on the ceiling and the room was silent but for the quiet chortling of the bubbling pot. They left the trays of dishes near the sinks, and Lirianna lit a candle and peered around the room to ensure they were alone. Once satisfied, she rejoined Alyen and Aaron at the massive oak table.

"All right, we should be able to talk here, but keep your voices down," she warned.

"Talk about *what*?" Aaron asked, frowning. "Are you suggesting they're lying to us?"

"No," Lirianna replied. "I'm suggesting they aren't telling us the whole truth."

"And what's your proof?" demanded Aaron.

"Weren't you watching?" Lirianna asked. "There's something they're hiding from us—something to do with us."

"It's true, Aaron," Alyen agreed. "And honestly, I think it

has to do with you in particular. It was all over their faces when you asked how you could help."

"I'm sorry, but I think you're imagining it," Aaron said. "I've known Morten a lot longer than you two have known Rowenna and Mother Brenwyn, and I just don't think he's that secretive."

Lirianna looked at Aaron with an expression bordering on pity. "Maybe you're right. Maybe he's not secretive when it's just the two of you. But maybe you also can't see it *because* you've had so much time with Morten."

"It's been going on for a while, too," Alyen said quietly. "Rowenna's been evasive with me about Ylvain and Illya before."

"Well, now she told us." Aaron sat back in his chair as if that closed the matter.

Lirianna pursed her lips and looked at Alyen who scratched at the back of her neck. "Look, Aaron, I'm sure that whatever they're hiding, it's with good intentions."

"Then we should trust them and let it be," Aaron said stubbornly.

"Maybe," Lirianna said gently. "But think of this, Aaron. Maybe not today, maybe not in twenty years, but eventually, *we* will be the Trianid. And these are apparently dangerous times we live in. I think we should take it upon ourselves to be as prepared as possible."

"What exactly are you proposing?"

"Well, obviously they'll be talking about it all right now," Lirianna said. "I propose we listen in."

"They'll never let us," Aaron said.

"I mean listen in *uninvited*," Lirianna said. "Eavesdrop."

"No," Aaron said flatly. "It's not honorable."

"But it could be important!" Lirianna pressed.

"It could be about Thor Lynn," Alyen said suddenly, surprising Aaron and Lirianna into silence.

"What do you mean?" Aaron asked after a pause. Alyen knew she'd hooked his curiosity.

"I mean that Rowenna seemed particularly interested in the fact that I read a book about Thor Lynn from the library. She even knew that Garret taught us the prophecy by heart and wanted to know if I remembered it. And they were all giving each other funny looks when Lirianna recited the legend for us last night."

Aaron said nothing but stared intently at the black, bubbling kettle. Alyen could see he was tempted.

"Aaron," Lirianna cajoled softly. "Don't you want to know?"

Aaron let out a puff of breath and looked back at the girls reluctantly. "All right. But how do we hear what they're saying? The walls are too thick, and the door's solid oak."

"Yes, how's that going to work?" asked Alyen.

"Obviously neither of you has older siblings to teach you things," Lirianna said dryly. "Take these and follow my lead. And above all, don't make a sound!" She handed each of them a delicately crafted wooden cup, blew out the candle, and headed out of the kitchen.

When they reached Mother Brenwyn's study, creeping slowly down the corridor on tiptoe, Lirianna turned and motioned for Alyen and Aaron to stop. They could hear murmuring from within, but the sounds were indistinct. Cautiously, Lirianna knelt down and very slowly set the rim of her cup against the door. Then, once she was sure it was in place, she pressed her ear against the bottom of the cup.

Alyen frowned, puzzled, but a satisfied grin appeared on Liri-anna's face, and she waved her friends forward before raising her finger to her lips. Aaron and Alyen settled on the floor in front of the door and each pressed their cups carefully and silently against the cool wood. Alyen held her ear to the bottom of her cup, and to her surprise, the voices from within were magnified. She could just make out Mother Brenwyn's words.

"But are you sure, Rowenna? Might we not be taking just as great a risk keeping it to ourselves?"

"I'm not sure at all," Rowenna said. "None of us is sure about anything anymore. But I still say we must err on the side of caution. What if we said something and it turned out we were wrong?"

"But what if we're not wrong?" Mother Brenwyn persisted. "Shouldn't he be preparing? And he seems so level-headed—mature even."

"That he is," came Morten's low voice, "but he's seventeen nonetheless, and the lure of that kind of power has corrupted men older and more experienced than he. Think of it, Bren-wyn. Imagine if the knowledge went to his head? Imagine how devastating it could be! I *am* preparing him every way I can, but to tell him outright? We can't risk it."

"If it's his destiny, it will find him without our help," Rowenna said.

"I suppose you're right," Mother Brenwyn conceded, though she still sounded unconvinced. "But there *is* one thing that they should hear from you, Rowenna—Alyen especially. You can't hide it from her forever."

"I know," Rowenna said, sounding tired. "I meant to tonight, but … If we can stop Ylvain in time, perhaps no one will ever need to know. I'd rather not feel like a traitor if it can be avoided."

"It's an understandably hard thing to tell," Morten said gently, "but it's their safety, Rowenna. And not only that—it could determine the outcome of everything."

"Yes, I know. I promise, if it comes to that, I'll tell Alyen. You have my word."

"Well, we shall hope it won't be necessary," Mother Brenwyn said. "And in the meantime, we'll prepare them as best we can without letting on our suspicions. Though for Aaron's sake, I hope we're wrong."

"As do I," agreed Morten. "Even if he *is* our last hope, Scala is a heavy blade to bear."

Alyen's head snapped around to Aaron's face and their eyes locked. For one frozen second the world was still, Morten's words hanging in the silence between them. An instant later, Lirianna was shooing them down the corridor on tiptoe, breaking into a trot once they turned the corner.

By silent agreement they all headed for Lirianna's room, not daring to speak until they had closed the door behind them. For a moment no one said anything; they stood in the dark, outlined by the moonlight filtering through Lirianna's window. Snow drifted softly, tiny specks of white against the blackness. Then Alyen spoke, her voice low and quiet.

"Did we just hear what I think we just heard?"

Aaron's face was a mask.

"Yes," Lirianna confirmed, her voice hushed. "They think Aaron is the Second Slayer."

There was a weighty pause.

"Can that be true?" Alyen asked.

"Whether he is or isn't," Lirianna said, "the fact that they think he is tells us something."

"Like what?" Alyen asked.

"Well," Lirianna continued, glancing at Aaron, "the Second Slayer isn't supposed to appear until the kingdom faces the darkest time it's seen since the age of Thor Lynn. That means whatever Mother Brenwyn, Morten, and Rowenna think Ylvain is up to, it must be really serious. Even more so than they're letting on."

"That's true," Alyen agreed, frowning.

"There must be a way to find out," Lirianna continued. "You know, we should look at the prophecy again and see if we can find any clues. Do you have it in your room?"

"It's back in the library," Alyen said. "But between Aaron and me we can probably …"

"I know the prophecy." Aaron spoke for the first time since entering Lirianna's room. His voice was quiet, and he was standing still, looking out the windows at the falling snow.

"You—you remember?" Alyen ventured tentatively.

"Of course. I never forgot it. Not since the day Garret taught us at Castle Dúr."

Aaron turned around and looked at the girls. "You won't find anything in it," he continued. "Nothing that will prove anything one way or another at least."

"What do you think?" Lirianna asked. "Do you think you're the Second Slayer?"

"I don't know," Aaron said, his voice tight. "None of us knows. But now I'll always be thinking about it, won't I? It will always be there in the back of my mind, and I won't know whether to feel proud or afraid. I'll always wonder if I've let it 'go to my head' or if it's corrupted me—not to mention trying to figure out how I'm supposed to save the world. And all before we even know if it's true or not!"

Aaron was trying to keep his voice down, but it was growing thicker with each word, and he glared fiercely at Lirianna. "This is why they didn't want to tell us! This is exactly why they wanted it kept secret, and it's exactly why we should have let it be!"

"But now that we know—"

"Now that we know, *I'm* the one who has to deal with it!" Aaron shouted in a hoarse whisper, cutting off Lirianna as he pounded his forefinger into his chest. He spun back around and continued to glare out the window, the rigid line of his shoulders black against the moonlit window.

Lirianna looked stricken as she exchanged a glance with Alyen and for a minute, silence filled the room again. Then on impulse, Alyen snatched up a candle from beside Lirianna's bed and strode to the window.

"Aaron, watch this," she commanded, and focused her attention on the stub of wax. "Fiery dancers in the night, help me now to make a light." Flame sprang to life, flickering on the blackened wick. A salamandar, lithe and graceful, swirled in the glow of its fire, visible only to Alyen.

Aaron's expression didn't change as Alyen whispered thanks to the salamandar, but he stared down at the candle, his features now glowing in its light.

"Aside from Rowenna and maybe Ylvain," Alyen said steadily, "I'm the only one who can do that. Someday, I'll be the only one at all. Does it make me special? It's hard for me not to think so." She paused and cleared her throat, gauging her next words. "You might be the Second Slayer, Aaron, and you might not. But you're already different. We all are. And if it hasn't corrupted you by now … I don't think this will change you whether it's true or not."

Aaron's face had softened. He raised his eyes to Alyen's. They shone gold and green in the candlelight and as Alyen looked into them, she felt her stomach flip.

"Aaron, I'm so sorry," Lirianna's voice was small as she approached the window. "We shouldn't have listened—it's my fault."

"No, Alyen is right." Aaron held Alyen's gaze for a second longer, then he broke off and turned to Lirianna. "I'm sorry for my outburst. It wasn't fair." He grinned crookedly and folded Lirianna into a warm hug that she readily returned. Alyen suddenly felt an unpleasant stab in her chest and turned brusquely to set down the candle.

"So, what do we do now?" she asked, a bit louder than she intended, and Aaron and Lirianna broke their embrace.

"Do we let on that we know?" Lirianna asked.

"No," Aaron said. "For now, I think we should stick to the plan. Lirianna, keep working on your weaving. I'll continue to train. And Alyen, see if you can get any hints at what it is that Mother Brenwyn thinks Rowenna should tell you."

"Oh, right," Alyen said frowning. In the excitement over Aaron, she had forgotten about Rowenna's newest secret. "What could that be about?"

"I don't know," Aaron said. "But it sounded important. And Lirianna is right—we need to be as prepared as possible."

But in the days and weeks that followed, there were no signs to be seen. A week after Midwinter, Morten and Aaron left, traveling west to the coast where Morten thought the merfolk would be wintering in warmer waters.

"They don't go near Castle Illya much anymore," he said to everyone as they stood in the courtyard to see the pair off. "But I'm hoping that maybe a few have ventured near enough to give us some new information."

Alyen hated goodbyes and stood scuffing her toe against the icy ground. The cold wind was making her nose run. She sniffed loudly.

"Are you crying?" Aaron teased. "There, there, I'll be back soon." He danced away from the punch Alyen aimed at his arm, then put out a hand to reassure his stallion, Soran, who was stomping at the commotion.

"Seriously, though, be careful, Aaron," Lirianna said in a low voice. "And do come back soon."

"Yes, take care of yourself," Alyen said, wishing she didn't feel so awkward saying it.

"I will," Aaron promised. "You have my word." He swung up onto Soran's back. He and Morten started down the path, waving behind them as they disappeared around the corner.

Rowenna stayed a few days longer, but soon it was time for her to leave as well.

"Where will you go?" Alyen asked her.

"West, I think, though not as far as the coast," Rowenna said. "I want to ask around the region and see if I can pick up Ylvain's trail after she left Ramsheath. With some luck, perhaps, I can find out where she's been all these years."

"I wish you didn't have to leave so soon."

"As do I," Rowenna agreed. "But I shall see you at night for lessons nonetheless."

Rowenna left at dawn the next morning. With the last of

the visitors gone, Alyen thought the abbey seemed empty and melancholy.

But there was little time to mope. Rowenna began to teach Alyen how to mix and brew dozens of tinctures, teas, poultices, creams, and salves to cure everything from minor burns to deadly pox. As the weeks progressed, the row of medicine jars in her room grew until she had to ask Mother Brenwyn for another small chest to store them all.

When half the abbey inhabitants came down with winter fever, Rowenna elected to stay away, giving Alyen her first chance to apply her newly gained knowledge. Enlisting Lirianna's help whenever possible, Alyen worked diligently, administering compresses, replacing water glasses and cool cloths, and instructing the abbey cooks in various broths and stews to prepare. None of the cases were dangerously serious. Still, Alyen felt a swell of pride when she was able to inform Rowenna that all had recovered—and most in far less time than was usual for winter fever.

At Rowenna's constant urging, she also practiced the singing speech as often as she could. This proved frustrating on numerous occasions. Since reciting the same lines over and over would not improve her skills, Alyen was constantly trying to invent new poetic ways to ask salamandars to start fires or undines to splash water over her hands in the lavatory. But as winter waned, she was pleased to discover that the words came to her much more quickly, and she was able to talk to two or even three elementals at one time without getting lightheaded.

Through it all, she watched for signs of anything amiss. But aside from the fact that it had been a colder winter than usual, she could find nothing out of the ordinary. Nor was she able to devise a way to ask Rowenna what she had kept from them. There was little to go on to begin with, and anything she could think to say sounded woefully contrived or would alert Rowenna to the fact that they'd been eavesdropping.

Lirianna had no more luck than Alyen.

"Nothing works!" she lamented as they sat by the spring in the gardens with their lunch. The snows had all melted, spring flowers were bursting through the wet earth, and it was the first day it felt warm enough to eat outside. "Once in a while I get a flash of color, but I still can't make out a single image. I must have woven yards and yards of plain black cloth by now."

"Could it be that there's just not much to see?" Alyen asked doubtfully.

"No, there's definitely something there," Lirianna said. "I can feel it. I just can't see it."

As the weeks passed and spring continued to blossom with no sign or word of disaster from anywhere, it was difficult to hold to the winter's sentiments of urgency and danger. Morten wrote to Mother Brenwyn regularly, and often Aaron would include a note to Alyen and Lirianna. *"No signs of anything new yet,"* his latest letter read. *"The merfolk won't go near Illya, which means Ylvain is probably still there. We're on our way south to the phoenix burning—will see how things go there."*

Spring melted into summer with still no new signs of growing darkness.

"I don't understand," Alyen confessed to Lirianna. "Rowenna was never able to find Ylvain's trail from Ramsheath, and she says that no more darklings have been seen since winter. Do you think it's possible that Ylvain's given up? She was obviously up to something, but maybe she failed and quit."

They had returned to their perch in the basin on Monstar's battlements and Lirianna frowned as she squinted out at the setting sun.

"I don't know," she said doubtfully. "I was sure something more would have happened by now. I'd like to think you're right, but we shouldn't let down our guard—carelessness could be dangerous. I think we have to assume that as much as we're watching Ylvain, she could be watching us as well."

Alyen looked out over Sheanen Crann. To her left the sun dipped below the horizon, sending shadows creeping over the tops of the trees. To the right she could barely make out the distant mountains in the Northlands. Straight ahead somewhere was Castle Illya, and as she gazed in its direction, with the shadows lengthening around her, she felt a shiver run down her spine. *It's just a chill from the night air,* she told herself, but she couldn't shake the feeling that in some distant place, a darkness was staring back at her.

12

THE DARKLINGS

Alyen woke to the flutter of tiny wings and a gentle breeze on her face, just as dawn was breaking. She scrunched open one eye and found three grinning sylphs hovering inches above her, fanning the air vigilantly in her direction. Alyen mirrored their smiles and mumbled her thanks before rolling out of bed, sending the sylphs scattering through her room.

Alyen yawned as she pulled her clothes over her head and glanced out the window toward the lightening eastern sky. It was earlier than she usually rose, and she'd asked the sylphs to wake her the night before. She was pleased they had complied. With still less than a year of training, Alyen couldn't always depend on the elementals to follow through on requests that weren't supposed to be immediately fulfilled.

Alyen splashed some water on her face, then gathered up an old map, a light shawl, and a small cloth bag, and quietly made her way to the kitchens, where she filled the bag with a chunk of bread, a wedge of cheese, and an apple. As an afterthought, she grabbed a second apple for Lusa and headed for the stables.

In a few minutes, Lusa was saddled and standing in the courtyard. Alyen packed the food into one of the saddlebags and carefully unrolled the map she'd found in the library the day before. It was old and the parchment crackled as it slowly unfurled to reveal the sprawling forest of Sheanen Crann. Alyen squinted at the fading ink in the dim light of dawn, but quickly found the spot she was looking for. Just to the west and slightly south of Monstar, a plateau emerged through the trees, represented by an open space enclosed by a somewhat shaky boundary line. Within the plateau, Alyen could make out a few dark blotches and underneath, the words "Ruins of Castle Enlair".

Alyen looked up from the map and turned to the left, but the plateau was hidden from sight by the walls of the abbey and the curve of the cliff; she doubted it would be visible even from the basin on the battlements. But if she descended the cliff and followed the base of the rock until it curved south, with any luck she could find the ruins before noon. She rolled up the map and tucked it into the saddlebag with the food. Then she swung up onto Lusa's back and clicked her tongue, nudging her horse toward the path down the cliff.

It was a perfect summer morning, mild yet warm, and Alyen was soon able to shed her shawl as the chill burned off with the rising sun. As Lusa continued to follow the base of the cliff, Alyen munched on her apple and let her mind wander, enjoying the freedom, the solitude, the woods, and throngs of elementals all busy with their tasks. She watched the tree elves painting the leaves of the forest a brilliant green as the hazy gray mist of the morning gave way to the lush colors of daytime. Occasionally, while passing a cave in the rocky wall of the cliff, Alyen caught sight of a gnome pushing a wheelbarrow filled to the brim with gemstones and crystals. Sylphs fluttered alongside butterflies, their wings changing to mimic those they were nearest to. None of it surprised her anymore—most of her summer days had been spent under the forest canopy. But it never ceased to delight her, and some days she found it hard to believe there had ever been a time when the elemental world had been blocked from her sight.

It was nearing midday when the cliff wall suddenly veered off to the left, and Alyen halted Lusa to consult the map once more. She turned them slightly south, heading away from the cliff, and after another quarter of an hour, the ground began to rise and the trees thinned, until the forest gave way altogether to a wide, grassy plateau. Alyen smiled in satisfaction as she surveyed her surroundings. At the far end of the clearing, a few crumbling stone walls and pillars were all that remained of Castle Enlair, but Alyen hadn't come to see the ruins. Scattered across the grassy expanse were dozens of lavender bushes, their tiny flower buds throwing a hazy violet wash across the hilltop and filling the air with a heavenly scent, heavy and fresh and soothing all at once.

Alyen slid to the ground and removed the saddlebags before feeding Lusa the second apple and setting her loose to graze freely. She was hungry as well, but lunch would have to wait. Lavender was best harvested in the late morning; Alyen guessed she had less than an hour before the sun crossed its zenith. She stooped down by the nearest lavender bush and quickly spotted its guardian—a wiry elemental with long, thin limbs, skin the dusty green hue of the lavender's leaves and each eye a deep, soothing pool of violet.

"These flowers with the purple hue—may I harvest some from you?" Alyen asked, and almost immediately the sprite bent the branches toward her. She felt the familiar tingle of magic in the air around her and was pleasantly surprised at how gentle it was.

Alyen thanked the sprite, carefully snapped off a few sprigs, and moved to the next plant. Slowly, she progressed across the plateau, asking each sprite for its flowers, careful not to take too many from any single plant. She was pleased there were so many bushes; she would have plenty harvested for her training purposes by the time she left, which meant she could leave the abbey lavender to the sisters who used it in sachets to keep moths out of the weaving rooms. She smiled thinking of how she would tell Rowenna in her lesson that night how successfully she'd located wild lavender on her own, thus solving the shortage problem.

By the time she was nearing the ruins of Castle Enlair, both her saddlebags were stuffed full of fragrant lavender sprigs wrapped in swaths of cloth to keep the buds from falling off. She straightened from her squatted position, wiping one arm across her forehead, and glanced up at the sun, now high in the hot blue sky. It was getting late to gather any more, but she thought she could collect from just a few more bushes before she stopped to eat and start the long ride back to Monstar.

She knelt again next to a lavender shrub that stood in the shadow of the crumbling walls of Castle Enlair. At once, she knew that something was not right. The plant was scrawny, half shriveled, and its flowers were a sickly brown color, sticky to the touch with an unpleasant, rotting odor. Alyen frowned and peered through the stems for the plant's elemental, but none could be found. She called for it in the singing speech, but no sprite came forth. *Strange*, Alyen thought, a feeling of unease sending a chill up her back despite the warmth of the sun. She hadn't failed to call an elemental in months. *Perhaps this plant has been abandoned?* she thought doubtfully, but dismissed the idea almost at once. An elemental would never abandon its charge, and if it did, the plant would surely die. This lavender wasn't dead, but sick, and unnaturally so at that.

Alyen scanned the area with growing dismay. She hadn't noticed it from the other side of the plateau, but up close she could see that the ruins stood at the center of a circle of diseased and putrefying vegetation. Alyen felt the hairs on the back of her neck rise as a cloud drifted in front of the sun, throwing a shadow over the plateau.

A noise made Alyen's head snap toward the top of the crumbling wall beside her. Just a few feet above, crouched on the top of the ancient stones, was a creature, hideous and strange. Alyen quickly took several steps back. It looked very much like the lavender sprites, thin and delicate, yet this creature's skin was ashen gray and its eyes, black as ink, held a gleam of malice. The creature leaned toward Alyen and bared its sharp, pointed teeth, hissing, and suddenly Alyen understood. Horror struck her heart as she realized that this creature had once been the lavender's elemental—but what she faced now was a darkling, twisted, devious, and unnatural.

Alyen's eyes swept the ground hastily. How many of the diseased plants were there? Tens? Hundreds? As if in response, more and more darklings appeared over the ridge of the ruined castle's walls. The air crackled—not with the nature magic Alyen had become used to, but with something far more sinister. The wind picked up, and at the other end of the plateau, Lusa whinnied and stomped in agitation. Fear surged through Alyen's body, but she forced herself to stand firm. *I can't run away, not if I'm going to be Keeper. A Keeper would be able to fix this—or at least try.*

One of the darklings above darted to the edge of the castle wall as if to leap down, and Alyen flinched. She needed to act quickly. She gathered her focus, ignoring the way her instincts screamed at her to run. Then she reached out with her mind to the darklings, opening her mouth to start the singing speech.

Her mind collided with the darkling magic with a force that drove her to her knees. Pain seared through her head and down her spine. She shrieked in agony as she clutched her head in her hands, gasping for air with lungs that felt as though they had been crushed. Dimly, she could hear the darklings hiss and chatter; she heard hard nails scratching the stones of the ruins above. They were coming for her.

Suddenly she was lifted bodily off the ground. Arms like steel carried her swiftly across the plateau toward Lusa and a black stallion. Still huddled in a ball and clutching her saddle-bags to her chest, Alyen was lifted to Lusa's back.

"Hold on." She heard the curt words and numbly grasped the reins pressed into her hands. She saw the black-robed assassin—her bodyguard—leap to the back of his stallion, then the horses were moving, eager to leave, making swiftly for the path back into Sheanen Crann. Just before they reached the trees, Alyen twisted in her saddle to look back. A few of the darklings had leapt down from the wall, but it didn't seem they were following. A moment later, the ruins were hidden from view.

They made swift progress through the forest, Alyen constantly looking behind her for signs of pursuing darklings. The pain in her head slowly faded as the distance between herself and the ruins grew, but her limbs still trembled with a chill deep in her bones. When finally they trotted through the abbey gates, the assassin lifted Alyen from her saddle and moved quickly through the tasks of stabling the horses. Alyen waited in the courtyard, exhausted and trembling, saddlebags still clutched in her arms. When he had finished, Nah'dar returned and hastened Alyen into the abbey, making straight for Mother Brenwyn's study.

"Alyen!" Mother Brenwyn exclaimed, rising from her desk at once upon seeing Alyen, pale and trembling in her doorway. "What on earth has happened?"

"Darklings," Alyen said in a weak voice. "Dozens of them at the Ruins of Enlair."

Mother Brenwyn's eyes flicked to Nah'dar who remained motionless in the doorway. Alyen swayed and suddenly Mother Brenwyn was steering her into a chair. "You're shaking, Alyen. Are you unwell?"

"I haven't eaten all day," Alyen said, noting the tremor in her voice and hands.

"Well, that won't do." Mother Brenwyn went to the door and called to one of the sisters to have food brought to her study. Alyen heard the abbess's voice drop in a soft question and the assassin's deeper voice in reply, but she couldn't make out the words. After a brief exchange the man was gone, and Mother Brenwyn had closed her study door.

In minutes, Alyen sat with a meat pie, bread with honey, and a glass of chilled raspberry juice. She ate far more quickly than was polite, and Mother Brenwyn sat at her desk, not speaking until Alyen had stopped shaking.

"Feel better? Good. Now, please tell me everything that happened, in as much detail as possible."

Mother Brenwyn listened intently as Alyen described everything: her journey to the plateau, the discovery of the lavender bushes, her confrontation with the darklings, and her rescue and hasty flight back to the abbey. "I've never been afraid in the forest before," she concluded. "If Nah'dar hadn't been there ..."

Mother Brenwyn's face was grim as she nodded. "Alyen, do you think you can fall asleep now?"

"I suppose so," Alyen said.

"Good. I need to confer with Rowenna and she needs to hear this from you before I do."

"I'll go up to bed now," Alyen said, rising slowly from her chair. She paused at the door.

"Mother Brenwyn?"

"Yes?"

"Will we have to confront Ylvain now?"

Mother Brenwyn regarded Alyen and did not reply immediately. "Perhaps," she said at last. "Now you need to sleep. We'll speak again in the morning."

Knowing she would get no further, Alyen left the study and headed for the dormitories.

——ڸ⌣——

Rowenna's face looked grave as Alyen described the darklings outside the dreamworld cabin.

"The Ruins of Enlair. So close to Monstar. How many were there?"

"At least twenty, but they kept appearing. There were likely more."

"And you're sure they were darklings?"

"Not entirely. I've never seen one before."

"Describe them again."

Alyen did so and Rowenna nodded grimly. "Yes, those are darklings. And you said the lavender was diseased?"

"They were all brown and withered and sticky. And they smelled rotten."

"They were blighted. It happens when an elemental turns darkling but remains near their plant. The plant begins to mirror the corruption of its guardian."

"What do you mean 'if the elemental remains near its plant?' Where else would it go?"

"Wherever its master asked it to," Rowenna replied, smoothing a hand over her head as she explained. "Speaking of which, what happened when they saw you?"

As Alyen told of her attempt to connect with the darklings, all blood drained from Rowenna's face. Her lips went white, and she suddenly cut Alyen off.

"You did *what?* Alyen, what were you thinking? Have you lost your mind completely?"

Alyen was taken aback at her mentor's reaction. "I thought I should try to fix them. Isn't that what a Keeper would do?"

"You are not a Keeper, Alyen. You are an apprentice with less than a year of training!" Rowenna's eyes snapped angrily.

"I'm sorry. I thought I could handle it."

Rowenna's voice was deadly quiet. "Oh. Did you now? You thought that you, with all your grand life experience of what—sixteen years?—could take on a legion of darklings, the existence of which you have known about for only a few short months, with zero knowledge or training whatsoever in the matter? You thought you would just ride home the hero, having singlehandedly rebalanced the world, conquering the greatest threat our kingdom has seen in generations without so much as wrinkling your dress? Alyen, do you have any idea how reckless, how naive—do you have any idea what could have happened to you? Do you know what you could have *done*?"

Rowenna's voice had risen steadily and by the end she was close to shouting. Alyen stood still against the tirade, her face a mask, but inwardly shocked and shaken by her mentor's reaction. When Rowenna was done, she spoke quietly.

"No. I don't know. Why don't you tell me?"

Rowenna's eyes narrowed as if she suspected Alyen was being impertinent. "For one, Alyen, you could have died. If not for Nah'dar, you would likely be dead right now. And lest you entertain any romantic thoughts of martyrdom, think about what that would mean for the kingdom. You are the only candidate we have for Keeper. To lose you now—particularly in so needless a way—would be a devastating blow not just to our cause, but to the stability of Dúramair and its people, who need you. I would have thought someone raised as a ruler would have more sense."

The comment stung and guilt swept over Alyen, but Rowenna continued without pause.

"If you hadn't been killed, you could have been captured.

Ylvain would easily glean from you any information she could want about us, our strategies, our talks, our fears, our positions —anything. As it is, she will likely know now that you are my apprentice and that you are at Monstar—something we have worked quite hard to keep quiet. Have I made the gravity of your actions clear?"

"Yes," Alyen said shortly, not meeting Rowenna's eye. She had never in her life been scolded in such a way, not as an apprentice, not as a princess, not even when she had fallen out of the tree. She had never before been a disappointment.

A silence stretched between them growing longer and more pronounced as the seconds ticked by. Alyen was almost surprised when Rowenna spoke again.

"Still, we may be able to salvage some good from the situation."

Alyen looked up and met Rowenna's eyes. They were stern, but no longer flashing.

"How?"

Rowenna sniffed and looked away thoughtfully. "Well, we know that she's making darklings in great numbers. And we know that they are far away from Illya, while she is most likely still there. That means we know for certain she's not working alone."

"Why?"

Rowenna shook her head. "One human could never possess the power to do that alone. We suspected this was the case all along, but I suppose confirmation is good."

Another pause filled the clearing.

"Rowenna, I—" Alyen broke off as Rowenna's eyes flicked back in her direction. She swallowed and glanced downward. "I apologize for … everything. I'm sorry."

There was a space of two heartbeats, then Rowenna stepped forward and lifted Alyen's chin so their eyes locked. "I know you are," she said softly. "But we can't afford to be sorry. Not right now." She lowered her hand. "So, from now on, until I say otherwise, you are not to go into the forest again under any circumstances. Not even close to Monstar. It's too risky and we can make do for now with the abbey gardens. Do you understand?"

Alyen nodded.

"And no more experimenting. Ever. You come to me first."

"I promise."

"Good. Now I need to confer with Brenwyn and Morten. I'll see you tonight."

Before Alyen could say anything else, Rowenna turned away and the mist rose.

Alyen woke in her room feeling disoriented and groggy. Why was it so dark? She glanced out her window trying to guess at the time. The sky gave her no clues, but her stomach began to growl loudly, indicating it must have been several hours since she sat in Mother Brenwyn's study.

There was a soft tap on her door, then Lirianna's face appeared, illuminated by a candle she carried on a tray piled with food. Alyen's room was filled with the smell of fresh bread and roasted meat.

"Sounds like you had quite a day," Lirianna remarked as Alyen sat up, rubbing her face.

"Lirianna, you are truly the best friend in the world," Alyen said. "What time is it?"

"A little after ten o'clock. I thought you might be hungry again."

"You thought right." She crossed her legs to make room for Lirianna on her bed with the tray between them. Lirianna sat and helped herself to a clump of grapes.

"So, what happened? Mother Brenwyn told me the gist of it, but I'd like to hear it from you."

Alyen retold the story once again between bites, not bothering to hide how angry Rowenna had been with her.

"She's right," Alyen admitted when she finished. "It *was* stupid. I could have really messed things up."

Lirianna shrugged. "We knew something would come up sooner or later. I'm just glad you're safe."

Alyen gave her friend a grateful smile. "What do you think will happen now?"

"Well, for one thing, Aaron is on his way here."

Alyen's heart gave an involuntary jump. "Really? When?"

"Soon. He's still south, so it will be a couple weeks until he gets here. It turns out your darklings aren't the only thing that's happened. Morten told Mother Brenwyn that two of the phoenixes didn't rise from the ashes after the burning. They're supposed to be immortal, you know. He and Aaron were going to stay in Brann Dala for the fall to try to figure out why, but since the darklings are so close to Monstar, Aaron's coming to protect us."

"So, they think something's coming?"

"Maybe. Rowenna and Morten are coming here too, but they'll get here later. They're going to meet up and search for more pockets of darklings along the way."

Alyen narrowed her eyes as she reached for more grapes.

"How do they talk with each other from different ends of the kingdom?"

"I'm not sure. Maybe they meet in the dreamworld, like you and Rowenna?" Lirianna stretched and yawned. "I think I'm going to bed. Mother Brenwyn wants me to start weaving early tomorrow. I don't know how it will help, but I suppose we have to try." The girls said their farewells, and Lirianna took the candle with her on her way out. The room was dark once more.

Alyen changed into her nightgown and slid back into bed, though she was now wide awake and doubted she would be able to sleep any time soon. And to be honest, she wasn't exactly in a rush to face Rowenna again anyway. The moon was rising outside her window and in its light, she could see the occasional owl or bat swoop by in search of food.

So, Aaron was coming back. Alyen knew the fluttering in her stomach *should* have been caused by the knowledge that danger was rising. But it wasn't.

It had been well over half a year since Midwinter, and she'd had plenty of time to think. She'd lived her whole life assuming her marriage would be arranged. Whatever was best for the good of the kingdom. And she'd been fine with that. But what if that didn't apply anymore? What if she was— free?

There was no way she could fool herself that the way her blood raced and her face flushed whenever she was around Aaron was the bonds of the Trianid anymore. It was happening now, just thinking about him. She supposed it was an easy mistake to have made; when Aaron was at Monstar they were *always* with Lirianna.

Alyen clamped down guiltily on the stab of unwelcome jealousy. Lirianna was wonderful. She was her best friend.

But … maybe this time she could find a way to be alone with Aaron. Just the two of them. Somewhere private …

It was a long time before Alyen fell asleep again, and when she did, the growing danger was far from her mind.

13

A DARK DREAM

Far away, another woman dreamt, but not of love.

"It is time," the voice hissed as a thin trail of black smoke wound its way, serpentine, into Ylvain's room. She flinched, her brow furrowing.

"Now?" her own voice echoed in her head. "It seems soon. Our army is not yet ready."

"They grow stronger," came the voice, closer now, malice lacing every word. "Soon they will combine their powers and then it will be too late for us. We must prepare to strike now, while there is still time." The smoke slid across the floor, up onto the bed, and Ylvain shivered.

"And it is necessary?" Her thought was small, almost unintentional, but the voice hissed dangerously.

"You doubt? You doubt even for a moment the task I have given you? There are many, you know—many who would die to take your place."

Ylvain's breath came shallow and fast. The smoke had

visited her only a few times since the birth of their army, but each time she sensed its cruelty ever closer to the surface. "I thought only that there might be a better way. An easier way—"

The voice thundered, echoing against the dark stone walls of the chamber.

"Cowardess! You have pledged to me your loyalty, your heart, your soul. But now, when we must act, I find you shrink back, afraid of the power I have given you! Do you fear the haunting of all-too-familiar ghosts? Or perhaps you find your heart conflicted? If you have hidden something from me, I shall tear it from you and turn you, willfully or no, to one who is not made a cripple by memories of the past."

Ylvain's head thrashed against the pillow, sweat beading on her face. "Please! I do not doubt! I am not afraid! I know you to be wise. I know the honor you have given me."

"Good," said the voice, quieting once again as the smoke slithered into Ylvain's chest, encircling the warm and fluttering heart. "Never forget what lies at the end of our plans, Ylvain. My power will be absolute, the world at my feet. And you shall be at my side, my sorceress queen, exalted and immortal. None more beautiful. None more revered. None more envied, more feared," the whisper purred, seductive as it slipped into a knot and bound the woman's heart in a dark embrace.

Ylvain no longer thrashed, but lay still on the bed, only her shallow breath and faint heartbeat betraying the life within her limbs. "I remember. Our desires are one, Master, my lord."

The smoke slid to the floor, a dark shadow as it crossed the room to the door. "Autumn is near, my queen. Before the leaves fall, the deed must be done. Do not fail me."

The stone chamber grew still and silent, the shadows of night filling each corner. It could have been empty, but for two sparks of light glinting from within Ylvain's open eyes as they stared, unblinking, into the darkness.

14

FIREFLIES

It was a hot afternoon late in the summer when Aaron rode into the courtyard, his bare arms and face glowing a golden tan from weeks spent in the Southlands. Alyen and Lirianna sat on hay bales in the barn while Aaron unsaddled Soran and stabled him in a stall next to Lusa. The two horses huffed air at each other and nuzzled their noses in greeting before turning to the oats Aaron was scooping into their feeding troughs.

"How long will you be here?" Lirianna asked.

"Not sure," Aaron replied. "Morten just told me to stay until he says otherwise. I've never seen him so worried. He hasn't said it outright, but I think they're preparing for an attack."

"An attack on the abbey?" Alyen asked doubtfully. Elementals or not, she had a hard time believing the darklings would have any effect on Monstar's massive stone walls.

"Not on the abbey exactly," Aaron said. "On Lirianna and Mother Brenwyn."

"What? Why?"

"Because of our Sight," Lirianna said, understanding more quickly. "Ylvain's blocked us for now, but maybe she can't hold us out forever and she can't risk us discovering her plans."

"You're in danger, too, Alyen," Aaron said seriously. "Ylvain most likely knows you're here. It would be highly convenient for her if she could bump off all three of you in one fell swoop."

"Then shouldn't we leave?" Alyen asked. "And why are Morten and Rowenna coming? We should be splitting up, not congregating together."

Aaron stroked Soran's nose absently. "You're right, it's a gamble. They did consider it—each of us going off to a different part of the kingdom. But the Trianid is always far more powerful together than apart. And Monstar is supposed to be nearly impenetrable. In the end they thought we'd have a better chance here together than scattered around."

Aaron came out of Soran's stall and latched the gate behind him.

"Which room are you staying in?" Alyen asked, standing up.

Aaron pointed one finger upward. "The hayloft."

"You're staying in the *barn*? Why? The abbey has hundreds of rooms!"

Aaron grimaced and looked away, scratching the back of his head. "I think Mother Brenwyn wanted to ensure that there wouldn't be any, uh, shenanigans."

Lirianna snorted behind her hand, but Alyen looked confused.

"Shenanigans?"

"You know," Lirianna said. "Secret romances, scandalous activities—*shenanigans*? And I can't say that I blame her. Half the occupants of the abbey look at our future Slayer as if he's the last slice of cake, and they're *nuns*. I'm not really sure how the barn is supposed to help matters, but still …"

Alyen felt her cheeks flush and hoped it wasn't noticeable. "But you stayed in the abbey at Midwinter."

"Morten was here with me most of the time at Midwinter," Aaron replied. "I guess he was my chaperone."

There was a pause, then Aaron cleared his throat. "Right, then I'll just go leave my things up there and get settled in."

"All right. I guess we'll see you in a bit." Alyen said. The girls turned back to the abbey while Aaron gathered his saddlebags and a blanket and headed for the ladder to the hayloft.

"That was awkward," Alyen said to Lirianna as they entered the abbey.

Lirianna shrugged. "It's a part of life. I don't see what the big fuss is."

"It's ridiculous that he has to stay in the barn. Is everyone really staring at him?"

"Of course. Didn't you notice?"

"No."

"Well, don't worry. He wasn't staring back."

Lirianna turned up the stairs, leaving Alyen to wonder if she should have been worried to begin with.

It was an uneasy feeling, to say the least, waiting to be attacked, and for the first couple days of Aaron's stay, Alyen was constantly on edge, jumping at every noise. But as the days progressed and nothing happened, she found herself gradually relaxing back into her regular rhythms. The onset of harvest season soon kept her busily distracted from thoughts of darkling attacks and brewing wars.

In fact, if she were to be entirely honest about it, Alyen was likely happier than if she had never seen the darklings and there was no threat of danger. With Aaron at Monstar, the evenings were filled once again with laughing, singing, and storytelling, though Mother Brenwyn kept them to a strict curfew after they stayed up in the gardens one night until it was nearly dawn and were barely able to function the following day.

The only downside to the situation was that Aaron grew restless as more and more time passed with no word from Morten or Rowenna on when they would arrive, or how long they would be staying at Monstar. They had decided that Aaron should not go to the Ruins of Enlair because he wouldn't be able to see the darklings to begin with, and if Ylvain was unaware of his presence in the abbey, they wanted to keep it that way. He tried to keep himself busy in the first few days by completing some minor repairs around the abbey, but since there really wasn't much to be done, he began to spend more and more time exercising in the courtyard. Before long, he had turned it into his own small training arena, complete with targets, obstacles, and a makeshift "enemy" that Alyen and Lirianna helped him to fashion from empty potato sacks, old rags, and a few sturdy tree branches.

It was with some annoyance that Alyen soon realized

Aaron's training sessions were becoming something of an attraction for the nuns and novices—particularly the younger ones. Suddenly, daily tasks seemed to require frequent rounds of the abbey's battlements and trips to the well; Monstar's wide stone front steps had never been so often nor so diligently swept. Alyen found herself gradually coming to approve of Mother Brenwyn's sleeping arrangement policy, but it didn't help the uncomfortable pinching in her chest whenever she saw one of the novices flip her hair away from her face as she crossed the courtyard while Aaron was training.

In truth, Alyen was just as guilty of ogling Aaron as the sisters, but, unlike them, she had a good excuse. As autumn approached, Alyen and Lirianna spent each sunset in their basin lookout on the battlements intending to soak up as much good weather as possible before the cold hit. Conveniently, this also coincided with Aaron's nightly training routine.

"He has good form," Lirianna commented one night as they sat, each with a mug of cider, watching as Aaron relentlessly assaulted the potato-sack man.

"Do you think we'll ever get to see him battle for real?" Alyen asked.

"I hope not," Lirianna replied seriously. "I hope we don't need to."

They sipped their cider in silence as the sun sank into the moor beyond Sheanen Crann. Slowly the fire of the sky and forest gave way to the muted purples and blues of twilight, and one by one, fireflies began to flicker and wink in the gloaming.

"Do you know what Rowenna told me about fireflies?" Alyen asked as one of the insects landed briefly on her knee.

"What?"

"It's the fireflies' job to mend the Balance."

"How do you mean?"

"Rowenna describes the Balance as an invisible weaving made of magic. Every living thing represents one string, and the way all the strings interweave makes up the tapestry of the world," Alyen explained. "When the tapestry is whole, the Balance is upheld. But in the course of a day, little tears or holes form in it, and the Balance gets off. That's where the fireflies come in; whenever one glows, it's fixing a tiny hole in the fabric."

"And where do the holes come from?"

"A tear happens when anyone does something that isn't in harmony with the Balance," Alyen explained. "Most holes are small—say, if someone speaks harshly or steals a pie from someone's window. Bigger wrongs make bigger holes."

"Hmm." Lirianna looked thoughtful for a while. "Can you … feel the tapestry?"

"Sort of. I'm getting better at it. Can you?"

"I think so. When I'm weaving—and sometimes when I'm not—I can feel stories and people and events stringing through the air like threads. Kind of like strands of spider silk borne on the wind."

But Alyen was distracted, squinting down at the dimming courtyard. "Isn't that the *third* time Lana has been to fetch water out of the well?"

"I don't know," Lirianna said, giving Alyen a sidelong glance. "*I* haven't been counting."

"Well, neither have I," Alyen said too quickly. "It just seems like she's spending a lot of time in the courtyard. No one in the abbey needs *that* much water tonight."

"Well, can you blame her? I mean look at him, Alyen! Aaron is quite a catch."

"That's beside the point. The point is, Lana's here to be a nun and—and so it's inappropriate. She shouldn't be thinking like that."

"She's just a novice, Alyen. She hasn't taken any vows. And even if she did, nuns are still people, you know."

Alyen was uncomfortably aware that her friend was giving her a long stare. When seconds had ticked by and Lirianna made no move to break it off, Alyen finally turned to face her. "What?"

"Oh, come on, Alyen. Admit it. You're in love."

"I—" Alyen broke off realizing that she didn't actually know what a truthful response would be. "I don't know. I might be. Is it really obvious?"

"Yes."

"Does Aaron know?"

A smile played about the corners of Lirianna's mouth. "I don't think so. He's too busy being in love with *you* to notice."

Lirianna's words lit a small flame just above Alyen's stomach, and she struggled to suppress the grin trying suddenly to push its way across her face.

"No, he's not. Stop it."

Lirianna simply waved her hand as she took another gulp of cider. "I'm right and you know it. Besides, if you both like each other, what's the fuss? You found someone; you should be happy."

Something in Lirianna's voice made Alyen pause and look at her friend closely. Lirianna had pulled the blanket a bit tighter about her shoulders, and was gazing out at the darkening sky, her face unusually blank. Alyen hesitated. She'd wondered if this would ever come up. She'd hoped to avoid it. But it would probably be better to get it out of the way now rather than later.

"Lirianna … do you love him, too?"

Lirianna smiled a little sadly and studied the contents of her mug before looking at Alyen directly. "No. But it wouldn't matter if I did. A Seer has to remain alone. It's part of the deal—Purity of Sight, you know. Otherwise, we might lose objectivity. It's not for no reason that the Seer lives in an abbey."

Alyen's eyebrows rose. "I—I'm sorry, Lirianna. I didn't know."

"Don't be," Lirianna replied. "I knew the rules before I ever came to Monstar, and I accept them. And it's not as if I'll ever be lonely. I have you and Aaron and all the sisters."

On impulse Alyen hugged Lirianna tightly. "You will always be my dearest friend. I won't let you be lonely."

"Thanks, Alyen." Lirianna gave her a squeeze, then let go. "Seriously, though, I would be so happy for you two if it worked out. The Keeper and the Slayer? It would be an epic love story."

Alyen paused in the middle of gulping her cider and lowered her mug. "Lirianna?"

"Yes?"

"You can't breathe a word of this to Aaron."

"Of course not." Lirianna's eyes were too innocent.

"I'm serious!"

"Yes, you are."

"Promise me you won't tell!"

"Don't you trust me?"

"Promise!"

Lirianna relaxed her face in a smile. "Don't worry, I promise."

Down in the courtyard, Aaron's sword made one final arc before he plunged it into the ground and stood breathing hard, sweat running down his face and shirt. He wiped his brow on his sleeve, tugged the sword out of the earth, and strode back into the barn as the last of the light faded from the courtyard, leaving only the fireflies winking in the darkness.

15

GREMLINS

"Alyen, is there an axe I can borrow?"

Aaron stood in the doorway of the library, looking agitated. Despite his scowl, Alyen felt her insides melt.

"I'm sure we can find one. Why?"

"Because I'm getting rusty," Aaron said, flexing his fingers in and out of fists. "I thought Morten would be here by now, so the only weapons I brought are my sword and a few knives. I'm getting out of practice with the rest and it's driving me insane."

Alyen set down the books she had been carrying and moved toward the door. "Let's go look in the tool shed. There must be one somewhere."

The tool shed was really a small cave with a door, built into the side of the mountain that edged the gardens. Alyen propped the door open with a rock to let in some light and they entered, squinting into the shadows.

For a moment, Alyen's heart leapt as she realized that she was finally alone with Aaron in a relatively private place. Then she saw the impatience lining Aaron's face as he scanned the walls of tools. It wasn't the time, or the place, really. And even if it were, what exactly had she meant to do about it? She sighed inwardly.

"Check over on that side," she said, gesturing to the opposite wall. "I'll look over here."

Alyen pawed through the racks of spades, hoes, and rakes, and the clunking noises from Aaron's side of the room told her he was doing the same with about as much success. She had almost reached the end of her wall when the noise behind her stopped.

"Alyen, come and look at this."

Alyen joined him at the back corner of the cave and peered in the direction of Aaron's stare. At first, she saw nothing but the walls of rock meeting each other in the shadowy corner. But then the dim light filtering from outside shifted; with a start of surprise, Alyen realized that the two walls of rock did not meet each other at all. Instead, a large crevasse, cunningly hidden in the shadows, flickered into sight. A black rip revealed itself in the rock before the light shifted again and it was gone.

"Did you know this was here?" Aaron asked.

"No," Alyen shook her head. "And I've never heard any of the sisters mention it either."

Aaron flashed her a grin, white and mischievous, and Alyen was reminded strongly of the day they had met at Castle Dúr when he'd convinced her to climb the tree.

"Do you feel like exploring?" he asked.

"All right," she agreed, feeling the same reckless excitement she had on that day so long ago.

"I'll go first," Aaron said. "You follow close behind."

Alyen watched as Aaron appeared to vanish into a wall of solid rock. She stepped up to the crevasse, turned sideways, and squeezed through the opening, expecting to run into Aaron at any moment.

But the crevasse widened immediately. Alyen found herself staring into a black expanse with only a tiny shard of white light cutting across the floor from the tool shed. The darkness was disorienting. She put her hand out to feel the rock wall beside her.

"Aaron?" she called.

"This is amazing!" came his reply, his voice reverberating against the stone. "I think it's some sort of tunnel ..." his words began to trail off and Alyen, who was quickly discovering that she did not like small dark spaces, felt a jolt of alarm as she realized he was getting farther away.

"Aaron, wait, I can't see anything!" she called, noting that her voice sounded high and pinched. Aaron must have noticed as well for she heard his footsteps returning and then he was at her side.

"I'm here," he said. "Don't worry." His hand came around her waist, so swiftly and naturally it seemed almost casual.

But it was not casual.

Alyen could feel the tension in his arm; he was suddenly so still. She heard his breath, heavier than she remembered it, and felt her own coming quicker to her throat. Trusting the dark to shield her boldness, Alyen looked up at his face, so close to hers, and saw how the single shard of light outlined his features in a thread of white. The line of his jaw was so strong and in the stark lighting, his nose and cheekbones looked chiseled yet soft. He was in front of her now, his hand sliding slowly, almost tentatively, from her waist to the small of her back, the other hand touching the hair near her temple softly, so gently. Warmth blossomed low in Alyen's stomach, spreading through her limbs, and she reached up to place her hands lightly on Aaron's strong shoulders.

"Alyen? Aaron? Where are you? We need you, quickly!"

It was Lirianna's voice calling from the gardens. Both Alyen and Aaron started. For a second, they froze, then Aaron squeezed Alyen's arm tightly for a second and he was gone, back through the crevasse, leaving Alyen to stumble out behind him.

"We're here, what's wrong?" Aaron was calling. Alyen was behind him and couldn't see his face, but she wondered if it looked as flushed as hers felt.

"There you are!" Lirianna cried, looking panicked. "Come quickly! The weaving rooms are being attacked!"

Lirianna turned and raced back toward the abbey, Alyen and Aaron sprinting after her. Once inside, Alyen could hear screaming coming from the corridors above and she saw Aaron reaching for the dagger in his belt as he ran in front of her. They burst through the door to the weaving rooms and stopped short, breathing hard.

The scene before them was one of total chaos. Shreds of yarn and string littered the floor. One loom had been completely overturned and a cluster of sisters stood cowering in the far corner, whimpering in fright. At one loom sat Sister Gwen, a young nun who was shrieking at the top of her lungs —and it didn't take Alyen long to see why.

Sister Gwen was hunched over her work, her face turned toward the wall, and her hair had been tightly knotted into the pattern of threads strung across her loom. She was surrounded by a dozen small, ugly creatures the color of rotting swamp slime, that hopped across her loom and her shoulders, pulling at her hair, twanging the threads of her weaving, and turning the gears of the loom, tightening the threads so they pulled the nun's hair tighter and tighter, causing her to scream even louder.

Several more of the creatures raced about the room pulling things off shelves and making loud chattering noises that filled the air with a constant racket.

"They just appeared out of nowhere!" Lirianna was shouting above the noise. "They tied up Sister Gwen's hair in a matter of seconds and we can't get rid of them!"

Mother Brenwyn, who had been hovering over Sister Gwen, torn between trying to calm the girl, scatter the creatures and shout largely ignored instructions to the huddle of sisters in the corner, abandoned her efforts and swooped down on Alyen and Aaron, eyes ablaze.

"Do either of you know what these creatures are?" she shouted. Alyen had never seen her look so fierce.

Aaron was shaking his head. "I've never seen these before!"

"Alyen?" Mother Brenwyn snapped. "Are they darklings?"

"I—I don't think so," Alyen yelled above the clamor. "They don't look like the ones I saw!"

Mother Brenwyn gave an impatient huff and without another word, strode briskly toward her private workroom and disappeared behind the door with the eye carved into the wood. Alyen, Aaron, and Lirianna looked at each other helplessly for a moment until Aaron said, "Come on, let's try to free Sister Gwen."

But they were no more successful than Mother Brenwyn had been. At first, all three tried to unravel the strands of hair from the warp of the loom, but the creatures kept running over their hands, scratching at their fingers, making it impossible to make any progress. Eventually, Alyen and Aaron took to swatting the creatures away while Lirianna continued to work at unraveling the hair. As Alyen smacked at several of the creatures trying to scratch at Lirianna's fingers, she saw that they had small but sharply pointed ears, sharp teeth, and tiny claws on their fingers. Their eyes held a wicked gleam and their mouths seemed too wide for their heads. Their limbs were thin and wiry and Alyen discovered with revulsion as she brushed one away that their skin was cold and clammy to the touch.

Alyen quickly realized that their interference was, if anything, making matters worse. Sister Gwen's shrieking had subsided to hysterical sobbing, but Lirianna was making little progress unknotting her hair. The creatures running about the room seemed to notice that their comrades were being confronted and more and more joined the battle. Soon Lirianna was forced to stop her untangling to aid Alyen and Aaron in simply keeping the creatures off Sister Gwen and themselves. Alyen by now was swatting at them left and right, her hands covered in tiny scratches, barely able to keep up with the onslaught of slimy undersized assailants. Next to her, Alyen saw Aaron draw his dagger swiftly from his belt, but before he could act, Mother Brenwyn's voice bellowed through the room.

"STOP!"

Alyen was momentarily impressed that such a loud noise could be made by such a small woman. The chattering of the creatures did not stop, but Mother Brenwyn shouted her instructions over the noise as she began to herd the whimpering nuns toward the door.

"Stop whatever you're doing!" she instructed. "Sit on the floor. Do not move. Do not fight back. Try to look bored."

These seemed like ridiculous instructions to Alyen, but Mother Brenwyn spoke with such authority that she obeyed. She sat on the thread-strewn floor, trying to keep her face as blank as possible. Beside her, Aaron and Lirianna did the same.

For what seemed an eternity, the creatures continued to race around them, making as much noise and chaos as possible, but no longer attacking. Then slowly the clamor began to die down as the creatures' enthusiasm waned and one by one, they began to disappear. Finally, the last creature vanished, and the room was empty and still, save for Alyen, Aaron, and Lirianna sitting on the floor, Mother Brenwyn standing in the doorway, and Sister Gwen sobbing softly, still hunched over her loom.

Mother Brenwyn found a pair of scissors and approached Sister Gwen's loom. She stroked the girl's head gently, crooning soft calming words, while she carefully cut the locks of hair as close to the threads as she could manage.

"Not to worry, dear," she murmured. "It will grow back in no time."

When Sister Gwen had been freed, Mother Brenwyn folded her in her arms, all traces of her blazing anger gone.

"Alyen," she said calmly. "Please take Sister Gwen and the

sisters in the hall to the infirmary. I want them all to have a calming draught. Then come back here and help Lirianna restore this room to order."

Lirianna rose from the ground and Alyen and Aaron followed suit.

"Aaron," Mother Brenwyn continued, "you and I will gather your things from the stable. We need a warrior inside the walls tonight."

Alyen and Lirianna exchanged a glance, knowing only serious circumstances could have persuaded Mother Brenwyn to abandon her sleeping arrangement rules.

"And Alyen," Mother Brenwyn added. "When you're done helping Lirianna with this room, eat your dinner and go to bed early. Rowenna wants to see you as soon as possible."

Rowenna was waiting near the cottage. Alyen started to speak before the mist had fully cleared.

"Rowenna, what were those things? Elementals? Magical Creatures?"

"Neither. They were gremlins," Rowenna replied. "Nasty creatures. And a troubling sign."

"Gremlins are real? I thought people just made them up to explain bad luck."

"Not at all," Rowenna replied. "Gremlins are creatures of chaos. They often show up wherever the Balance has been disturbed."

"And they're evil?"

"No, not necessarily; just inconvenient. But the fact that

they showed up inside Monstar and attacked a person directly is quite seriously alarming."

"Why?"

"For one, gremlins don't naturally attack people—they only tamper with objects and try to break things to create trouble. Secondly, they usually stay out of sight. I've never heard of them acting out in the open like this. But apart from all that, I'm shocked that they appeared in Monstar at all. The abbey is the safest place in the kingdom and one of the areas where the Balance is the strongest. Honestly, I don't know how they managed to get in and it worries me greatly."

"But Mother Brenwyn made them disappear. Did you tell her how to do that?"

"Yes, it's fairly simple. The gremlins' goal is to increase chaos and to spread frustration in those around them. So, if you refuse to react to their efforts, they'll soon grow bored and move on. But it's not actually the gremlins I'm worried about. What we suspect is that they were sent ahead to breach Monstar in preparation for a larger attack that's on the way."

"On the way—*now*?"

"Perhaps even tonight," Rowenna said, her brow furrowed. "Morten and I will hurry, but we're still a couple of days away from each other and I fear we may reach Monstar too late to stop an attack. Now listen carefully because this is important. I'm going to teach you how to ask the elementals to defend you inside a protective circle. It can be a bit flashy, so you don't want to do it if you're trying to stay hidden, but it will work well in your situation. Did Brenwyn ask Aaron to stay in the abbey tonight?"

"Yes," Alyen confirmed.

"Good. I want the circle protecting all three of you, so you must all sleep in the same room tonight."

Alyen nodded, and suddenly, unbidden, the image of Aaron in the cave earlier that afternoon flashed into her head, and she started to blush. Horrified, she turned her head, but Rowenna noticed and one of her eyebrows rose.

"Will that be awkward?" she asked, her eyes searching Alyen's.

"No," Alyen replied, but her voice sounded unnatural, and she was finding it hard to maintain eye contact.

Rowenna didn't say anything for a moment but stood in the clearing studying Alyen's face with a strange expression. Finally, she motioned to a bench in front of the cottage.

"Come sit, Alyen. We need to talk about something before I show you the circle."

Alyen groaned inwardly as she sat beside Rowenna on the bench, cursing her cheeks for giving her away. She braced herself for an awkward conversation but was surprised when she reluctantly looked up to see Rowenna's face suddenly sad and etched with lines of regret.

"Did I ever tell you that I didn't meet Morten until I was about your age?" Alyen shook her head. "It's true. I was traveling south to a village where I heard there had been an outbreak of a bad fever. I was staying at an inn in a town near the border of Sheanen Crann to the west of Monstar, and Morten happened to be traveling back from the Southlands and booked a room in the same inn. Our mentors had intended for us to meet later that year, but destiny had other plans—as she often does.

"I first saw Morten across the room at breakfast. I remember feeling as though I'd been struck hard in the stomach. He was a young man then, of course—tall, muscular, and handsome with a glittering sword at his side. He was on his first solo journey to the Northlands. It didn't take long for us to realize the connections between us and—well, you know how strong the natural bonds are amongst the Trianid. We spent the whole day together and then the next, and the one after that. Both of us had places to be, duties that were pressing, but we kept putting off our departure for just one more day. Soon two weeks had passed, and we'd barely noticed. They were the happiest weeks of my life, and by the end of them, we were very much in love. Eventually, though, my conscience caught up with me, and I insisted that I really did need to reach the village to cure the fever, so Morten offered to ride with me.

"When we reached the village, I found that a third of the villagers were ill and four had died from the fever in the previous week—exactly during the time Morten and I had been avoiding our responsibilities in exchange for a few nights of romance. The guilt was unbearable. It was made worse by the fact that all the villagers treated me as a hero as I worked tirelessly to cure those still infected, not knowing that had I continued my journey as I should have, I would have arrived in time to save those who had died. It was a grave mistake, and one I have never forgiven myself for."

Alyen didn't know what to say. It was, indeed, an awkward conversation—though not for the reasons she'd thought it would be. She had always thought of Rowenna as unerringly wise. Now, she didn't know how to respond.

"Morten was distraught, too, and after the fever was under control, we had a long talk. We decided that we could never allow such a thing to happen again, but we knew that the temptations of a normal life would always be there as long as we were together. For the sake of the kingdom and all its people, we vowed to never again be together as lovers, and we promised we would never again seek anything from each other apart from what was needed in our roles as Keeper and Slayer. And we have kept that promise to this day."

"But—but you *loved* him," Alyen protested, seeing where Rowenna was going with her story and not liking it.

"As I still do and as I will until the day I die," Rowenna confirmed. "But it's better for the Keeper to remain alone."

Alyen frowned as she stared at the ground. "Are you telling me that I'm not allowed to fall in love?"

"Of course not," Rowenna said calmly. "You can't help falling in love. But I am cautioning you against acting on love in any way that will compromise your duties as Keeper. As I said, it's easier and better to avoid complications altogether. And Aaron would be very complicated."

Alyen felt her limbs starting to tremble. She couldn't remember ever being so angry in her life. Rowenna saw her expression and continued before Alyen could say anything.

"But surely this can't be too large a shock, Alyen. You were born a princess—chances are you were never going to marry for love anyway. If you had stayed at Castle Dúr, eventually a suitable marriage would have been arranged for you. With you as the heir to the throne, there would have been few sons with families prestigious enough to pick from. Surely you knew this. Why this sudden expectation of romance?"

"I don't know. I thought maybe it would be different now. Maybe I could choose …" Alyen was blinking rapidly, unsure herself why she was so upset.

"Look at Lirianna," Rowenna continued. "One day she'll

be an abbess and will never marry. It's part of what it means to be the Seer."

There it was. The reason for her anger.

Alyen looked up at Rowenna, her face like a stone. "You should have told me."

Rowenna gave a small shrug. "I suppose I—"

"No—you should have *told* me. Mother Brenwyn told Liri-anna about this *before* she agreed to be Seer. *You* never did. You knew if you told me before the binding ceremony I might not want to agree, and that would have been inconvenient for you."

"Alyen—"

"I had a right to know!"

"Alyen, you never asked—"

"*I never asked?* How could I have asked? How could I have known *what* to ask? Don't blame this on me. You should have told me and you didn't. That's it!" Alyen angrily dashed her hands against her eyes.

Rowenna was still for a moment before she replied softly.

"You're right, Alyen."

She said nothing more for a while and Alyen continued to sniff, refusing to look at Rowenna. Eventually Rowenna stood and said, "I'm going to make us some tea and give you some time. We'll return to this conversation soon, I promise, but tonight there isn't time. I must teach you the protective circle, and then you have to wake to make it at Monstar."

Rowenna rose and took a few steps before turning to pause at the door. "For what it's worth, I never meant to deceive you. I'm sorry, Alyen. Truly I am. I know what it is to lose love."

She went into the cottage and Alyen continued to seethe

on the bench. It was easier to be angry than heartbroken. The horrible thing was that, if not for the cave at Monstar that very afternoon, none of this might have bothered her even half as much. And the worst part was that, despite the betrayal, she knew that Rowenna was right.

16

PROTECTIVE CIRCLE

When Alyen woke in her room, the sun had just set, and she could still see a thin golden line on the western horizon resting below the first twinkling stars. She sat quietly for a moment, watching the last of the light fade to darkness, not yet ready to join the others. Her mood was heavy, but she would have to disguise it since she wouldn't be able to explain in front of Aaron.

It had taken her several tries before she had mastered the protective circle in the dreamworld, not because it was especially difficult, but because she was too distracted by her anger at Rowenna and thoughts of Aaron. And, though she didn't want to admit it, she was embarrassed and upset with herself as well. She needed time to sort it out, but not now, not with Ylvain's army of darklings potentially on the way. She closed her curtains against the darkness and went in search of the others, hoping her face wouldn't betray her turmoil.

She found them in one of the studies near the center of the abbey. Already the tables and chairs had all been removed, and three mattresses had been placed in the middle of the floor with piles of blankets and pillows. Lirianna and Aaron were trying to convince Mother Brenwyn to stay with them inside the protective circle, but she insisted on staying in her own rooms so as not to alarm the nuns, and to ensure that the sisters could reach her quickly if need be. She saw Alyen enter the room and looked grateful for the interruption.

"Alyen, we're all ready for you. Do you know how to make the circle? Do you need anything?"

Alyen tried for a confident smile but managed only a thin stretch of her mouth with a nod.

"You all right?" Lirianna asked with narrowed eyes, perceptive as always.

"Yes, fine." Alyen brightened her expression and scanned the room for available resources. "Just a little sleepy. I'll need a pitcher of water, but that's all. We already have plenty of candles."

Lirianna fetched a pitcher from the lavatory, then she and Aaron moved into the center of the room, each sitting on one of the mattresses.

"You're sure you won't stay with us?" Alyen asked Mother Brenwyn. "Everyone has to be inside before I draw the circle."

Mother Brenwyn smiled, but her words were firm. "I'll stay until I see the circle drawn and then I'll be just down the hall if you need me." She moved to the door, well outside the area where Alyen would trace the protective boundary and stood quietly to watch.

Alyen swallowed and concentrated on focusing her mind.

She had never worked so much magic with others watching before and she knew she mustn't let it distract her. She took the pitcher and moved slowly in a large arc, trickling a thin trail of water around the three mattresses, careful not to leave any gaps in the wet circle that formed around the center of the room. When she was confident the circle was whole, she set down the pitcher and closed her eyes, collecting her thoughts. *Address each group one at a time*, Rowenna had said, *and start with fire. Fire is always the first line of defense.* Alyen opened her eyes and stretched her hands over the arc of her circle.

"Bearers of the fire's spark, protect us on this night so dark. Our enemies are fast advancing, guard this circle with your dancing. Save us from the threat of night."

As Alyen spoke, the candles in the room flared. One by one the salamandars leapt to the floor, swirling and multiplying until Alyen, Aaron, and Lirianna were surrounded by a wall of flames. Alyen saw Mother Brenwyn step back from the wave of heat, but inside the circle the air was merely warm and comfortable. It would be impossible to sleep with so much light flickering in the room, so Alyen whispered, "The enemies are not yet here. Calm your flames until they're near." At once the flames shrank to the ground until the room was lit only by the candles lining the walls and a ring of bluish flame surrounding the pile of bedding.

Alyen continued, calling next upon the undines who raised a wall of water in seconds from the thin, wet circle Alyen had traced on the floor. As with the salamandars, Alyen quieted the undines, and the shimmering wall shrank back to the ground to await attack. When Alyen turned to the sylphs, Mother Brenwyn was driven into the corridor altogether as a raging vortex of wind rose. The three apprentices sat undisturbed in the eye of the storm, but the wind, too, died down to a gentle breeze at Alyen's bidding.

Alyen hesitated before making her final request to the gnomes. Twice in the dreamworld, she had not asked delicately enough, and a ravine had opened in the earth in front of the cottage. It would not do for Monstar to be ripped apart by an earthquake, leaving Alyen and her friends on an island of rock amidst the ruins of the abbey. It was why the gnomes were always asked last—it took the greatest amount of time and careful wording to ask correctly, and their method of defense was always a last resort. Alyen crouched and rested her hands against the stone floor.

"Gnomes who dwell within the stone, this abbey has become my home; I do not wish to see it fall, but if our enemies breach the walls, protect us from their evil will—until then may the ground lie still."

Alyen held her breath and braced herself, but she felt only a slight tremor rise from the earth deep below the abbey. The circle was complete; all was quiet.

"Well done, Alyen," Mother Brenwyn said from the doorway as Alyen sank back onto her mattress with a sigh of relief.

"Truly, that was impressive," Aaron said, sounding legitimately surprised as Lirianna patted Alyen's back. Alyen was about to say something to the effect that she was pleased she hadn't torn down the abbey, but thought better of it and merely said, "I just hope we don't need it after all."

Mother Brenwyn circled the room, blowing out candles until only the blue flames of the circle were left, then bid them goodnight.

"Try to get some sleep," she said. "I think it's likely that nothing will happen, and we'll all have a good laugh about it in the morning."

Within a few minutes, Alyen, Aaron, and Lirianna had arranged the mattresses so their heads all faced the center of the circle and they lay propped up on their elbows under the blankets, whispering in the faint blue light from the circle's flames.

"I'm glad you brought your sword," Lirianna said to Aaron, noting the scabbard tucked close beside his bed. "Even if it is just a precaution."

"Better to have it and not need it than be caught without it," Aaron replied.

"By the way," Lirianna said, "what were you two doing in the tool shed this afternoon? I looked everywhere for you."

Alyen kept her eyes glued to the floor and was surprised to hear Aaron's calm answer.

"Alyen was helping me find an axe for training."

"And did you find one?" Alyen thought she sounded skeptical.

"No, but we did find something else," Aaron replied. He told Lirianna about the tunnel leading into the mountain. "Did you know about it?" he finally concluded.

"No," Lirianna said, now sounding surprised. "And you don't know where it leads?"

"No, we were just going to look when we heard you calling us," Aaron said.

Alyen ventured a glance at Aaron's face, but he wasn't looking at her at all and didn't seem the least bit uncomfortable. For a moment, Alyen wondered if she'd terribly misread the events in the tool shed. Had she imagined it? The way his arm had come around her waist, pressing her closer to him? The way his fingers had brushed her hair and her cheek in the dark?

"Well, good to know," Lirianna joked. "Because you know how it looks when two people come bursting out of a tool shed together."

Aaron laughed, his voice sounding horribly carefree in Alyen's ears. "Sorry to disappoint you, Lirianna, but nothing of the sort. We can show you the tunnel tomorrow if you like. We'll explore it together—what do you say, Alyen?"

For a second their eyes met and Alyen saw it. The quick flash in his gaze and the nearly imperceptible quirk of his smile. She hadn't misread. She hadn't imagined a thing.

"Sure. Sounds fun," she replied hollowly. She managed another of her thin smiles.

"Alyen, are you sure you're all right?" Lirianna said, frowning. "You haven't been yourself since you woke up."

"I'm fine, really. Just a little nervous I expect."

"Don't worry," Aaron said. "I'm sure this will all blow over in a couple days."

"Yes, nothing can get by your circle. And we have Aaron here as backup," Lirianna said. Well-intentioned as their reassurances were, they just made Alyen feel worse.

"You're right," Alyen said. "I'm probably just tired. Maybe I'll try to get some sleep."

"Good idea," Lirianna agreed. "We should all try to get some rest."

They exchanged goodnights and settled into their pillows. Aaron and Lirianna were soon breathing deeply. But Alyen buried her head under her blankets so the others wouldn't notice the tears running down her cheeks.

The mist began to lift from the dreamworld and Alyen ground her teeth, wishing she could escape into the oblivion of a dreamless sleep. The last thing in the world she wanted to do at the moment was focus on another lesson, another plant, another cure for another disease. But even in her distracted state, it took only seconds to realize something was amiss.

The fog was not thinning as usual, instead swirling in chaotic, restless flurries around her. The glimpses of the forest she could see were fragmented, and they quivered like reflections on the surface of a pond disturbed by ripples. The ground was shuddering; Alyen had to crouch and throw her hands out to keep her balance as the clearing heaved below her feet. And where was the cottage? She should be able to make out the roof through the mist to her left, but she saw nothing but a dark void beyond the roiling fog.

"Rowenna?" Alyen called, frightened. "Rowenna, are you here?"

She couldn't see her mentor anywhere and there was no reply to her shouting other than the eerie moan of wind through branches she could barely see. Alyen gulped against the panic building in her chest. Did this have something to do with the attack on Monstar? Had she somehow been trapped here without Rowenna? What if she couldn't wake up? Were her friends in danger? Perhaps she should try to wake herself?

But just as she was about to attempt to force herself awake a shadowy form began to materialize in front of her. Alyen froze in fear. She watched as the shadow grew more and more solid, forming itself from the swirling fog and flickering like the glimpses of the forest beyond the mist. Gradually the shade began to take on a familiar form and Alyen almost sobbed with relief when she realized it was Rowenna materializing in the air before her.

"Rowenna! What's ha—?" Alyen began to say but stopped short as she realized that something was terribly wrong with her mentor. Rowenna's face was gray, and her eyes were wide with shock and remorse. Both her hands were pressed over a spot near her heart, and beneath her fingers Alyen could see a dark, wet patch spreading slowly across the front of her dress.

"Alyen," Rowenna said, her voice a sigh, rough and ragged. "Alyen, I don't have much time."

"What's happening?" Alyen cried, now terrified as she hurried to Rowenna's side. "Where are we?"

"We're in the clearing. Just barely. I have to tell you … Have to warn you …"

"But what happened to you?"

"Alyen. I've been killed. Morten, too." And with these words Rowenna sank to her knees. Alyen struggled to support her, to soften the fall.

"No. No, that can't be. The darklings—the gremlins. They're all coming to Monstar."

"All a ruse," Rowenna said, her breath coming fast and shallow. "We waited too long. Didn't know we were being tracked. And now we've left you such a burden, Alyen. I'm sorry."

This was a nightmare. It had to be. Another tremor shook the ground and Rowenna's glazed eyes focused on Alyen's.

"Alyen, you must listen to me. Are you listening?"

Her hand gripped Alyen's as her head sank back into the crook of Alyen's arm.

"Ylvain will start a war. I'm sure of it. And when she does, you must be wary of Garret."

"Garret? Why?"

"He was the one who ... loved Ylvain. The one she tricked ... with the fire."

"W-what?"

"Garret would never betray you ... not on purpose. But Ylvain is devious. She will try to use him ... she will ..."

Rowenna began to cough, her breath coming fast and ragged. Alyen saw the wet patch had spread throughout the front of her dress.

"Rowenna, I can help you. Tell me what to do—what medicine do you need? I can ask the elementals ..." Her eyes scanned wildly around her, but she could not see even a single sylph in the mist. All at once she realized she could no longer glimpse the forest, the clearing, not even the ground beneath them—nothing but a sea of fog and black emptiness beyond it.

"No use, Alyen. You can't heal me here. And I ... can't hold on any longer."

"Yes, yes you can!" Alyen said, unaware of the tears streaming down her cheeks. "You can't leave now. I don't know what to do!"

"Go to Brenwyn," Rowenna whispered. Her form was beginning to flicker and fade. "Brenwyn will tell you what to do."

"But I need *you*," Alyen sobbed. "I can't do it without you."

A shadow of a smile flickered on Rowenna's face. "You will be a great Keeper of Scales, Alyen. I'm sorry I couldn't teach you more ..."

Rowenna's image was faint now. Alyen tried to grasp at her hand, but it was like grasping at the mist. "No! No, please, don't go, Rowenna. Please!"

"Alyen ..." Rowenna's voice was like the whisper of the wind. Then it was gone and Alyen's arms were empty.

ESCAPE

Alyen bolted upright with a cry of dismay, sweat and tears pouring down her face, glistening in the blue light of the protective flames. Aaron and Lirianna were awake as well, one on each side, their hands gripping her arms and shoulders, shaking gently.

"Mother Brenwyn," Alyen gasped, struggling to stand. "I need to see Mother Brenwyn!"

"Alyen!" Aaron said, restraining her with his firm grip. "You can't leave without breaking the circle. You just had a bad dream, that's all."

"No!" Alyen cried, her eyes wild as they met his. "It wasn't a dream! Aaron …" and she felt her throat close around the words she couldn't bear to utter. "Aaron, it's Morten. And Rowenna." She was sobbing now, and Aaron was searching her face with his eyes, fearing her words and already not believing them. "They've been killed, Aaron. Ylvain … she …" But she could not go on.

Aaron's face went hard, his expression strangely blank. "Alyen," he said firmly. "You had a nightmare. A bad dream."

Alyen shook her head, wishing with all her heart it was true, but knowing it was not. A small ache had started in her chest, and she remembered Rowenna's words just before her binding ceremony a year ago. *The binding is permanent and can be broken only by death.* Now, with the empty loneliness gradually spreading, Alyen knew her connection with Rowenna had been severed.

"Aaron, she may be right." It was Lirianna who spoke and as Alyen looked, she saw her friend with her hands pressed against her temples, her eyes closed tight.

"What's wrong?" Aaron asked.

"My Sight," Lirianna said. "It's come unblocked and it's all flooding in at once. I really think we need to go see Mother Brenwyn."

Aaron hesitated a moment then nodded, snatching up his sword before stepping over the flames and leading the way into the corridor. As soon as his foot touched the stone floor outside the circle, the fires vanished.

The cool breeze in the corridors soothed Alyen's tears and she was no longer weeping when they met Mother Brenwyn hurrying toward them in the halls. She wore only a nightgown and slippers, silver-streaked hair in a loose braid over one shoulder. Without her wimple, Alyen thought she looked even smaller in the looming darkness of the corridor.

"What's happened?" Mother Brenwyn asked sharply, and Alyen saw she had one hand massaging her heart. "What's wrong?"

"Alyen says Rowenna and Morten have been killed by Ylvain," Aaron said, his face still a blank mask.

Mother Brenwyn froze, then turned to Alyen. "Is this true?"

"Yes. Rowenna told me. Just before she died." How calmly she said the horrible words, and Alyen could see in Mother Brenwyn's eyes that the news did not entirely come as a surprise. The abbess fumbled with the front of her nightgown until she was clasping the flashing pendant she always wore. She froze for a moment as if listening intently. After several silent moments, her face drained of color.

Suddenly Lirianna cried out, collapsing to her knees, her hands pressed against her forehead.

"What is it, Lirianna?" Mother Brenwyn asked, hurrying to kneel at her student's side.

"My head," Lirianna moaned. "It's going to split!"

"She said her Sight is back," Aaron supplied. "Isn't yours?"

"No," Mother Brenwyn replied, a quaver in her voice. "But if Rowenna and Morten are truly gone, it's not surprising. The shock of our bonds being severed would surely compromise it."

A sob escaped Lirianna's lips. Mother Brenwyn turned to Aaron.

"Help me get her up," she instructed. "We need to take her to the weaving rooms."

Aaron scooped Lirianna easily into his arms and followed as Mother Brenwyn headed quickly down the corridor, Alyen hurrying at her side.

"Mother Brenwyn, you do believe me, don't you?" Alyen asked as they reached the stairs leading to the weaving rooms.

"Yes. But we need more information before we take any action. And Lirianna needs to weave."

Alyen did not question her further. They had reached the weaving rooms and Mother Brenwyn was leading them between the empty rows of looms that threw stark shadows across the moonlit floor. They approached the door where the carved eye stared unblinkingly into the darkness, eerie in the gloom.

Mother Brenwyn drew a key out of a pocket in her nightgown and twisted it swiftly in the lock. The door opened, and Alyen followed the others inside, glancing about at the room she had never entered.

She was surprised to find it was round, and Alyen realized they must be in one of the abbey's towers. Tall arched windows circled the outer wall and moonlight streamed in, bathing the room in a pale, white glow. Shadows of clouds crossing the moon drifted slowly across the floor and over the two looms that stood in the center of the room.

Mother Brenwyn was helping Aaron settle Lirianna on the chair before the smaller of the two looms. Alyen saw it was threaded with a warp of black string and beneath the loom, yards of black woven cloth wrapped around and around a wooden beam showing months of Lirianna's unsuccessful efforts to see past the darkness that blocked her Sight.

Aaron was dragging a small table to Lirianna's side, careful not to disturb the objects carefully arranged across its surface. Alyen went to help him and saw that the table was covered with an array of shuttles, each loaded with different shades of red, blue, green, gold, violet, and every color between. At Mother Brenwyn's instructions, Alyen and Aaron positioned the table so that Lirianna could reach each of the shuttles easily, then they stood back as Mother Brenwyn took up the shuttle attached to Lirianna's work and placed it gently in her hands.

"Look to the past, Lirianna," she instructed softly. "Focus your mind on Rowenna and Morten and look back to earlier this night."

Lirianna's hand closed around the black-threaded shuttle. For a moment she was still, staring straight ahead, her eyes clouded and unfocussed. Alyen knew that whatever her friend was seeing, it was far away from the room in Monstar's tower. For some reason the sight chilled her, and she moved a step closer to Aaron, almost wishing she could look away.

Suddenly, Lirianna's foot snapped down on one of the loom's treadles and the threads sprang to attention. She began to weave, the black shuttle flashing from side to side, treadles working in rhythm beneath her feet, her arm pounding the beater against the black cloth.

"It's dark—so dark," Lirianna murmured in a horribly altered voice, thin, hollow, and dry as the falling leaves. Her hand flew to the table and grasped a shuttle threaded in a deep green. The pattern of her feet on the treadles changed and soon both shuttles were working across the warp.

"They're asleep among trees. Not together. Far apart. Each alone." She continued to weave, never looking at her work but staring blankly into the air in front of her until her hand once again darted to the table, snatching up a shuttle of steely gray.

"There are knives—wicked knives," she said, her voice quivering eerily as she added the new shuttle to the mix. The speed of her weaving increased and soon her hand was reaching once again for another shuttle, this one a deep crimson red.

"And there is blood—so much blood!" she cried, her hands and feet pounding the loom in its rhythm as sweat began to bead on her forehead. "Rowenna is slain! Morten tries to fight, but there are too many. He falls, he falls! His sword is taken …"

Her hand fell on a shuttle of vibrant yellow that began to interweave with the red, the colors standing out starkly against the black cloth.

"Fire," Lirianna moaned, her cheeks now streaked with tears. "Fire burns the Keeper and the Slayer. They burn … they burn!" Her voice rose into hysteria and her limbs began to shake, sobs racking her chest. Mother Brenwyn was at Lirianna's side quickly, arms encircling the girl's trembling body, interrupting the rhythm of the loom, and pinning Lirianna's arms to her sides.

"Leave the vision, now, Lirianna," she spoke into her ear. "Come back to me, to the present, to our room where you are safe. There's no need to finish this tapestry."

Slowly, Lirianna's fingers unclenched from the shuttles she clutched in her hands and her eyes cleared, though her sobbing continued. Alyen thought Mother Brenwyn's face had never looked so old, so tired, as she stroked Lirianna's hair and rocked her until she quieted.

"So, it's true?" Aaron asked, his voice sounding strange and mildly surprised.

Mother Brenwyn nodded. "It is true—and it's worse than anything we feared. We must act quickly."

"What do we do?" Alyen asked, feeling numb and distant. It was as if the whole night were happening in another world, and she were merely observing curiously from a space high above or far beyond.

Mother Brenwyn was helping Lirianna away from her loom and into a more comfortable chair. Thankfully, Lirianna was beginning to look like herself again, though weak, and badly shaken.

"It's my guess," Mother Brenwyn began as she straightened from Lirianna to address Aaron and Alyen frankly, "that the gremlins and the darklings we've been tracking were merely a distraction. With all our focus on preventing an attack here, we didn't give sufficient attention to the possibility of an assault on Morten or Rowenna—which was Ylvain's true goal. Still, there is yet the possibility that we remain in great danger. With both the Slayer and the Keeper gone, Ylvain may now turn her attention here to finish the job."

"But if Ylvain was planning more attacks, wouldn't she still be blocking Lirianna's Sight?"

"It's my hope that, in her arrogance, Ylvain has wildly underestimated the skills of you three, early as you are in your training. She likely knew that with the deaths of Rowenna and Morten, my Sight would be severely compromised and so lowered her defenses, not accounting for Lirianna. As it is, you three are now the last remaining hope for Dúramair. We cannot afford to make any more mistakes. Aaron and Alyen, you must leave Monstar tonight."

There was a stunned silence before Mother Brenwyn bustled toward a small chest resting beneath one of the arched windows.

Alyen recovered her voice first. "Leave? Leave to where? I thought Monstar was the safest place in the kingdom."

"It is," Mother Brenwyn confirmed, fumbling in her pocket as she knelt by the chest. "But holing up in here won't do anything to stop Ylvain—it will only delay the inevitable.

And besides, after today we already know the walls can be breached."

Mother Brenwyn drew a small iron key from the pocket of her nightgown and unlocked the chest. From inside she took out something small enough to be concealed in her hand. She closed one fist around the object while her other hand returned to her pendant. With eyes closed, she muttered several words under her breath. Then she opened her eyes, relocked the chest, and dropped the key back in her pocket.

"Aaron," she said as she stood and addressed him with a serious expression. "Considering this terrible turn of events, I'm afraid only one person remains who can hope to best such power as Ylvain's and whoever she may be consorting with."

Aaron's face was grave. "The Second Slayer."

"Yes," Mother Brenwyn whispered, seemingly unsurprised at his quick response. "You and Alyen must travel north to Norhelm. You must seek out the Tomb of Thor Lynn, claim Scala, his blade, and return to Castle Dúr to offer the sword and yourself in defense of Dúramair."

"And if I'm not the Second Slayer?"

"We must hope that you are," Mother Brenwyn said simply.

"I want to go with them." It was Lirianna, her voice still weak but determined. "I don't want to stay behind. I want to help. We're most powerful when we're all together."

"That's true," Mother Brenwyn said shaking her head. "But you will be much greater help to them here at your loom. Since I no longer have my Sight, we must all rely on yours to watch Ylvain and warn of her movements. In fact, we will need you to start weaving again tonight."

"But if they leave, how can I warn them?" Lirianna cried.

In response, Mother Brenwyn stretched out the hand that still held the secreted contents of the chest. Her open palm revealed three small stones, each a milky gray, that flashed when the moonlight hit. Each hung threaded on a silver chain.

"These were to be your gifts from us this Midwinter," Mother Brenwyn said softly. "They're hearing stones, all connected to each other. Hold them in your hands, and without voicing anything, think of the person—or people— you wish to speak with and then do so using only your minds."

Frowning slightly, Aaron, Alyen, and Lirianna each took one of the pendants and held the stones tightly in their fists. No sooner had Alyen closed her fingers around her stone than she gave a start at Aaron's voice sounding clearly inside her head.

"Alyen? Lirianna?"

"I'm here," Alyen thought, amazed.

"So am I," came Lirianna's voice. They all looked up at each other in surprise.

Mother Brenwyn smiled faintly and held out her pendant. "I have one as well, also connected to yours. Wear them around your necks for now. They turn warm when someone is trying to contact you, but you will only be able to hear them and reply if you hold the stone in your hand. Eventually you may choose to keep them in some other way; Morten had his mounted in an armband, and Rowenna set hers in a brooch. It's how we communicated with each other across the distance. In any case, you three will be able to speak to each other and to me whenever you wish, and Lirianna will be able to warn you should her visions show any danger."

Aaron was frowning. "But isn't this dangerous? If one of

us is captured—or killed—won't our enemies be able to eavesdrop?"

"Capture is a risk, yes," Mother Brenwyn conceded. "It's not a foolproof system, so you must guard your stones well. But should the owner of a hearing stone *die*, all the connections in its loop will instantly sever. It's a safety measure all hearing stones possess and offers some peace of mind.

"Now, Alyen, Aaron, gather your things. Take only what you need, but Alyen, make sure you have your healing things. Lirianna and I will fetch you some food and meet you in the gardens."

"The gardens?" Aaron asked. "Should I bring the horses around?"

"No, there's no time. I'll contact Nah'dar and see that your horses come to you by morning. Besides, you can't leave down the cliff path. If Ylvain *is* planning an attack on you, that's where her forces will be waiting. There's another secret way in and out of Monstar through a tunnel in the back of the tool shed. Do you know it?"

With only the briefest of glances at each other, Alyen and Aaron nodded. "We know of it," Aaron confirmed. "But we don't know where it leads."

"The tunnel leads back into the mountain, curves around, and eventually comes out in another cave a few miles to the east. It's a steep path, but from there you can make your way down into Sheanen Crann and turn north for Norhelm. Now go. We have little time to lose. Meet us in the garden in fifteen minutes."

Mother Brenwyn hurried them out the door and down the corridors, and suddenly Alyen found herself in her room with an empty bag, wondering what to take, not believing she was leaving, not knowing if she would ever come back.

She decided to change her clothes quickly and pulled on plain but warm garments, along with sturdy boots and her winter cloak. She stuffed one change of clothing into the bottom of her bag along with some extra undergarments, and strung her hearing stone around her neck, tucking it beneath her clothes next to her skin. She turned to her chest of medicines and began sifting through the jars and supplies, trying to decide what would be best to take. The jars would be too heavy to bring more than a few; Alyen cursed the fact that winter was coming and there would be limited time left to find medicine growing in the forest in a pinch.

In the end, she packed a roll of bandages, her mortar and pestle, an ointment for healing wounds, and some dried lavender to calm nerves. She sighed, hoping that with any luck, it would be a long autumn and they would be back south before the cold hit.

Alyen was about to close the chest and head for the gardens when one small, dusty jar caught her eye. It was the jar that contained the three leaves of deadly nightshade, the first plant she had gathered herself from an elemental. She picked it up, remembering how Rowenna had been impressed that she'd managed the nightshade on her first try. A lump suddenly rose in her throat, and her eyes burned. She dashed the tears away, thrust the jar into her bag, closed the chest, and glanced once more around her room in Monstar before closing the door behind her and heading for the gardens.

She was the last to arrive. Lirianna was already handing Aaron a sack of food and a torch to light the way through the tunnel. Alyen saw a sword and dagger belted around his waist, and from watching him train she guessed he had at least one or two more knives hidden in his boots or in his sleeves. Mother Brenwyn gave Alyen a second bag with blankets and two skins of water.

"Be careful and be brave," Mother Brenwyn said as she gave each of them a quick, firm embrace. "Keep off the main path and stay hidden, but go as quickly as you can. I'll rest better when I know you're back safe."

"You must remember to check in with me often," Lirianna said, her voice catching slightly. "I'll worry if you don't." She gave Alyen and then Aaron a tight hug, then they were entering the tool shed, Aaron's torch throwing dancing shadows across the cave walls.

"Travel well," Mother Brenwyn said. "May your journey be blessed and your path safe."

Aaron nodded briefly before disappearing through the crevasse. The tool shed was plunged into darkness, save for the orange glow of the torch from the other side turning the tunnel entrance into a thin shard of light.

"Goodbye," Alyen whispered into the dark. She turned away, shoved her bags through the crevasse, then squeezed herself through to join Aaron and begin the long journey north to Norhelm, and the Tomb of Thor Lynn.

18
REVENGE

It was done.

Ylvain stood gazing toward the shore of Dúramair, knowing that somewhere in the forest darkness, Rowenna had breathed her last.

"How does it feel," the voice whispered as smoke curled around her neck to her ear, "knowing you have at last attained revenge?"

Ylvain's face was a mask, her voice hollow. "I feel nothing. Only pleasure that we are but one step closer to our goal."

The orange glow within the smoke flickered with satisfaction. "Then you are ready."

"Ready?"

"It is time for you to assume command of our army. It will be you who decides our movements, our strategy, the timing of our next attack. It is you who will lead the march on Castle Dúr. And it is for you to ensure that no threats to our cause remain."

Ylvain's brow furrowed. "The Keeper and the Slayer are dead. Without them, the Seer is crippled and powerless. What other threat can there be?"

The smoke churned, rippling over Ylvain's shoulders, twining about her arms. "You know the ancient legends, my queen. We must not forget the possibility of the Second Slayer."

"The Second Slayer?" Ylvain scoffed. "He is but a myth."

Suddenly the smoke lashed itself tightly around Ylvain's chest and she gasped in surprise and pain. "*I* am a myth, Ylvain," the voice hissed in anger. "And you have found me to be real enough. It was I who made you what you are—do not presume to question me and do not let your ambition be compromised by arrogance."

Ylvain's breath pressed against the constriction in her chest. She suppressed the instinct to fight for air—he would calm more quickly if she did not resist. "I would never question you, my lord," she said. "But with Morten gone, who is left to claim the blade of the Second Slayer?"

"The Trianid had apprentices, did they not?"

"Yes, but they are young and untried—practically children."

"Then it will be easy for you to dispose of them and ensure our success. Or do you intend to gamble with the power I've given you?"

Ylvain heard the dangerous edge in the whispered voice and closed her eyes. "No, my lord. It shall be as you say."

The tightness in her chest eased as the smoke unfurled itself and Ylvain breathed a silent sigh. The black smoke hovered near the edge of the tower as if gazing down on the army below, now nearly mature.

"The time has come, my queen. I must take up permanent residence deep in the hearts of our army to ensure they reach their full and final strength. After this night, you will not hear from me again until we achieve victory at Castle Dúr. But know this …" The smoke swirled and Ylvain had the impression that the being within now faced her directly, holding her in a chilling gaze. "I will be watching you. I shall know all that transpires—every success and every mistake. And if you fail me, the world will know of it by the undying scream of your soul on the wind."

The smoke swirled once again and rippled over the tower edge, disappearing into the darkness. Suddenly from below, shrieks pierced the air sending chills up and down Ylvain's spine. They did not die down but continued to echo and swell —an endless and terrifying cacophony encircling the black tower in the sea.

In the center of the chaos, Ylvain remained motionless, her eyes still fixed on the shores of Dúramair.

19

AARON'S STORY

The tunnel smelled musty with earth and rock and damp. Aaron took the lead, holding the torch aloft and brushing cobwebs out of their way while Alyen followed silently behind. As Mother Brenwyn had said, the tunnel went back into the mountain, then gradually curved around for what seemed like ages. It was long past midnight and Alyen was thoroughly exhausted when they stumbled out of the cave and Aaron immediately thrust the torch into a puddle. They stood still, waiting for their eyes to adjust to the darkness. Slowly, the night took form around them, and they could begin to pick out boulders, trees, and the path that led down into the forest beneath.

"Can you see well enough yet?" Aaron's voice sounded strange and hollow in the silence.

"I think so," Alyen replied. They picked their way slowly down the side of the mountain in silence, concentrating on the task at hand. After an hour, the crags and cliffs melted into the thick forest of oak and ash. Aaron spotted a small clearing just off the path somewhat hidden by the trees, and they finally stopped, dropping their packs, and finding seats on a half-rotted log.

Neither of them spoke. Alyen dropped her head into her hands, not knowing what to think, what to feel, what to do. Time had stopped. Reality was gone. She felt she must be caught in a horrible nightmare, only she knew she hadn't had a regular dream since she had arrived at Monstar.

Rowenna.

Gone.

She couldn't grasp it. It was hard to believe that only a few hours ago she had gone to sleep in her chamber at Monstar and Rowenna had taught her how to cast a protective circle. It seemed so long ago; so much had changed. From the moment she had awoken in the study, everything had been all shock and confusion and abruptness. Yet in the time spent walking through the tunnel and the silence of the forest, Alyen had begun to think once more. Rowenna's words began to sink in, and in her chest Alyen felt the horrible emptiness grow larger in the place Rowenna had once occupied. And without her to fill it, without her to guide, to teach, to reassure, it began to fill instead with grief.

Alyen drew a breath that shuddered involuntarily as the first of many tears she would shed for Rowenna spilled silently down her cheeks. She raised her head to dry her face and saw Aaron also sitting with his head in his hands on the log beside her.

She felt she should say something. After all, he, too, had lost a mentor. And Aaron had been with Morten far longer than Alyen had been with Rowenna. As wretched as she felt, she supposed it must be much worse for him.

Only then did Alyen realize she had no idea where Aaron had come from. He had never told her—and she had never thought to ask. Her voice cracked as she broke the silence.

"Are you all right?"

He didn't look up, but after a pause he nodded briefly. Alyen wasn't sure whether she should continue or leave him to his thoughts, but her need for something to distract from the spreading ache in her chest finally convinced her to press on.

"Aaron, how did you come to be Morten's apprentice?"

Aaron sniffed and cleared his throat gruffly. He raised his head, revealing brightened eyes and a telltale wetness about his lashes. He was silent for so long that Alyen thought he was ignoring her, and was startled when he spoke, staring into the distance without seeing anything.

"I never knew my father. My mother and I lived in a shack near the fishing docks in Doclann. It was usually cold and there wasn't much to eat. I never really knew how my mother managed to feed us and everything. She told me she sewed, and I thought ... I thought that explained the men's clothes I would find strewn about now and then when she was ... um ... with a customer in the bedroom. Sometimes I would pretend that maybe they belonged to my father. That he had come back for us, or, you know. Something."

Aaron dropped his gaze and studied his hands, his face impenetrable.

"Then she started coughing, and it got worse and worse. I told her I would go for a doctor, but she told me it was just a cold, and she that would be better in no time. One day she went out—to work she said—and never came back. I was eight," he added offhand, as if it were a small detail that mattered little.

"Oh, Aaron," Alyen breathed as she watched him scowling stoically at a scar on his palm. She couldn't think of anything else to say.

"She tried, you know. I mean, she did her best. She was a good mother, and it couldn't have been easy with me and no husband ..." He trailed off, shrugging. Alyen felt another stab of pain in her chest, this time for him, as he tried to defend the only parent he had ever known and lost so young.

The woods were still and silent in the darkness around them. Wind rustled the leaves softly in the branches above. Neither of them moved, until finally Aaron swallowed and continued softly.

"Anyway, I wandered around for a couple weeks looking for her. No one would take the time to tell me exactly what had happened, and no one had food to spare for another mouth that wasn't theirs.

"Then one day, Morten found me. Actually, he caught me trying to steal a fish from the market. He took me aside and asked me to go with him. When he gave me some bread and cheese, I agreed."

They sat in silence for a time, Aaron still not looking at Alyen, who sat huddled in a ball with her arms wrapped around her knees to ward off the night's chill.

How could I not have known? Aaron was eight when they had first met. It must have been not long after his mother's death. So much now made sense: the way he had always seemed older than his years. His fierce loyalty to Morten.

"What was her name?" Alyen asked, suddenly feeling it

was important to know. Aaron was silent for a moment, and when he spoke it came as a whisper.

"Lillah."

Another awkward pause.

"Morten must have been like a father to you, then?"

Aaron smiled ruefully. "He was. And I suppose now that means I'm twice orphaned. Back to having no one again." He tried to say it casually, but Alyen caught the tightness in his voice and the rigid lines of his shoulders and face.

"You have me," she offered, feeling utterly inadequate.

Aaron finally looked at her, his expression unreadable. She reached out and placed a tentative hand on his shoulder.

They stayed that way for the space of three heartbeats until Aaron dropped his gaze, once more clearing his throat. He got up and pulled a large blanket from one of the packs and spread it on the ground beneath a tree. He sat down on one side of it, looking out into the darkness and the trees. "I'll take first watch."

After a moment Alyen moved to the blanket, lay down, and covered herself with her cloak. She closed her eyes and felt her heart lurch as she realized Rowenna would not be waiting for her when she crossed into the realm of dreams. But as she drifted toward sleep, Alyen felt something that lit a small glow of warmth in her stomach, despite the danger, despite her grief.

It was Aaron's hand closing over her own where it lay outstretched on the blanket between them.

20

NAH'DAR

Aaron was still sleeping the next morning when Alyen heard the sounds of hoofbeats through the trees. She tensed and reached to wake Aaron, but before she could touch him, he sprang up from the blanket. In one fluid movement he snatched a dagger from his things and positioned himself between Alyen and the edge of the clearing, half-crouched, muscles tensed.

The undergrowth shivered, then a black stallion broke into the clearing bearing a familiar, black-robed rider. A scimitar hung at his side, and one hand held the reigns of Lusa and Soran who followed behind.

"Aaron, it's all right," Alyen said, relaxing beside him. "It's Nah'dar, my bodyguard."

Aaron straightened, lowered his dagger, and opened his mouth to speak, but in a sudden flurry of motion, Nah'dar leapt from his saddle, whipping his scimitar out of its sheath with a ringing flash. Alyen felt herself hurled to the side, and she landed hard against the roots of a tree. When she looked up, Aaron was lying flat on his back in the leaves, his dagger knocked away, with the point of the assassin's blade hovering a hair's breadth from his throat.

"You are far too quick to trust, Slayer," the assassin snarled, speaking with deadly precision in an accented voice of silk and steel. "What if the girl had been mistaken, or bewitched? What if I had been disguised? Lower your defenses before an unproved stranger so readily, and you will not see the next season. Lesson one."

"Lesson one?" Aaron asked, his eyes narrowing.

Abruptly, the assassin sheathed his scimitar, reached down, and helped Aaron to his feet.

"I am Nah'dar, First Assassin of the Bahari and protector of Princess Alyen. In addition, I will be continuing your training, Slayer, as you will soon find yourself facing foes you have not been prepared to defeat. Finally, I will act as your guide as we travel north to the Tomb of Thor Lynn, then on to face the battle at Castle Dúr."

"What do you mean, battle at Castle Dúr?" Alyen asked sharply.

"And Mother Brenwyn never said anything about you coming with us," Aaron added, a challenge in his voice.

Nah'dar's face was impassive. "The young Seer spent long hours at her loom as you slept. There can no longer be a doubt that war is coming, and the fate of the Balance rests in your hands alone. One careless move, one thoughtless mistake, and all hope could be lost forever. As these things came to light, the abbess and I concluded that my assistance will be not only beneficial, but necessary."

When neither Alyen nor Aaron said anything, Nah'dar

nodded in grim approval of what he assumed was distrust. He reached beneath the neck of his robes and pulled out a thin silver chain from which dangled a small pendant that flashed in the light. "I carry a hearing stone. The abbess connected it to both of yours, as well as to the stones held by herself and the young Seer. If you try to communicate with me, you will see that it works."

Alyen's hand rose instinctively to her chest, and she fished the flat stone disk out from beneath her dress. She clasped it in her fist and, looking toward Nah'dar, she thought, *"Can you hear me?"*

"Yes," spoke Nah'dar's voice in Alyen's head. She glanced at Aaron, but he was still reaching for his pendant. She sent her thought out again.

"Mother Brenwyn?"

"Yes?"

"Did you tell Nah'dar to come with us?"

"I did. Listen to him well, Alyen. He has skills that can't be found in Dúramair."

She looked back to Aaron, and he gave her a brief nod. There was a moment of silence, then Alyen concentrated on Aaron and Nah'dar.

"All right. What now?"

"We have stayed in this place too long already. Gather your things. I will prepare the horses. We ride north."

Abruptly, Nah'dar dropped his stone back beneath his black robes and strode to their mounts at the edge of the trees. Aaron moved to Alyen's side, a frown on his face as they watched Nah'dar across the clearing.

"What do you think, Alyen? Do we just let him come along?"

Nah'dar was adjusting the straps of his saddle, his movements deft and ruthless.

"Mother Brenwyn says we should. And honestly, I don't think we really have a choice."

They traveled most of the day in silence, Aaron and Alyen riding behind Nah'dar through Sheanen Crann. They stopped only briefly at midday to water the horses and pass a small loaf of bread and cheese among themselves before pressing on beneath the leafy canopy. As the shadows grew longer late in the afternoon, Alyen began to watch for signs of the Moor of Moin between the trees, recalling her journey to Monstar the year before. But they had gone a different route—one that led deeper into the wooded hills off the narrow common road—and the moor never appeared. Ferns and undergrowth slapped against Lusa's legs until finally the trio stopped in a small clearing not far from a spring that trickled from between two large boulders.

Nah'dar reined in his stallion and slid to the ground. "We stop here for the night. Alyen, light a fire and prepare a meal. Aaron, gather firewood and then ready yourself for training."

Aaron's face tightened, but he moved toward a pile of brush after securing Soran to a low branch. Alyen, affronted at being bossed and ordered to cook, scowled but said nothing and began clearing a space for the fire.

The elementals in the clearing were more plentiful than in the more traveled parts of the wood. Amid the trees and shrubs Alyen spotted several elves, a few undines splashing in the spring, and a pair of nettle nyads tending to the stinging leaves of their plants. Thinking there must be at least a few salamandars nearby, Alyen stretched her hands over the small pile of twigs and dried grass she had collected and whispered softly to the forest.

"Salamandars—fire dancers, carriers of sparks and light. Will you help me warm the night? Come and light my sticks and grasses, dance until the darkness passes."

As Alyen whispered, tiny sparks appeared, flickering around the kindling. Suddenly, small flames rose to lick about the twigs, snapping as more and more salamandars appeared in the firelight. A sudden movement from the direction of the horses distracted Alyen and she looked up to see Nah'dar watching her from the corner of his eyes, his expression uncharacteristically wary. *Hmm. Could the cold-blooded assassin of the Bahari be superstitious?* Alyen wondered. She lifted her hands a bit theatrically, whispering words of encouragement, and the flames swirled and flared higher. Glancing toward Nah'dar, Alyen saw his lips tighten. He turned sharply so his back faced the unnatural flames. Alyen chuckled quietly to herself, feeling suddenly much more cheerful.

Aaron soon returned, his arms full of firewood which he heaped beside Alyen's now steadily burning fire. He moved to sit on a nearby rock, but suddenly sprang up to catch the sword Nah'dar sent hurtling through the air in his direction.

"On your feet, Slayer," Nah'dar said. "We will train while it is still light."

"I've already been trained," Aaron said coolly. "Morten schooled me in combat using fourteen different weapons against every known opponent, man or beast."

Alyen heard the edge in Aaron's voice, and it didn't go unnoticed by Nah'dar.

"Do not let sentiment make you arrogant or stupid, Aaron," Nah'dar said sharply. "Morten was indeed a gifted warrior, perhaps the best since Thor Lynn, and no doubt he trained you well—for everything he ever thought you would need. But Dúramairians have long turned a blind eye to the shadows of the world. Did Morten prepare you to stand against enemies whispered of only in the ancient legends? Did he teach you to confront creatures spawned in the darkest corners of the earth?"

"Exactly what are you talking about?" Aaron asked, and Alyen was relieved to hear him sound unimpressed. "No one has seen a dark creature for centuries—not since the time of Thor Lynn. For all we know, they never existed at all."

"Oh, they are very real," Nah'dar said softly. He moved across the clearing toward his unwilling pupil. "They are real, and *you*, Slayer, will undoubtedly find yourself facing one or many before long. It should interest you to know that even now as we speak, Ylvain is breeding a hoard of morkshai larger than any army this kingdom could ever hope to raise."

Aaron's face turned slightly pale and his grip on the hilt of his sword tightened. "Morkshai? Those are creatures only of stories and nightmares."

"Again, they are real—and you must face them. Preferably not unprepared."

Aaron stiffened and squared his shoulders. "I have trained to combat dragons and giants my whole life. If the morkshai really do exist, I'm sure I can handle them."

"Are you?" Nah'dar asked, sounding mildly interested. "Then you should have no problem besting me as well."

In a sudden flash of movement, Nah'dar lunged at Aaron, who barely had time to raise his sword to block the gleaming scimitar that had appeared in Nah'dar's hand from somewhere in his robes. The two warriors circled, ducked, lunged, and danced. Alyen, holding her breath, could see that Aaron was indeed skilled. Nah'dar attacked ruthlessly, but in one swift motion, Aaron rolled away from a sweeping blow, snatched a dagger from his boot, then leapt up, spinning in mid-air to confront Nah'dar double-armed. But the assassin had also pulled a dagger from his own belt and was already advancing furiously, both blades darting about Aaron's head while well-aimed kicks repeatedly connected with Aaron's stomach and knees. Within seconds, Aaron was once again on his back, staring down the crescent of Nah'dar's scimitar.

"That is as close as a man can come to simulating the attack of a morkush. The real thing will be much worse," Nah'dar said, breathing heavily. He lowered his scimitar and helped a scowling Aaron to his feet. "Come," he said, motioning to the fire. "There are things your mind and heart must know before your hands can obey them."

"How do you know Ylvain's breeding morkshai?" Aaron asked heatedly as he and Nah'dar found seats on two large rocks near the fire. "Did Lirianna see them?"

"She did," Nah'dar replied calmly as he wiped his sleeve across the blade of his scimitar. "She has seen much since her Sight was restored."

Alyen went back to extracting food from one of the saddlebags, watching Nah'dar's face closely. "What are morkshai?" she asked. "I've never heard of them."

Nah'dar looked at her across the crackling flames, his eyes dark and glistening. "The morkshai are some of the foulest monsters known to this world. They have no place in natural creation—they can only be spawned and bred using dark magic. They are covered in scaly skin as black as night and have the body of a horse, although they are much bigger than a horse when fully grown. Each leg ends in a paw with razor-sharp claws, and they have long whipping tails that end in a deadly spine. In the place of a head, a morkush sprouts three to six snakes out of its neck, each mouth filled with poisoned fangs and eyes that burn like hellfire. Most terrifying, the morkshai are regenerative. If one head is cut off, another simply grows in its place. This makes them virtually immortal."

"*Virtually* immortal?" Aaron asked.

"There is only one thing that will kill a morkush: fire," Nah'dar answered as he stared into Alyen's cooking fire, unaware of the salamandars swaying in the flames. "The only way to defeat a morkush is to somehow get past its writhing heads close enough to stab it deep in the breast with a sword and then thrust a flaming torch into the wound, burning out the heart."

Alyen made a face and recoiled in disgust, but Aaron's eyes merely narrowed.

"I'm sorry it's not a pretty picture, Princess," Nah'dar said dryly. "But if you haven't the skill or the stomach to kill a morkush, then knowledge of its one great fear might at least buy you time at some point."

Alyen scowled. "It seems to me that if these morkshai are as terrible and invincible as you say, they wouldn't be afraid of anything—certainly not a little campfire."

"There you are mistaken," said Nah'dar. "It is because of their near immortality that the morkshai fear death far more than we mortals, who know with certainty that it awaits us all. Since we have little control over its circumstances, humans generally give death little thought, but the morkshai, knowing that fire is their only ambassador to the realms of the dead, fear it intensely."

Nah'dar rose, the fire making his face glow red. "If you refuse to believe me, Princess, then ask the young Seer yourself. And heed her words. Disbelief is a luxury you no longer have." He turned and left the clearing, disappearing in the shadows that had overtaken the forest as night fell.

Alyen shifted uneasily on her rock and met Aaron's thoughtful gaze. She glanced in the direction of the horses, where Nah'dar had disappeared, and discretely pulled her hearing stone from beneath her dress. Aaron understood and reached casually for his own stone.

"I don't like him. He's creepy." Alyen sent her thought out to Aaron.

"I don't care for him either," came Aaron's voice in her mind.

"Do you think he's right?" Alyen asked. *"Do you think the morkshai are real?"* It was easy to believe in the darkness of the night with the trees looming black all around them.

Aaron paused. *"Like he said, we should check in with Lirianna. I wouldn't have believed it possible—but I wouldn't have believed a lot that's happened in the last day."*

They sat a moment in silence, staring into the crackling flames.

"Alyen?" Aaron's voice sounded tentative. *"I've been thinking. You know the prophesy of the Second Slayer?"*

"Yes."

"Do you remember the part at the beginning: 'two suns shall set to leave but one'?"

Alyen gasped inwardly, realizing where Aaron's thoughts were leading. *"Do you think it means …?"*

"I was wondering if it meant the deaths of Morten and Rowenna. Leaving just Mother Brenwyn behind." Aaron sounded uncomfortable, but Alyen's mind was racing.

"And now we're heading north! To get the sword of Thor Lynn! Aaron, do you think …?"

"Do you *think?"* Aaron asked, his voice almost pleading. *"Is it … could I really be … the Second Slayer?"*

Alyen was silent for a moment, staring into the flames before she met Aaron's eyes. *"I hope you are,"* she sent her thought seriously. *"Because if you're not, I have no idea how we can hope to win."*

The rain fell in a mist the following day as the party pressed its way north through the forest. Nah'dar insisted they stay off the main road and often the horses, used to more open terrain, stomped and snorted impatiently at the undergrowth that pulled and scratched at their legs. They made slow progress though they rarely stopped, and conversation was kept to a minimum.

Alyen and Aaron had confirmed Lirianna's vision of the morkshai with her the evening before. The terror in their friend's voice as she described the monsters had given their quest a whole new sense of urgency, and Alyen chafed at their slow plodding through the forest. Although the day passed uneventfully and the forest seemed quiet and peaceful, Alyen could not shake her anxiety and was exhausted and frazzled by the time they stopped to make camp.

The evening passed much as the previous one had; Alyen was relegated to cooking duty while Nah'dar trained Aaron vigorously in morkshai combat. This time, Nah'dar gave Aaron a fair chance to fight, shouting instructions as they dueled. Despite herself, Alyen could not resist glancing up frequently from her work to watch Aaron as he spun, ducked, and attacked, his chest bare to the waist, one hand wielding his sword, the other brandishing a flaming torch that traced fiery patterns in the gloom, throwing flickering shadows up the tree trunks. At one point the fight became so fierce that Alyen forgot her work altogether and sat, her mouth slightly open, staring at the two men circling and shouting, blades clashing, fire roaring, until at last, Nah'dar once again had Aaron clutching his side on the ground. Nah'dar, his face fixed in a fierce scowl, raised his head, and glared into Alyen's eyes, making her start. She quickly turned back to her work, embarrassed at having been caught.

She had not given much thought to Rowenna's warning concerning her feelings for Aaron since their escape from the abbey, and now as the memory came swimming back to her, she felt her eyes prickle and a sharp pang of remorse in her breast. It had been one of their last conversations. She had been angry and bitter when Rowenna was only trying to help. Refusing to give in to grief and guilt, she blinked hard and took a deep breath, resolving to shove the memory and the emotion aside for later. She had no time to grieve and no space for thoughts of love.

They had been traveling almost a week when the attack came.

As on each day prior, the trio stopped in a small clearing for the night, this time in a place where the trees were thinner, and the undergrowth had given way to soft turf and moss. Aaron headed into the trees in search of firewood. Nah'dar glanced around warily, as if uncomfortable with the more open terrain, but said nothing and began his ritual of securing the horses for the night. Alyen had just stooped to gather dry leaves and twigs into a pile for the cooking fire when two strong hands clamped about her neck, cutting off the air to her lungs.

Alyen tried to scream but no sound came; her eyes watered and bulged as she thrashed violently, prying at the thick fingers at her throat. Her vision began to go black, and she felt her mind slipping when her heel connected with something hard. She heard a grunt and the hands loosened their grip around her neck. Alyen twisted, screaming and choking at the same time. Suddenly Nah'dar was there, his black robes swirling, his face in a snarl, his eyes burning. He picked up Alyen's assailant by the throat with one hand, slamming him into the trunk of a tree. Alyen kept screaming and Aaron was sprinting toward her, firewood abandoned. Now it was the attacker's face turning blue, his legs beating frantically against the tree trunk, his cloudy eyes rolling back as a gurgle issued from his lips.

He's going to murder him, Alyen realized, a sudden dread mixing with her terror.

"Stop! Nah'dar, stop!" Alyen shrieked as she struggled against Aaron's suddenly firm grip around her arms and waist. Nah'dar glanced once her way, then threw the man across the clearing, where he crumpled on the ground. Relieved, Alyen stopped yelling and watched as her attacker struggled to rise to his feet. But his face froze in surprise and Alyen watched in horror as Nah'dar's scimitar flashed, a deadly silver arc sweeping over his head, then curving upward to lodge itself to the hilt in the stranger's gut.

"*No!*" Alyen screamed. The man's back arched and he slid off Nah'dar's blade to the ground, where his blood poured into the moss and he twitched until at last the light left his foggy eyes.

"*You!*" Alyen shouted at Nah'dar, who stood over the dead man's body, his face emotionless. "What were you *thinking?*"

"What was I thinking?" Nah'dar asked. "I was thinking that he attacked us—*you* actually. Clearly, he is an agent of our enemy; did you not notice how his eyes were clouded? The man was likely bewitched. In all probability he, himself, had no notion of what he was doing."

"But you *killed* him! You didn't have to do that!"

"And what would you have suggested as an alternative?" Nah'dar asked coldly.

Alyen forced her eyes away from the man's staring, bloodied face. She began struggling again and shouted at Aaron, "Let go of me!" To her surprise he did, and she rounded on Nah'dar.

"We should have questioned him. We should have used the opportunity to gain information we have no other way of getting! You didn't just waste a life; you threw away a chance to get ahead of Ylvain!"

Nah'dar sneered. "Question him? And then what, Princess —let him go? This man knew nothing worth our time, and I would have killed him either way."

Alyen trembled with rage. "You are no warrior. You're a murderer. Ignoble and cold-blooded, with no respect for life!"

Nah'dar stared at Alyen in silence, his features cold and unmoved. Finally, he said softly, "On the contrary, Princess, I think there are few in this world who respect life more than I."

Without another word, he turned and headed in the direction of the stream to wash his stained blade.

"Alyen," Aaron's voice was quiet and gentle. "He has a point. The man would have killed you."

Alyen whirled to face Aaron, her eyes on fire. She was shaking now from head to toe, shock rattling against her teeth. "You side with *him*? I was raised to rule, Aaron. I know how to judge when an enemy is worth more alive than dead. And anyone who advocates for sticking a sword into everyone who gets in your way is an uneducated, immoral idiot!" she spat.

Aaron looked as though she had slapped him. In an instant Alyen regretted her words and wished he would argue back. But Aaron's face turned stony. He turned his back on Alyen and walked away. Alyen, unable to keep the horror at bay, fled the clearing to retch behind the trees.

21

THE BLACK BASIN

An icy rain slashed at the black rock of the island castle as lightning cracked the sky and pierced the heaving waves. Atop her tower, Ylvain stood before a jet-black pedestal hollowed at the top to hold a pool of inky water. The wind whipped strands of dripping hair about her face as she raised her hands above her head; in one she held a raven, terrified past the point of struggle, and in the other a knife of sharpened black stone. Her incantation was lost to the howling wind. Her hands rushed down, the raven went limp, and three drops of scarlet blood dripped into the basin's pool of murky liquid.

Still clutching the dead bird, Ylvain leaned over the basin, staring into the waters as the surface cleared and images floated up from the depths.

She saw a clearing in an autumn wood, three horses tethered to the trees. She saw the girl crouch down, saw the man creep up behind her. Watched as the clumsy oaf tried to

205

strangle her, watched as the black-robed man killed him, while the young warrior did nothing but hold the girl back. She sneered as the girl screamed, lashing out at her protectors before the images clouded and the waters of the basin returned to black.

Stupid girl. She was weak. And the Slayer? No more than a lovesick boy, overconfident and under-skilled. Her fears were assuaged—the new young Keeper and Slayer would be no threat at all. But the black-robed man—he could be problematic if left alone too long.

Ylvain wandered to the tower's edge and gazed down at the scene below. On all sides from the castle to the shore, the rocks were covered with a mass of black, writhing worms: the snaking heads of her vast army of morkshai. Their screams were drowned by the fury of the storm, but Ylvain could sense their hunger, their thirst for blood as they writhed and twisted in the rain.

Two should be enough, Ylvain thought. More than enough to put an end to two pathetic children and one assassin, skilled though he may be. With a shriek, Ylvain raised the dead raven above her head, ripped the carcass in two and hurled the pieces to the hoard below.

The monsters surged upward, clawing each other viciously as dozens of snake heads snapped at the falling, bloody meat. A brief struggle, then two rose victorious, shredding what remained of the unfortunate bird with dripping teeth as fiery eyes rolled in their scaled heads.

Ylvain felt the spell latch onto the two morkshai, linking them to her will through the blood of the raven's forced sacrifice. She surged her thoughts down the invisible thread of magic. Images of the girl, the boy, and the man in black filled the monsters' minds with thoughts of hunger and hate and blood. When she sensed they were well-fused with the darkness of her own heart, she sent them plunging into the sea, where they made swiftly for the farther shore. There they would emerge at a run, their steps racing toward an autumn wood.

22

BROTHER HUGH

By the time Alyen returned to the fire, the slain man's body had been removed. Alyen avoided looking toward the dark wet patch of moss where he had fallen, and refusing to speak or even look at Aaron or Nah'dar, she curled up in her blanket without eating, her back to the fire.

She'd put on a good show, claiming her reaction was rage at the loss of an opportunity to gain information. But in the quiet of her heart, she knew that wasn't the real reason. In truth, watching a man be murdered had horrified her. The scimitar, the sounds, his bulging eyes—she couldn't erase them from her mind where they continued to spin, making her stomach clench and heave. *Pull yourself together, Alyen,* she thought. *If you can't handle this, how will you be able to face a war?*

Aching for a distraction, Alyen peered into the shadows, looking for any sprite or elf she could watch. But the clearing was completely devoid of elementals—likely they had all fled from the horror that had happened there. Only fireflies flickered in the darkness, healing the fabric of the Balance from Nah'dar's dark deed. The absence of the elementals made the world seem cold and empty, and a single tear escaped from beneath Alyen's lashes.

Suddenly, one tiny undine appeared, hovering in the air just inches from Alyen's nose. In a flash of silvery blue, the tiny creature darted forward, both arms outstretched, and caught the teardrop before it could fall from Alyen's cheek. The undine hovered, holding the watery globe in both hands. For a moment, their eyes locked, blue gazing into blue. Then with a sudden smile, the undine heaved the teardrop into the air and let it fall, splashing over her head. The undine laughed, a sound like tinkling bells in a gurgling stream, then disappeared in a flash.

Alyen smiled weakly, her spirits soothed somewhat by the undine's playful antics. Taking a breath, she quietly withdrew her hearing stone from beneath her dress and clasped it in her fist.

"Lirianna?" she thought. *"Lirianna, are you there?"*

There was a silence, then Lirianna's voice sounded in her head. *"Alyen! Where are you? Are you all right?"*

The words rushed through Alyen's thoughts before she could stop them. *"Everyone's fine. But some man attacked me and Nah'dar killed him, and it was horrible. I just feel sick."*

"Wait—you were attacked? Slow down, go back."

Alyen took another deep breath and recounted the events to Lirianna, who, once she realized no one was in current danger, listened, sympathized, and comforted her friend.

"What about Aaron?" Lirianna asked when Alyen told how she had screamed at Nah'dar.

"He agrees with Nah'dar," Alyen replied, noting the bitterness in her thoughts. *"He sided with him and then I—I yelled something horrible, and now we're not speaking."*

"I see," Lirianna's thought was quiet.

There was a moment of silence before Alyen thought again. *"Lirianna, we think Aaron might really be the Second Slayer."*

"Yes, I've been wondering about that myself. How do you feel about it?"

Alyen didn't answer right away. *"I don't know. At first, I was excited, but I'm not so sure anymore after today. I mean, a Slayer is just that—someone who kills things. Kills people. How can I—how could anyone love a murderer?"*

She hadn't meant to think it, it had just slipped out. The question hung in the silence before Lirianna replied. *"Don't worry about it. At least not yet. Remember Thor Lynn? He was the greatest of all Slayers, but he didn't kill Nimrath, and that's what made him so great. Don't let the title of 'Slayer' cloud your judgment of Aaron, and don't punish him for something he hasn't done yet."*

"Yet?"

"My weavings are still unclear." Lirianna sounded tired. *"It's obvious that Aaron will play some role in the future—a very important one—but I can't tell for sure what it is yet."*

"So, you can't see if he'll be able to get the sword?"

"No. That's why you shouldn't worry yet. Aaron might not even be the Second Slayer. And remember, we need to stick together, now more than ever."

"I know, you're right. I'll try," Alyen agreed. *"I miss you."*

"I miss you, too," Lirianna thought back. *"Get some rest."*

"You, too," Alyen agreed, and tucked her hearing stone back against her chest.

Alyen lay in the darkness listening as Aaron and Nah'dar

ate and prepared their beds, foregoing training for the night. As the men settled and the quiet of night fell over the clearing, thoughts of the prophecy ran through Alyen's head. She thought of Aaron, of the unknown man who had attacked her, of the morkshai, and of Ylvain, somewhere out in the night amassing an army, preparing to march on Castle Dúr, her home. She remembered her life as a princess, when her word was final, when she'd always felt in control—not outnumbered and unheeded by two warriors in the middle of a forest. Then she thought of the undine catching her tear, and she thought of Faer Dinnán, the faerie king she had never seen. Finally, she rolled over and closed her eyes, resolving to wake early the next morning. There was something she had to do.

Alyen rose as dawn was breaking, grateful to see that Aaron had taken the last watch, and that Nah'dar lay sleeping in his blankets. Quietly, she went to the fire and blew on it until flames sprang from the coals. Using a stick of wood and a bit of cloth, she fashioned and lit a small torch and moved silently to the edge of the clearing where Aaron sat watch.

His expression didn't change as he saw her approach, and Alyen felt a pang of guilt for her words the day before. *Never mind that now*, she thought. *It will have to wait for later.* She stopped in front of him and said rather stiffly, "I'm going down to the creek to wash."

Aaron studied her. "To wash?"

"Yes, wash."

"As in a bath?"

"Yes, of course."

Aaron glanced to the east where the rays of the newly risen sun shone through the trees and raised an eyebrow. "With a torch?"

Alyen swallowed and said nothing.

"It's too dangerous to go off alone," Aaron said flatly.

"I won't be long," Alyen said testily. "We still get privacy to relieve ourselves, don't we? I just thought I'd let you know where I was going." They were wasting time, but Alyen wanted to be sure she wouldn't be interrupted. "I'll come right back," she added.

Aaron looked at her another minute; Alyen could see he was still angry with her. "Fine. But if you aren't back in fifteen minutes, I'm coming to fetch you and I won't care if you're dressed or not."

Alyen made a face at him and headed in the direction of the creek.

It didn't take her long to find what she was looking for. The path led her to a wide mossy bank leading down to the water, where large boulders rested in the sandy soil. The creek was bordered by weeping willows trailing their branches in the water, and the ground was dotted here and there with late-blooming wildflowers. Even a few bushes laden with plump red berries stood near the bank, and as Alyen looked about her, she saw undines, tree elves, flower sprites, gnomes, and sylphs all busy at work or play. Alyen looked at the torch she held in her hand and saw two salamandars swirling in the flame. She nodded in satisfaction; it was a perfect spot.

Knowing she had little time, Alyen walked gently to the creek and knelt on the mossy bank. She half-closed her eyes, reaching out with her mind and heart to the forest around her, tugging at the strings that wove together in the fabric of the Balance.

"Hear me, spirits of the trees, undines of the rain and seas, salamandars burning brightly, sylphs who fly and flutter lightly ..."

The forest stilled. Alyen could feel the air quiver as the elementals gathered around her.

"... gnomes who tend to earth and stone, sprites who call the forest home: to all who guard the land and sea, a favor I must ask of thee."

Even the stream seemed to quiet as elementals of all varieties clustered about Alyen. The air hummed as they hovered and crouched, peering out from bushes and tree branches, listening intently to Alyen's whispered words. She took a deep breath, strengthening her hold on the building magic. The time was now.

"A darkness spreads throughout our land. A mighty battle is at hand, and lest all fall to endless night, together we must bear the light. While never have I heard or seen the ruler of the wood, your king, for good to have a chance to stand, I need the help of Faer Dinnán."

The bank and bordering forest exploded with commotion as the elementals began chattering excitedly, jumping about, and scurrying along the tree branches. Alyen winced at the surge of magic that hit her, and she knew it wouldn't be long before it would overpower her and break free of her grasp. Sweat ran down her face and back; it was all she could do to hold the elementals on the bank with every ounce of her concentrated will, and she prayed her final words would be heard through their clamor.

"Hear me, elementals all! Hasten to the faerie hall. Ask

Faer Dinnán to join the fight, to stand with me, restore the light. The Balance hangs upon a thread—I beg you, do as I have said!"

With a gasp, Alyen released the magic that had built on the riverbank. There was a roar in her ears and a rush of wind; her torch snuffed out and she dropped it in the moss at her side. Then suddenly, all was silent save the faint rustle of leaves and the gentle trickle of the stream.

Alyen slumped over, letting her forehead touch the cool moss in front of her. It was the most magic she had ever gathered at one time, and she felt drained, hollow, and dizzy. With her eyes closed, she steadied her breathing until she felt strong enough to sit up and look around. The forest was empty, not an elemental in sight.

There was no way to know if her plan had worked—if the elementals really would take her message to Faer Dinnán. But it was the best she could do.

A twig snapped somewhere in the forest behind her and Alyen gave a start; most likely Aaron was coming to find her as promised. She rose shakily and stumbled to the creek, where she hastily splashed water on her face and wet her hair to make it look as though she had washed. She rose and turned just as Aaron appeared between the trees, one hand on the dagger in his belt. He stopped when he saw Alyen and looked her up and down, taking in her slumped shoulders and the drops of water trickling down her ashen face into her clothes. He raised an eyebrow, and Alyen lifted her chin an inch, returning his gaze. Aaron frowned.

"It's time to go," he said coolly.

"Fine, I was just coming," Alyen replied. As she approached the edge of the wood, she stumbled, exhaustion overcoming her, and Aaron, on instinct, stepped quickly to support her, one hand on her elbow, another at her waist.

"Are you all right?" he asked gruffly.

"I'm fine," Alyen answered, cursing herself for sounding so breathless. "I just tripped."

Aaron was not fooled. "Alyen, what did you just do?"

"Nothing." She shrugged away from his grip. "Like I said, I just wanted a bath. Come on, let's go."

Aaron snorted but said nothing more and followed closely behind Alyen as they wove their way through the trees back to camp.

Alyen couldn't say for sure why she didn't want to tell Aaron about her attempt to contact Faer Dinnán. She had promised Lirianna that she would try to mend things with him, and she did mean to. But Nah'dar was getting out of hand. He was supposed to assist them, not take control of the quest itself, and if Aaron was going to align himself closer with the assassin than with her, Alyen was in desperate need of a solid ally. For a royal, the well-being of the kingdom always—*always* —came first. Personal matters came later. So, until she felt more in control, she would just make do with the chilly courtesy that laced any words exchanged between herself and the future Slayer.

Moreover, Alyen didn't know when, how, or if she would hear from Faer Dinnán. Perhaps the elementals would take him her message, perhaps not. If they did, Faer Dinnán may or may not agree to help her. Assuming he got her message and made a decision one way or the other, would he inform her of it? There was no way to tell and nothing more to do but wait.

It was late in the morning when Alyen, Aaron, and Nah'dar rounded a corner to find a crude wooden sign stuck on a stick in the ground in the middle of their path. In black letters painted across the weathered wood were the words:

HERMIT WANTED
INQUIRE WITHIN

Alyen looked up past the sign and saw through the trees a tiny hut with cheerful puffs of smoke issuing from a slightly crooked chimney. Curious, she nudged Lusa in the direction of the cottage. At once Nah'dar and his black stallion were blocking her way.

"Don't be a fool, Princess. We'll double back and circle around unnoticed."

Fury boiled in Alyen's stomach as she looked at the assassin, his bloodied scimitar emblazoned in her memory. When she spoke, her voice was low and calm.

"You are my guide and bodyguard, Nah'dar, not my master, and I'll go where I please. Now stand aside." Her eyes locked on his dark ones.

"Go where you please?" Nah'dar repeated scornfully. "There is far too much at stake for you to risk your life on a whim, Alyen, and as your *bodyguard,* if you cannot control yourself then I will have to do it for you. Turn your horse around."

Alyen opened her mouth to retort, but Aaron cut in from behind her.

"You may as well let her go, Nah'dar. I'm sure you and I can take on anything that could be waiting in that little hut."

Alyen turned toward Aaron, her heart warming with gratitude, but he was not finished.

"Besides, one way or another Alyen will find a way to get what she wants," Aaron's eyes settled on her own. "All royalty assume they can do or say whatever they please, no matter how stupid or selfish it is."

The words were like a blow to her stomach, and she struggled not to let it show. Perhaps she deserved no better after what she had said, but she wouldn't give him the satisfaction of making her upset. Besides, she was still too drained from magic overload to fight with him now. She turned her back on Aaron, rounding once more on Nah'dar.

"I'll go where I like, Nah'dar, and if you won't move of your own will, then I'll call on my magic to force you. You know I can!"

It was a gamble—Alyen doubted she actually could do much at the moment—but she was satisfied to see the flicker of fear in Nah'dar's black eyes. They darted from Alyen to Aaron and back. Finally, he drew the corners of his mouth down in disgust.

"Then you are both fools!" he spat and wheeled his stallion out of Alyen's path.

Alyen didn't look back but sat tall in her saddle and rode straight for the hut.

Probably she *was* being stupid, she admitted to herself as she passed the weathered wooden sign. But Nah'dar's objections had given her an excuse to exercise some control—and Aaron's jab made it final.

Bringing Lusa to a halt by a wild cherry tree, Alyen saw

that the stone-thatched hut was surrounded by a neatly tended garden that displayed a surprising number of vegetables and herbs, considering the lateness of the season. Boxes of red and yellow flowers hung below the hut's two windows, and a few fruit trees nestled beside the oaks and aspens of the forest.

Alyen dismounted and secured Lusa to a tree branch. Aaron and Nah'dar unenthusiastically followed suit. A narrow path led to the front door; from within, she heard the sounds of robust singing. She knocked loudly, uncomfortably aware of Aaron and Nah'dar standing close behind her with their hands on their weapons.

The singing stopped abruptly and there was a long silence. Alyen knocked again and heard a brief commotion before the door flew open to reveal a brown-robed, quivering monk gazing at them with wide eyes and a hesitant smile twitching up one side of his face.

"Oh, my heavenly stars, would you look at this, Ferdinand? It's people! Real honest to goodness *visitors*!"

The monk fidgeted with the rope tied around his slightly plump waist, the end of which dangled just above two large and rather dirty duck-footed, sandaled feet. Alyen noted that though the crown of his head *was* technically shaved, several tufts of wispy, graying hair sprouted up randomly across the top, giving him the look of one who had been recently struck by lightning.

"Uh, hello," she stammered. "Are you the hermit?"

The monk's smile grew wider, crinkling his eyes into delighted slits.

"Yes! Yes, I *am* the hermit—I'm Brother Hugh! Please, please do come in! Ferdinand, make room for our guests to enter."

Ignoring the sharp intake of breath from Nah'dar, Alyen moved cautiously into the hut, peering around the single room. It was slightly cluttered and contained only a small table, one chair, and a simple cot against one wall. A fire crackled merrily in the fireplace and Alyen was surprised to see it filled with salamandars—more than she had ever seen in one fire before. But aside from the salamandars and several sylphs, the room was empty.

"You must excuse the mess," Brother Hugh was saying. "The garden, forgive my boast, is immaculate, but I'm afraid neither myself nor Ferdinand is much of a housekeeper."

Like Alyen, Nah'dar and Aaron were peering around the empty room with puzzled and suspicious expressions.

"I would ask you to sit, but as you can see, there's really nothing to sit upon!" Brother Hugh said with a high-pitched giggle. "Not good for visitors—not good at all. And how did I come to be a hermit given my love of company, you must be wondering, yes, of course you are! Well, actually, it really was all Ferdinand's fault, wasn't it, Ferdinand? Not that I blame him, but still—entirely his doing."

"Excuse me," Alyen cut in, seeing that the monk showed no signs of ending his monologue, "but who is Ferdinand?"

"Aha!" Brother Hugh exclaimed, thrusting his fist into the air, one finger pointing toward the ceiling. "You can't see him, can you? Any of you!" he added, looking around at his three guests. "Right here in the room with us and you can't see him! Well, don't feel bad. No one can but me, and that's really the whole problem, isn't it?"

At these words, Aaron's eyebrows shot up and Nah'dar's face went flat. Both turned to Alyen with near identical expressions of annoyance, but before anyone could say anything, Brother Hugh had resumed his prattling while he scurried around the hut, stuffing food and seemingly random objects into a large, tattered satchel.

"Yes, I'm afraid I ended up here precisely because no one but me can see Ferdinand. You see, I used to live in a monastery a bit to the west of here, home to the Brotherhood of St. Thymus, the patron saint of cooking. Wonderful saint, I must say. He could work miracles in the kitchen with nothing but a spoon and a peach pit, he could! Anyway. I was working in the gardens, peaceful as you please, when one day along comes Ferdinand. He seemed a decent fellow, so we got to talking and soon became fast friends. He's quite the expert on culinary herbs.

"The problem was none of my fellow brothers could see him. They began looking at me strangely when I mentioned his name—some avoided me altogether. Finally, they concluded I had gone quite mad! They'd never say it to my face, of course, but I overheard some of them just the same. One day the abbot called me in … I tried to explain, but to no avail, and he sent me from the monastery to take up life as a hermit. *No matter*, I thought. I assumed the solitary life would be a blessing—a quiet way to live a godly life. But I was wrong!"

This was punctuated by a solid pound from Brother Hugh's fist on the tabletop, and the monk stood looking at his guests with a wild expression.

"The solitary life is no blessing at all! It's the most ungodly way in the world to live! I don't care how romantic the idea sounds, let me tell you—people were meant to be with other people. Living alone, no one to talk to—if I wasn't mad before, I'm certainly well on my way now."

Nah'dar was beginning to look dangerously irritated, and Alyen found herself wishing the men had left their weapons with the horses.

"Of course, I'm not *completely* alone," Brother Hugh explained as he resumed his activities, stuffing a fresh loaf of bread and several jars of spices into the bulging satchel. "I still have Ferdinand, but he does tend to come and go quite a bit and honestly, you can't go on forever with only one flighty friend, can you? So, I made up my mind to give up the life of a hermit and posted the sign for a replacement. And now, two months later, here you are! Can't tell you how thankful I am."

With this he shouldered his satchel with a grunt and, looking Nah'dar up and down, asked, "Are *you* going to be the next hermit?"

Nah'dar's lips curled into a snarl and Alyen jumped in quickly.

"Actually, we're not here about the position. We're just passing through."

"Splendid!" Brother Hugh cried without skipping a beat. "I shall come with you!"

If possible, Nah'dar's look of dislike intensified even more. Aaron glanced at him and said, "But what about your post? You can't leave without another hermit to replace you. Besides, it's very dangerous where we're going. You wouldn't want to come."

"You could be *killed*," Nah'dar added through clenched teeth, and Alyen wasn't certain he was referring to the dangers of the road.

"No matter, not to fear!" Brother Hugh raised a reassuring hand. "I'm finished with the hermitage, replacement or no, and what's an adventure without a dash of danger, eh? Besides, Ferdinand insists we come."

It would be ridiculous to bring him along, Alyen thought as she watched the monk argue his case with Aaron and Nah'dar. *Stupid, even.* But if she could convince Aaron and overrule Nah'dar, authority would shift back to her. And if she advocated for the monk, he'd likely back her in the future. Besides, it wasn't as if they would have anything to worry about from a hermit …

"All right, you can come," Alyen cut in, shocking Aaron and Nah'dar. Both heads snapped toward her, Nah'dar's expression furious and Aaron's incredulous.

"He can't come, he has no horse!" Nah'dar almost shouted, sounding, to Alyen's satisfaction, more agitated than she had ever heard him.

"Alyen," Aaron said leaning toward her. "He has an *imaginary friend*!"

"Yes, I've gathered as much," Alyen replied acidly. "He can take turns doubling up on our horses."

Nah'dar was gripping his scimitar so tightly that his knuckles turned white. Aaron looked at Alyen squarely.

"What's this about, Alyen?" he asked bluntly. "You know he has no business with our quest. Why do you want him along?"

Alyen stared back at him, gauging her words. "Did you see what he packed in that satchel, Aaron? Bread, spices, vegetables, nuts—he's a devotee of the patron saint of cooking for heaven's sake! If I have to eat one more meal of half-cooked beans and moldy bread, I'll scream. This way we at least have some decent food."

Aaron didn't immediately reply, so Alyen raised her voice,

looking over his shoulder at Nah'dar. "This isn't a debate. He comes with us." She stared meaningfully at the assassin, hoping his fear of her supposed magic would hold strong enough for a few more minutes.

It did.

With unmasked hate, Nah'dar spat, "That man will *never* ride my horse!" He swirled out the door and stalked toward the horses.

Aaron shrugged, shaking his head, and followed suit. Alyen smiled at Brother Hugh and led him out of the cottage into his garden, which was teeming with sprites.

"Come along, Ferdinand—a new horizon awaits! Oh, I really should pinch a few basil leaves before we're off. They're wonderful with fresh cheese."

Brother Hugh straightened and looked ahead, his face glowing. "What splendid horses!" he exclaimed. "May I ride the black one?"

"You'll come with me on the white one for now," Alyen said, hoping she had not just made a rather large mistake.

23

THE MORKSHAI

Brother Hugh liked to sing. Loudly.

This became painfully apparent within the first hour of the party's departure from the hermitage. Bouncing along on Lusa's back, sweaty hands clasped tightly around Alyen's waist, Brother Hugh belted out song after song to the trees, blissfully unaware of anything but his newfound freedom. Much to the interest of Alyen's empty stomach, most of the lyrics seemed to be about food, and while some may have been legitimate songs, Alyen suspected that a good number of them were made up by Brother Hugh himself.

"Ooooooooooh, I sing a song about a fish,
A derry derry dally,
I served him up on a golden dish,
'Tis lunchtime in the valley!

"Ooooooooooh, a sauce I poured across the meat,
A derry derry dally,
'Twas made of herbs and butter sweet,
'Tis lunchtime in the valley!

"Ooooooooooooh …"

Abruptly, Nah'dar turned his stallion off their path and came to a halt by the stream. Everyone dismounted to let the horses drink. Brother Hugh began splashing about while bellowing a new chorus to his fish song. Alyen was about to bend over the water herself when Nah'dar's rough hand on her shoulder spun her around to meet his burning eyes. One vein in his temple throbbed visibly.

"Get that monk to stop singing or I will do it myself," he said through his teeth. He released Alyen's shoulder and stalked away before she could reply.

Alyen didn't care to think about the method Nah'dar would use to silence Brother Hugh, but she knew he was right. She was uncomfortably aware that Brother Hugh was broadcasting their exact whereabouts to the entire forest. Sighing inwardly, Alyen approached the monk, who was jabbing his arm in and out of the stream, apparently attempting to catch a fish. She saw him take a deep breath, presumably in preparation for bursting once more into song, and cleared her throat loudly.

"Brother Hugh?"

The monk looked up, beaming. "At your service, my dear!"

"I think it's easier to catch a fish if you're very, very quiet."

"Really? Why?"

"You might scare them away otherwise."

"Fiddlesticks!" Brother Hugh exclaimed and threw open his dripping arms. "All of creation rejoices in music!"

From the corner of her eye, Alyen saw Aaron and Nah'dar looking their way, Nah'dar glowering and Aaron's expression skeptical. She closed her eyes momentarily and tried again.

"Brother Hugh, I think it would be much better if you didn't sing."

"Really? Why?"

"Well, this adventure we're on—it's a secret. We have to stay hidden and make sure no one finds us."

Brother Hugh's eyes widened. "Is that so? Bless my soul, I've landed myself in a proper secret mission! Am I correct in understanding that we need to employ the use of *stealth*?"

"Yes," Alyen replied warily. "Stealth, and above all, *quiet*."

Brother Hugh, the fish forgotten, splashed out of the water and stood on the bank, the hems of his robes dripping in a circle about his feet. He rubbed his hands together, eyes darting suspiciously from side to side, peering into the trees.

"Never fear, my dear," he said in a low voice. "Your secrets are safe with me!"

"Thank you." Alyen was turning back to Lusa when Brother Hugh called after her in a strangled voice, "And don't worry—I'll tell Ferdinand to keep it down, too!"

Alyen could think of no reply to this, so she merely smiled tightly and turned to retrieve her horse.

Impressively, Brother Hugh did manage to quiet down considerably. While true silence was an obvious impossibility for him to achieve, he transformed his explosive singing into a steady stream of lyrics uttered in a breathy half-whisper. As he still rode behind Alyen on Lusa, only she could hear that the theme of his songs now often switched away from food to adventure and secrecy.

> *"Ooooooooooooh, I mustn't sing nor make a peep,*
> *A derry, derry dally,*
> *Our quest I must a secret keep,*
> *Adventure in the valley!"*

The only times Brother Hugh was truly unable to monitor himself were during Aaron and Nah'dar's training sessions. As Alyen had hoped, the monk took over the role of the party's chef, which greatly improved the quality of their diet. However, while he cooked, Aaron and Nah'dar would begin their sparring, and Brother Hugh would become so excited by the clashing of swords and swirling of torches that he would leap onto a boulder or tree stump, brandish his cooking ladle, and shout encouragement that inevitably turned into advice.

"Here now, boy, watch it on your left! Oh, well done, that was a mighty thrust, that was! Careful now, don't let him trick you like that. Jump! Or duck! Say, you in the black, watch where you're swinging that thing!"

At these times, it was not so crucial for Brother Hugh to keep his voice down as Nah'dar and Aaron were already shouting and clashing, so Alyen would only intervene if their dinner looked about to burn, or if it appeared that Brother Hugh was himself in danger of being thrown in the fire by Nah'dar.

The group pressed forward day after day, and gradually

the forest began to change. Thick, gnarled pines began to replace the oak, ash, and aspens, and the terrain grew steadily rockier. The air held a frosty chill, whether from the nearing Northlands or the promise of winter, Alyen was not sure. Winds rushed through the tops of the evergreens, producing a high, lonely sound, and they carried the smell of mountains— granite, pine, and distant snow.

A week after they had come across Brother Hugh's hermitage, the four sat around the fire sharing a delicious soup the monk had made from beans, herbs, and a bunch of wild onions he had found growing near their camp. With the exception of Brother Hugh's tuneless humming, the group was silent, Nah'dar not being much of a conversationalist, and Alyen and Aaron having yet to thaw the chill that had settled between them. Eventually Nah'dar set down his empty bowl and announced, "By sunset tomorrow we will reach the edge of Sheanen Crann. Thor Lynn's tomb is half a day's journey from there."

Brother Hugh stopped humming. "Did you hear that, Ferdinand? We're going to a tomb! Creepy sort of adventure, isn't it?"

Nah'dar looked toward Brother Hugh with dislike, then moved to the shadows to prepare his bed before taking the first watch.

The rest soon followed suit, spreading their blankets a safe distance from the fire that cast an orange glow on the trunks of the towering pines surrounding their camp. Alyen thought briefly of checking in with Lirianna before sleeping, but the crackling of the fire and the dance of the salamandars in the half-light were already making her eyelids droop. She pulled her blanket up to her ears and closed her eyes.

A scream split the night—a scream neither human nor animal, but something far more sinister. Alyen bolted upright, chills running up and down her spine. Nah'dar and Aaron were already on their feet, swords drawn, standing black against the firelight.

"What was that?" Alyen asked, her voice high and pinched. The horses were stomping and whinnying in fright and Brother Hugh sat wide-eyed, clutching his blanket about his head like a woman's scarf. Aaron looked to Nah'dar.

"That was the scream of a morkush," Nah'dar replied quietly. "It has caught the scent of its prey."

The scream came again, closer this time. Alyen shuddered, pressing her palms against her ears. Nah'dar swooped down and lit the end of a long branch he and Aaron had used in their training earlier.

"Guard the camp, Aaron," he said, and moved out of the clearing. They followed the path of his torch with their eyes as it flickered in the woods, growing smaller and smaller until it disappeared altogether.

Aaron, Alyen, and Brother Hugh sat frozen in the clearing, not daring to speak or breathe, ears straining, bracing themselves for another blood-curdling scream. But the forest remained silent.

Without warning, the scream came again, this time from the very edge of their camp. The horses reared and shrieked as the trees directly across the clearing from Alyen exploded; a black monster leapt out of the darkness. Alyen let out a sob of terror as she looked up at the beast before her. The morkush was far worse than Nah'dar had described: three hideous snake heads whipped through the air, each with burning red eyes and dripping fangs, claws ripping at the ground. With an evil hiss, the morkush lunged at Aaron, one snake going for his head, one for his gut, the third for his sword arm. In a flash, Aaron rolled, missing the morkush's fangs by inches, and snatched up the second torch as he righted himself. He thrust the end of the torch in the fire; the momentary flare of the flames bought him seconds as the monster flinched.

"Alyen, get close to the fire!" Aaron shouted. With a roar, he leapt over the blaze, blade flashing, torch carving fiery ribbons of light as he swung it overhead.

Alyen began to crawl toward the campfire and caught sight of Brother Hugh frozen in place, unable to move. She dashed to the monk, yanking on the front of his robes until he stumbled forward. She half-dragged him to the fire, where they crouched to watch the battle in terror.

Seeing Aaron fight the morkush made the training sessions with Nah'dar seem like a child's game. The morkush's heads whipped and jabbed at him from all sides, one by one, then all at once as its claws repeatedly raked the air, missing Aaron's skin by a hair. Aaron never stopped moving; he spun, leapt, ducked, and rolled, lunging off tree trunks and boulders, his sword constantly flashing, his torch just keeping the monster at bay. Twice Alyen saw his sword connect, then retract, dripping with black blood. But the monster would only scream without flinching and within seconds, the wound would close and heal seamlessly of its own accord. Horrified, Alyen realized that Aaron's job might be easier if he stayed closer to the fire, as the morkush wouldn't dare to come too near; but he was purposely keeping the battle as far from it as possible, knowing that Alyen and Brother Hugh were crouching in its shelter.

As the battle raged on, rivers of sweat ran down Aaron's face and arms, his shirt drenched and his arms shaking. A pit of dread formed in Alyen's stomach as she realized that while the morkush would fight on until victory without a scratch, Aaron would tire and eventually make a mistake. Alyen tried to think of something, *anything* she could do to help. Could she summon salamandars to build or spread the fire? Desperately she searched her mind for words that would call up the flames, words that would draw the salamandars, despite the evil in the clearing. But she was unable to focus as her eyes darted back and forth from Aaron to the three hissing snakes writhing around him.

The morkush had Aaron cornered against a boulder, his waving torch the only thing keeping it at bay. In an instant, Alyen realized that it was over: there would be no escape. The morkush would devour Aaron, then turn on her. Alyen clutched at her face, letting out a wail of terror and grief for her lost life, for Aaron—Aaron, who would now never know how she felt, the things she had wanted to say …

But Alyen's thoughts were cut short as, without warning, Aaron sprang once more to action. In a final effort, he leapt to the top of the boulder. As the morkush reared its heads to strike in unison, he hurled himself at the monster headfirst, both sword and torch outstretched before him. Startled, the morkush swept at Aaron with its claws, but the tip of Aaron's sword was already plunging into the heart of the beast, the torch ramming in just after it. The three snake heads screamed and jerked as the morkush fell, dragging Aaron down. Aaron released his hold on his weapons and rolled clear of the monster before coming to a stop and lying still upon the ground. The morkush twitched and writhed for a few moments, then lay motionless and dead, steam issuing from the sword and torch protruding from its breast.

For a long moment, no one in the clearing moved or spoke. Finally, Aaron stirred, rising slowly to his feet, and Alyen let out a breath of relief. He walked over to the slain morkush, tugged his sword out of the wound and wiped it clean on a patch of drying grass. He turned then to face Alyen, his expression unreadable.

Alyen stood slowly and walked out from behind the crackling fire. She crossed the clearing, her eyes locked on Aaron's until she stood right before him. Then she placed her right hand over his heart, her left hand over her own, and bowed her head—the ancient gesture of thanks when one's life has been saved.

"Well fought, Slayer," she said softly. Beneath her palm, tension drained from his body. She felt her chin lifted gently by his hardened hand, and though exhaustion traced deep lines in his face, Aaron smiled weakly.

"Indeed," came Nah'dar's voice. "Well fought, indeed."

Aaron and Alyen turned and saw Nah'dar standing at the edge of the clearing, his robes also sweat-drenched, his face reflecting the same exhaustion Aaron's wore, his scimitar still wet and shiny with black blood. He was looking at Aaron with a strange expression that Alyen could only describe as something close to pride.

Near the dwindling fire, Brother Hugh rose slowly, clutching his blanket to his chest. "Oh, my," came his voice, sounding small beneath the dark trees. "Oh, my, my, my."

24

A BATTLE LOST

Ylvain's pale fingers clutched the sides of her black basin as she watched the boy battle against her morkush. *He's more skilled than I anticipated*, she thought grimly, and snarled at the images in the inky liquid.

"No—*no!*" she shouted as the impossible unfolded before her eyes. Ylvain stared unbelieving as the boy launched himself at her morkush, felt the connection between their minds fade and sever as the monster lay dying on the ground. She scanned the scene frantically, looking for signs of the black-robed man; she knew he had slain her other morkush, but with any luck he may have been killed or fatally injured as well.

Ylvain's eyes narrowed with hate as the girl crawled out of hiding with her revolting display of thanks; at least she had proven herself to be pitifully weak. But—*Curses!* Ylvain swore as the assassin came into view unscathed. She slammed her hand on the basin in fury and let out a chilling shriek that

233

ripped at the stars. Glancing once more into the water, Ylvain watched as all three figures—no four, they had some idiot monk trailing along—faded. She turned away in disgust.

I underestimated them, Ylvain thought as she approached the battlements overlooking her army of morkshai. Not for the first time since Rowenna's and Morten's deaths, she felt a shiver of fear in her heart as she contemplated her plans. *He* was watching. He would know her attempt had failed. He would not be happy, and if one day he turned his wrath upon her … She brushed the thought firmly away, pushing the fear down into the dark reaches of her heart. There would be no further mistakes. She must simply proceed with greater care.

She had not intended to strike until the spring, but that might prove too late—the enemy was already too strong for comfort. Not that two warriors alone could stand against an army of morkshai, but why give them time to plan, train, recruit? Victory was still hers for the taking, but her strategy must remain fluid. She would keep her head cool. She would be cunning, calculate her steps carefully. And the next time she made a move, she would not fail.

25
CHOICES

"How's your arm?" Alyen asked Aaron at breakfast the next morning. In his final dive toward the monster, one of the morkush's claws had grazed Aaron's shoulder. Luckily, it had not been one of the poisoned fangs, which would have almost certainly been deadly, but it had still left a deep, bloody gash across his arm. Alyen had stopped the bleeding, wishing she had brought needles and thread to stitch the arm properly as Rowenna had taught her. Instead, she found a patch of comfrey growing in the clearing and asked the nyads to boost its healing properties before making a poultice and bandaging the arm as well as she could.

"Much better," Aaron replied, smiling as he gently rotated his shoulder. "You truly have a healing touch."

"I'm sorry, it'll likely leave a scar."

"That's all right. I hear some women think scars are attractive." Aaron's grin was slightly wicked.

Alyen felt her face flush as she smiled, aware that Nah'-dar's watchful eyes were narrowing at them from across the campfire. She couldn't bring herself to care about Nah'dar's disapproval. While it was clear that he didn't relish the thought of chaperoning two infatuated youths through the wilderness, the victory over the morkshai and the resulting renewal of Alyen and Aaron's friendship had left Alyen feeling giddy and invincible.

They broke camp quickly and prepared the horses, but as Alyen reached up for the saddle to mount Lusa, Aaron caught her wrist.

"Brother Hugh has been riding double for days now. Why not let him take Lusa, and you can ride in front of me on Soran."

Alyen's stomach fluttered as she agreed, all while trying to avoid looking too directly into Aaron's face. Nah'dar looked toward them with suspicion as they moved together toward Soran, but Brother Hugh could not have been more delighted at his change of circumstance.

"Oh, my, we've the horse all to ourselves, Ferdinand!" The monk puffed as he scrambled onto Lusa's back and righted himself in the saddle. "Now we're proper adventurers! And what do you make of those two riding together, hmm? It's just as I suspected; love blooms even in the most desperate situations!"

Alyen turned to scowl at Brother Hugh with a finger over her mouth, reminding him of the need to travel stealthily. Brother Hugh ceased his talking, a stoic expression overcoming his face, but Alyen caught Aaron smiling quietly to himself as he tightened Soran's bridle.

Aaron helped Alyen onto Soran's back and swung up

behind her, his bandaged arm sliding around her waist. He clucked at Soran to move ahead but held him back at a slower pace until several yards separated them from Nah'dar's black stallion. Brother Hugh trailed behind them, blissfully oblivious to anything save the sound of his own humming.

"Are you feeling all right?" Aaron's voice came low in Alyen's ear.

"Yes, fine. Why?"

"The last time there was a battle you were very upset. I think you were sick?"

"Oh, right," Alyen said, her spirits dropping a notch. "I'm fine. I just—it was hard to see a person being killed. It's easier when it's a monster."

Alyen could feel Aaron nod behind her. "So, you don't hate me, then?"

"I don't hate you. I never hated you," Alyen said softly. She took a breath and let it out, her face troubled. "I don't like feeling like I'm not in control. I lived my whole life expecting to be in charge of everything and now … I know I made quick progress with my apprenticeship, but I've had a lot more training in how to handle a crisis. And now we're in one, but Nah'dar won't listen to me, and I thought you were just going to side with him because you're both warriors. I'm sorry for what I said to you. It was terrible and I didn't mean it. You were right about royals—we *do* do whatever we want. But that's because it's what we're trained to do—what we *have* to do."

Aaron was shaking his head. "No, I'm sorry, too. I was angry and I didn't mean what I said either." There was a pause, then Aaron's arm tightened on Alyen's waist. "Consider this," he said. "You were trained to lead the kingdom through troubled times as a royal, and now you have the added benefit of knowing how to do it with elemental help. I was raised learning how to protect the kingdom as well, just from the standpoint of Slayer. So, in a sense, we've actually had very similar childhoods. We've both been prepared for this moment, and we can both benefit from each other's perspective. So, from now on, we lead as a team. This is *our* quest—not mine, not Nah'dar's. We make decisions together and I promise to listen to you if you'll do the same for me. What do you think?"

Alyen relaxed, feeling a weight lift from her shoulders. "Perfect. It's a deal." Tentatively, she leaned back to rest her head against Aaron's uninjured shoulder. He didn't object.

For a time, they didn't speak as they watched the forest pass by and listened to Brother Hugh hum. Alyen was content to let her mind drift, enjoying the warm sensation of Aaron's arms conveniently around her. Eventually, Aaron broke the silence.

"So, do I get to know what you did down by the stream?"

Alyen grinned, no longer feeling she had to keep the secret from him. "I was trying to send a message to Faer Dinnán. I wanted to ask him for help."

"Really?" Aaron sounded surprised. "Did he agree?"

"I don't know," Alyen replied. "I asked a whole army of elementals to take him my message, but I haven't heard a word. And I can't go to him directly. Only he decides when and if he'll appear to mortals. What's so funny?"

Aaron was chuckling behind her, making Alyen's head jostle against him. "Nothing, really. It's just not what I thought you were doing."

"And what exactly did you think I was doing?"

"I thought you went to put a curse on me and Nah'dar."

"I wouldn't put a curse on you!" Alyen said indignantly. "I don't even know how to do curses. That's dark magic."

"Well, that's a relief. You know, you can be a bit frightening when you're upset."

"Well, you're not exactly pleasant when you're angry either."

"True. So, we're friends again?"

"Yes," Alyen agreed, though she felt her heart sink upon hearing the word *friends*.

The rest of the day passed pleasantly and without incident. The sun shone cold and white, brightening the sky despite the chill. Around them the land became more and more rugged, and their pace slowed as they guided the horses on a narrow, winding path that twined through the pines, skirting around cliffs and boulders. Eventually the shadows began to lengthen, earlier and more slanted than they did farther south, and Alyen and Aaron began to speculate on the obstacles that could be waiting for them the following day.

"I can't imagine the tomb will be very easy to reach physically," Aaron said. "And it must be guarded as well; it's right in the heart of dragon territory. In fact," he said, glancing toward the sky, "I'm a bit surprised we haven't seen any dragons overhead thus far. We've been in their lands for a couple days now."

"I thought they only lived in the mountains," Alyen said, scanning the sky herself.

"They do," Aaron confirmed. "They're far too big to fit between the trees in the forest. But they still fly over the lands surrounding their habitat that were granted to them as part of the Dragon Treaties."

"Have *you* ever dealt with dragons?"

"Only once. Not long after we met, actually. Morten and I were on our way here when we stopped at Castle Dúr."

"Oh, yes, I remember," Alyen said softly, noting the sudden touch of sadness in Aaron's voice. She hesitated a moment before asking the question at the back of her mind. "So, you know how to fight a dragon … right?"

"I do," Aaron replied simply. "But honestly it's foolish to try, and usually unnecessary. You see, while dragons may be fierce and extremely cunning, they're also deeply magical and incredibly wise. They can live up to five hundred years, so time moves more slowly for them and they usually value wit and honor over brute force. It takes a lot to rile a dragon to violence—but if you do, you best watch out."

Alyen was unsure whether to be reassured or not. Making off with the sword of Thor Lynn sounded like it might be the kind of "a lot" that might indeed rouse a dragon's ire.

"Don't worry," Aaron said, guessing Alyen's thoughts. "I would be surprised if it came to a fight with the dragons tomorrow. I'm guessing the tomb is guarded by ancient dragon magic, not the dragons themselves. Besides, if I really am the Second Slayer, I'm supposed to be able to get the sword, right?"

Alyen grinned at the confidence in Aaron's voice. *What am I worrying about?* she thought. *What couldn't Aaron handle after a morkush?*

They camped that night at the edge of the forest beneath a rocky overhang that heralded the entrance into Norhelm—the stark, circular range of mountains ruled by the dragons that rose like an island out of a sea of pines. Aaron and Nah'dar sparred with each other as usual, but there was a marked difference in Nah'dar's attitude toward his opponent. He no longer riddled Aaron with biting criticisms, nor dismissed Aaron's skill as mediocre. If an opportunity arose to show Aaron a new tactic, Nah'dar did so without the condescension that had been so characteristic of his instruction thus far. Indeed, Alyen thought, it was as if Aaron's victory over the morkush had proven him in Nah'dar's eyes, and Nah'dar now regarded Aaron as a true fellow warrior. The mood in camp was light, and Alyen smiled, watching the mock battle as she helped Brother Hugh with their evening meal.

Despite the buoyancy of the day, Alyen felt her spirits begin to falter as the sun slipped below the horizon and shadows crept over the campsite. The darkness brought with it memories of the night before, and without the daylight to ward it off, Alyen felt fear begin to creep back into her stomach and up her spine. She lay wide-eyed near the fire as the moon rose higher and found herself starting at each snap of a twig, shivering when the wind rushed ominously through the pine boughs and around the cold, barren cliffs. She thought about talking to Lirianna, but she didn't want to worry her unnecessarily and did not quite trust herself to keep the fear out of her mind's voice.

Aaron had taken the first watch, and Alyen could just make out his silhouette at the edge of the firelight. Finally, with the moon high in the sky, and herself no closer to sleep, Alyen tentatively pulled out her hearing stone from beneath her dress and clasped it tightly in her palm.

"Aaron?" Even her thought seemed to quaver in her mind.

"Alyen?" He sounded surprised. *"Are you all right?"*

"I can't sleep," Alyen thought, trying not to sound like a

child afraid of the dark. *"I just wondered if you heard anything unusual or—or anything,"* she finished weakly.

"No," his reply came, calm and reassuring. *"I think it will be a quiet night tonight."*

"Oh, all right then," Alyen replied quickly. There followed, in her opinion, an awkward silence, and she kicked herself for being cowardly.

"Alyen?" Aaron's thought came again, sounding hesitant.

"Yes?"

"Do you remember that day in the tunnel at Monstar?"

The question surprised Alyen, and the flip in her stomach had nothing to do with her fears of morkshai. A string of images raced through her mind: the void of darkness, the cool stone walls, Aaron standing close, his fingers light and careful as they touched her hair …

"Of course."

"Well, I was wondering what you would think about … I mean, I care a lot about both you and Lirianna, but I …" he cleared his throat gruffly. *"I think things are different with you and I wondered if you felt the same way?"*

Aaron had not moved as he kept watch, his back still straight and solid across the campfire, but Alyen could sense the tense line of his shoulders. At the same time her own heart was racing, and the sudden surge in her chest surprised her with its strength. How desperately she wanted to say yes, to throw all caution to the wind and grasp at happiness! For one brief and glorious moment she let herself picture it as she bit down on her lip, closing her eyes to savor the longing. But when she answered, her words were careful.

"Aaron, I—I just don't know if it's a very good idea." She felt

wretched saying it, and Aaron's reply sounded just as flat and dejected.

"I see. Do you mind if I ask why?"

"It's because of Rowenna," Alyen replied. *"When she started to suspect that—that I might have certain feelings about you, she warned me against getting involved with anyone. She said it would risk the safety of the kingdom—and then told me all about her and Morten and how they stayed apart just for that reason. Aaron, if you were just another boy and I was just a—a milkmaid or something …"*

"Yes, I know," Aaron cut her off. *"Morten gave me the same talk."*

"He did?"

"He did."

"But you still want to …?"

Aaron took a deep breath. *"I do. Think about it, Alyen. I know they had good reasons for their choices, but I think they would have been stronger together than apart. If they had been together, they could have stood against the darkness as one. Maybe they would still be here today. But more importantly, isn't it our purpose to uphold the Balance and all that's good and natural? And what could be more natural than loving and acting on that love? How can we claim to be champions of the Light if we deny its greatest expression in ourselves?"*

Alyen paused, frowning. It was a good point. A very good point. But Rowenna had been wise. Morten had been wise. They had been known as the most powerful Keeper and Slayer in generations. And these were no ordinary times. Given the prophecy, their destiny, the fate of the world and all that lay ahead—could they really risk taking a chance on love? Just as importantly, could they risk not taking one?

"I think …" Alyen sent her thought slowly, *"that you speak truly. But I need some time."*

"I agree to that," Aaron replied, sounding brighter. *"Take as much time as you need to think about it."*

There was silence for a minute as Alyen lay staring seriously into the flames and Aaron continued to watch the darkness. Suddenly his voice came into Alyen's head again.

"So have you thought about it?"

Alyen snorted out loud with laughter before catching herself and slapping a hand over her mouth. Aaron's chuckle sounded in her head, and she could see his shoulders shake subtly beneath his blanket.

"Sorry. Couldn't resist," he said. *"No pressure, really."*

"That's all right," Alyen replied, still giggling in her mind.

"Seriously, though," Aaron added, *"I think Morten regretted it. I always sensed that he wished they'd made a different choice."*

Alyen thought of Rowenna and the special sadness that had filled her eyes as she spoke of Morten. *"Yes, I think Rowenna regretted it as well."*

Alyen sensed that Aaron was about to say something more, but after a moment he merely said, *"Well, then—do you think you can sleep now?"*

Alyen smiled, realizing that her fears were gone. She snuggled deeper into her blanket. *"Yes, I think so. Thank you."*

"Any time." He shrugged his blanket closer around his shoulders as he continued to watch the night.

Alyen's eyelids were drooping as the fire burned low, her hearing stone still clasped in her hand when Aaron's voice came once more.

"Alyen?"

"Yes?"

"I don't want to live with regrets."

An ember crackled in the fire, sending a shower of orange sparks skyward.

26

THE TOMB OF THOR LYNN

They awoke in the morning to blankets stiff with frost, their breath rising in thin clouds of steam. Alyen blew on her cold hands as Aaron stoked the dying embers enough to warm a small breakfast, but no one, with the exception of Brother Hugh, seemed to have much of an appetite. The mountains of Norhelm loomed above them, stark and gray; somewhere hidden in the maze of canyons, cliffs, and ravines lay the Tomb of Thor Lynn. No one had a thought for much else.

Camp was broken quickly, the horses harnessed, and dirt thrown hastily over the last of the fire. There was no trail through Norhelm as none was needed by dragons, so the party was left to pick its way over boulders and skirt the towering cliffs, climbing always steadily upward toward the crisp white sky. The terrain was too rough for riding, so Nah'-dar, Alyen, and Aaron led their horses, traveling in single file with Nah'dar in the lead, followed by Alyen and Brother Hugh, and Aaron coming last to guard the back.

It was a rigorous climb, and soon Alyen was panting. Even Brother Hugh was no longer humming; Alyen could hear him puffing with the effort of hoisting himself up the mountain. For hours they picked their way toward the center of Norhelm, choosing paths the horses could follow, always on guard for dragons or whatever else might be set to guard the tomb. But aside from the strenuous climb, they met no opposition, nor did they see another living creature amidst the barren, gray cliffs.

The sun was nearing its peak and a cold wind whipped at the travelers' cloaks, moaning as it raced through the canyons. Alyen felt that soon she would be unable to move another step forward. Her legs were like jelly, and she noticed that Lusa, too, was quivering, her flanks slick with cold sweat. She had just made up her mind to call out to Nah'dar for a break when they rounded the corner of a cliff and found themselves on a wide, rocky plateau encircled by the mountains of Norhelm. In the center of the strange arena, the plateau dropped away suddenly forming a crater, easily a mile wide, sunk twenty feet into the rock. And on the far side of the crater, Alyen could just make out two natural pillars of rough, white marble framing a great slab of stone that concealed an entrance into the rock: the Tomb of Thor Lynn.

The four paused, catching their breath and scanning the wide expanse for any signs of dragons, but the plateau was just as deserted as the rest of their path through Norhelm had been. Aaron was frowning. Even Nah'dar's usually stony face looked uneasy.

"I thought we would've run into some sort of obstacle by

now," said Aaron. "We're nearly there; it seems much too easy."

"Maybe it's because you really are the Second Slayer?" offered Alyen. "Maybe the dragons are just letting you through because they know you're the one?"

"Maybe," said Aaron, sounding unconvinced.

Nah'dar gestured to a low overhang on a nearby cliff. "We will leave the horses under there," he decided. "They cannot make it down into the crater, and I don't want them spooked if we do run into anything."

They secured the horses as best as they were able to small boulders and jutting rocks and threw warm blankets over their backs. The group hastily ate a few bites of food, and Aaron took his dagger from his saddlebag and slid it into his boot. He and Nah'dar checked the rest of their weapons, and Brother Hugh, apparently not wanting to feel left out, snatched a pointed shard of rock from the ground and waved it about experimentally before tucking it in his rope belt. With nothing more to prepare, all four turned to face the crater. There was no point in trying to conceal themselves on the exposed terrain, so after glancing about at each other and with a curt nod from Nah'dar, they struck out onto the barren plateau.

It wasn't long before they reached the edge of the crater, though to Alyen, who kept glancing sharply at the sky and cliffs for signs of dragons, it seemed much longer. Peering over the edge, Alyen could see that the sides of the crater were smooth as glass, allowing for no handholds to accommodate a climb to the bottom. Scanning the perimeter of the crater, she could see no way down unless they attempted to shimmy down one of the pillars of the tomb itself.

"Will we have to climb down the tomb?" she asked doubtfully.

"I'd rather not," replied Aaron. "We don't know how the tomb is protected and for some reason, I doubt that whatever is guarding it would appreciate us clambering all over it. I don't want to risk it."

"Then how are we supposed to get down there?" Alyen feared whatever answer Aaron might give.

Brother Hugh was looking over the edge, shaking his head solemnly. "Dear, dear, Ferdinand, it's quite a drop, isn't it?"

Aaron looked at Nah'dar. "I'll go first," he said, and Nah'dar nodded. Aaron unbuckled his short sword, removed the dagger from his boot and another from inside his tunic, wrapped them in his cloak, and tossed them over the edge. They landed with a soft thud, then Aaron crouched. With a gasp, Alyen suddenly realized what he planned to do, but before she could cry out to stop him, Aaron had sprung over the edge of the cliff. Alyen threw herself on the ground to peer over the edge and saw him hit the rock below, tucking in his knees and head so that he rolled several feet before straightening again.

"Are you all right?" Alyen called.

"Of course. It's really not that bad," Aaron replied, grinning as he straightened his tunic and brushed loose strands of hair from his eyes.

Alyen scowled. "Maybe not for you, but how am *I* going to get down there? I'm not jumping!"

"Yes, you are," came Aaron's matter-of-fact reply.

"No, I'm not! I'll be killed!" Alyen called down shrilly.

"You'll be fine. You jump down, and I'll catch you. It'll be easy!"

Obviously, these words were meant as reassurance, but the worried look on her face told Aaron they seemed to have had the opposite effect.

"What's the matter?" he called up, his arms outstretched as if to catch her. "Don't you trust me?"

"Um," Alyen hesitated. "It's just—are you *sure* you can do it?"

Aaron's expression darkened and he dropped his arms. "What's that supposed to mean? I'm the next Slayer of Monsters, I've defeated a *morkush*, and to be honest I'm pretty strong. Of course I can catch you!"

"It's just that you've missed twice before," Alyen said, still peering over the lip of the cliff from the ground.

"What!?"

"Well, you have! You said you would catch me climbing the tree the day I met you and you didn't, and you didn't exactly catch me when I fell off the ladder in the library either."

Aaron glared fiercely up at Alyen. "I was *eight* when I met you, Alyen, and unless you're planning on throwing another pile of books on my head as you jump, the second time doesn't count either! Now, come on—isn't this one of those things princesses are supposed to enjoy?"

"We don't have all day, *Princess*," Nah'dar said shortly. Alyen pursed her lips but rose to her feet. This made Aaron seem even farther away, and she gulped.

"Are you ready?" she called down, a quaver in her voice.

"I'm ready," Aaron confirmed, now trying to sound reassuring. "Don't be scared, just jump right toward me. You'll be fine."

Alyen tried to make herself jump, but her legs would not

move. *It's really not that far down*, she told herself, but she remained rooted to the spot. She had never thought she was afraid of heights, but faced with the prospect of hurling herself off a cliff, albeit a small one, she found herself going dizzy as she looked down at the drop. Nah'dar let out a huff of impatience.

"Alyen, look at me. Look in my eyes," Aaron called, reaching his arms up to her again. Alyen looked into Aaron's eyes. They were clear and steady. "Alyen, I'm going to count to three. I want you to take a big breath, and on three you jump. I *promise* I will catch you, and then it'll be over."

Alyen nodded, not looking away from Aaron.

"All right, one … two … three!"

Alyen gulped a breath of air and, not allowing herself to think, her eyes glued to Aaron's, she leapt off the edge of the cliff. She felt herself tilting sideways in the air and she shut her eyes tight with a small cry, then felt a jolt as strong arms clasped around her. All was still for a few seconds and finally she dared to open one eye and squinted up into Aaron's grinning face. His hazel eyes were dark and sparkling.

"You did it," he said softly.

"So did you," Alyen said, smiling.

Aaron's face was very close. Alyen could see the rough stubble on his cheeks from weeks of shaving crudely with his dagger. She glanced up to his eyes again, but Aaron was distracted, his gaze lifting once more to the top of the cliff.

"Oh, curses," he said, his eyes no longer sparkling.

Alyen looked up quickly to see a beaming Brother Hugh inching to the edge of the cliff, his arms outstretched, ready to be caught.

In the end, Nah'dar lowered Brother Hugh over the edge of the cliff with the monk's rope belt until his wildly kicking feet were only a few yards from the crater floor. At that point, Brother Hugh was supposed to let go and drop, with Aaron waiting below to spot his landing, but when Brother Hugh refused to relinquish his grip on the rope, Nah'dar promptly dropped it. Brother Hugh fell with a *whoop* and landed unharmed, and Alyen, glancing at the grim satisfaction lining Nah'dar's face, suspected that the assassin had relished the chance to cause mischief to his third and most annoying companion. Nah'dar discarded his weapons and leapt down as gracefully as had Aaron, and after the two warriors had retrieved their effects and Brother Hugh had retied his belt, all four turned to face the tomb at the opposite end of the crater.

The terrain they set out to cross was an expanse of dry rock covered in a film of chalky gray silt. They had not walked far in the direction of the white-pillared tomb when Alyen's mouth suddenly felt parched, and a thirst began to gnaw at her stomach and throat. She swallowed hard, trying to ignore the fact that her tongue felt like sand, but a growing panic was beginning to rise in her chest. She looked around at her companions in alarm.

"Does anyone have water?"

"No," Aaron replied, also sounding worried. "We left it all with the horses."

"What?" Alyen cried. Her heartbeat was beginning to race, and her breath was coming quick and shallow. "Why did you leave it? Why didn't you bring it along?"

"You didn't bring it either!"

They were no longer walking and Alyen saw that Nah'dar and Aaron were casting about for any sign of water, looking just as panicked as she felt, and Brother Hugh was fumbling in the pockets of his robe, muttering to himself. Alyen whirled around in circles, scanning their surroundings, but instead of finding water, her eyes landed on something white lying pale and twisted on the ground.

It was a skeleton. The skeleton of a person, its jaw gaping in a silent scream, one ghastly arm outstretched toward an oasis that was not there. Alyen gasped in horror and in that second, she knew that the same fate awaited them unless they left the crater immediately. Terror clutched at her heart as she scanned the rock wall with its glassy sides rising high into the air. How were they to get out? It was far too high to jump, and there wasn't a foothold in sight to aid in a climb.

Alyen gulped in fright and looked back at the skeleton, but there were now many skeletons littering the ground around them. Alyen shrieked, clutching at her throat, already feeling the deadly thirst shriveling her stomach as her tongue swelled. How had they not seen the skeletons before? Why hadn't they brought water? She didn't want to die; not like this, not now. She was still screaming as she fell to her knees, dimly registering the shouts of her companions behind her. Then one by one their voices ceased and hers was the only one still raised in terror, her eyes closed tightly against the horror of the bones closing in on her. *They've all died*, Alyen thought. *They've died of thirst and any minute, I'll die, too.*

And suddenly someone had grasped her head and was shoving something hard and smooth into her mouth. She struggled, choking, trying to clench her teeth against the foreign object, but her assailant was firm and within seconds, her mouth had closed around the small round object. At once a cooling sensation filled her mouth and trickled down her throat, filling her stomach and sending waves of cool relief through her body. Alyen stopped screaming, her limbs trembling, and instinctively sucked furiously on the object in her mouth. She began to breathe deeply once more, her heart slowed, and slowly she opened her eyes. The skeletons were gone and, blinking around, she saw Aaron and Nah'dar sitting near her, each sucking intently. Brother Hugh was crouching nearby smiling benignly as his tongue worked at something in his own mouth.

"What happened?" Alyen asked in a hoarse voice.

Aaron shook his head looking perplexed, and Nah'dar reached in his mouth and pulled out a small, smooth stone the pale blue color of a robin's egg. His eyebrows lifted in surprise, and he looked at Brother Hugh.

"Rain stones?" he asked.

"Of course," Brother Hugh beamed. "They're terribly useful on long journeys. Much lighter to carry than water bags, you see."

"Yes, but they are also magical and quite rare," Nah'dar replied, placing the stone back into his mouth. "Where did you come by them?"

"Found them in the river on the way here," Brother Hugh replied as he stood, brushing off his robes. "I thought they were just pretty, but Ferdinand showed me how useful they are. Lucky I brought them I'd say. It gets dreadfully thirsty in here, doesn't it? You lot were in a right state!"

Alyen reached into her mouth and pulled out the light blue stone. It was not large, perhaps the size of a grape, but the moment it left her mouth she felt the thirst begin to creep back and the bleached skeletal bones began to flicker once more in the corners of her eyesight. Alyen quickly placed the stone back in her mouth and the bones vanished instantly along with the thirst.

"This isn't a normal thirst," Alyen commented as they rose from the ground, brushing themselves off as much as possible.

"No, it's not," Aaron agreed. "I doubt regular water would have done anything for us even if we did have it. Like I said, dragons prefer mind games and magic over battle. This was probably a strong and ancient enchantment—effective, too, I'd say. Did the rest of you feel you had to leave this place at once, no matter the cost?"

Everyone nodded.

"Exactly," said Aaron. "Anyone coming for the sword would go mad with panic and imagined thirst before they ever got near the tomb. We'll have to be on our guard for more magic from now on. Let's stick close together, and speak up the second you feel, see, hear, or smell anything strange."

They continued cautiously, their senses straining for anything out of the ordinary, but aside from a yelp from Brother Hugh when a pebble got caught in his shoe, they traveled uninterrupted until they had nearly reached the entrance of the tomb.

The tomb was larger than it had appeared from the far side of the crater. As the group approached, they gaped up at the towering marble pillars framing the equally dazzling stone doorway that marked the entrance to the final resting place of Dúramair's greatest Slayer. The sun, high in the sky, blazed onto the white marble and scattered into their eyes, so they didn't see the tomb's guardian until they were almost upon her.

Not twenty paces from the doors, Nah'dar suddenly hissed, throwing one arm out to stop the others while his other arm darted for his scimitar. In a flash both he and Aaron were armed. Alyen, looking around wildly, spotted what had caused the alarm. Resting on a low, rocky outcrop just feet away, motionless save for the swish of her golden tail, sat a lion with the head of a woman, her full, black hair matching her dark, shining, almond-shaped eyes. Her alabaster face held no expression, but she gazed on the travelers with an unnerving intensity that made Alyen want to avoid her stare.

"What is it?" she asked.

"It's a sphinx," said Aaron, sounding amazed. "There are few left, and I thought they only lived far to the south, in Sandamar."

"Is it dangerous?" Alyen asked warily.

Nah'dar scowled, his teeth barred. "It is a beast, and it is a woman. Of course it is dangerous," he growled.

Alyen, feeling a bit affronted at this statement, frowned and asked, "What does it do?"

Glancing at Nah'dar, Aaron explained, "The sphinxes are riddlers and they're also soul searchers. With one look, their eyes can penetrate down into your deepest thoughts, feelings, memories—it's impossible to lie or hide anything from them. They make excellent guardians because you can only pass them if you solve their riddles correctly. If you don't, they attack."

Alyen peered doubtfully at the razor-sharp claws extending from each of the sphinx's paws, but Brother Hugh seemed unbothered by this news.

"Riddles? How exciting! I've never solved a riddle before. I expect it will be very tricky, won't it?" he said happily.

Nah'dar glowered at the monk, then turned to Aaron. "The odds are not in our favor with the beast. I suggest we find another way to gain entrance."

Aaron frowned and surveyed the landscape, shaking his head. "I don't think there *is* another way, Nah'dar. The tomb is carved into the rock, and this is the only door."

"Besides," Alyen added, "it can't be that bad if we get the riddle wrong, can it? I mean, you *have* both defeated morkshai."

Nah'dar's scowl deepened. "You misunderstand the danger, Princess. To seek passage from a sphinx is not merely to have your soul searched, but to risk it entirely. The beast's riddles speak to the quester's darkest fears, their most painful memories—those realms of the heart that are kept secret from the world, hidden even from the seeker's own mind. Answer the riddle rightly, and all is well. But answer incorrectly, and even if you survive the attack, your soul will be forever tormented, haunted by the riddle that sprung from within and lives there still. The madness will spread until you are consumed by it entirely—until you long for the death you escaped. And when it finally comes once more to claim you, it will seem as an angel of mercy." Nah'dar turned to face Aaron. "Think well before you approach this beast, Aaron. Do you know your soul so well that you are willing to risk facing it?"

All were silent following Nah'dar's dark words. After a time, Aaron spoke softly.

"Be that as it may, Nah'dar, I don't really have the luxury of cowardice. I *have* to enter the tomb, and I don't see another way in. If I have to risk my soul, then that's how it is."

Nah'dar, his face like stone, said nothing.

"So, we pass the sphinx, then," said Alyen bracingly, feeling, despite Nah'dar's warning, that she would still rather chance the riddle than battle morkshai or dragons. "What do we do?"

"We just approach," said Aaron. "Slowly and respectfully. She'll take it from there. And Brother Hugh ..." Aaron regarded the monk nervously. "Try—just try not to say anything." As Brother Hugh smiled and clamped his mouth shut, Aaron muttered in an undertone to Alyen, "I don't want him blurting out nonsense that the sphinx takes as an answer."

Cautiously, the group stepped toward the sphinx's outcrop. The riddler didn't move except for an occasional swish of her tail, nor did her face show any sign of expression as she regarded the travelers approaching her. Alyen found herself avoiding the sphinx's black stare.

They stopped before the outcrop, Aaron looking determined, Nah'dar defiant, and Brother Hugh naïve and expectant. Alyen hoped she did not look how she felt, which was acutely nervous. In an attempt to appear brave, she lifted her eyes to the sphinx's alabaster face. The sphinx spoke at last, her voice liquid steel.

"To each, one riddle shall I give.
Answer well if you would live
To pass beyond my guarded gate;
Answer wrong and death awaits."

Alyen gulped and glanced at her companions; Aaron's face was tense, and Nah'dar's had darkened considerably. Only Brother Hugh seemed unconcerned, rocking back and forth on the balls of his feet excitedly.

The sphinx turned her head slowly to Aaron. Their eyes locked and Alyen saw Aaron's widen as his face drained of color. Looking back at the sphinx, Alyen saw a glow in the fathomless eyes, then the sphinx gave her first riddle.

"Burning brighter than the flame,
Always found yet lost again.
Its further loss, your greatest fear
Because of one your heart holds dear."

The glow in the sphinx's eyes extinguished and Aaron gave an involuntary shudder as he staggered back a step. Immediately he threw an agonized glance toward Alyen, then just as quickly looked away, his head bowed, his eyes on the ground.

But there was no time to console or ask questions. As Alyen watched Aaron's reaction, she felt the back of her neck prickle and sensed that the sphinx's eyes now rested on her, waiting for Alyen to meet her gaze. Taking a shaky breath, Alyen turned her head and stared into the twin pools of glowing onyx.

It felt as though she had been plunged into icy water. Alyen gasped as the sphinx's eyes glowed with a light that pierced to the center of her heart. She felt every memory, every emotion, every thought or experience she ever had flee from her, pouring into the sphinx's gaze as the riddler regarded her life and her soul, cool and unyielding. She was a small child at one of her father's feasts, she was studying a map of the kingdom with Professor Glibb, she was looking up at Aaron in the tree at Castle Dúr, Garret was teaching her to ride Lusa, Monstar Abbey loomed on the cliff above her,

Rowenna was explaining the properties of mugwort, Lirianna was laughing on the battlements of Monstar, she was in the hidden cave in the tool shed and Aaron was standing very close … his hand was on her arm as she staggered on the river bank … his arms held her tightly before him on Soran …

The few moments it took for the sphinx to collect the whole of Alyen's life felt to Alyen like hours, and finally, still held petrified by the sphinx's eyes, she heard the terrible, beautiful voice ring in her ears, in her heart, in her bones.

> "Blooming sweeter than the rose,
> Deep within its yearning grows.
> Yet at its sight, you shy away
> Lest it should lead your heart astray."

Suddenly the eyes, the cold, the rush of memory was gone, and it was Alyen's turn to shiver, feeling that her heart was empty, all its contents now held captive by the sphinx. She glanced hollowly toward Aaron. He seemed a bit recovered, but his expression as he returned Alyen's gaze was unreadable.

The sphinx had turned toward Brother Hugh, and the monk was standing very still under her glowing eyes.

> "Purer than the morning dew,
> Freely does it flow from you.
> And though your value few may see,
> It never fails to comfort thee."

Brother Hugh gave a dancing wiggle that would have made Alyen laugh if she did not know firsthand how it felt to be held under that stare. Finally, the sphinx turned her magnificent head toward Nah'dar, who stood waiting with a snarl on his face, one hand clenched on the hilt of his scimitar. Alyen thought she saw the sphinx's eyes flash when they met his, and the light they held was more a burning flame than a glow.

"Wounding deeper than the blade,
It shall not breach the walls you've laid.
But if you would avoid attack,
Tell me what your mother lacked."

By the end of this speech, all color had drained from Nah'dar's face, and while he did not move when the sphinx released him from her stare, Alyen thought she had never seen him look so gray. No one spoke or moved for a moment, then Brother Hugh broke the silence.

"Well, I think I've got mine all figured out. It seems to me the answer should be—"

"NO!" shouted Alyen and Aaron together, startling Brother Hugh out of finishing his sentence.

"Don't say anything, Brother Hugh," Aaron said sternly. "We have to be very sure of this. Perhaps if we discuss together, carefully. Don't make anything you say sound like a definite answer. Now, does anyone have any *thoughts* on their riddle?"

Alyen thought on her riddle. There was no danger of forgetting it; she felt as though each word had been burned on her soul with a hot iron. And it felt as though the answer was there with it, but hidden, just beyond her reach, and something told her that perhaps she didn't want the others to know what that answer was, to know the secret that whispered in her heart. She decided to be vague as she mulled it over to herself.

"Mine has to do with something I want," she said. "Something I want, but I'm not sure I should have it, maybe? What about you Aaron—didn't yours say something about something you're afraid of?"

"Yes," Aaron replied with an awkward glance at Alyen, and she got the impression that he was no keener to let her in on his soul's secret than she was. "But honestly, that could be many things. Any kind of monster to face, the morkshai, certainly, bees … these are *not* answers yet," he said to the sphinx who was regarding him with a faintly hungry expression.

"Bees?" Alyen said incredulously. "You're the next Slayer of Monsters and you're afraid of *bees*?"

"Not *much*," Aaron said defensively, his cheeks faintly flushed. Alyen suspected he had not meant to add bees to his list out loud, and smirked.

"Anyway," Aaron continued, sounding mildly flustered, "the riddle specifically referred to losing it as my *greatest* fear, and that's not bees."

"So, what is it?"

"I really do think I have mine figured out now," piped up Brother Hugh. "If you'll just let me answer—"

"Just wait, Brother Hugh," said Aaron firmly. "We'll get to yours in a minute. Nah'dar, yours seemed fairly straightforward at the end. Something about what your mother is missing?"

Nah'dar still hadn't moved, nor did he look at all recovered from the delivery of his riddle. When he spoke, it seemed to take great effort to force the words through his clenched teeth.

"I have not seen my mother for over twenty years. If she is missing something, I know nothing of it."

Such was Nah'dar's tone and expression, that neither Aaron nor Alyen dared to inquire further. After a brief awkward pause, Alyen said in a voice rather higher than usual, "So then, we're back to something I want, and something Aaron is afraid to lose. Now, Brother Hugh, what—"

"Brother Hugh, no!" Aaron shouted, but it was too late. Brother Hugh had locked eyes with the sphinx once more. Spreading his arms wide, he shouted, "The answer is love!"

There was a horrified silence as everyone waited for the sphinx to spring, but no attack came. Instead, the glow slowly left the sphinx's eyes and Brother Hugh, grinning broadly, bounced past the sphinx's outcrop toward the entrance of the tomb.

"Truly?" asked Alyen. "That was really the answer?"

"Of course!" Brother Hugh called as he turned back to them. He spread his arms once more, his face jubilant. "The answer to *everything* is love! I'll see you inside!"

And with that, he squeezed himself through a crevasse in the marble and disappeared into the Tomb of Thor Lynn.

Again, silence. At last Aaron spoke.

"I've had a thought," he said, throwing a hasty glance at Nah'dar. "Did you hear what Brother Hugh said—that love is the answer to *everything*?"

Alyen's mouth formed a silent "oh" and her eyebrows rose as she caught what Aaron meant.

"You think all our riddles have the same answer?"

"It's possible. Why don't we all think over our own riddle and see if it makes sense."

There was silence again as the three contemplated. Alyen began to scrutinize hers in her mind, line by line, but she knew in her heart that it was so before she had started. It was as if the answer that was already there, buried beneath the layers of riddle, surged forth as it heard its name called, and there was no longer room for doubt with her heart trumpeting its truth.

"Blooming sweeter than the rose." It made sense. The feeling of love *was* sweet, and the rose was a symbol of love. "Deep within its yearning grows." That was true as well. Alyen looked almost guiltily toward Aaron, then looked away quickly as she saw him glance at her. "Yet at its sight you shy away, lest it should lead your heart astray." Also, true. Hadn't she just told Aaron the previous night that she didn't think they should be together? It might not be right. It might ruin everything. Not just for Dúramair, but for them as well. If she was going to be completely honest with herself, Alyen knew she feared ruining their friendship almost more than she feared ruining the kingdom. A pang of guilt stabbed at her hollow heart. She was supposed to be the Keeper of Scales and was raised to rule, yet here she was, strongly considering putting the desires of her own heart before her duties to her kingdom. And when Rowenna had tried to warn her, all she'd given in return was anger. Yes, love was her answer. But was it anything to be proud of? And did she have to admit it in front of Aaron and Nah'dar?

Alyen finally looked up and was relieved when Aaron spoke first.

"The answer works for mine," he said softly, a strange look in his eyes.

"For mine as well," she mumbled.

They looked to Nah'dar with the same thought in their minds: was love the thing Nah'dar's mother had lacked? Neither wanted to ask, and Nah'dar remained silent.

"Well, then. There's only one way to know if we're right," said Aaron. He placed himself before the sphinx and looked up into her eyes. Alyen saw him tense once more, but his voice was strong as he announced, "My answer, too, is love."

Again, the glow faded from the black eyes. Alyen watched with relief as Aaron passed safely by the sphinx and stepped up to the tomb's white marble entrance. He paused to look back toward Alyen and Nah'dar, then with a crooked smile, edged through the narrow crevasse and disappeared within.

Any lingering doubt Alyen may have had that the answer to her riddle was the same as the others' was extinguished, and she was thankful that Aaron had passed into the cavern before her. Although she knew the meaning of her riddle would likely become clear to Aaron in the days to come, she was still glad not to admit it to the sphinx in front of him. Hoping she would be able to give her answer in private by going last, she turned to Nah'dar.

"Do you want to go next?" she asked. But Nah'dar didn't answer. He was staring at the sphinx, every muscle in his body clenched, and his face held a look upon it more terrible than any Alyen had ever seen. It was an expression of burning hate, of fury, of pain—and of fear.

Alarmed, Alyen took a step back from Nah'dar but still he did not move. She hesitated for a moment, watching him closely, unsure of what to do, and finally decided to address the sphinx herself. Tearing her eyes from Nah'dar's rigid form, she moved in front of the sphinx and raised her eyes to meet its gaze.

Once more Alyen felt the sensation of being struck by icy water as she fell into the black glowing pools of the sphinx's eyes and her voice came out in a rush of breath.

"Love," she gasped. "My answer is love."

At once the cold vanished. A feeling of warmth blossomed in her chest and spread outward through her limbs down to her fingertips and toes. Alyen's heart suddenly felt full to the point of bursting, yet lighter than it had been in weeks. The sphinx's features softened into the shadow of a smile, which Alyen returned as she passed to stand before the tomb's door.

At the entrance Alyen turned to look at Nah'dar. He was watching her now, his face a mask, but he made no move toward the sphinx.

"Go on, Princess. I will stand watch here until the sword has been retrieved."

"But aren't you …"

"I said I shall remain here!" Nah'dar almost shouted, then turned on his heel and stalked several paces away, his robes swirling around his ankles. The sphinx watched him retreat, her face as expressionless as ever.

Alyen watched Nah'dar's back for a moment until she was sure he didn't mean to follow, then sighed and slipped through the narrow crevasse into the Tomb of Thor Lynn.

27

SCALA

Alyen paused just inside the doorway of the tomb, momentarily blinded in the dim light after the blaze of the sun-struck marble outside. As her eyes adjusted, she saw that she stood at the top of a few stone steps hewn out of the rock leading down into a small cavern on her right. The chamber was empty save for a great marble sarcophagus raised on a stone dais at the far end of the room —and the weapon that hung above it.

Scala. The undefeated sword carrying a ruby of dragon heart blood. The blade of Thor Lynn—and of the Second Slayer.

Brother Hugh was sitting at one end of the cavern, perched on a rocky ledge, looking peaceful and almost sad.

"So, our friend in black has decided not to join us?" he asked and nodded ruefully. "It doesn't surprise me. Some wounds are too great to face."

The monk hopped off the ledge and headed toward the

tomb's entrance. "I think I shall leave the sword to you two and wait outside with Nah'dar."

Alyen opened her mouth to protest, convinced that Brother Hugh was the last person who should be left alone with Nah'dar at that moment, but the monk put a reassuring hand on Alyen's arm and smiled a sad smile. His eyes were more lucid than Alyen had ever seen them.

"Don't worry, my dear, we'll be fine. You just concentrate on the sword. It's quite pretty, isn't it?"

With a final glance toward the mounted blade, Brother Hugh patted Alyen's arm, and squeezed his way back into the sunlight.

"There's something very odd about that monk," Aaron said. He was standing near the dais looking at the crevasse through which Brother Hugh had just disappeared, a slight frown on his face.

"Yes, he's full of surprises today, isn't he?"

Aaron grunted, then turned to contemplate the sword.

Brother Hugh had been correct. It *was* beautiful. The long, double-edged, steel blade pointed downward, glinting in the dim light. Its hilt, also steel, was adorned with delicately interwoven designs inlayed in gold, and at its very center rested the great ruby, blood-red and infused with dragon magic.

Both Aaron and Alyen stared at it in awed silence. Until this moment, Scala had been a thing of fantasy and legend, yet here it was before them, a legend turned real, beautiful and deadly, waiting to be claimed by its next true master.

"It doesn't look like it will be hard to take it off the wall," Alyen finally said in a hushed voice. "Why don't you try it?"

Aaron looked flushed, both excited and nervous. He took a deep breath and glanced at Alyen. "All right. Here it goes."

He stepped up onto the dais, slowly reached up, and grasped the hilt of the sword in his hand. He closed his eyes and Alyen saw the muscles in his arm contract as he willed it to lift the sword from the wall.

Nothing happened.

The blade didn't budge, and for a moment, neither did Aaron. Then he reached up with his other arm, placing both hands on the hilt and tugged at the sword, much less ceremoniously than his first attempt, but with no better result. Aaron backed down from the dais almost hastily. His face was no longer flushed, but white.

"It won't move," he said unnecessarily.

"Well, maybe it's just not that simple," Alyen offered, quick to reassure. "There must be some kind of clue here."

She began scanning the walls, the ceiling, the floor of the cavern, and Aaron followed suit.

Alyen's eyes soon rested on the marble sarcophagus. She had been so focused on the sword that she hadn't given a thought to the second relic the tomb held—the remains of the greatest of Slayers, a legend himself, even without his sword. Alyen suddenly felt awed standing there before the dais, and she respectfully bowed her head.

It was then she noticed the words engraved in the marble running around the rim of the coffin's lid. Alyen dropped to her knees on the dais, her fingers tracing the etched letters.

"Aaron, look! It's the prophecy!"

Aaron knelt swiftly beside her, his hands mirroring Alyen's as he confirmed her discovery. The rhyme Garret had taught them so long ago was embedded in Thor Lynn's stone encasement.

"Perhaps there's a clue hidden in the prophecy?" Aaron suggested, excited once again. "Let's take it line by line." They read aloud together.

> *"Let all be warned! A time shall come*
> *Two suns shall set to leave but one*
> *When shifting scales foretell our doom*
> *And from below a darkness looms.*
>
> *Our only hope in darkest night*
> *To turn our world back to the light*
> *Shall lie with one who seeks to win*
> *The weapon of the knight Thor Lynn.*
>
> *Oh, Second Slayer, ye tread a path*
> *Of villains' snare and monsters' wrath*
> *Past riddles and spells of magic laid;*
> *Alone ye cannot claim the blade.*
>
> *Yet let none crave this hero's lot*
> *Though fame be prized and glory sought,*
> *For if on you the fate should fall,*
> *Remember this: death changes all."*

Aaron looked at Alyen with gleaming eyes to match her own. "Alyen, so much of this makes sense! Why didn't we think of this before?"

"I know!" Alyen agreed eagerly. "Start again from the top."

"'*Two suns shall set to leave but one.*' Well, we've already agreed that probably refers to Rowenna and Morten."

"And we already know a darkness is looming, and that we were told to claim the sword in order to have a chance at victory."

"And look, '*Past riddles and spells of magic laid*'—that's the sphinx and the spell of thirst."

"And before that it says '*ye tread a path of villains' snare and monsters' wrath.*' That's the assassin and the morkshai Ylvain sent to stop us."

"The last verse is just a warning," Aaron continued, his breath coming quick. "Like you always hear about glory not being as good as it sounds. But look at the last line of the verse right before that."

"'*Alone ye cannot claim the blade*'," Alyen mused, then looked up at Aaron. "Do you think it will work if we try it together?"

"I'm certain," said Aaron, his eyes sparkling. "It all fits."

"It's worth a try," agreed Alyen, and they rose to approach the sword once more.

Again, Aaron stepped onto the dais and gripped the hilt with both hands. Alyen placed her hands over Aaron's and, with a nod, they both tugged and strained at the weapon. But they could just as easily have been pulling at the wall of the mountain itself for all the sword would move.

After several moments of tugging, twisting, and straining, Aaron threw his hands off the hilt, sending Alyen's hands flying as well. His face was now a blotchy red, all the eager excitement from their interpretation of the prophecy erased from his features.

"Let's face it, Alyen. I'm obviously not the Second Slayer."

His words hung in the air.

"Don't say that," Alyen said quietly. "What about the prophecy, how it all fits?"

"It could fit with *anyone* who can solve a riddle and get their hands on a rain stone! It doesn't mean anything except that we came all this way for nothing."

"But maybe we just haven't found the right way yet. I'm sure if we just keep looking …"

"It's no use, Alyen!" Aaron's voice was loud as it cut her off. "The Second Slayer is supposed to be able to claim the sword, and I can't so it's not me. It's that simple."

Aaron stalked to the other end of the cavern and leaned against the ledge Brother Hugh had sat upon, scowling with his arms folded.

Alyen said nothing. She didn't know what she *could* say. All evidence indicated that Aaron was right, but what that meant for Dúramair and the danger coming, Alyen didn't want to think. And the prophecy did seem to fit so well …

Alyen looked back up at the sword, her eyes fixing on the ruby in the center of the hilt. It seemed to draw her in, invite her touch, and she felt her arm raise almost by itself. She hadn't actually touched the sword yet, she realized. She had only touched Aaron's hands as they pulled at it together. As if in slow motion, she gripped the hilt of the sword.

Scala began to glow a silvery light, and a hum rang through the cavern. Alyen's eyes widened as her arm pulled upward and Scala arced fluidly through the air in her grasp as she turned to face the center of the room. The humming grew louder, the silvery light blazed brighter, and suddenly the sword was so hot, that Alyen yelled and dropped it as if it were on fire. It clanged on the stone floor, and in the same instant, the hum disappeared, and the silver light was extinguished.

Alyen stared at the sword where it lay and finally looked up at Aaron. He was staring at her, his face blank.

"It just—came off," Alyen said lamely.

"You better pick it up off the floor," he replied, his expression still a mask.

"I can't, it burned me," Alyen protested, though when she looked at her hands, there was no mark on her skin.

"Try it again," said Aaron.

Alyen stepped down from the dais and knelt by the sword. It looked exactly the same, except it was on the floor rather than the wall. Alyen reached out a tentative hand and touched the hilt. There was no glow of light, nor ringing hum, but the blade still burned to the touch, and she jerked her hand back.

"I'm telling you, I can't touch it, Aaron! Come see for yourself."

Aaron knelt on the other side of the blade and placed his hand on the hilt. Alyen waited for him to snatch it away, but it remained, lying gently across the ruby. Aaron looked into Alyen's face.

"It's cool to my touch," he said, and Alyen thought there was an accusatory note in his voice.

"Well then, you take it," Alyen said. "I don't want it."

"I can't take it," Aaron objected. "It should be carried by the Second Slayer, and I'm not the Second Slayer."

"Oh, how do you know?" Alyen said crossly. "*I'm* certainly not the Second Slayer, so you can stop acting like you're angry with me."

Aaron looked sheepish and troubled. "I'm not angry with you. I just really thought I was the Second Slayer. And now I don't know what to do. I shouldn't carry it if it didn't let me claim it."

"Look, Aaron," said Alyen more gently. "It won't even let me touch it anymore, but it fits your hand perfectly. It can't hurt to have it with us in the coming battle either way, so why don't you just take it for the time being and we can figure out the Second Slayer part later?"

Aaron sat looking down at the sword for a long moment, his fingers tracing the ruby and the adornments on the hilt. Finally, he gripped it in his hand and rose.

"I'm not sure," he said looking at Alyen. "But I'll carry it for now. I think it's time we headed for Castle Dúr."

They squeezed back out the crevasse, squinting at the bright sunlight. Blinking, Alyen saw that Nah'dar hadn't moved from the spot she had seen him last, but that his scimitar was drawn, and he was tensed for battle. At the same time, Aaron stopped short, and in the next second Alyen saw why.

The entire rim of the crater was lined with dragons.

"Hello!" called Brother Hugh who seemed, as usual, unconcerned as he traced figures in the sand in the shade of the sphinx's outcrop. The sphinx was nowhere to be seen. "Oh, good, you have the sword! I think they've been waiting for you."

Alyen felt her legs turn to liquid as she scanned the dragon-lined crater, noting that each one seemed bigger than the last. Claws, horns, spikes, and fangs could be seen in every direction, and smoke trickled skyward from scaly snouts.

Dragons don't eat people, dragons don't eat people, Alyen repeated to herself. She tried to focus instead on the beauty of the dragons' scales, each one a different hue of green, silver, black, and occasionally red.

Then without warning the dragons, as one, lifted their heads and let out a bellow that shot columns of fire to the sky and shook the floor of the crater. Indeed, the crater walls began to crack and suddenly the ground surged, and a column of sand and rock exploded into the air. Alyen shrieked and ducked, closing her eyes, dimly aware that Aaron had thrown his arms over her, pushing her to the ground, shielding both their faces from the worst of the dust. The dragons' resounding call continued to ring in the air as the earth shuddered; there was a loud crack, then quite suddenly, all grew still and quiet.

Slowly, Aaron and Alyen raised their heads and gaped in astonishment at the transformation of the terrain before them. Only feet from where they stood, a wide stone stair rose from the earth, leading all the way back to the other end of the crater where they had descended. Each marble stair was not high, but very long and wide, forming a gradual incline over the mile of crater floor. The dragons had fallen silent but did not move.

Brother Hugh peeked over the sphinx's outcrop at the stair, then stood up with a grin. "Well, this will certainly make things easier," he said brightly.

Nah'dar rose slowly from where he had been crouched, his black robes gray from the dust. "You have the sword?" he asked Aaron shortly. Aaron placed his hand on Scala's hilt and Nah'dar nodded. "Then let us leave this place."

Without a backward glance, Nah'dar turned and began to traverse the marble stairway, his scimitar still drawn.

The other three followed, Alyen still glancing nervously at the dragons monitoring their progress. As they neared the edge of the crater, Alyen saw that Nah'dar was stopped at the end of the stair, blocked from exiting by the largest dragon present, an enormous creature with scales of midnight black, three great horns, a spiked tail, and claws and fangs of glinting steel. Despite her best efforts, Alyen trembled as they drew even with Nah'dar, but Aaron was calm as he mounted the final step. Alyen was dimly aware that Brother Hugh had tucked her hand into the crook of his elbow, smiling serenely as he patted her fingers.

Aaron stood before the dragon, drew Scala from his belt, and knelt to one knee, both his hands on the sword's hilt, the tip touching the ground before him like a squire taking his vows of knighthood. The dragon regarded him, and Alyen could see Aaron's figure reflected many times in its gaze as his image scattered through each facet of eyes that shone like jet-black jewels. Then the dragon spoke, and its voice rang through the mountains of Norhelm, a deep resounding tone.

"Hail, Aaron of Doclann, Second Slayer, true heir to Scala, the blade of Thor Lynn, who was mightiest of Slayers, and humblest of men."

"Hail, Visrath, King of Norhelm, wisest and most powerful of dragons. I seek your blessing to claim the weapon of Thor Lynn, though it chose the hand of another to remove it from its place of rest," Aaron intoned.

There followed a profound silence as the dragons stood motionless, all gazing intently at Aaron. Finally, Visrath spoke again.

"If not you, then who is the one who took Scala from the tomb's wall?"

"It was Alyen of Dúr," Aaron said, motioning to the figure at Brother Hugh's side. "Princess of Dúramair and future Keeper of Scales."

"And if it was she who first took up the blade," Visrath continued, "why is it you who carries it now?"

Aaron swallowed. "Once removed, the blade burned like fire at Alyen's touch," he said. "Yet it remains cool in my grip."

Another silence followed. Alyen had the distinct impression that the dragons had not anticipated this turn of events and possibly didn't know what to do about it.

"I don't claim to be the Second Slayer," Aaron continued suddenly. "I ask only your permission to bear this noble blade in defense of Dúramair. To wield it against the darkness that threatens our land."

There followed the longest silence yet. So long that Alyen heard Brother Hugh start to hum softly beside her and she quickly squeezed his arm to hush him.

The massive black dragon finally spoke again. "And in claiming this blade, will you swear to honor the legacy of the one who first bore it? Will you swear to carry it to preserve the Balance of our shared world, to wield it for truth, to strike every blow in the name of justice?"

"I swear this upon my heart," replied Aaron, and Alyen heard in his voice that they were not empty words.

"Then you may pass from this place with my blessing. So may the woman, as her destiny also is bound to Scala. But what of your other companions? They, too, have penetrated deep into our secret realms, but they do not share your destiny, nor can they share your oath. The one in black, in particular, carries unrest within."

Nah'dar looked thunderous at these words, but Aaron hesitated only slightly before he answered.

"My companions are all true of heart, and each has helped us on our quest. Nah'dar has been our faithful guide and taught me how to defeat ancient forces of darkness. And without Brother Hugh, we would surely have perished, either from drought, or at the hand of the sphinx."

Visrath fixed his glittering gaze on each of them before speaking, his voice ringing through the cliffs. "So be it. I grant all four safe passage through Norhelm. Go with my blessing, and through your hands, may the scales once more be balanced."

With a deafening roar, the dragons all leapt into the air, giant leathery wings beating at the sky in a sudden flurry of dust. Within moments, they had all disappeared into the mountains of Norhelm. The air was still once more, and the rocky plateau was empty.

Aaron rose from his knee as Alyen nearly sank to hers. They walked slowly back to the horses, who were stomping and snorting in agitation from the arrival and departure of the dragons. Alyen, feeling the strength slowly return to her legs, looked up at Aaron's face. "Was that enough to convince you?"

"Of what?"

"That you're the Second Slayer."

Aaron frowned slightly. "Should it have? I—"

But he cut his sentence short as he suddenly groped for his hearing stone and in the same moment, Alyen felt hers burning against her skin beneath her dress. Quickly, she fished the stone out and clutched it in her hand.

"Lirianna?"

"*Alyen? Aaron? Are you there*"? Lirianna's voice sounded panicked in Alyen's head.

"*Yes, we're here. What's wrong?*"

"*I've only just seen it. Everything changed. A great black army, and mountains, not the moor …*"

"*Lirianna, what does it mean? What's happening?*"

"*It's Ylvain. We thought she was coming to Castle Dúr in the spring, but she's changed her mind. She's coming now, and straight for you!*"

28

A DESPERATE MOVE

The wind whipped at Alyen's cloak as she grasped Aaron's arm and pulled herself up the last few inches onto the flat cliff top. They turned to join Nah'dar, who was already gazing solemnly to the west. Norhelm rose from a sea of pine green, and at the edge of the forest, a wide grassy plain stretched to the horizon. And on the plain, not more than a day's ride away, a sprawling black army glistened in the cold sunlight, inching its way closer and closer to the edge of Sheanen Crann.

"Are all those morkshai?" Alyen asked, horrified.

"They are," Nah'dar confirmed, his voice devoid of expression.

"Can we outrun them?"

"We could, Princess, but we would not reach Castle Dúr with sufficient time to prepare a defense before the army would arrive."

"Then we need a way to delay them," Aaron said.

Nah'dar turned his head to look at him. "And how do you propose we do that?"

"I don't know. What about some kind of barricade? A wall of some sort?"

"Anything large enough to stop that army would take months to build, if not years," Nah'dar said flatly.

"Well, what's your suggestion, then?"

"I have none," Nah'dar said simply, turning his face back to the plain. "I no longer see that there is any hope for Dúramair. I suggest we ride for the coast and book passage on a ship to the Eastern Kingdoms. With any luck, the darkness will not follow."

"And what about Dúramair?" Aaron asked hotly. "We can't abandon everyone here!"

"We have no choice, Slayer. There is nothing we can do."

"So, your solution is to give up?" Aaron shouted.

"A true warrior knows when he has lost. As I said, there is nothing we can do."

Aaron continued to shout but Alyen had stopped listening. Was it her imagination, or could she hear, faintly, the screams of the morkshai, carried on the wind that whipped about her ears? She stood, her gaze fixed on the black army, sensing that somewhere within the sprawling mass, Ylvain was inching her way ever closer. With a chill that ran down her spine, Alyen reached out across the distance between them and felt the bonds of dark magic leashing the morkshai tightly to Ylvain's will, holding them in check until she would loose them in a wave of destruction and death. *She's powerful,* Alyen thought. *But so am I. Think, Alyen, there has to be something you can do.*

Nah'dar was right. There was no time to build a wall.

But perhaps …

It would be incredibly risky—and far beyond anything she had ever done or even thought to try. But it wasn't as if she was taking on the whole army—or even just Ylvain—by herself. All they needed was a bit of time, an obstacle, a delay. And if it worked, it could save the entire kingdom. If not …

But either way, there didn't seem to be another option.

Alyen knelt on the cliff top and spread her hands on the cold granite rock, sending her thoughts down, down, deep into the earth. She pushed all doubts out of her mind—she could not afford to worry about the consequences of what she was about to do. She must simply focus and act.

She closed her eyes, stretching her mind farther and farther downward until at last she felt the faint, telltale tingle she sought. She locked onto it, took two steadying breaths, and began to whisper.

"Gnomes who dwell in places deep, beneath the earth, below our feet …"

The tingle from below surged upward, touching on Alyen's mind, nearly overwhelming her, but she gritted her teeth and harnessed it. The sudden wave of power was immense, vast, and heady, and she gasped with surprise and elation as her chest and arms expanded, invincibility coursing through her veins.

"I come to you in greatest need and beg of you my words to heed …"

Alyen continued her fervent whispering, unaware of the sweat beginning to bead on her forehead, not noticing when her outstretched arms began to shake. So, *this* was what real magic felt like! Fierce and blazing, boundless and *wonderful*. She pushed her mind again, farther than ever before, reaching ever deeper into the earth and farther outward toward the plains and Ylvain's advancing army.

She was unaware when the earth began to tremble, causing Aaron and Nah'dar to cut off their argument abruptly and look about wildly in alarm. She didn't hear their shouts or see them fall to their knees as the trembling from below increased to a rumble, then a roar.

"… help me stop this evil's path, crack the earth, delay its wrath! You alone are our last hope …"

Alyen strained to contain the massive force she had gathered until the very last second, blind and deaf to the world around her, pouring sweat, veins throbbing and bulging from her forehead. There was a deafening crack, the earth heaved, and Alyen crumpled. All was black.

Hours could have passed, or days—Alyen had no way of knowing as she flitted restlessly in and out of consciousness. Her world was a black void, a chaotic swirling of half-heard voices, glimpses of faces, and the nightmarish sensation of running while mired in mud, screaming only to find she had no voice. Now and then she caught a flash of what might be reality—a glimpse of trees moving above her against a bright white sky, Aaron's and Brother Hugh's familiar faces hovering above her. She could hear their voices … they were worried. She tried to focus, strained to grasp onto the sounds with her mind, to use them as an anchor … but the effort was too great and she would slip back into confused oblivion, the voices and faces fading to black.

When her eyes at last did open, Alyen was certain she was

hallucinating. She was in her own bed in her old room at Castle Dúr. There were the familiar walls, the arched doorway; there was her hearth with a fire crackling merrily within. She stared at it a moment, her mind slowly registering the salamandars dancing in the flames. *That's a good sign*, she thought, although her mind couldn't quite latch on to the reason she would think so.

Alyen flexed her fingers experimentally, feeling the soft blankets covering her, tracing the small furrows of stitches running in patterns through the quilting. *Perhaps I should try to sit up*, she thought, noting curiously how large an endeavor some part of her seemed to think such an undertaking would be. After contemplating it a few more minutes, she decided to give it a try, and awkwardly struggled to prop herself up on her elbows.

A wave of vertigo hit her full force as spots danced before her eyes, her arms trembled under her weight and she fell back onto her pillows, her breath absurdly labored. The attempt, however, seemed to trigger a chain reaction of commotion throughout her room.

"Alyen!"

"Your Highness!"

"Bridget, quickly! Fetch a cool cloth and some broth. Alyen?"

"Right away, Your Majesty."

"Alyen, love. Can you hear me?"

Cool hands touched her cheeks and forehead, then her mother's face swam into view, tear-streaked and beautiful, and Alyen could only blink and swallow, trying to find her voice to reply. A tray clinked on the table by her bed, then Bridget's rosy, anxious face appeared beside her mother's. A cool, damp cloth was draped across her forehead and one of her mother's arms came around her back, lifting her gently as Bridget propped an extra pillow behind her.

"Here, Alyen, try to take just a sip of this."

A spoon touched her mouth and Alyen managed to part her lips, letting the warm broth trickle down her dry throat. After several minutes and a few more spoonfuls, Alyen managed to speak, her voice a hoarse croak.

"Mother?"

"Yes, my dear." Relief etched each line of her mother's face.

"How ... how long?"

Her mother's voice was gentle as her fingers lifted strands of hair away from Alyen's eyes. "It's been at least three weeks, love."

Three weeks. She had lost three weeks. What had happened, what had she been doing? Her mind struggled to remember, her brow furrowing. The queen was quick to soothe.

"Shush, now, don't worry about anything right now. Everything's going to be fine, and everyone got back safely— Aaron, Nah'dar, and Brother Hugh are all here.

Aaron. Nah'dar. Brother Hugh. Norhelm and Scala and the dragons. Memory snapped into place.

"Ylvain," she croaked anxiously. "The morkshai ..."

"Shh," her mother reassured. "All delayed and, for now, a safe distance away. We can go over all the details later, but now you need to rest and eat and regain your strength."

"So ..." Alyen whispered, already exhausted from the effort of forming words. "It worked?"

Queen Réanna smiled. "It seems so, Alyen. You almost killed yourself in the process, but it appears you saved us all."

After swallowing more broth, Alyen slept once more and awoke as the sun was sinking low in the sky outside her windows. At Bridget's urging, she managed another bowl of broth and even a few nibbles of bread. Though still tired, her head felt much clearer after the food, and she managed to struggle up into a sitting position before Bridget left to clear her soup tray.

Alone, Alyen surveyed her room carefully. The salamandars still swayed in the hearth and several sylphs were drifting in the air. A basin by her bed held a small pool of water, and one or two undines splashed around the rim. Alyen breathed a sigh of relief, but her thoughts were serious. This had been close. Far too close. Not only had she almost died, but her mind could have been completely broken. Her connection to the elemental world could have been lost forever. She had tried to control too much magic at once—stretched far beyond her powers, which were, after all, still quite new. She had been lucky, but she must not rely on such luck again. At least her plan had worked, and no permanent damage had been done.

But what had she done? She knew what she'd *meant* to happen—she had meant to split the earth around Ylvain and her hoard, trapping the morkshai on an island of rock. Certainly, it would not hold them forever, but it would have given Alyen and her companions time to escape and make a new plan. Alyen strained to recall what had actually happened when she called upon the gnomes from the cliffs of Norhelm.

In her memory, there was just the earth shuddering, then blackness.

That, and power. And the fierce *joy* of harnessing it.

A soft tap interrupted her thoughts. Aaron's head peered cautiously around her half-opened door.

"Aaron!" Alyen croaked. She hastily cleared her throat.

"Can I come in?" he asked, stepping just inside the door.

"Of course."

"I heard you were awake. Bridget didn't want to let me up, so I waited until I saw her leave. If you're too tired I can go."

"No, come in," Alyen said, motioning weakly at a nearby chair. Aaron pulled it to the edge of her bed, sat, and to Alyen's surprise, grasped her hand in both of his and kissed her fingers, squeezing tightly.

"Alyen, we were so worried. I—was so worried." His face was grave and Alyen noticed that it looked more drawn than the last time she had seen him.

"I'm all right now," she said, feeling suddenly shy. "What happened? How did we get here?"

"Well," Aaron began, "you fell. You were shouting in the singing speech and suddenly the ground was shaking and you just … fell. We thought you had died. When we realized you were alive, we tried to wake you. Brother Hugh even waved some sort of smelly plant under your nose, but nothing worked. We waited until nightfall but when there was no change, we decided to try to get you back to Castle Dúr as quickly as possible. We bought a wagon in the nearest village and arrived here a few days ago."

A disturbing realization was slowly dawning in Alyen's mind. "We were on the road for three weeks?"

"Roughly, yes."

"So, you must have fed me?"

"We managed to get a little broth and water down your throat every now and then. Brother Hugh rode with you in the wagon. He took really good care of you, considering the circumstances. I helped, too, whenever we stopped."

"And … and when I had to be … washed?"

Alyen felt herself blush, wondering how much of her Aaron may have seen while she was unconscious, and in what state.

Aaron's cheeks flushed as well, and his eyes flicked downward. "Brother Hugh insisted on taking care of it himself. He was very protective. Especially around me."

Alyen nodded, feeling somewhat relieved. "And Ylvain? Has she been held up long enough for us to plan?"

Something shifted in Aaron's eyes as he raised them once more to Alyen's. A chill raced down her back.

"Oh, yes," he said, his reassuring smile slightly too tight to be natural. "Ylvain won't make it here for at least another month."

So long? At best, my plan would have held her up only a couple weeks …

"Aaron, what happened? What did I do?"

Aaron quickly began rubbing Alyen's hand in his own. His face relaxed, but the strangeness was still in his eyes. Was it fear?

"Don't worry, everything's fine. You stranded Ylvain, just as you wanted. You gave us time to escape and make a plan. As far as everyone's concerned, you're a hero."

Then what is it you're not telling me? Alyen wanted to ask, but at that moment, Bridget's voice cut across her thoughts.

"I thought I told you to wait until the Princess is feeling stronger?"

"It's fine, Bridget, I asked him in ..." Alyen tried to say, but Bridget would hear none of it and Alyen realized as a wave of exhaustion suddenly hit that she was too tired to argue.

"I'll come back as soon as I can," Aaron assured her as he stood to leave. Alyen smiled weakly. She closed her eyes to rest as Bridget bustled about, tidying the room, feeling she didn't really want to talk anymore. If no one would tell her what had really happened in Norhelm, she would have to find out for herself—and she would need her strength to do it.

WAR COUNCIL

The next day Alyen woke feeling stronger and more alert. She felt around her neck and was relieved to find her hearing stone still hanging on its chain against her skin. She grasped it in her hand and sent her thought out. *"Lirianna?"*

"Alyen!" Her friend's voice exuded relief. *"I heard you were awake. Are you all right?"*

"I've been better," Alyen replied honestly. *"But I think I'll be fine."*

"I'm so glad. I've been worried sick for weeks."

Alyen decided to get straight to the point. *"Lirianna, what happened in Norhelm? What did I do?"*

There was a slight pause and Alyen's mouth tightened in a thin line as her stomach knotted. Lirianna wasn't going to tell her the truth either.

"You did just what you meant to do. You held up Ylvain."

Alyen knew it was futile but decided to press once more.

"Yes, but what exactly *did I do? No one will tell me and everyone's acting strange."*

"Well, you called up the gnomes, didn't you? They cracked the earth and ... and now Ylvain's delayed and ..." Alyen could hear the faint note of panic in Lirianna's thoughts as she scrambled for words.

"All right, thanks, Lirianna," she broke in. *"That's all I needed to know. Can we talk more later? I think I need to rest some more."*

"Of course." Lirianna sounded relieved. *"I'm here whenever you need me."*

Alyen dropped her hearing stone and let out a long breath. Lirianna's awkwardness had confirmed her fears—something had happened in Norhelm she didn't know about, and it wasn't good.

Slowly, Alyen hoisted herself into a sitting position, her bare feet dangling off the edge of her bed. They looked pale and thin, she thought—probably all of her looked pale and thin. Undoubtedly, she would be weak and would need to pace herself, but first she must concentrate on getting out of her room. Bridget was nowhere to be seen, but Alyen knew it wouldn't be long before she appeared with food or freshly cleaned clothing, or a basket of knitting—or any number of other excuses to keep Alyen trapped where she was.

Alyen found a simple gown in her wardrobe and clumsily fumbled through dressing herself. Once on, the dress felt loose; a glance in the mirror confirmed her suspicions—she did, indeed, look drawn and sickly. But aside from dragging a brush through her hair once or twice, she didn't waste any time trying to remedy the situation. Instead, she slid her feet into a pair of warm slippers and half walked, half stumbled into the corridor.

Dúramair had been at peace Alyen's entire life—in fact, it had been at peace for almost a century. So Alyen wasn't entirely sure what the routine was supposed to be in a time of war. However, she suspected that if plans were being devised to fight Ylvain and her morkshai, likely everyone would be meeting in the war council room. Given her weakened state, Alyen knew she could never simply walk into the council and hope to discover anything before being sent away back to bed. But if her father *was* meeting in that particular room, there was hope.

Alyen walked slowly through the halls, choosing routes she hoped would have little traffic, and eventually came to one narrow corridor she knew hadn't been used in years. She slid a torch out of a sconce and turned down the dark twisting passageway. She followed the corridor deeper and deeper into the castle until finally she stopped in front of an old wooden door on her left, cobwebs limply draping its iron handle.

Alyen slid her torch into a nearby sconce and frowned at the rusty door hinges. If she remembered correctly, the war council room lay on the other side of this door, which once had been a servants' entrance. If Alyen followed the corridor farther, she would eventually reach the kitchens. However, with the servants' entrance so long out of use, eventually a large tapestry had been hung across the wall of the war council room, covering the door completely from the inside. Alyen had hoped to prop the door open and listen through the tapestry from the corridor, undetected—but she had not counted on rusty hinges, which would surely give her away if they squealed as she opened the door.

Alyen gripped the door handle and, holding her breath, slowly depressed the latch and began to inch the door open.

Peeking through the crack, she saw that her memory had served her well. A tapestry hung across the doorway inside the room and from the other side she could hear a murmur of voices. Alyen managed to prop the door open a couple feet before the hinges began to groan, making her quickly release the handle and freeze. She listened intently, but the murmuring voices did not break. After several tense moments, Alyen released her breath and sidled through the partially opened door, careful not to disturb the tapestry.

The weaving was old and thin, and Alyen found that if she focused her eyes in a certain way, she could dimly make out the scene in the room before her through the aging threads. There were six—no seven people present: her father sat at the head of the table next to her mother, Nah'dar and Aaron sat to one side and on the other sat Garret, Yoran, Captain of the Guard, and Finn, the Master Armorer. On the wall opposite from Alyen hung a large map of the kingdom—but, no, it couldn't be a current map. There was a long, dark gash across it where Alyen knew the towns of Corin and Plinth and a number of villages stood. She tried to squint harder through the tapestry but could get no clearer view and focused instead on the discussion around the table.

"With so many morkshai to control, Ylvain will have to advance slowly." Nah'dar was speaking. "Even so, once she has circumvented Alyen's obstacle, which should happen within the next week or so, we will have four weeks at best until she reaches Castle Dúr."

So, it was true, Alyen realized. Whatever Nah'dar meant by her "obstacle," it was delaying Ylvain much longer than she had anticipated. With a shiver of apprehension, she continued to listen as her father spoke.

"In that case I want us to count on one month for preparations—no more. Merrith has already been sent south where we've arranged passage for him and his family on a ship to the Eastern Kingdoms. Evacuations of the northern settlements will begin immediately. I want no one caught in Ylvain's path as she advances. Queen Réanna will oversee the arrangements. Nah'dar, can you train our knights to fight the morkshai within that time frame?"

Nah'dar's voice was unenthusiastic as Alyen listened intently through the tapestry.

"If I had one month with one highly skilled warrior, I may be able to give him a chance at defeating one morkush, maybe two. But to train an entire army with few skills to begin with against Ylvain's entire hoard? I would need a year at least, and even then, the attempt may be futile."

Yoran's gruff voice cut in, sounding ruffled. "I would hardly say our knights are unskilled ..."

"I mean no disrespect, Captain, but in this particular case they most certainly are. This will not be the kind of fight any of you have been trained or prepared for. Frankly, I see little hope for our victory."

An awkward pause, then Garret's voice. "Nah'dar is right. If we can't hope to defeat the morkshai in hand-to-hand combat, then we shouldn't waste our time and resources preparing to do so. But perhaps there's another way? Some way to streamline our attack against them without placing our knights directly in their path? A trap, perhaps, or a new kind of weapon?"

Finn spoke next. "You say the only way to kill a morkush is to burn out its heart with fire, correct?"

Nah'dar nodded.

"Then what if we could design a machine that would launch burning spears at the morkshai from a safe distance? The calibration would have to be delicately built since we'll need a high degree of aiming accuracy, but if it worked, we could potentially wipe out dozens of morkshai with a line of machines from the battlements without a single knight ever setting foot on the battlefield."

There was a general stirring in the room and Alyen heard a note of hope in her father's voice. "Nah'dar, do you think this plan could work?"

"It is … untraditional." He sounded doubtful.

"I think it's worth a try," Alyen heard Aaron say, and she strained to listen even more closely. "We must try something, after all, and we know the traditional ways won't work. I propose that construction on the machines begin immediately, and in the meantime, Nah'dar and I can train the knights in hand-to-hand combat, as a backup in case the launchers don't work. We'll likely need some warriors on the ground in any case, to fight the morkshai that get too close to the castle for the launchers to aim at their hearts."

"Agreed," King Stephan's voice was firm. "Nah'dar, Aaron, you will work with Yoran to establish a training strategy and schedule to begin immediately. Likewise, work should begin in the armory at once to design and build the launchers. Finn, use whatever resources are necessary. As to the evacuations, we must predict the route that Ylvain is most likely to take and concentrate on clearing those areas first."

Aaron rose to stand by the map on the wall, gesturing at the wide area in the Northlands that was blotted out. "Alyen's barrier stretches from the edge of Norhelm all the way to the western coast. Ylvain will either have to find a way to cross it

—unlikely—or navigate her hoard through Norhelm itself. I doubt she'll choose that path either, as she would risk further delay from an altercation with the dragons. This leaves her only one option: travel due west until she reaches the coast, swim her morkshai past the barrier, then continue on to Castle Dúr across the Searing Plain and the Moor of Moin."

Alyen's barrier? Reaching from Norhelm to the coast? A feeling of dread stole into Alyen's heart.

"And you're sure there's no way for Ylvain to cross the barrier directly?"

"I don't think so," Aaron replied. "The gorge Alyen created is several hundred feet straight down and almost a mile wide. Even if Ylvain were to find a path down, the morkshai aren't strong climbers."

Alyen's breath had stopped, panic erasing all caution. She whipped the tapestry aside and stumbled into the room, her eyes desperately scanning the map. A startled silence filled the room, then the king and queen were quickly on their feet.

"Alyen!"

"What are you doing out of bed?"

"This black area you've crossed off the map—what is that?" Alyen demanded, her voice trembling. Her question was met with silence.

"Is that the gorge? Is that my *barrier*?"

More silence.

Alyen spoke slowly and deliberately. "What happened to Corin and Plinth? All the rest of the villages?"

"Alyen …" her father started to say gently, but the softness of his tone threw Alyen into an even greater panic.

"What happened to all the people *living* in Corin, Plinth, and the villages?" Her voice was high and shaking now.

Her father was saying something. Her mother was crossing the room toward her. But their faces answered her question.

"No! No, I didn't mean … I never wanted … I …"

Alyen ran blindly from the room, deaf to the shouts behind her.

It was freezing on the battlements, and Alyen hadn't brought a cloak. She stood huddled against the frigid wind, looking out across the moor to the north where, somewhere beyond her sight, countless people and their homes had been devoured by the earth at her bidding.

She'd always known, at some level, that being a ruler meant she had to be prepared to sacrifice her subjects—her people—for the good of the kingdom if things ever came to war. But war hadn't been a reality for so long, she'd never thought it would actually happen. And even if it did, the people she would supposedly be sending to their deaths would be warriors—those who'd chosen to serve, knowing the risks involved and willing to take them on.

But she hadn't knowingly sacrificed these people. She'd lost control and killed them. And they hadn't been brave and willing knights. They'd been mothers, fathers, farmers, grandparents—children and babies. They'd been eating and working and playing, enjoying the day and planning for the future and suddenly … Alyen's face sunk into trembling fingers.

A hooded cloak fell about her head and shoulders. Strong hands turned her around and Aaron's arms came around her. Alyen didn't return the embrace but stood still and dry-eyed, her cheek pressed against the wool of Aaron's tunic.

"You shouldn't hug me," she said at last.

"Why not?"

"I don't deserve it."

"I don't think that's true."

"I'm serious. You shouldn't love me at all."

"But I do," was Aaron's simple reply. It was silly, Alyen thought, after all their past tentativeness to speak so plainly now. Absurdly, her eyes began to prickle, but she didn't deserve the comfort of crying and blinked the sensation away.

"I wasn't lying when I said everyone considers you a hero," Aaron said after a time. "Everyone knows you did what you had to do to save the kingdom."

"But I *didn't* have to," Alyen protested, pulling away and looking up into Aaron's eyes. "And I didn't mean to. All I meant was to trap Ylvain's army on a little island. Just to slow her down. I was so sure I could do it. But it was so *big* and overwhelming and I couldn't control it. And now hundreds of people are dead! I *killed* them! Do you think *they* all think I'm a hero? Or anyone else living in Dúramair for that matter? I'm not a hero, I'm a monster!"

"You're not a monster," Aaron said calmly. "You're a gifted healer and the next Keeper of Scales. You just happen to be very powerful, and you're still learning."

Alyen was staring bitterly at the moor again, shaking her head. "I can't be the Keeper of Scales after this, Aaron. I don't think I would even be allowed."

"Have the elementals disappeared?"

"No."

"Wouldn't they have, if you had really ruined things?"

Alyen paused before replying. "I don't know. Maybe."

Aaron hesitated. "You should cry, you know. Just let yourself be sad. We all know it's a terrible thing for you to deal with. It's why we didn't want you to know until you were stronger. I know it might seem tempting to walk away from it all, but you're still the next Keeper. You still have work to do. You need to grieve, and then move on."

Alyen's mouth began to tremble, and her eyes filled with tears. "But how can I?" she whispered. "Everyone will be afraid of me. *I'm* afraid of me."

"I'm not afraid of you," Aaron replied and pulled Alyen into his chest again as she began to cry. "And those who are won't be forever."

"There's nothing I can ever do that will make up for this!" Alyen sobbed, clutching the back of Aaron's tunic.

"Actually, the king and queen were hoping you would help with the refugees when the evacuations start. It's a lot to organize—everyone will need food, shelter, and certainly many will need the services of a healer. It might make you feel better to help the people you saved, and it will give them a chance to see your true nature."

Alyen was crying too much to reply, and Aaron didn't press the issue. They stood on the cold battlements until Alyen's sobs began to subside into shuddering sighs, and eventually Aaron pulled back and looked at Alyen's face.

"I probably look horrible," Alyen commented.

"You look exhausted. And cold. Let's get you back inside to your room."

Alyen nodded and allowed Aaron to lead her back into the castle and slowly down the corridors. "The launchers are a good plan," she said suddenly, with a loud sniff.

"I think so," Aaron replied, sounding encouraged.

"It didn't seem like Nah'dar thought they would work, though."

Aaron frowned. "Nah'dar hasn't been the same since Norhelm. Not because of you," he added quickly, seeing the look on Alyen's face. "I think it has something to do with the sphinx. He never answered her riddle. And remember what he said about the answer eating away at someone's soul if they didn't say it?"

"Do you think he'll be all right?"

"I hope so. We need to count on his help now. But he doesn't seem to care much about anything. And he always seems distracted."

Alyen hesitated. "So, did I miss anything else from the council? After I … left?"

"Not really," Aaron replied. "Mostly just plans for bringing Mother Brenwyn and Lirianna to Castle Dúr."

"They're coming here?"

"Yes, in fact they're going to arrive here later this week to help prepare for the battle; it will be easier to defend everyone if we're all in one place. Garret and a few of the knights are leaving for Monstar tomorrow to escort them."

A memory tugged at Alyen's mind, and she suddenly realized she'd never told anyone about Rowenna's final words the night she died.

"Aaron, I completely forgot—Rowenna warned me just before we left Monstar …" And she proceeded to tell Aaron about Garret's history with Ylvain.

"So that's what Rowenna's secret was," Aaron mused as he pulled a chair around to the bed. They had reached her room, and Alyen immediately burrowed into her warmest quilt. "I'm glad you told me."

"I still trust Garret. *Completely*." Alyen gave Aaron a hard stare. "Rowenna said herself that he'd never knowingly do anything to betray us. I just don't trust that Ylvain won't try to use him somehow."

Aaron nodded his understanding. "Don't worry, my faith in Garret is intact. But even the most honest person in the world can be manipulated by their past. Rowenna was right to warn us." He hesitated. "It might not be a bad idea to talk with him once he's back."

Alyen groaned. "That's not a conversation I want to have."

"I know, the two of you are close." Aaron's voice was gentle. "And it's messy and personal—in any other situation it would be none of our business. But we can't leave Ylvain any openings without checking. And you won't have to talk to him alone. Maybe all three of us should go?"

Alyen nodded, feeling suddenly weary. Aaron noticed and patted her leg through the thick quilt. "I think you should try to get some sleep," he said. "Besides, Bridget will probably be up with food soon and she'll kick me out again anyway."

Alyen gave him a tired smile and he stood to leave. "Will you be all right?" he asked, his eyes searching her face.

"Yes," she assured him. "I just need to rest."

Aaron nodded and left her room, promising to be back later in the day.

Alyen lay on her bed, still huddled in the quilt, staring into the fire in her hearth where salamandars swayed hypnotically. Despite what she had told Aaron, she was not all right. She wasn't sure she could ever feel all right again. She knew everyone expected her to feel better after the initial shock wore off since she had, after all, saved the kingdom. But none of them knew what it was to wield such power, to be so sure it could be controlled, that she could save everyone—and then to fail. There was no way to redeem what had happened. The only thing she could do was to bury her guilt deep within and, as Aaron suggested, try to help and protect as many people as possible—both from Ylvain, and from herself.

For if it happened once, it could happen again.

Never again, she vowed silently to herself and to the flames. *I must never let this happen again.*

30

PREPARATIONS

Alyen woke from her nap later that day and lay motionless in her bed, staring at the ceiling. There were two things she knew she must do: First, she must rally her strength and find her mother to begin preparations for the refugees. She would leave that for tomorrow morning, as her mother would probably send her back to bed today anyway. Second, she must speak with Lirianna. Alyen sighed. That one would not be so easily put off.

Knowing Aaron as well as she did, Alyen suspected he would have already spoken with Lirianna about the events of the morning, and likely told her Alyen was resting and not to be disturbed. Knowing Lirianna as well as she did, Alyen knew her friend would not be content to remain silent for long once she knew Alyen had learned the truth of her actions at Norhelm and would be all too eager to talk the whole thing over and make Alyen feel better. But Alyen didn't want to be made to feel better. In fact, she didn't want to talk with anyone about anything that had happened since leaving the Tomb of Thor Lynn ever again.

But it had to be done. And if Alyen reached out first, perhaps she could steer the conversation in a different direction than the one she knew Lirianna would want to take.

Alyen reached under her gown and pulled out her hearing stone.

"Lirianna?"

"Alyen! How are you feeling?"

"I'm fine, just tired."

"Aaron said you were sleeping …"

"I was."

"He said you had a rough morning?" Lirianna's voice was wary.

"Lirianna, I'm sorry, I just really don't want to talk about it. I'm fine, really."

"All right." Lirianna sounded doubtful, but thankfully she didn't push the issue. *"Just—I'm here if you need me."*

"Thanks. And I'm glad you're coming soon." It was true, and the comment had the distracting effect on her friend Alyen had hoped for.

"So am I! The abbey's in an absolute flurry getting everything ready for us to leave. You'd think we were heading off for the Eastern Kingdoms."

Alyen smiled. *"There can't be that much you need to bring. You are coming to a castle after all."*

"Yes, but we have to bring our looms and all our weaving things so we can continue working while we're there. Especially leading up to and during the battle."

"I see. How's your weaving been going lately? Have you seen anything?" Alyen asked, half hoping for news of Ylvain's plans and half afraid of what Lirianna might report of the north.

"*No, nothing really.*" Lirianna sounded tired. "*It's been mostly black for a while now—since Norhelm. Once in a while I get a glimpse of … of your gorge, but usually it's blank and all I get is the same unsettled feeling with nothing to show for it. I know everyone keeps hoping I'll find the answers we need — how Ylvain is working her magic, who she's working with … I feel like I'm failing.*"

"*You're not failing, Lirianna. You're a gifted Seer—I've watched you weave. And it shouldn't all rest on you. It's not your fault all records of dark magic were destroyed …*"

Alyen's voice trailed off and she paused, realization hitting. "*But they weren't all destroyed, were they? Not all of them. If Ylvain could find out about dark magic and how to use it, the information is still out there. And I know one of the places it's kept.*"

Alyen quickly described to her the shelf she had found so long ago in Monstar's library, just before Aaron had startled her off the ladder. The shelf that bore the heading "Dark Works."

"*Do you think you can find it?*" Alyen asked.

"*Yes, I think so,*" Lirianna replied. "*You want me to bring all the books?*"

"*Yes, just bring them all. It's not a very big shelf.*"

"*If you think they'll help …*"

"*I know it's a slim chance—it won't be the same as whatever Ylvain found—but it's the only idea I have. And we need to figure out who the real enemy is.*"

And if I can figure that out, Alyen thought to herself, momentarily releasing the hearing stone from her grip, *perhaps I have a chance at some tiny bit of redemption after all.*

⌘

Snow was falling over the moor when Alyen woke the next morning. It was odd, she thought, to look out at the peacefully drifting flakes beyond the walls when inside the castle, everyone was tensing for war. *What stupid games we humans play*, she thought as she dressed and swallowed some of the porridge Bridget had left by her bedside. Then, eager to distract herself before her mind had a chance to start tormenting her with its brooding, she left her room in search of her mother.

Queen Réanna was in one of the smaller studies, leaning over a map spread out across the table, occasionally jotting down numbers and notes on a sheet of parchment. She straightened when Alyen entered, smoothing back a wisp of hair that had escaped her crown. Alyen braced herself to ward off the expected flurry of maternal concern and caring she dreaded, but surprisingly it didn't come.

"Alyen," the queen said calmly. "How do you feel?"

"Tired," Alyen said truthfully. "But ready to work."

"If you need to rest a few more days, you're certainly entitled to it. I can manage here while you recover."

"No, I'd rather keep busy. Honestly I can't stand the thought of sitting around with nothing to do but think."

Queen Réanna nodded and crossed to Alyen, cupping her daughter's face in her hands. "You were raised to be a ruler, Alyen. Sometimes that means making sacrifices—even terrible, unintentional ones—for the greater good of our people. You saved thousands of lives. Remember that and try to focus on the blessings of your actions rather than the losses."

Alyen could think of nothing to say but nodded, and to her surprise, her mother said no more on the subject. Instead, she led Alyen to the table and began pointing out various refugee stations she had marked in red.

"Here's my plan thus far. The first refugees from the closest towns and villages will begin to arrive sometime next week. I don't want to settle anyone nearby with the battle coming, but Castle Dúr *will* serve as a temporary camp for everyone to pass through so we can count them, replenish their food and clothing, and care for the sick or injured. Then, we'll assign them to one of the long-term settlements farther south. Orphans, the elderly without families, or those needing the most medical care will be sent on to Monstar Abbey. The rest will be sent to one of these five main settlements ..."

My mother is strong—perhaps stronger than my father—and a wise ruler, Alyen thought as she listened and nodded her agreement. *Why did I never see that before?*

"I was hoping," Queen Réanna concluded, "that if I focus on overseeing the registration process and setting up the long-term camps, that you could coordinate food, clothing, and medicine for the temporary camp here. You can set the maids making extra socks, cloaks, and the like, and see if anyone skilled in leatherwork can be ready to make or repair shoes and belts. Tell everyone that all regular responsibilities are hereby put on hold and all efforts should turn toward whatever's necessary to aid the refugees. Food will be easy—we have plenty of stores and you'll just need to establish a plan with Nellie and Brother Hugh ..."

"Nellie and Brother Hugh?" Alyen cut in.

A smile played at the corners of the queen's mouth. "Of course, you wouldn't know. Brother Hugh joined the kitchen staff not long after you arrived. Apparently, he and Nellie are *quite* taken with each other."

Alyen was speechless. "*Nellie?* And *Brother Hugh?*"

Her mother laughed. "Yes. He still insists on wearing his monk's garb, but I don't think anyone has any doubt that Brother Hugh's monastic days are over."

Nellie and Brother Hugh? Alyen thought to herself as she made her way through the castle later that day. *I didn't see that one coming.*

As she approached the doors to the kitchens, she couldn't help smiling at the all-too-familiar sounds issuing from within between the clanging of pots and pans.

> *"Ooooooooooooh, a bonny girl I chanced to meet,*
> *A derry derry dally,*
> *She bakes me pies and cakes so sweet,*
> *I've found love in the valley!"*

Alyen pushed open the doors and was welcomed by Brother Hugh's round beaming face and a smiling Nellie whose cheeks were flushed more than was warranted by just the heat from the stoves and fires.

"Alyen, my dear girl! I can't tell you how glad I am to see you up and about!" Brother Hugh exclaimed as he threw his arms around her shoulders, completely mindless of the spots of sauce dribbling down the front of the flowery apron he had tied around his brown robes.

"Brother Hugh!" Alyen said, surprised herself at how glad she was to see him. "I owe you a 'thank you' for taking care of me on the way back from Norhelm. I think you saved my life."

"Oh, my dear, don't even mention it. It was the least I could do to return the favor."

"Favor?"

"Of course! I don't expect I can ever properly repay you, but I am glad I could be of some help."

"Repay me for what?"

"Why, for convincing the others to bring me along on your adventure, of course!" Brother Hugh explained as if it were obvious, and he leaned in conspiratorially as Nellie bustled about the kitchen making preparations for dinner. "Perhaps you haven't heard," he continued in a loud whisper, "but I have happened upon love in the most unexpected of circumstances. I have met my match, one could say—and it's all thanks to you!"

"I ... oh! Well, I can't take credit for that, but I'm glad you're happy."

"Happy? I'm beyond happy, my dear!" Brother Hugh crowed. "I'm downright jubilant! Blissful! Really, when I think that only months ago, I was alone in the forest with only Ferdinand as company—well, let's just say this is more than I ever hoped for in life," he finished, smiling contentedly about him.

"And—how is Ferdinand?" Alyen asked, to be polite.

"Ferdinand? Haven't seen him in days. Doesn't come around much anymore—prefers the outdoors I expect. Ah, well. I do wish him well."

"I see. Well, Brother Hugh, I need to talk to you and Nellie about preparing food for the refugees."

"Oh, yes! I heard we're about to have quite a bit of company. Nellie, my dear!" he called across the kitchen as he led Alyen to a seat at the table. "We must plan with Alyen. There's a feast to prepare!"

Alyen smiled, shaking her head inwardly. *At least Brother Hugh is happy*, she thought. *And maybe even sane.*

Mother Brenwyn and Lirianna arrived three days later, escorted by Garret and a few knights of the castle guard. Behind them creaked a wagon, heavily loaded with both Seers' looms, personal effects, and a crate of old, dusty books that Aaron gallantly lugged through the corridors to one of the smallest and least-used studies.

"Are you sure you don't want this in your room?" Aaron puffed as he heaved the crate up a stairwell. "Or in the library?"

Alyen nodded firmly. "I'm sorry it's so far to carry, but there are too many servants everywhere else, and I don't want anyone picking through them."

"Yes, these are some seriously unpleasant-looking books you made me bring, Alyen," Lirianna commented from behind.

"I just hope they have something useful," Alyen said. "We can start going through them this evening after you and Mother Brenwyn get settled."

"And in the meantime," Aaron said with a glance at Alyen, "we should decide how we want to approach the issue with Garret."

Alyen's heart sank. They had briefed Lirianna on Rowenna's warning about Garret and Ylvain via hearing stone before the party had left Monstar. They had all agreed to keep the secret between themselves—after all Mother Brenwyn already knew, and they didn't want to risk Garret's reputation further. But Lirianna had agreed that doing nothing was too risky, and it seemed that a discussion was inevitable.

"I don't want to do it alone," Alyen said. "But I don't want him to feel attacked if we all confront him at once either."

Lirianna pursed her lips. "Why don't just you and Aaron go. He knows you two best and he might be more open with fewer people there. I'll help Mother Brenwyn get everything settled in here and you can fill me in when you're done."

They had reached the study and Aaron hoisted the crate of books onto one of the desks with a thud. He turned to Alyen. "We might as well get it over with."

Alyen sighed and nodded. "All right. Let's go."

The stables were warm with the heat of horses and braziers of coals; still Alyen rubbed at her arms and hands nervously as they entered. Aaron pushed the wide doors closed behind them and Garret emerged from the tack room at the noise.

"Hello, Garret," Alyen said, fighting for a smile. "Welcome back."

"Your Highness." Garret looked at Aaron, his eyes flickering over the closed stable door. He nodded. "She told you, then. You've come to ask about Ylvain."

Alyen looked down guiltily.

"We have," Aaron said, his voice sounding much more confident than Alyen felt. "We were hoping you would tell us about her. About how she thinks, or how she might work ..."

"We wouldn't dream of asking you," Alyen said raising her face. "It's just that ..."

"Just that you have a kingdom to protect, and you have to make sure that I can be trusted," Garret said, his voice gentle and resigned. Alyen's brow knit together, and she opened her mouth to protest, but Garret raised his hand stopping her.

"It's all right, cailínna. I was half-expecting you to show up. You wouldn't be doing your job if you didn't. Why don't you both come back and have a seat."

They all filed into the tack room and found seats on stools and crates. For the first time Alyen could remember, Garret made no move to busy his hands with repairs or polishing, but sat across from them, his face calm. Only the constant tracing of his fingers along the scars on the backs of his hands told Alyen that perhaps he wasn't as collected as he appeared.

"All right then," he said. "What would you like to know? You have my word that I'll not hold anything back."

Alyen glanced at Aaron and swallowed. "Well, firstly, please know that we trust you completely, Garret. We're just worried that Ylvain might try to—to use you somehow. To influence you, or trick you, or … Has anything happened recently that was out of the ordinary? Has she tried to contact you at all?"

Garret shook his head. "No. I've not heard from Ylvain since I left Ramsheath in my youth." His voice was steady, but Alyen noticed his fingers tightening around his hands.

"That's good," Aaron said. "Then we just need to watch for anything she might try as the battle nears." He paused. "Would you be willing to tell us what happened between you two? I know it's personal, but if we all know the history she has to pull from, it might help us spot trickery we would otherwise miss."

Garret took a long breath and nodded, squinting out the window at the pale winter sun. "There's not a lot to tell, actually." He shrugged. "I fell in love with Ylvain. It was foolish I suppose, but no one knew her cruelty then. So, I asked her to marry me and, to my delight and surprise, she agreed. She told me to light a fire at midnight atop a nearby hill and said that when she saw the flames, she would come so we could seal our betrothal vows. It was just the kind of dramatic idea she would suggest, and I was eager to please her, so I did as she asked.

"I climbed the hill that night, lit the fire, and suddenly the flames blazed and leapt out of control. The fire spread faster than anything I've ever seen—covered the whole hilltop in seconds and then started making toward the village. Luckily it was spotted, and everyone rushed out to douse it before any serious damage was done."

Garret fell silent. Alyen saw that his hands were clasped tight enough to turn his knuckles white, contrasting sharply against his scars. "Garret," she said quietly, "is that what happened to your hands?"

Garret looked down and unclenched his hands, his face bitter for the first time Alyen could remember. "Aye, cailínna. It all happened in a second when the fire spread. It was well for me that Sylvan and Rowenna were there; had lesser healers tended me, I likely would have lost the use of them. As it is ..." He flexed his fingers and shrugged.

"And what happened then?" Aaron asked. "Where was Ylvain?"

"Ylvain was nowhere to be seen until the fire was out. Once the danger had passed and everyone learned what had happened, I was ridiculed as a fool and ostracized. Ylvain wept and brokenly declared our engagement ended—no one would expect her to marry an idiotic boy who almost destroyed the village. And I almost believed it. I almost thought it really was my fault.

"But once we were alone, Rowenna started asking questions. Had I seen Ylvain during the fire? Had the blaze seemed ordinary? Had the grass been dry? It was the question about the grass that opened my eyes. The grass wasn't dry. It had been a rainy spring and it had stormed earlier that day. The grass was as lush and green as it could be. It shouldn't have caught fire at all, let alone spread so quickly—not without elemental help. So, we knew it must have been Ylvain."

"And that's when Rowenna told Sylvan she'd been teaching her," Alyen supplied.

"Aye, Rowenna and Sylvan left and I decided it would be best for me to leave, too. I found work in the stables of a noble family away from Ramsheath."

"But why?" Alyen asked. "It wasn't your fault. Didn't anyone else realize the grass was wet? Didn't you tell everyone it was Ylvain?"

Garret shook his head. "The damage was already done, cailínna. Ramsheath is a small village. When crisis hits, everyone looks for who to blame the quickest and no one asks too many questions. Even if I *had* accused Ylvain I would have been known forever as the boy who almost burned the village and then tried to blame it on a girl and her faeries. Besides, I didn't exactly fancy living too close to Ylvain after that." Garret looked intently at Alyen and Aaron, a fierce glow in his eyes. "I'll have nothing more to do with Ylvain. Not in this life or the next. I give you my word."

Alyen was quick to nod. "I know, Garret. And I'm sorry we had to ask."

"We'll stay alert for anything unusual—as much for *your* protection as anything else," Aaron assured. "And if anything happens, or if Ylvain tries to contact you, please tell us right away."

Garret nodded solemnly, features etched with unhappiness. Alyen's heart ached as they thanked him and took their leave. She hunched into her cloak with her head down as they walked back across the courtyard.

Aaron glanced at her. "He calls you cailínna?"

Alyen nodded. "He's never called me that in front of anyone else before. He must consider you very close."

Aaron said nothing. They walked in silence for a moment before Alyen continued.

"I hate this. Garret is like family to me. I know we did what we had to do, but now he's miserable. And I don't think we have anything to worry about from him anyway."

Aaron sniffed against the cold. "I'm not sure. I know Garret would never betray us intentionally," he added quickly, seeing Alyen stiffen. "But I'm worried that Ylvain may have an easier time influencing him than he thinks."

"Why?"

"He loved her. Even after the fire, I think a part of him still loved her."

"What? Didn't you see how angry he still is about it?"

"Yes, but he never told anyone it was her fault. He saved her reputation, even after she had destroyed his. What he said about it being better to just leave is probably true, but I think deep down he still loved her."

"How could he?" Alyen whispered.

Aaron looked at her, his eyes a flash of color against the

bleakness of winter. "She was his first love. First loves make a strong mark. You can't get rid of them easily."

For a second Alyen held his gaze and felt her insides race and melt at the same time. A yearning raged through her, and suddenly she wanted to cry. Abruptly she looked down again.

"Don't worry too much about it," Aaron said, his eyes taking in the slump of Alyen's shoulders. "I think Garret knows we trust him. We'll just be watchful and focus on getting everything ready for the battle."

Alyen nodded and straightened a bit. "Yes, the best thing we can do is figure out who Ylvain is working with. I just hope we'll find something in those books."

"We'll start searching tonight," Aaron promised as they reentered the castle's stone walls.

But leafing through the musty crate of books turned out to be a more difficult task than Alyen had anticipated. Many of the books were in poor repair, the writing so faded and the pages so tattered that only scattered sentences could be deciphered. At least half were in languages unknown to Lirianna and Aaron, and with Alyen possessing only passing skills, translation was made slow and arduous. Those that *were* legible were often written in such cramped, spidery script that it took forever to get through a single page, let alone a whole massive tome, let alone a whole crate of them. Midnight found Alyen, Aaron, and Lirianna red-eyed, exhausted, and discouraged, having discovered several unpleasant topics, but nothing that seemed relevant to the looming battle.

"Alyen," Lirianna yawned, rubbing her eyes, "we need to stop for tonight."

"I know," Alyen admitted. "But we only made it through a few books. We'll need to spend more time on it tomorrow."

Aaron and Lirianna exchanged a glance. "We can come back tomorrow night," Lirianna suggested. "But I have to weave with Mother Brenwyn all day, and Aaron needs to train with the knights."

"And you'll have refugees arriving any day now," Aaron added.

"But this is *important*," Alyen insisted. "Morten and Rowenna and Mother Brenwyn *knew* that Ylvain isn't acting alone, and without knowing who we're really fighting, everything else could be a complete waste of time. These books are the only chance we have of figuring it out!"

"But Alyen," Lirianna reasoned. "The dark magic is a *huge* subject. Ylvain and whoever she's working with—they could be doing *anything*. The chances of us finding it in one of these few books are …" Lirianna trailed off and shrugged, her face apologetic.

Alyen turned to Aaron, hoping he would take her side, but the silence that filled the room as he hesitated answered her question. Alyen bit down on the disappointment that filled her mouth. She reached for a lamp and stood to leave.

"It's not that we don't agree with you, Alyen," Aaron protested. "We can still help in the evenings."

"Yes, there's just a lot to prepare, and I might have more luck finding something with my weaving anyway …"

"It's fine," Alyen said flatly as she reached the door. "I'll see you both tomorrow."

Alyen closed the study door behind her, a bit louder than she had intended, and stalked down the halls to her room. *It doesn't matter*, she told herself. *If the answer is here, I can find it without their help. And I'm the one who needs to redeem myself anyway.*

31

THE OTHER PROPHECY

The refugees started to arrive at Castle Dúr, first in small groups, then in larger numbers each day. Soon Alyen found that most of her time was spent tending to wounds and illnesses, and mixing new batches of medicines, salves, and poultices to replenish her constantly depleting stock. She found there was some truth to Aaron's words—the act of helping and healing those in need did take a slight edge off the guilt she carried with her at all times, and she was relieved to see that, apart from the occasional wary glance or half-concealed whisper, the refugees were mostly just grateful for the shelter, food, clothing, and medicine Alyen could give them. But though the elementals were always present around her as usual, Alyen could not bring herself to utter a word in the singing speech; even the thought of reaching out to ask for help with her medicines felt like a knife twisting in her belly. She tried to convince herself she wasn't afraid—that no challenge she faced in the castle walls was more than she could handle without magic. Bad coughs, sprained wrists—they might have healed a few days faster with the help of the elementals, but if the end result was the same, did that really matter?

As the refugees began to demand more and more of her time, the crate of books in the study niggled more insistently at the back of her mind. Alyen found that Aaron and Lirianna had been correct: soon the only time she could spare to escape to the study was in the evenings, and progress remained maddeningly slow. True to their word, her friends returned each night to help, though Alyen knew they didn't really expect to find anything and came only to humor her. She began to stay in the study late into the night, long after the other two had retreated to their rooms. Still, she found nothing.

More than two weeks had passed when scouts began to arrive with the news that Ylvain had reached the western coast and had swum her morkshai past Alyen's barrier.

"That gives us about two weeks until they reach Castle Dúr," Aaron said when he brought her the news. Alyen looked up from the pot of salve she was stirring in alarm.

"But that's not enough time!" she exclaimed. "We still don't know who the enemy is."

Aaron flung his arms out in an exasperated shrug. "I know, but what else can we do? Lirianna's weaving constantly, I'm doing all I can to prepare the knights, and the refugees have to be out of the way before the battle starts."

"We need more time with those books," Alyen said, pursing her lips and cutting Aaron off with a glare when she saw he was about to argue. "It's our best chance, Aaron. Our *only* chance."

But as the days passed and the stack of books in the study dwindled, even Alyen began to lose heart. The nights she spent poring over horrible stories of monsters, demons, and dark magic grew longer and longer until she was barely getting any sleep at all before rolling out of bed at dawn. Her face, thin already from her weeks spent unconscious, became haggard and gray, but she shrugged off any show of concern from her friends or family.

"Alyen, *please* go to bed," Lirianna pleaded one night, well past midnight, as she and Aaron rose to leave. "You look *terrible.*"

"Thanks," Alyen said dryly, not looking up. "But no."

"You won't be able to help anyone if you run yourself into the ground," Aaron said.

Alyen looked up with a sharp glance. "And if I don't find what we're looking for, there won't be anyone left to help," she snapped. She turned her eyes back to her book, missing Lirianna's exasperated look at Aaron and his defeated shrug in return.

"Just don't stay up too late," Aaron said as they exited the room. Alyen did not reply.

The minutes ticked by, and Alyen shoved aside one book, then another. Eventually, she glanced at the hourglass; dawn would come in a couple hours, and she had not slept. Five books remained in the crate. She wanted to weep, but she was too exhausted and defeated for tears.

She reached down to retrieve the first text: a small book with a red cover and no title. Glancing inside, she registered what appeared to be an index of spells and incantations—not likely her best bet. The next book was a history of the founding of the Academy of Ancient Arts—she tossed it aside as well. Beneath that one …

The moment Alyen's finger brushed the book, a chill of recognition ran down her spine and she froze momentarily. She pulled the black-bound tome from the crate, set it on the desk, and pulled her lamp closer. Faded gold lettering formed a title in a language she couldn't read. She remembered this book. This was the one she'd been looking at when Aaron interrupted her in the library.

All traces of exhaustion gone, Alyen slowly opened the cover and began carefully flipping through the brittle pages. Just as before, the text was completely foreign. The illustrations, though, were beautiful and terrible, depicting raging giants and ogres, witches feasting from cauldrons filled with stews made of human flesh, and demons in black chariots riding ruthlessly over the naked bodies of peasants.

Suddenly she stopped turning the pages and sucked her breath in sharply. The illustration before her showed a cloud of black smoke, two fiery eyes burning orange from within. It was hardly graphic compared to the other drawings she'd flipped past, but for some reason this one sent a jolt of fear coursing through her bones. Alyen forced her eyes away from the picture and focused them on the text beside it. If only she could make out the words—even just a few of them—anything that might give them a clue. Aaron especially would need all the information he could get if he really was the Second Slayer …

Her eyes traced line after line, her mind sounding out the syllables in her head. *Tun vulnerisai feri a Thonus Fulmar exstitore…*

"*Alyen? Alyen what are you doing?*"

Alyen jumped. Aaron's voice in her mind had startled her into dropping her hearing stone she'd been absently fingering as she pored over the book. She quickly took it back into her hand.

"Aaron, I'm sorry, I didn't mean to wake you. I was just reading, and I must have been fiddling with my stone—"

"But what are you reading? I've never heard that story about Thor Lynn."

Alyen froze and didn't reply for a long moment.

"Alyen?"

"You can tell what I was reading?"

"Of course. My hearing stone woke me up—might have even burned me a little. And then I heard what you were just reading about the treachery of Thor Lynn coming to light—"

"Aaron, I had no idea what I was reading. It's in a language I can't even identify."

There was a long pause.

"Hang on, I'll be right there."

Minutes later Aaron hurried through the doorway, hair slightly rumpled but eyes sharp and bright. "Show me."

He sat beside Alyen and she shoved the book over to rest between them. Aaron's eyes scanned the page for a few moments in silence until Alyen couldn't restrain herself from asking, "Can you understand it? All of it?"

Aaron looked up, confusion lining his face. "Yes. Every word."

"How?"

"I have no idea. But it's as easy as reading Dúramairian. It's as if my brain doesn't even register the difference."

"Read it to me."

Aaron swallowed and began to read.

THE TREACHERY OF THOR LYNN

At the height of our Golden Age had the demon hoards conquered the Kingdom of Nethermair and all were under the dominion of the Demon Lord Malscath, most powerful, feared, and ruthless in all the forces of Darkness. Determined to bend all the kingdoms of the world to his rule, Malscath turned his attention to the eastern kingdom of Dúramair and sent forth his monsters to prepare the way for his armies. But though his monsters spread fear and terror throughout the realm, the warriors of Dúramair were skilled, and for three generations they succeeded in holding Malscath's forces at bay.

It was then that Malscath heard of a young magician from Dúramair who had forsaken his homeland to study those most ancient and noble arts in Nethermair's newly founded Academy. Malscath summoned this magician, thinking to make him an ally who would provide power and information, and so gain the upper hand in the coming war. The young magician, Thor Lynn, did indeed become Malscath's closest council and informed Malscath in all matters concerning Dúramair's forces, tactics, and weaknesses. Slowly did darkness begin to spread throughout the east.

When it seemed that Malscath's victory was certain, he gathered unto him his armies of demons. So valuable had Thor Lynn proved himself, that Malscath made the magician his general, bestowing upon him power over all his demon hoards. The vast army made ready to cross the sea to the island called Illya, whose castle was to be Malscath's fortress in the east. But before the ships of Malscath could sail, the traitor Thor Lynn did show his true loyalties. With words of magic that caused the earth to crack and the sea to rise, Thor Lynn did banish Malscath and all his demon hoards to the depths of the earth where they were to be entombed in cold stone for all of eternity. So great was the wrath of

Malscath, that earthquakes did plague the western lands for years, caused by his shrieks and howls of rage deep within the earth. But over time, the earth ceased to shudder and all presumed that Malscath had perished within his stony tomb.

But not even Thor Lynn himself knew that Malscath, the Lord of Demons, could not perish merely by means of force and time alone. Instead, a new prophecy was born, whispered through the stones that entombed the Demon Lord. Words that calmed the flame of Malscath's rage, though his hatred of Dúramair and its warriors would burn for all times. Patiently, then, does Malscath endure the passage of time, awaiting the day when he will once again be released by a true ally from the east and rise to sow his vengeance throughout Dúramair, seeking this time not to rule, but to destroy.

Aaron paused and glanced at Alyen. "It looks like they have the prophecy it mentioned as well." He read again.

Prophecy of the Second Rising

Though for centuries as a slave
You dwell entombed in stony grave,
Bide well thy time and nurse thy hate
For victory comes to those who wait.

A black star rising in the east
Shall be the key to night's release.
The scales will shift—a time will come
Two suns shall set to leave but one.

Then free at last, shall Malscath reign!

> *Yet, lest the light should rise again,*
> *Beware the one who wields the blade*
> *That was in peaks of Norhelm made.*

> *For unto this last hope light clings,*
> *And if the blade its victory brings,*
> *Shall darkness in the depths remain,*
> *Nevermore to rise again.*

Aaron's eyes stopped. Alyen's breath was coming fast and shallow, her fingers icy as they gripped the edge of the table in front of her. They looked at each other a long moment, neither finding the right words to express the enormity of the discovery. Suddenly Aaron's hand came fast to the back of Alyen's head and pulled her into a brief but fierce kiss, his lips nearly bruising her own. All too soon it was over, and when he released her, Aaron's eyes were shining.

"You found it, Alyen! This has to be it."

"*We* found it," Alyen corrected, her face flushed. "It's practically a sister prophecy. And it tells us who's really attacking Dúramair."

"We should call the others."

Alyen nodded, flustered, but Aaron was already pushing back his chair and getting to his feet. Alyen hastily scooped up the book and fumbled for her hearing stone.

"*Lirianna, Nah'dar, Mother Brenwyn!*" she sent her thought out urgently. "*Wake up!*"

"*Alyen?*"

"*What time is it?*"

"*Are you all right?*" came the confused and sleepy replies.

"*We found it. We know who we're fighting. You all need to meet us in the king and queen's chambers immediately. Aaron and I are already on our way."*

She didn't wait to hear an answer but dropped the hearing stone back beneath her gown. "Let's go," she said and hurried down the hallway, Aaron close behind.

Seconds later she was pounding on the door to her parents' rooms. It opened to reveal an alarmed and disheveled King Stephan in his dressing gown and slippers, holding a candle and squinting into the dark corridor.

"Alyen! And Aaron? What on earth is the matter?"

"I've called an emergency meeting," Alyen replied and held up the black leather book. "I think we've discovered who's really behind Ylvain's war. Lirianna, Nah'dar, and Mother Brenwyn are on their way now."

Within minutes the lamps and fires had been lit, and the whole group had gathered in the king and queen's sitting room. Dressing gowns and shawls had been hastily thrown over night shirts and everyone had bits of hair sticking up or flying loose—everyone, that is, but Nah'dar who looked as he always did in his black robes. All eyes were alert and focused on Alyen.

It didn't take long for Alyen and Aaron to explain what had happened, and once the book had been passed around for inspection, Aaron read the passage aloud once more to the assembled crowd. After he had read the final lines of the prophecy, silence filled the room. For a terrible moment, Alyen was afraid no one believed the story was true.

"It does all seem to fit," Mother Brenwyn said at last, and Alyen breathed a sigh of relief.

"Yes," agreed Lirianna. "I'm guessing that Ylvain is the 'dark star' the prophecy mentions—the 'true ally from the east.' After she left Ramsheath, she probably continued to dabble in dark magic, and eventually she went far enough that Malscath somehow got hold of her."

"They plotted from Illya—the place he originally intended to use as his fortress in Dúramair," Aaron continued. "And he used her to kill Morten and Rowenna, who would have been his most powerful enemies."

"'Two suns shall set to leave but one,'" Mother Brenwyn whispered sadly.

King Stephan suddenly held up his hand. "Wait, please, everyone. Let's not get ahead of ourselves. As astounding as this all may seem, there are a few questions that must be answered before we can take any action on the basis of this discovery. First, we must determine the authenticity of the book itself and whether the text is meant to depict an actual historic event. It baffles me that such a story involving our greatest hero would have been lost to us. And second, we must seek to uncover the reason for Aaron's understanding of the language. I, myself, can find no similarities to any language in current use."

"We must send for Professor Glibb," Queen Réanna decided. "He's our most renowned and learned scholar and if anyone can shed light on this book, he can."

King Stephan rang a bell, and a bleary-eyed page was sent to wake and fetch Professor Glibb.

The room was tense as they waited for the professor's arrival. No one spoke, and Alyen spent the time gazing out the windows, where a thin gray line on the black horizon announced that dawn would soon break over the moor.

"Professor Glibb," the king said, stirring Alyen from her thoughts. "Thank you for joining us at such an early hour."

"I was told it was a matter of some urgency, Your Majesty?" Professor Glibb drawled, sour as ever, though being woken up likely did nothing to help his disposition. He, too, was wrapped hastily in a dressing robe. Alyen noted the familiar ink spots still flecked his long nose. Apparently, they didn't wash off.

"Yes, we need you to examine a document. A book, actually, and one excerpt in particular that may concern the war we're facing. We need to know the origin of the text, whether or not it contains authentic, historic information, and anything else about it you may deem significant. As the kingdom's most learned scholar, any insight you can give us will be most gratefully received."

The compliment was artfully placed, and Alyen smiled inwardly as she saw her father's flattery ignite a spark in Professor Glibb's eyes, banishing most of the surliness from his features. Alyen handed her old tutor the leather book and watched Professor Glibb's face closely as he began his examination. His eyebrows rose quickly upon seeing the title and he spent several minutes examining the leather, the binding, and inhaling the aroma of the crackling pages before he turned his attention to the text itself.

His eyes roved over the pages Alyen indicated several times, and he flipped through the remainder of the book, studying the illustrations and lettering. Alyen was bursting with the desire to pepper him with questions, but she knew the professor well enough to know that interrupting his examination would only cause irritation, making him less willing to give them the full answers they needed.

After the better part of an hour had passed, Professor Glibb gently closed the book and finally looked up.

"You say this book was found in the library at Monstar?" he asked Alyen.

"Yes."

Professor Glibb turned to Mother Brenwyn. "Do you have any idea how such a text may have come to be acquired by the abbey?"

Mother Brenwyn shook her head. "I'm afraid not. Most of the books were collected generations ago and, to my knowledge, no records were kept of their origins."

"I see," Professor Glibb said, looking down again at the cover of the book, stroking it almost reverently.

"Can you tell us anything about it?" the king pressed. "Do you at least recognize the language?"

"I do. Astoundingly, this book is written in ancient Nethermairian—ancient enough to have been completely out of use for at least one thousand years. I myself know very little of it. It will unfortunately take several weeks of translation before an evaluation of its content and its historical accuracy can be presented."

"Well, fortunately, we have a way around that," Alyen said. "Aaron can read every word."

Professor Glibb's gaze focussed on Aaron as if seeing him for the first time. His expression was unreadable. "You can read this text?"

"Yes," Aaron replied.

"Have you somehow made previous study of ancient Nethermairian?"

"No."

"Then how have you come by the ability to read it?"

"I have no idea. We were hoping you could tell us."

Professor Glibb's eyes had narrowed slightly. Without

taking them from Aaron's face he held the book out to him. "Will you be so kind as to read for me the passage in question?" Alyen thought she detected a hint of accusation—or perhaps jealousy—in his voice.

Once more, Aaron read the text aloud, this time following the words with his finger as Professor Glibb watched over his shoulder. When Aaron had finished, the professor retrieved the book and began pacing slowly, muttering to himself under his breath. After a few moments, King Stephan interrupted. "Professor?"

Professor Glibb stopped pacing and looked up as if he'd forgotten the others were present. "Yes?"

"The text—is the book historic? Authentic?"

Professor Glibb's nose twitched. "Authenticity, Your Majesty, is not a thing to be declared lightly or in haste. Before I could state with confidence that the text is authentic, it would have to undergo a much more rigorous examination by myself, the results of which must then be corroborated by at least three other scholars, preferably from different kingdoms. The entire process would take months if not years."

Professor Glibb's voice took on a slight quaver of excitement as he continued, and his long fingers repeatedly stroked the cover of the book as if they could not remain still. "However, after my very brief and unconfirmed examination, I believe that what we have here may be one of the original tomes of historic records from ancient Nethermair that were kept under lock and key in the Academy of Ancient Arts for centuries. No one except for the high priests were allowed access and only one copy of each book was made. How this one ended up in Monstar is beyond my grasp, but if I'm correct, we are looking at one of the greatest scholarly discoveries to be found in Dúramair since —well *ever*, really."

"So, the events described in this book are likely true?" the king prompted.

"Recording these books was not merely a secretarial task in ancient Nethermair," Professor Glibb explained. "It was considered more of a sacred endeavor. The true texts themselves would be extremely accurate and the forgery of one would be considered the highest form of blasphemy, punishable by death. In addition, the lettering, binding, and illustration styles of this particular book are all congruent with those found in other western texts from antiquity. So, yes, the events it describes are likely accurate, at least from a Nethermairian point of view."

"But how is that possible?" Mother Brenwyn asked. "Everyone knows the legend of Dúramair's greatest Slayer, and this is the first anyone has ever heard of these events. How could we not know such a significant chapter of his life?"

Professor Glibb smiled. "History marks the passage of time, Abbess, but time is not always kind to history. Knowledge is often and easily lost, especially from times so long past. The legend of Thor Lynn, as widespread as it is, relates only a brief moment in the life of its hero, and it's a moment that occurs when Thor Lynn was well into manhood. The void that shrouds Thor Lynn's youth has long been one of the greatest scholarly mysteries, and many have searched their entire lives for any record of who the Slayer was before he took on that role. This, of course, only adds to the magnitude of this book's discovery, as I'm sure you can see."

"And do you have any idea why I can read it?" Aaron asked.

There was a pause as Professor Glibb studied Aaron again. "I have but one theory. May I be so bold as to inquire about your lineage?"

Aaron immediately stiffened beside Alyen. "My lineage? You mean—my parents?"

Professor Glibb nodded. "Your parents, yes, or the origins of other ancestors?"

"Why? What does that have to do with anything?" Aaron's voice was tense and Alyen understood why. He'd never mentioned his parents to her before that terrible night in the woods—and he likely only had as a result of the shock of Morten and Rowenna's deaths. Alyen wouldn't be surprised if she was, at least as far as Aaron knew, the only one in the room who knew the story of his childhood.

Professor Glibb gave an apologetic nod. "I only ask, Slayer, because it may explain your inherent talent for deciphering a long dead language. You see, Nethermairians have always claimed to possess a phenomenon they refer to as "blood memory." Essentially, they believe that knowledge can be inherited by blood and lie dormant in the brain, unbeknownst to the carrier, until such time as it is needed—usually in a time of hardship or crisis. So, for instance, when faced with a gravely ill child, a woman may suddenly "remember" a life-saving remedy last known by her great-grandmother one hundred years prior. Now, granted, confirmed cases of this actually occurring are quite rare and mostly unsubstantiated. However, it *would* explain things in this specific case, *if* ...""

There was a pause, then Aaron asked, "Are you saying you think I'm *Nethermairian*?"

"I watched closely as you read," Professor Glibb said. "And though it's impossible for me to confirm without further study the total accuracy of your translation, the few words that I was able to compare in the moment were indeed correct. And if you truly have had no prior study of the language, then the only explanation I can offer is that you are, at least in part, Nethermairian."

Aaron was looking intensely uncomfortable. "I—I don't know," he stammered. "My parents ... my mother ..." he looked up at the ceiling.

Alyen's heart ached for him. She knew he was struggling to find a way to address the issue without sacrificing his privacy or his mother's reputation. She wanted to help him, but it would have to be done carefully.

"Aaron," she cut in. "Didn't you tell me once that you didn't know much about your father's side of the family?"

Aaron met her steady, knowing gaze and the look he gave her was filled with gratitude. "Yes. That's true. I always assumed I was just Dúramairian, but I never learned much about my father's ancestors. I suppose it would be entirely possible that I carry Nethermairian blood on that side."

There was a long and thoughtful silence as everyone absorbed this information. Finally, King Stephan drew in a deep breath and looked up from contemplating the rug in front of him. "Thank you, Professor Glibb. Your expertise has been invaluable."

Professor Glibb nodded, recognizing the dismissal, but hesitated before leaving, his gaze lingering on the black book he'd left lying on the table before him.

"If I may, Your Majesty, what shall become of the book?"

King Stephan smiled. "We'll need to keep it on hand until the war is over. But should all come out well, I shall have it delivered to your study for further examination at that time."

Professor Glibb bowed again, tearing his eyes away from the book only at the last possible second as he turned to leave.

The room was silent again as the first rays of early sunlight began to filter through the windows. At last, the king sighed.

"Alyen, Aaron, it would seem that you're right. It appears that our true enemy is the Demon Lord Malscath, aided by Ylvain and a hoard of morkshai."

Alyen's heart soared. She had done it. She had discovered their enemy, and now they could prepare, fully informed, for the battle ahead. They might even have a chance of winning.

But the king's next words cut Alyen's jubilation short.

"Unfortunately, this knowledge does little to help us in the coming battle."

"What do you mean?" Alyen demanded. "Now that we know the truth, we can prepare!"

"Your father is right, Alyen," Mother Brenwyn said softly. "You're forgetting the prophecies. Only the one who wields the sword of Thor Lynn can hope to defeat Malscath. Ylvain and her morkshai are merely distractions—dangerous and deadly, but distractions, nonetheless. Aaron, it appears that all hope for Dúramair now lies with you."

All eyes turned to Aaron who was looking disconcerted.

"But—I don't know how to defeat Malscath," he said bluntly. "How's anyone supposed to fight a demon?" He looked to Nah'dar, but the assassin's face remained blank. The room remained shrouded in uncomfortable silence.

Finally, Queen Réanna spoke. "I suggest we continue as planned. We'll face the morkshai with the new machines and on foot as it becomes necessary. But above all, it's vital that Aaron be kept safe prior to meeting Malscath. If our enemies know of these prophecies, which I'm sure they do, then they'll be targeting Aaron from the onset—probably through Ylvain. I suggest he remain sequestered in the castle until the demon appears."

Aaron's face darkened. "Absolutely not. Second Slayer or not, I won't hide inside while everyone else is out risking their lives."

Before the queen could reply, Nah'dar spoke.

"Aaron is one of our only warriors capable of effectively battling a morkush, Your Majesty. I don't think we can afford to keep him out of the battle. However, I will appoint myself as his personal guard and will fight at his side until he is victorious, or I am struck down."

Aaron looked stunned. Alyen felt her eyebrows rise seemingly of their own accord.

"Nah'dar—you don't have to do that," said Aaron, looking rather embarrassed.

"It is always an honor to fight alongside a true warrior, and a duty to protect those with whom you are closely aligned," Nah'dar said quietly. "This is my final lesson for you. Your training is now complete."

32

GARRET'S DREAM

The forest was dark and shadowy, only faint slivers of moonlight threading through the tangle of bare winter branches above. Ylvain whispered the needed words and watched from behind a tree as Garret materialized before the Ancient Oak. He glanced about him, a confused look on his simple features, then gazed upward at the tree's massive trunk, stark and black in the gloom. Ylvain's mouth drew into a sneer—if Garret was even half as blind and trusting as she remembered, it would be far too easy to weave the web of lies she needed. She pulled the hood of her cloak closer about her face and stepped out into the moonlight. Garret took a step backward, alarm rising in his eyes.

"Who's there?" he asked, his voice unnaturally loud in the quiet forest.

"Do you need to ask?" Ylvain replied, pitching her voice low and velvety. "Or has it been too long?" She pulled back her hood to reveal her face, a face she knew was still proud and beautiful through the signs of age.

"Ylvain," Garret said flatly, the scars showing white on his hands as his fingers instinctively clenched.

Ylvain lowered her eyes, pulling her mouth into an expression of resignation. "You aren't happy to see me. I suppose I deserve as much."

"Why are you in my dream, Ylvain?" Garret's voice was icy and his eyes hard.

"To make amends." Ylvain stepped forward, the edge of her cloak slithering lightly over the forest floor. "The thought of what I did to you has haunted me for years. I was unspeakably cruel and a fool to turn my back on your love. I've come to beg your forgiveness."

"I don't believe you."

Ylvain filled her face with regret as she shook her head. "I don't blame you. But I've changed, Garret. I'm not the same arrogant, ambitious girl you knew. Life broke that girl long ago. Please give me a chance to regain your trust."

"Trust," Garret scoffed, his voice bitter. "Ylvain, you're marching on Castle Dúr with an army of morkshai as we speak. How can you possibly expect me to trust you?"

Ylvain continued to walk toward Garret, her eyes pleading as they held his. "You're right. I've no right to hope for anyone's trust, not after my past. But I'm afraid you've all greatly misunderstood. I don't want to make war. I want to come home! I made a mistake, and now the morkshai are tethered to me and I can't rid myself of them alone. I'm not coming to Castle Dúr to conquer. I'm coming to ask for help."

"You always did deal in lies, Ylvain," Garret said, a note

of sadness in his voice. "Even down to staging your own death."

"But you can understand that, can't you, Garret?" Ylvain pleaded, her dark eyes filling artfully with tears. "A mother's grief at losing her child, a marriage without love, and the judging eyes of all the village following me … It would drive anyone to seek out a new life. Surely you can see that. Your heart was always kind."

Garret's face was troubled, anger waging war with pity across his features. "What do you want from me, Ylvain?"

"A simple meeting is all I ask," Ylvain said quietly, now standing directly before him. "I know I'd never be received at the castle, at least not yet. But perhaps if I could explain to just one person—perhaps Alyen? We both know the secrets of the elemental world. It may be that she possesses the power I need to banish the darkness that binds me so that I can begin life anew. A second chance. Doesn't everyone deserve a second chance?"

"I still don't know what you want me to do about it."

"Just ask Alyen to meet with me. Here, by this oak. It's the only thing I ask of you. Except, well … speaking of second chances …" Ylvain lowered her eyes to the ground.

"What is it?"

Ylvain reached out hesitantly and took hold of Garret's hands, her fingers gently stroking the white scar lines. "Let me show you the person I've become, Garret. A better, kinder person. A person worthy of your love. Let me show you it's still not too late … for us."

Ylvain lifted her eyes, tearful and shining, and relished a surge of triumph as Garret gazed into their depths, blind to the shadows that moved behind them.

33

THE BATTLE

"But I should be helping. Maybe I can do something with the elementals?" Alyen protested, knowing she only half-meant the words.

"You, of all people, shouldn't be involved in the battle," Mother Brenwyn said firmly.

"Yes, you have Sanctity of Life to uphold," Lirianna agreed.

"You need to stay safely inside to help with the wounded afterward," Aaron added, his tone final. "Stay in your room and don't come out until it's finished. Don't worry—we'll keep you updated with the hearing stones."

Sanctity of Life. Healing the wounded. They were good excuses. But Alyen knew they weren't the real reasons everyone wanted her inside, away from the action. *They're afraid of me. Afraid of what I might do if I try to do anything.* She didn't blame them, and honestly a part of her was relieved.

She was terrified herself of ever trying to harness the elemental magic again.

"And what if we don't win?" she asked bluntly. "Where am I supposed to go then?"

The silence that followed was uncomfortable.

"I do not think it will matter where you are if we do not win," Nah'dar said at last. King Stephan glanced at him, his brow furrowed. He seemed to come to a decision and stood abruptly.

"Come with me, Alyen."

Alyen rose, curious, and followed her father through the castle and out a small door into the courtyard. "Where are we going?"

"Hush," the king said seriously. "What I'm about to show you is of the highest secrecy. Right now, we must act as if we are simply taking a leisurely stroll around the castle."

They walked together, circling the castle, talking of trivial things, Alyen's curiosity growing with each step. When they made a turn that brought them to one of the more remote ends of the castle, King Stephan glanced upward, confirming they were not being watched by the guard, and suddenly pulled Alyen close to the castle wall underneath an overhanging gargoyle.

He placed his hand on the wall, feeling under one partic-ular stone and nodded in satisfaction.

"Place your hand here, Alyen, and tell me what you feel."

Alyen obeyed, feeling beneath the rough stone, realizing now that it jutted out slightly farther than those around it. She felt nothing unusual until suddenly her fingers felt the smooth, cold touch of metal. She looked up at her father in surprise.

"An iron bar?"

The king nodded. "Pull it to the left."

Alyen tugged at the iron, which grudgingly shifted until she heard a soft *click*. All at once, the wall before Alyen was moving, swinging inward to reveal a dark tunnel, wide and high, leading back into the castle.

Alyen looked at her father in awe. "How does that work?"

"The architect of Castle Dúr was a gifted master who invented a way to make the door open itself with weights and wheels and the like. This passage was designed as a secret escape route for the royal family in times of great danger or war. The secret has been passed down from ruler to ruler for hundreds of years. Your mother and I, and now you, are the only ones who know it exists."

"But it just leads back into the castle."

"That's only how it appears from here. If you enter, you will see that it soon tilts downward, deep underground, where it turns and leads under the moat and out beneath the moor. If you follow it to the end, it resurfaces and comes out in a cave in the Royal Wood."

Realization dawned slowly in Alyen's mind. "That's why the Royal Wood is forbidden, isn't it?"

The king smiled. "Our ancestors wanted to keep anyone from stumbling upon the tunnel, so the Wood was banned. Faerie stories about stolen children and enchanted waters were invented and spread to discourage outlaws and adventurers."

The king sighed then and looked at Alyen, his expression grave. Alyen suddenly noticed the tired lines around his eyes, and his hair seemed far more gray.

"Alyen, if we don't win the battle—if it begins to seem that all is lost—I want you to take Lusa and escape with her through this tunnel. Once you get out, ride hard to the coast and make for the Eastern Kingdoms. If you can't get to Lusa, you must go on foot and travel as quickly as you can."

"But what about everyone else?" Alyen asked. "What about Mother Brenwyn, Lirianna, Aaron, Garret—what about you and Mother?"

King Stephan smiled sadly. "We can't know what the future holds, Alyen. But now you know what to do, should the worst happen. Keep the secret safe—not even Aaron and Lirianna may know. Now shift the lever back to the right to close the door. We mustn't linger here any longer."

Several tense days passed as Castle Dúr awaited the arrival of Ylvain's army. Alyen was distracted at first, busily helping the last of the refugees to make their way south, but eventually they had all gone, there was no one left to help, and all she could do was stalk the battlements, her eyes fixed northward, waiting.

At last, one morning she saw it. At first just a dark smudge against the cold horizon, but then it grew until a black swarm seemed to carpet the moor, creeping ever closer to the castle. She could hear the guards sounding the alarm, but she reached beneath her dress to clasp her hearing stone anyway.

"She's here."

"Finally," Aaron said aloud behind her, and Alyen turned in surprise. "I don't think I could keep up this waiting much longer."

Alyen turned back to the moor, her brow furrowed, and Aaron came to stand behind her. His arms circled around her waist, his chin resting against her hair. *I shouldn't let him do this,*

Alyen thought. *I shouldn't lead him on. It's cruel.* But she made no move to stop him and even leaned back slightly into his embrace. They watched in silence as the black army slowly inched its way toward the castle.

"How long will it take them to get here?" Alyen finally asked.

"A day at least," Aaron replied in her ear. "An army that size can't move very fast."

"So, the battle will begin tomorrow?"

"Yes."

"I don't want to stay inside, not knowing what's happening."

"I know. But the castle's the safest place for you. And protecting you and Lirianna is my highest priority."

"I'm not sure it should be," Alyen said. "I think defeating Malscath may be more important at this point."

Aaron didn't reply.

"Are you scared?" she asked.

"Yes. I think I would be less scared if I knew for certain the task was meant for me."

"Do you really still doubt you're the Second Slayer?"

"Honestly? I'm not sure. I've been thinking—do you remember the last lines of Thor Lynn that Lirianna played for us at Midwinter?"

Alyen shook her head.

"It says that the Second Slayer will be the one to complete Thor Lynn's work when darkness comes again. Everyone always thought it meant something about the dragons, but I think what it really meant was the Second Slayer would be the one to defeat Malscath once and for all."

"Well, we know Malscath's coming, and you have Scala. What more proof do you need? Who else could it be?"

"There were two of us in the tomb, Alyen, and it wasn't me who took Scala from the wall."

"It's not me, Aaron. Be serious."

"Well, why not?"

"For one, I can't touch Scala without being burned. For two, I can't fight. For three, even if I could, there's the Sanctity of Life law." The words stuck in Alyen's throat as she said them, but she swallowed the lump of guilt and continued. "That likely wouldn't apply to Malscath, but still, I wouldn't want to risk losing the elementals' trust. Four, the prophecy says the Second Slayer is the one who *claims* the sword, not the one who takes it from the wall. As I recall, *you're* the one who asked the dragons for permission to carry it; therefore, you claimed it. And finally, the prophecy also says the Second Slayer can't claim Scala by himself, which explains why I had to be there to assist *you*—the Second Slayer."

"That's a pretty convincing argument," Aaron said, and she felt his face twist into one of his crooked half-smiles. He sighed, and she felt his shoulders slump slightly.

"What's wrong?"

Aaron hesitated. "I think they knew," he finally said softly.

"Who knew what?"

"Morten and Rowenna. I think they knew—or at least suspected—that they were going to die."

Alyen was surprised and didn't reply for a moment. "Why do you think that?"

"Just a feeling," Aaron replied vaguely, then added quickly. "I mean, they were studying the prophecy for years. *Two suns shall set to leave but one*—they must have had some theories as to what it meant. And maybe that's why Rowenna was in such a hurry to train you. She knew she didn't have much time."

"I suppose," Alyen agreed. "What made you think of this now?"

"I don't know. Probably just the battle coming up." Alyen could tell there was something he wasn't saying.

"I'm not sure death is the best thing to be thinking about before a battle," she offered, trying to sound light.

Aaron chuckled. "Probably not. But it can't really be helped." He paused, then said seriously, "What do you think it feels like—knowing you're going to die."

There was a note in his voice that Alyen didn't like.

"You're not going to die, Aaron," she said, sounding more forceful than she had intended.

"But if I did …" He gently turned Alyen around to face him, searching her eyes with his hazel ones.

"Aaron, stop it," Alyen interrupted, alarmed. "You shouldn't be thinking this way."

"There are things I'd want you to know. Things I want to say."

"Aaron!" Alyen said firmly, gazing fiercely into his eyes. "You can tell me tomorrow. After the battle. Once we've won."

Aaron's hands were gripping her arms, his face so close. *Is he going to kiss me again? I shouldn't want him to kiss me.*

For a moment Alyen thought he would. But then Aaron's shoulders sank again, and the urgency went out of his eyes. He smiled his half-smile, but it didn't keep him from looking sad.

"You're right. Tomorrow. Once we've won," he said. He leaned forward and his lips brushed her brow between her eyes. Then before Alyen could reply, he had turned away and disappeared back into the castle.

Alyen remained on the battlements for most of the day. She watched as the black army swarmed ever closer over the moor. She saw the moat turn an ugly black as oil was poured into it. If the new machines failed to stop the morkshai, the oil would be ignited, forming a wall of fire around the castle. *I should have offered to make a protective circle*, Alyen thought, knowing no one would want her to, and that she lacked the courage to try.

As the day wore on and a cold wind picked up, Alyen retreated indoors, pacing the halls. She watched through the windows as the war machines were rolled into position along the top of the outer wall. Long wooden spears were coated with oil and stockpiled at every station, waiting to be loaded, lit, and shot into the hearts of the oncoming hoard.

It was a restless night. As the army approached, the shrieks of the morkshai could be heard echoing across the moor through the darkness—a chilling, ghostly sound. Alyen cowered beneath her quilts, sleepless as the hours passed, remembering all too well the night in the forest when she had come face-to-face with just one of the monsters. She trembled, sick to her stomach, thinking of all the knights, the guards, Nah'dar, and mostly of Aaron, all of whom would be facing Ylvain's entire swarm once morning came. She clutched her hearing stone tightly in her fist as the darkness and the shrieking pressed around her, but she sent out no thoughts to her friends. Better to let them sleep if they could.

The day of the battle dawned cold and dry, the sky white

over the frozen gray moor. Alyen sat up in her bed, her fist still wrapped around her hearing stone. The shrieking of the morkshai was louder now, clear even through the castle's thick stone walls.

"They're nearly here," Aaron's voice finally sounded in Alyen's mind. *"They should be within range of the machines in half an hour or so."*

"Can you see any sign of Ylvain? Or Malscath?" Nah'dar's voice asked.

"No, not at all. Mother Brenwyn, Lirianna, are you both ready?" Aaron asked.

"Yes, we'll start weaving now," came Mother Brenwyn's voice.

"We'll try to find them and let you know if we see anything," Lirianna promised.

"And Alyen?" Aaron asked.

"Don't worry," Alyen assured him. *"I'm here in my room."*

But she had no intention of staying there.

She would have to act quickly. She was certain Bridget would appear at any minute, sent by her parents to keep her company—and to ensure she didn't leave. Alyen snatched up a piece of parchment and hastily scribbled a message.

> *Bridget —*
> *Mother Brenwyn and Lirianna have asked for my help, so I've gone to their rooms. I don't know how long it will take, so will you please begin preparing bandages? Just rip these old linens into strips. I'll be back to help soon.*

Alyen reached under her bed and began tugging out a stack of bed linens she had gathered over the course of the week. She piled them in a heap on her bed and set the note on top. Bridget would never dare interrupt Mother Brenwyn to verify Alyen's story, and hopefully the bandages would keep her occupied, away from anyone who might ask about Alyen's whereabouts.

It took longer to reach the battlements than usual, as she took a route she knew would be little traveled. After a quick glance to make sure none of the guards were posted nearby, she crept to the edge of the wall and cautiously peered over.

The sight below was terrifying. The morkshai had arrived and were charging across the moor toward the castle, their claws tearing at the earth, their snake heads writhing and shrieking to the sky. They moved as one body, undulating over the landscape, though Alyen could see no sign of Ylvain, or of any leader to control them at all. Glancing along the outer wall, Alyen saw Aaron stationed front and center at his machine atop the drawbridge, Nah'dar at his side. She jumped as she felt her hearing stone burn and quickly fished it from beneath her gown.

"It's starting," Aaron's voice said tightly.

"Be careful," Alyen replied, not daring to say more lest she give away her location.

Aaron raised an arm with a shout and the machines were loaded and aimed at the charging monsters. At another signal from Aaron, the spears were ignited; at his cry, they were launched into the air.

It wasn't completely unsuccessful. A few of the flaming spears found their marks, plunging deep into black, scaly flesh, and a handful of morkshai screamed as they fell to the ground as their hearts burned. But even Alyen could tell it was not enough. The machines were quickly loaded and fired again and again, each time felling a few more monsters, but the numbers of the black army were too great, and the majority reached the edge of the moat unscathed.

Aaron shouted again and torches were hurled into the moat, igniting the oil that glistened in greasy patches along the surface. As the flames erupted from the water, the hoard screamed and recoiled, giving the machines time to claim more victims. For a moment, Alyen grasped at a wild hope that the morkshai would simply stand at the water's edge, paralyzed with fear as the machines picked them off one by one. But as the battle raged on, the oil began to deplete, and the wall of fire began to flicker and fade. Gaping holes appeared and the morkshai, sensing the weakness, began to plunge into the moat, at first only a few but then more and more followed until the water was filled with writhing black snake heads making for the outer wall. Alyen gasped as the leading monsters began to scale the wall, claws digging into the wood of the drawbridge and finding footing among the cracks and crevasses of the stonework. They were clumsy and awkward, ill-suited for climbing, but Alyen could see that it was only a matter of time before they reached the top and began pouring over the wall into the courtyard.

And where is Ylvain? Alyen thought in a panic. Her eyes scanned through the hoard and out to the moor beyond, but she could see no sign of the sorceress or of the demon that supposedly accompanied her. Had they perhaps not come?

In the courtyard, foot soldiers scrambled into position along the inside of the wall and the cavalry hastily mounted their horses. Along the top of the wall, torches were being lit and passed around and swords were being drawn, the machines abandoned at such close range. *It's no use*, Alyen realized. *These soldiers aren't prepared for this. Aaron barely defeated one morkush and he's probably the best warrior in the kingdom.*

Then suddenly, Lirianna's voice rang out in Alyen's head.

"I've found Ylvain! She's nearby—somewhere with lots of trees."

"That's probably the Royal Wood," Alyen suggested.

"Can you tell what she's doing? Is anyone with her?" Aaron asked, his voice a shout as Alyen watched him racing along the wall preparing for combat.

"I think she's alone. She was saying something, but I couldn't see anyone else. I'm not sure what she's doing."

"In that case, I'm going to have to deal with her later," Aaron said. *"I can't leave the castle now, and we still don't know where Malscath is."*

"I'll keep looking," Lirianna said.

Alyen stood very still, knowing she had seconds to make a choice. She knew she suspected what the others had failed to consider: if Ylvain was speaking alone in the Royal Wood, it was likely in the singing speech which would mean that soon the morkshai would be joined by some "natural" disaster, caused by Ylvain's misuse of elemental magic. Alyen would be the only one able to see what was truly happening. And she was the only one who had a chance of stopping it before it happened.

Clenching her hands into fists to stop their trembling, Alyen turned from the battlements and raced back into the castle. She wove swiftly through the corridors, doubling her efforts to remain unseen. Eventually she came to a small service door leading outside. She carefully cracked it open, scanning the courtyard beyond.

She needed to get to the stable. Looking in its direction, she saw Garret hastening among the cavalry, double checking saddles and straps, helping the knights to mount. He would be busy for several minutes, she guessed—just long enough for her to run in the back of the stable and sneak Lusa out.

Alyen ducked low to the ground and dashed across the courtyard. She burst into the stable and threw herself behind a stack of hay bales, breathing heavily and listening for sounds of pursuit. When she was sure no one was coming to stop her, she crept from her hiding place, grabbed a saddle blanket and a harness, and stole softly into Lusa's stall.

Lusa snorted and stamped her foot when she saw Alyen, her ears back and her eyes rolling at the sound of the mork-shai's screaming. Alyen hushed her, patting her soft neck as she threw the blanket over her back and fastened the harness to her head.

"Come on, girl," she whispered as she led her horse out of the stall and toward the back doors of the stable.

"She said she'd be waiting for you by the Ancient Oak."

Alyen started and whirled around to find Garret standing in the middle of the stable, a pair of damaged reins hanging from one hand. Alyen was suddenly wary.

"You've known all along where Ylvain is?"

Garret nodded.

"And you didn't say anything?"

"I know, I promised I would. But I feared it was a trap. I fear it still. And I've been tricked by her before." Garret was shaking his head, frowning at the reins in his hands.

"If you think it's a trap, why aren't you stopping me?"

Garret's voice was quiet. "Because she must be defeated. And you're the only one who can do it, cailínna."

He crossed the stable to stand in front of Alyen. He placed his hands gently on her shoulders and looked earnestly into her eyes.

"Rowenna was my sister and my best friend in the world," he said hoarsely. "Ylvain's killed her, and no amount of childhood love can overlook that. I tell you about the Ancient Oak so you can be warned of her trap. Do you believe me?"

Alyen paused only a moment before nodding sincerely. "Yes, of course I do."

"You must be careful. And you must win. I'll want to see Lusa back by sunset."

Alyen gave him a weak smile and nodded. Garret patted her shoulder and released her, and Alyen clucked softly to Lusa and turned to exit the stable.

"Alyen," Garret said. She paused to look back. "You will remember Sanctity of Life, won't you? It's just—she wasn't always evil. Not when she was a girl."

Alyen looked into his face etched with sorrow and nodded again. "I will," she promised. She led Lusa out of the stable, leaving Garret with the broken reins still hanging from his hand.

SANCTITY OF LIFE

It took some coaxing to convince the trembling Lusa to enter the tunnel at the far side of the castle, but eventually her trust in Alyen won out over her fear of the enclosed space and the screaming of the morkshai. Alyen lifted a torch she had snatched and felt along the back of the door until her fingers found the small iron bar once more. She shoved it to the side and the door swung closed, leaving them in the darkness lit only by Alyen's flickering torch.

She was about to set off down the tunnel, but a sudden thought made her halt in her tracks. Reluctantly, she pulled her hearing stone out from under her gown and after a moment's hesitation, she lifted its chain over her head, cradling the pendant in her palm.

She didn't have a plan, she realized. Even if she had never made the gorge, even if she was fearless and brave and completely confident in her abilities, even if she'd had a lifetime more to practice and train—she was going to confront Ylvain with no plan.

It wasn't the best idea. But she had no time, and therefore no choice.

I have to be realistic about this, she thought, though she shivered at the prospect of what she was considering. *I have to be responsible this time.*

If Alyen failed and Ylvain defeated her … Being killed would be bad enough. But if she was *captured*, she couldn't have her hearing stone with her, ready to be claimed by Ylvain, who could then hear everything Aaron and Lirianna and all the others were saying. Leaving it meant that she would have no backup to her lack of plan—no method to call for help or to hear what was happening at Castle Dúr. She would be utterly alone. But it was the way it must be.

Alyen tore a strip of cloth from the hem of her gown, wrapped the stone in a tight bundle, and set it gently against the wall of the tunnel. *I'll come back for it as soon as I'm done*, she thought. Trying not to think of the alternatives, she gripped Lusa's harness tightly and began to lead her down the dark tunnel beneath the moor.

Alyen couldn't say how long the journey took. Time meant nothing within the quiet of the earth, with the darkness pressing around her. Eventually she realized she could no longer hear the faint echo of the morkshai, though Lusa remained skittish and fretful. On and on, one step after another, she trudged forward, trying to formulate some sort of strategy but succeeding only in coming up hard against the familiar wall of fear and guilt as she imagined calling on the elementals to help her.

At last, Alyen felt the ground beneath her begin to tilt

upward and gradually a faint gray light could be seen ahead. Despite her fear, she quickened her pace, eager to emerge above ground and gulp the fresh forest air. Suddenly, the tunnel veered sharply to the right, and rounding the corner Alyen found herself in the back of a large cave. She dropped her torch in a puddle of water and led Lusa out of the entrance; the horse snorted and tossed her head in relief. Alyen tied her harness to a branch and patted her neck.

"Stay here, girl," she whispered. "I'll be back for you soon."

She hoped it was true.

It took a minute for Alyen to orient herself, but she quickly got her bearings and turned toward the center of the Royal Wood. *This is probably stupid*, she thought. *If Ylvain told Garret she would be at the Ancient Oak, I'll walk right into her trap if I go there.* But what other option was there? It would be useless to wander aimlessly through the forest looking for Ylvain and, trap or not, at least she would likely find her if she went to the oak. Alyen took a shaky breath and headed for the center of the wood.

It had been a long time since she had been in the Royal Wood. Now she could feel that the forest was filled with elemental magic, but there was something different about the tingle in the air and it filled her with foreboding. The feeling grew worse as she approached the center of the forest, and gradually Alyen began to suspect that it was not being caused solely by her feelings of guilt and fear. There was something familiar about the way the crackle in the air was changing, the way the forest around her felt hostile and sick. As the Ancient Oak came into view, Alyen realized what it was.

Darklings. Ylvain's poisoned the Royal Wood, and I'm surrounded by darklings.

She could see them now, dozens of them, gray and sickly and evil, peering at her from between the branches of the surrounding trees and bushes. Alyen's breath quickened, and she gulped, her mind reaching for the singing speech, knowing she at least had to call on whichever elementals hadn't yet been corrupted to defend her from the darklings.

"Elves who care for branch and limb ..."

She could feel the distant tingle of pure magic, but it was so far away, hidden deep within the trees.

"Sylphs who flit on waves of air ..."

She couldn't reach them; the darklings were too many, their corrupt magic too distracting. And she was so afraid. She gasped, straining, sweat trickling down her face.

"Undines flashing in the dew ... Sprites who ... Elves..."

That's when she heard the laughter—a low, mirthless chuckle that sent the trees shivering. A woman stepped out from behind the Ancient Oak, robed and cloaked in black, her face terrible, beautiful, and proud.

"Oh, Alyen," Ylvain said, her voice dripping with contempt. "Just stop trying. You needn't make yourself look so pathetic."

Alyen's eyes darted back and forth between Ylvain and the darklings half hidden in the shadows. The attack she expected never came, and Ylvain spoke again.

"Relax, Princess, I'm not going to waste my time attacking you. Honestly, you take yourself so seriously for such a weak, sorry excuse for a Keeper."

Alyen struggled to keep her face neutral, hiding her confusion and the small voice in her head that whispered, *She's right, you know. You* are *weak and pathetic—you could never be a good Keeper, not after what you've done.* With an effort, Alyen kept her voice level.

"If I'm so weak, why did you tell Garret to send me here?"

Ylvain laughed outright then, a cruel sound, and tossed her head, shaking her long dark hair free of her hood. Her eyes narrowed and she grinned wolfishly at Alyen. "You're here as bait, Princess."

All at once, she realized what Ylvain had planned. "Aaron," she stated. "You think Aaron's going to come for me."

"Oh, well done, you solved it!" Ylvain's voice dripped with sarcasm, but Alyen's mind was racing.

"He won't," she said over Ylvain's laughing. "He's defending Castle Dúr against your morkshai. He doesn't even know I'm here!"

"Yes, well, I've always been able to count on Garret's stupidity and the idiocy of men in love. I doubt either will let me down this time."

As if on cue, Aaron's voice rang through the Royal Wood. "Alyen! Alyen!"

"No!" Alyen cried as Ylvain crowed with glee. Without thinking, she sent her mind outward, strong and hard, pulling every bit of elemental magic to her, but before she could open her mouth to say a word, Ylvain shouted and flung her arms forward. As one, the darklings sprang into the clearing and fell upon Alyen, pinning her against a tree, their arms cold and thin but strong. Alyen's concentration was broken.

"Well, well," Ylvain said softly, her dark eyes calculating as they studied Alyen as if for the first time. "That's quite a bit of power hiding in you. A shame you let it all go to waste."

"It shouldn't be news to you," Alyen said through gritted teeth, straining her arms against the grip of the darklings. "I did stop you at Norhelm."

"And how did that feel?" Ylvain purred.

"It shouldn't have happened," Alyen said. "I killed innocent people."

"Yes, yes, how terrible, *Sanctity of Life* and all that. Rowenna's mark is all over you," Ylvain said bitterly. "But what I meant was, how did it feel when you *did it?*"

Alyen said nothing, her eyes hard and defiant under Ylvain's gaze. Aaron shouted again in the distance and Ylvain smiled.

"It felt good, didn't it? You liked the feel of the power, didn't you? The way it fills you, makes you more than you are —the heady rush, knowing that you are the sky, the stars, the earth, the trees, knowing that you alone are *invincible.*"

I mustn't listen! Alyen thought desperately, realizing where Ylvain's speech was leading. *I mustn't believe her!*

"That's really what's been bothering you, isn't it?" Ylvain continued as she slowly stepped closer to Alyen. "That's what's at the bottom of your guilt: the fact that you *liked* it. That you *enjoyed* the act that killed all those people. And you won't admit it even to yourself because if that's true, then maybe that makes you just … like … *me.*"

Ylvain's face was directly in front of Alyen's now, her smile wicked and triumphant as she saw the despair that crept into Alyen's eyes. And for one terrible moment, Alyen realized she had lost. Ylvain would kill her, then Aaron; Castle Dúr would fall along with everyone she loved, and Malscath, wherever he was, would destroy Dúramair forever.

"Stand down, Ylvain," Aaron's voice rang out. Alyen

raised her eyes to see him standing at the edge of the clearing, Scala drawn and leveled at Ylvain's heart. Ylvain turned calmly, satisfaction settling over her face. With a flick of her hand the darklings hissed and tightened their grip, two of them stretching their sickly hands to clutch at Alyen's throat.

"Let's not be too hasty, young Slayer," Ylvain said softly. "Not if you value the life of your princess."

"Alyen, come behind me," Aaron instructed. Alyen looked at him incredulously, then realization struck. *He can't see the darklings. He thinks I'm just standing here.*

But before she could say anything, Ylvain flicked her hand once more and the darklings tightened their grip on Alyen's throat. Alyen coughed and gagged, gasping for air. She saw the alarm rise in Aaron's eyes as he grasped the situation.

"So, you see how it is, Slayer. I have your love's life in my hands, and the only way you can save her is by doing exactly as I say. One false move and she dies before your eyes—but we both know it won't come to that, don't we? No, you would never risk Alyen's safety, even if you weren't hopelessly in love with her. You're far too noble for that. Instead, you're going to place your sword slowly on the ground and step away from it with your hands where I can see them. *Now.*"

For a moment Aaron hesitated, frozen where he stood. Ylvain's eyes narrowed and Alyen made a choking sound as the darkling's grip tightened around her neck once more. *Don't do it*, Alyen thought desperately. *Don't give in!* But to her dismay, Aaron crouched down slowly, placing Scala gently on the forest floor, and rose again, his hands stretched in front of him. He began to move away from the sword, but in an instant the darklings released Alyen and hurled themselves at him. Aaron gave a shout as the unseen force hit him, pinning him against a tree, his arms straining in vain against their grip. Alyen lurched forward, gasping for air, and stumbled, landing hard on the ground. She looked up to see Ylvain pulling a second sword out from beneath the folds of her robes. Aaron's face went white with rage.

"You recognize this sword, don't you?" Ylvain taunted with a smile. "Morten's choicest weapon upon which he swore to protect the kingdom and all its people from evil. How ironic that the last hope for Dúramair will perish on its blade."

Aaron struggled again against his captors and Ylvain threw her head back with laughter.

"I must say, Aaron, you come as a disappointment. Morten at least put up a good fight when they came for him. Not that it did any good in the end, but still, at least he tried. I'm afraid this will be over far too quickly—and to think we considered you our greatest threat. Now, any last words for your true love?"

For a second, Aaron's eyes met Alyen's, his expression filled with anger and helplessness and regret. He opened his mouth to speak, but suddenly Ylvain moved, Morten's blade arcing over her head, her face wild with triumph as she moved in for her victory.

"She loved you, Ylvain!" Alyen screamed. Ylvain froze, Morten's sword still poised in the air. For a moment Alyen was paralyzed. She hadn't worked this through at all—hadn't realized she *thought* the words, let alone planned to say them. But her distraction was the only thing keeping Aaron alive, so she stood and began talking once more as she slowly came around to face Ylvain.

"Rowenna loved you. I could tell every time she talked

about you. She was never angry, never hated you—she was just sad."

Alyen could see Ylvain's face now. It was blank, but her eyes held something that looked like confusion, as if she was listening to something inside or far away.

"She called you her best friend. She told us how she had tried to teach you the magic you wanted. She told us how she tried to save your baby. She felt guilty about not helping you more."

Alyen stopped walking not far from where Scala lay on the ground. Ylvain was staring at her now with a look Alyen couldn't decipher. She didn't dare come any closer but continued to speak.

"If Rowenna loved you, that means there was something in you to love. And it's probably still there. It's not too late to stop this. It's not too late to make a different choice."

It was over in seconds. For the rest of her life, Alyen would never know if Ylvain had meant to follow through with her dark intent, or if she was lowering her defenses to stand down. She registered only the flash in Ylvain's eyes and the smallest movement of the arm that still held Morten's sword aloft. But when Alyen saw that movement, she acted on instinct without thought or hesitation.

She lunged to the side, her hands closing around Scala's hilt. The metal burned in her hands, but she barely felt them as she twisted and plunged the blade deep into the sorceress's breast. Easily it slid through skin, muscle, and bone until Alyen was standing inches from Ylvain's shocked face, their eyes locking, her hands still clutching the hilt protruding from Ylvain's heart. For a frozen moment, Ylvain stared at Alyen, mouth open, her face registering disbelief, then despair. Her mouth moved as if she would say something, but a gush of blood choked the words back. She slumped backward, sliding off the crimson blade and crumpling to the forest floor. Her eyes fixed on Alyen once more before it seemed a shadow left them; they stared blankly, seeing no more.

In shock, Alyen dropped Scala to the ground, unable to look away from Ylvain's frozen face. Dimly she registered that Aaron was at her side—he was saying something, words she could not understand. *The darklings must have gone*, she thought numbly. She glanced about distractedly, looking for any sign of them. There was none, and it should have been a relief, yet something was bothering her; something was still amiss. When the realization came, it hit her stomach like ice. Not only was there no sign of the darklings, there was no sign of *any* elementals. No tree elves, no sprites, not a single sylph drifting on a breeze. Alyen couldn't feel even the smallest tingle of the magic that had filled the forest just minutes before. *I've lost them*, she realized. *I'll never see them again.*

Her legs gave way, and she sank to the ground, her face in her hands, trembling as the truth settled in beneath the shock. In the air around her, fireflies began to wink and glow, mending the Balance where she had destroyed it with an act that had closed the elemental world to her forever.

35

THE SECOND SLAYER

lyen couldn't remember how they got back to Castle Dúr. She didn't remember leaving the clearing by the Ancient Oak or retrieving Lusa from the entrance of the secret cave. At some point she realized she was riding hard across the moor on Soran, Aaron's arm hooked around her waist; Lusa charged along at their side, her harness held firmly in Aaron's grip. Above them, storm clouds were gathering and rumbling, and the wind stirred restlessly across the moor. Aaron slowed to a canter as they approached Castle Dúr and Alyen gazed around at the empty landscape with a detached confusion.

"Where are the morkshai?" she asked flatly, hearing the monsters' shrieks fill the air once more.

"They must all be inside the outer wall," Aaron replied bleakly.

"How are we going to get in?"

As if in answer, the drawbridge began to lower. Before it

364

had fully extended, soldiers leapt out the entrance into the moat, heedless of the oily surface that still burned with patches of flame.

"It doesn't look like it's going very well," Aaron commented.

"You weren't supposed to follow me," Alyen said distantly.

"You weren't supposed to leave," Aaron replied, though there was no accusation in his voice. He pulled Soran to a halt in front of the bridge and helped Alyen to dismount. He took her firmly by the hand and led her, half-running with Scala drawn, across the bridge and up the narrow stairway leading to the top of the outer wall.

The sight that met their eyes as they gazed down was bleak. Morkshai swarmed across the entire courtyard, which was littered with the bodies of fallen soldiers. Few warriors were left to keep up the fight, and those who did were falling quickly. Several morkshai were already attempting to smash in the castle windows or scale the walls. Alyen looked about for Nah'dar but she couldn't see him anywhere. The battle, it seemed, was lost.

Aaron swore, smashing his fist down on the top of the wall's battlements. He brandished Scala in the air as the wind whipped about them and roared in frustration.

"Malscath! *Malscath!* Stop cowering behind your monsters and fight me face-to-face!"

That won't work, Alyen thought. *It's too late.*

But a strange thing was taking place. As one, the morkshai abandoned their pursuits and amassed in the center of the courtyard. They pressed together more and more tightly, writhing and clawing at each other until they could pack themselves no closer together. Then, suddenly, their screaming stopped. A hush fell over the battlefield. From the midst of the morkshai, a black smoke rose, small tendrils expanding rapidly into a billowing plume. It grew and grew until it covered the entire hoard of monsters, then continued to rise upward, a great column of darkness reaching for the sky. Aaron and Alyen watched in silence as the storm clouds above seemed to descend to meet the rising smoke, lightning striking within its center as thunder roared, breaking the silence.

The smoke began to morph, pulling away from the storm and spreading out, taking shape, growing more hideous by the moment. Within seconds, the form of a demon rose from the courtyard, its horned head reaching the turrets, its clawed arms raking the air from the castle to the outer wall. Then the smoke began to thin and Alyen saw in horrible surprise that the demon was formed not of smoke, but from the hoard of morkshai itself: the monsters writhed and twined together to form the massive limbs and torso, crowned by a head whose eyes glowed with orange fire. The demon turned toward the outer wall where Aaron and Alyen stood, spread its arms, opened its mouth, and roared, a terrible sound magnified by the echoing screams of the morkshai.

Aaron and Alyen ducked down behind the battlements, knowing they had only moments before the outer wall would be torn apart. Alyen looked at Aaron and saw from the expression on his white face that he had not expected his challenge to be met, had not expected Malscath to appear at all once the castle was won. Aaron returned her gaze, panic in his eyes.

"Alyen—I don't know how …"

He stopped speaking mid-sentence and stared at her. Gradually the fear drained from his face and was replaced with a calm comprehension and something that resembled sadness.

"What is it?" Alyen asked.

"I know what to do," Aaron replied simply. "I know how to win. You were the key all along."

And before Alyen could ask what he meant, Aaron stood up, squaring his shoulders, his head held high. He faced the raging Malscath with Scala held before him, its tip pointed to the storming sky. Then he closed his eyes, and began to speak haltingly, to Alyen's shock, in the singing speech.

"To all the spirits who tend these lands: please … hear my words and lend your hands. I ask you clothe my blade in flame … and to my body do the same. Make of us a flaming light, to burn into the heart of night. Then open wide the earth below and so entomb our demon foe."

Alyen watched disbelieving as fire began to lick at Scala's tip, spreading quickly down the length of the blade, then down Aaron's arms, shoulders, back, engulfing his body until Alyen no longer saw a man and a sword but only a single blazing beacon standing atop the battlements. Then Aaron stepped to the very edge of the wall, and from within the flames Alyen heard his voice rise in a roar of agony and triumph. He launched himself into the air, just as he had done battling the morkush in Sheanen Crann, and plunged head-first, Scala outstretched into Malscath's heart.

The demon roared first in surprise, then fury, then anguish as the fire spread within his chest. Malscath began to collapse; the ground beneath his feet lurched and split, ripping a jagged scar in the earth across the courtyard. As if in slow motion, the demon swayed before toppling backward into the crevasse, still bellowing its howls of death. The earth swallowed

Malscath with a shudder, then the chasm shivered to a close, the ground resealing itself where it had torn apart.

There was screaming in the air, a human scream, and Alyen realized it was coming from her own throat as she watched the last of the earth close over the demon's grave. She did not register that the battle was won, that the morkshai were gone, or that Malscath had been slain. She knew only that she was a murderer, the elementals had abandoned her, and that Aaron was dead.

36
FERDINAND

A cold rain was falling, but Alyen didn't notice. Drops spattered against the stones of the castle wall, slowly forming puddles and tiny rivulets that ran down into the ugly black moat.

Lirianna knelt beside her, speaking urgently. Her face was wet—was it tears or the rain that ran down her cheeks? Now Lirianna was tugging at her arm, trying to force her to stand.

"What?" Alyen asked blankly.

"You have to come, Alyen," Lirianna sobbed. "He'll die for sure if you don't."

"Who?"

"Nah'dar! A morkush fanged him and the poison's spreading fast."

"No hope for him then," Alyen said. "He's going to die, too."

A sharp crack exploded below Alyen's right eye. For a

moment the haze that pressed about her lifted, and in surprise she realized that Lirianna had struck her.

"You hit me!" she accused.

"Alyen, you've got to pull yourself together. You have to come now!"

"Aaron's dead."

More tears poured down Lirianna's face. "I know. But he would still want you to try. Please, you're the only healer we have."

Slowly, Alyen stood. "I'm not a healer. I'm a murderer."

But Lirianna was pulling at Alyen's hand, leading her down from the wall and across the courtyard to the castle.

"They took him to the infirmary," she was saying. "I've already sent for your healing bag. I didn't know what else you'd need."

They entered the infirmary to find Alyen's parents, Mother Brenwyn, and strangely, Brother Hugh, all gathered around a bed where Nah'dar lay, his skin pale and waxy.

"What happened?" Alyen asked. She was dismayed to see the relief on the faces that turned toward her.

"Alyen, thank goodness," Mother Brenwyn said, hurrying over to lead her to the bedside. "Nah'dar was trying to protect Brother Hugh—who was fighting off a morkush through the kitchen window with a frying pan."

Brother Hugh's face was almost as pale as Nah'dar's. "I was defending my lady love," he said in a quavering voice.

A page ran into the room and placed Alyen's bag in her hands. Alyen looked at it in despair. "I can't do it," she whispered, feeling her palms sting where the burns from Scala pressed against the cloth.

"Don't be afraid, Alyen," Mother Brenwyn encouraged.

"It's a bad wound, but with the elementals, there may still be time."

"No," Alyen whispered, meeting Mother Brenwyn's eyes with her tearful ones. "I mean I *can't*. The elementals won't help me anymore because ... because I killed Ylvain."

There was an audible gasp and then silence in the room. Mother Brenwyn held Alyen's gaze for only a moment before she reached out and pressed the healing bag to Alyen's chest.

"It doesn't matter right now. Elementals or no, you're still a healer and Rowenna taught you well. You might be able to save him, and you might not, but the greater mistake would be not to try at all."

There was a sudden jerk from the bed and everyone's attention diverted to Nah'dar, who began to tremble violently. Alyen automatically stepped closer, seeing the wound clearly for the first time. Nah'dar's black robes were ripped open from the top to the waist, baring his chest where a gaping round hole lay just below his heart. From the edges of the wound, Alyen could see a black, inky substance slowly spreading outward under the skin—the morkush poison that would kill the assassin in minutes.

I don't know what to do for this, Alyen thought as she fumbled to open her bag. *Even if I* could *ask the elementals, I wouldn't know what to ask for.* She rummaged through the contents of her bag, searching for anything that might help, trying not to be distracted by Nah'dar's trembling and twitching on the bed beside her. She pulled out bandages, creams, and small jars of lavender, comfrey, and rose hips, plus all manner of dried leaves and bark, but nothing emerged that would stop the spreading poison.

Finally, she pulled out the last jar from her bag and examined the contents within. It was her first sample—the three small leaves of deadly nightshade. Alyen stared at the jar. What had Rowenna said about nightshade? *When a body shakes from an illness and is unable to stop, nightshade will relax the muscles and help the body to lie still.* And there was something else—something about poison. *…it has even been known to help in cases of poisoning from mushrooms.* That was it.

This was infinitely worse than mushrooms.

But the nightshade was all she had. She carefully opened the jar and tipped the three leaves into her mortar. She crushed them quickly, her hands trembling slightly, and mixed the powder into a healing cream. Smearing the ointment around the wound on Nah'dar's chest, she focused on covering any place where the poison coursed visibly beneath his skin. As she worked, Nah'dar's shaking began to subside; by the time she finished, he lay still once more. *Maybe there's already enough magic in the nightshade for it to work,* Alyen thought, hopeful despite herself. But Nah'dar's skin continued to gray, and Alyen soon saw threads of poison seeping past the edges of the cream she had applied.

"I don't think it's working," she said aloud, not meeting anyone's eyes.

No one replied.

Why Nah'dar? Alyen thought as tears began to spill down her cheeks. She had already failed at so much. Must she lose Nah'dar, too?

It was too much. All her energy drained away and, exhausted, past fear or remorse, Alyen surrendered to her last hope for Nah'dar. In a quiet voice, she began to speak.

"I know I have no right to ask for help with any healing task. And I know that I can never be the Keeper as was meant for me. But here before me lies a friend, and without your help his life will end. So, to any who can hear my plea, I beg you lend your gifts to me. For though my deeds you can't condone, I cannot heal this man alone."

"It is a strange request you make."

Alyen didn't recognize the voice. She lifted her head to see that a stranger had appeared in the room. He was both young and old, dressed all in green, a wreath of leaves crowning his dark hair. His black eyes were fathomless as they studied Alyen, his expression mildly curious.

"Faer Dinnán?" Alyen asked, hesitant and barely believing.

"The same."

"Can you save him?"

"Perhaps. But why?"

"What do you mean, why?"

The faerie king stepped closer, regarding Alyen keenly from across the bed. "This man is an assassin. He has caused suffering and ended countless lives before their time. To many in this world, his name is cursed and feared. Yet you wish him to be saved. Why?"

It was true, Alyen knew. Yet Nah'dar had also guarded her, taught Aaron to fight the morkshai, guided them, and helped to defend Castle Dúr. Now he lay dying after trying to protect a friend.

"He's a good man," she said helplessly.

"A good man," Faer Dinnán mused, studying Nah'dar's ashen features. He looked back at Alyen. "And you? Are you a good woman?"

Alyen faltered. "I ... I don't know."

There was silence in the room. Alyen felt Faer Dinnán's

eyes search her face while she watched the life fading from Nah'dar's body.

"Please," she whispered, tears standing in her eyes.

Finally, Faer Dinnán spoke again, his voice like the wind. "A fascinating mix of light and dark you are. How very curious."

He stretched his hand over the wound in Nah'dar's chest. For a moment, a green light glowed from his palm, then ever so slowly, the black streaks of poison began to recede.

Alyen let out the breath she had been holding, relief flooding her body. "Thank you," she said, looking up at Faer Dinnán's face once more. His expression was intrigued and slightly amused.

"I think we will meet again," he said, and suddenly he was gone.

A stunned silence filled the room, then Brother Hugh's voice piped up cheerfully.

"Well, it seems I'm not the only one who can see Ferdinand after all!"

It took a moment for Alyen to register what he had said, then she whirled around to face the monk. "Wait—what? Your invisible friend is *Faer Dinnán*?" she asked incredulously.

For the first time that Alyen could remember, Brother Hugh's expression showed annoyance. "Well yes, my dear, it's as I've been saying all along. *Fer-di-nand!*"

SECOND CHANCES

Castle Dúr had held, but not without sacrifice. Alyen surveyed the courtyard and the moor from the battlements as snow fell, seeming gray against the white sky. She watched as the remaining soldiers built a bonfire and dragged the bodies of the slain morkshai to burn. The warriors lost were more numerous; their fallen bodies were covered with ceremonial cloaks and laid in wagons to await burial with honor. Among them were the two guards who had escorted Alyen to Monstar. Captain Yoran lay still beneath Dúramair's banner of green and gold.

There was no cloak for Aaron. He was simply gone.

Death changes all. Those were the final words of the prophecy. The words that meant the most, and the ones Alyen had paid the least attention to. Fate had played a cruel trick, making them excited over some stupid prophecy only to leave their lives in ruin and death when it was fulfilled. *It's true*, she thought bitterly. *Death changes everything. It changed me when I killed Ylvain, and nothing will ever be the same again now that Aaron is dead.*

The sky darkened as the sun set, unseen behind the blanket of clouds. Alyen shrugged the snow from her shoulders and turned away from the wall. She had finished patching up what wounds she could, and now wanted nothing more than to go to sleep and sink into nothingness, to a place where she could not think or feel or hurt and remain there forever. But her duties for the day were still not done.

Nah'dar had been moved back to his room. Alyen entered quietly, hoping he was asleep. The assassin lay still on his back, but his eyes were open, reflecting the glow from the hearth near his bed.

"Nah'dar? Your bandages need to be changed. Can I come in?"

Nah'dar turned his head and studied her for a moment, then nodded silently. He watched quietly as Alyen helped him to sit up, unwound the stiff bandages and examined the wound near his heart. It looked much better already, and Alyen delicately reapplied more healing cream before wrapping fresh strips of white cloth around his chest. Throughout the procedure she avoided Nah'dar's gaze, hoping to likewise avoid the conversation she dreaded.

But there was no escaping it.

"I understand it was you who slew Ylvain?"

Alyen nodded, still not meeting his eyes.

"I am sure you fought honorably."

"It doesn't feel honorable," Alyen said softly, blinking against the tears so quick to rise.

"It never does," Nah'dar replied.

There was a pause, then he continued.

"I am sorry about Aaron. He was a noble warrior."

Alyen didn't trust herself to speak, and so she merely nodded, redoubling her concentration on the bandages beneath her hands. Nah'dar let Alyen work in silence for a time before he spoke again.

"I also hear that you took great pains to save my life."

Alyen shrugged. "It was Faer Dinnán, not me."

"I prefer to think of it as you," Nah'dar said, and Alyen almost smiled, recalling his unease around magic.

"Everyone was … pleased that I did not die?" Nah'dar's voice was soft.

"Of course," Alyen said, fastening the last of the bandages and cleaning her hands on a towel.

"You all felt—concern?" Something in Nah'dar's tone made Alyen stop and finally meet his gaze. His eyes, usually so fierce, held a searching look she had not seen there before.

"Yes," Alyen replied, managing a watery smile as she helped him recline back on the bed. "We were all terribly concerned."

Nah'dar held her gaze a moment longer before he turned his head toward the ceiling above him and closed his eyes. "Thank you for saving my life."

"Try to get some rest," she replied and turned to leave. She had almost reached the door when Nah'dar's voice made her stop in her tracks.

"It was love."

"What?" Alyen asked, turning.

"What my mother lacked," Nah'dar whispered, his eyes still closed. "She did not love me."

His chest rose and fell as a great breath left him and his body seemed to sink into the bed in relief. Alyen was spared the need to reply as the assassin's deep, even breathing told her he had fallen asleep. She turned away, wondering if it was a trick of the firelight, or if the corners of Nah'dar's eyes were moist.

There was one more person Alyen needed to see before bed—one more person who deserved an explanation.

She entered the stables from the back again, lifting her lantern high to banish the gloom from the shadowy interior. She was relieved to see Lusa munching quietly on grain in her stall—someone had brought her in from the moor. Lusa whinnied softly as Alyen hung her lantern on a nail and leaned against the gate to stroke the horse's face.

"Oh, Lusa," she whispered brokenly. "I'm so sorry." It seemed easier to say it to the horse, who would still love her, than to the man who might not.

"Sorry for what, cailínna?" Garret's gentle voice asked.

"Garret," Alyen said, turning to see him standing in the doorway of the tack room. "I didn't mean to. I wanted to uphold Sanctity of Life and I never meant to … I didn't want to …" then his arms were around her, the strong arms that had always been there to catch or to comfort, arms that smelled of horses and leather and home. Alyen sobbed as Garret held her tight, shielding her from the world.

"There now," he said when her tears began to wear themselves out. "You've nothing to be sorry for. It seems to me you've lost more than anyone this day."

"How can you say that?" Alyen asked, her voice muffled against Garret's shirt. "I killed the woman you loved."

"The girl I loved was lost long ago, Alyen, and you'd nothing to do with it. If you ask me, there's no shame in defending the one you love against evil, no matter the outcome. If anything, it's I who should be asking *your* forgiveness."

"What do you mean?"

Garret opened his arms and looked at Alyen's tear-streaked face, his eyes troubled. "I told Aaron where to find you, cailínna. After you left, I dashed atop the outer wall before the morkshai came over and when I told him where you'd gone—I've never seen a man so enraged or fearful for a life that wasn't his own. He cut down three morkshai fighting to get through the gate to go after you. And if he hadn't gone —perhaps you never would have killed Ylvain. I fear it's my fault you've been broken."

Alyen was shaking her head. "No, Garret. If Aaron hadn't come, I would be dead, too. It's not your fault I'm broken—I broke myself at Norhelm, and now there's nothing left of me but weakness, fear, and guilt."

Garret's face was filled with compassion as he gave Alyen a half-smile. "I've known you a long time, Alyen. You're many things, but weak isn't one of them. It's no weakness to have low moments or make mistakes, and it's only human to be afraid—especially of ourselves. As for the guilt, let it go, cailínna. It can't change the past and brings only shadows to the future."

Night had fallen and the stables were dark save for the small circle of light from Alyen's lantern. Garret lifted it from the nail on Lusa's stall and placed it in Alyen's hand.

"Go to bed, cailínna. As dark as it seems now, things always look better in the morning."

The snow had stopped. Stars twinkled above as Alyen left the stables. She stopped to look up, wondering how they could be so unaltered when everything else had been so changed. It was hard to believe that only hours ago she'd been crossing the courtyard with Lusa, entering the tunnel to the Royal Wood …

Her hearing stone.

Alyen sighed. She had left it in the tunnel and forgotten to retrieve it. *I can't just leave it there*, she thought, though the idea of holding the cold stone, knowing Aaron's voice would never again warm it or sound in her head, sent pain stabbing through her chest once more. Wearily, she blew out her lantern to let the darkness hide her and turned her steps to circle the castle.

It took a few minutes of groping in the dark before her fist closed around the small bundle tucked against the wall of the tunnel. She stepped back outside and closed the secret door behind her, leaning against the wall beneath the watchful gargoyle. Slowly she unwound the long strip of cloth and felt the smooth stone settle between her palm and fingers.

"Lirianna?" she sent her thought out.

"Alyen?" Her friend's voice was sleepy; she'd waken her.

"I'm sorry, go back to sleep. I'm not sure what I was going to say anyway."

"Are you all right?"

"I think I will be. Eventually. Get some rest."

"Are you sure? We can talk—"

"No, I'm fine, really. I'll see you in the morning."

"All right."

Alyen dropped her hand still clasping the stone to her side and closed her eyes. For a moment she stood still and silent, feeling the cold of the winter air and the colder stones of the castle at her back.

Then her eyes flew open.

The stone had worked.

And if Aaron had died, it shouldn't have worked.

Her heart began to pound as her fingers scrambled over the hearing stone once more, nearly dropping it in her haste. She hadn't even thought before contacting Lirianna—but if the link between their stones still worked, then Aaron was alive.

"Aaron? Aaron!" her mind screamed. There was no answer, but Alyen was already racing across the grounds, making for the place where the earth had swallowed Aaron at his bidding. *"Aaron, hold on, I'm coming!"*

She screeched to a halt in front of the castle and dropped to her knees, clawing at the snow. She looked around wildly for help, knowing already that it would come too late. She pounded at the ground, barely holding back a howl of frustration.

"Isn't it a bit chilly for gardening?"

Alyen whirled at the sound of the voice and almost sobbed with relief. "Faer Dinnán! Oh, please, *please* open the ground again—Aaron is alive down there!"

Once again, Faer Dinnán's expression was curious and amused. "Another warrior you would save today? Yet you seem so much more desperate about this one."

"Please, I need to get him out *now!*"

"And what is so different about young Aaron? Is it that he is the Second Slayer? Surely a fine prize for any maid—even a princess."

"No, it's not that! Please—"

"Then why are you accosting the ground in such a panic?"

"Because … because I love him."

"Ah. Love. Human love." Faer Dinnán's expression changed, and he stepped closer to Alyen, his eyes intent. "And what if I should refuse to help you? What will you do to save Aaron then?"

Anger surged through Alyen and she almost snarled out her words. "I will do whatever I have to do! Whatever it takes!"

Faer Dinnán's eyes snapped. Alyen felt the wind rustle restlessly around her. "Will you, then? You'll do whatever you must, so long as your desires are fulfilled? Without my willing help, will you ensnare the elements by force? Create your own darklings and rip the earth apart by will alone? Will you do this, Alyen?"

Alyen paused, trembling with rage and cold and perhaps a bit of fear. "No. No, I won't do that. I'm not like Ylvain, if that's what you're asking."

The wind subsided and suddenly the air was very still and clear. Faer Dinnán was standing close to Alyen now, his black eyes searching hers with a strange look.

"This human love is strange to me," he mused. "To bind oneself to one person for all time—does it not seem limiting? Why give love to only one when you could share it with many?"

"It just doesn't work like that," Alyen said desperately. "Not if it's real love. Please, will you help or not?"

Faer Dinnán continued to study her face. Alyen had the sudden urge to squirm under his gaze.

"I admit, Alyen, that you intrigue me. Such power straining between joy and pain, love and fear, all in one person. What if I told you that I would save Aaron—if you agree to come with me and be my Faerie Queen?"

"What?"

Faer Dinnán lifted a hand to Alyen's cheek, and his fingers were like cool water on her skin. "I am curious about this human love. Leave Aaron and choose me instead."

"I can't. You can't choose who you love."

"Perhaps if I looked like your Slayer? I can, you know." Faer Dinnán shimmered and suddenly Aaron stood before her in place of the faerie king. For a second, Alyen felt her heart lurch and she wanted to throw her arms around him, but then she quickly stepped backward.

"No! You don't understand—it doesn't matter what he looks like. I love Aaron for his heart, for who he is inside. If the only way to save him is to be your queen, then I'll do it, but I will never love you, can never love you, not like that."

Alyen turned away from the illusion of Aaron but was stopped by Faer Dinnán's cool fingers on her wrist.

"You will lose him, Alyen."

Alyen didn't turn to look at him, but felt ice hit her stomach with his words.

"What?"

"Human love. It is finite. Whether it's today or tomorrow, some future battle, accident, or merely the progression of time leading you both to old age and death—you *will* lose him. Why begin something that can only end in the agony of loss?"

Alyen turned. Aaron's face was gone, and her eyes locked with those of the faerie king. "Because it's the thing that makes the living worthwhile.

For a moment time froze as Alyen held steady under Faer Dinnán's gaze. Then suddenly her wrist under his fingers burned. Alyen snatched her hand back; the cool winter air rushed over her skin, easing the sting. When she looked down to examine the burn, she saw the mark of a green leaf glowing faintly in the moonlight. "I think you will do well, Keeper of Scales," said Faer Dinnán, amusement once more dancing across his features. "Let us, together, rescue your Slayer, so your living may be worthwhile."

All at once, the courtyard was filled with elementals. Sylphs darted through the crackling winter air, whirling with undines through the drifts of snow; brown elves flitted through the branches of the bare trees. Alyen's heart swelled with joy, and she felt her own power rush through her veins stronger than it had ever done before. Faer Dinnán offered his hand; as Alyen clasped his fingers, she felt her power mesh with the enormity of his own. She felt herself grow, expanding outward in all directions—they were the earth, the oceans, every tree and every mountain, every pebble on the sandy shores. There was no need for singing speech as Alyen rode the wave of their combined magic, delving deep into the rock below, finding the cave and the small light within that was Aaron. Then gently, like a caress, they eased the earth open. Aaron was lifted up and out, set onto the snowy ground, and the earth closed again with a sigh as the magic subsided. Alyen felt her power retract within and realized that Faer Dinnán was gone—her fingers clutched empty air. *Thank you,* she thought silently, and the wind rustled in reply.

Aaron was stirring. Alyen hurried to his side, scanning his features for signs of injury, but he stood, and their eyes locked. Aaron reached out a hand and Alyen gasped to see its palm red and raw with burns from Scala; no wonder he hadn't been able to clasp his hearing stone. Aaron held his hand out until it hovered a hair's breadth from Alyen's heart as his other hand covered the space in front of his own, his head bowed in gratitude. Then suddenly his arms were around her, hands still held awkwardly away; her fingers wound themselves into his hair as her feet left the ground and she felt his breath warm on her neck in the winter chill. And high in the tree branches above, she heard the soft sounds of laughter.

EPILOGUE

"How did you know to use the singing speech?" Lirianna asked through a spoonful of pudding.

"Honestly it was mostly luck," Aaron replied, gesturing toward his pudding bowl with one heavily bandaged hand. "I was trying to think of what Thor Lynn could have done when *he* defeated Malscath, and I remembered the text in the book we found saying that he spoke words that cracked open the earth. Alyen, you were standing right there, and I just sort of realized that he must have used the singing speech."

"I wonder how he learned it," Alyen mused as she scooped pudding onto a spoon and held it toward Aaron's mouth.

"Who knows? Maybe Professor Glibb will figure it out."

"Yes, uncovering the rest of Thor Lynn's history is his life's mission now." Alyen chuckled. "No one will ever get that book away from him again."

"Whatever happened to Scala?" Lirianna asked.

"Not sure, but I think it burned up with Malscath," Aaron replied.

"That's too bad," Alyen said. "It was such a beautiful sword."

"Probably just as well," said Aaron, shaking his head. "Unbeatable weapons really shouldn't be floating around."

Lirianna pushed aside her spoon and sat back in her chair. The kitchens were cozy with warm fires in the hearths, stews bubbling, the scents of dried herbs and onions, and the sounds of Nellie and Brother Hugh cooking. "So, what happens now?"

"Well, now that Faer Dinnán's approved me, I guess I'll have to start working," Alyen said, licking the last of the pudding off her spoon. "Once spring comes, I think I'll head north and help the refugees resettle along the way."

"If you don't mind, I think I'll join you," Aaron said, his eyes twinkling. "I'm sure Ylvain's army left a trail of damage. I can help everyone rebuild. Besides, I need to get to Norhelm eventually. I think the dragons deserve to know what happened to Scala."

"And I'll be heading back to Monstar," Lirianna added. "But not until after Brother Hugh and Nellie's wedding. You won't leave before that, will you?"

Alyen smiled as Nellie's peal of laughter floated from the pantries, echoed by Brother Hugh's hearty chuckle. "Of course not. I wouldn't miss that for the world."

"Do you think Nah'dar will come, too?" Aaron joked.

"I think he has to," Alyen laughed. "He's taking Yoran's position as Captain of the Guard. I guess he doesn't want to be an assassin anymore."

"It's not fair, you know," Lirianna complained. "Everyone

has new things happening for them and I'm still just an apprentice."

"When do you become the Seer?" Aaron asked.

"Whenever a tapestry I've woven from a foresight vision has come to pass."

"But hasn't that happened?" Alyen asked, frowning. "I mean, you saw the morkshai and the battle here and everything."

Lirianna shook her head. "It's not quite the same. I saw the visions, but I never completed a tapestry. My loom is just filled with snippets of weaving, mostly of things that were happening in the present, or very near future. I can't be Seer until a *completed* tapestry from a foresight vision has proven true."

It sounded like a technicality to Alyen, but Aaron was looking thoughtful.

"Lirianna, I think that's happened," he said. "Didn't you weave the one that hung in Alyen's room at Monstar? The girl in the forest with the sword and the little lights everywhere?"

"Yes, but that hasn't—" Lirianna's posture went rigid, her eyes wide. "But that hasn't happened yet. Right? I mean— when did that happen?"

Realization bloomed on Alyen's face. "He's right, Lirianna! Just after I killed Ylvain in the Royal Wood, the fireflies surrounded me and started lighting up to heal the Balance. I can't believe I didn't realize …"

"It's true," confirmed Aaron. "I had to keep brushing them aside to get Alyen back on her feet. And Scala was on the ground beside her."

"That's it, then!" cried Lirianna, clapping. "I've woven a true foresight, Alyen's been accepted by Faer Dinnán, and

Aaron's the proven Second Slayer. We can all be initiated in the Ceremony of Three."

"But what about Mother Brenwyn?" Alyen asked.

"Oh, she'll still be the abbess of Monstar for as long as she wants," Lirianna said. "She just won't be the Seer anymore. Honestly, I think it might be a relief for her now that Morten and Rowenna are gone."

"Doesn't it seem a little strange, though, to think of us as Morten, Rowenna, and Mother Brenwyn?" Alyen mused. "I mean we're still so young ..."

Aaron smiled. "Listen, Alyen. I think Brother Hugh has the right of it." He nodded toward the pantries where Brother Hugh's voice could be heard booming out the latest version of his favorite song.

"Ooooooooooooh, I'm glad that we've the battle won,
A derry derry dally,
And the best of life is yet to come,
Rejoicing in the valley!"

THE
ANCIENT
OAK
BONUS SCENE
ANNE MOLLOVA

ACKNOWLEDGMENTS

In high school, I had a class in which we studied Wolfram von Eschenbach's *Parzival*, a medieval romance detailing the famous quest for the holy grail. The symbolic moral of this story, so we were taught, is that one cannot reach the grail alone: It is achieved only through companionship and empathy for others. This stuck with me, and I am reminded of it when I think of the many people who have contributed their talents, expertise, time, and support in the making of this book.

First and foremost, to my husband: You were the first to read my initial attempts at writing this story—none of which, thankfully, made it into the actual book. But, from the start, you've been a constant source of support with your unwavering love, your faith in me and my writing, and, most significantly, the gift of time. I love you.

To my children: Thank you for bringing me purpose, structure, and direction and for filling my life with unbelievable love.

To Mom and Dad: Thank you for giving me a childhood and an education that taught me to believe that the world holds magic, that creativity is a good and noble purpose, and that anything is possible. And thank you for being two of my earliest readers, reviewing the same book over and over through all its multiple drafts.

To my editor, Rebecca Heyman: This book is many, many times better than it would have been without your guidance, honesty, professionalism, and encouragement. Thank you for believing in my work often more than I did myself and making me stretch to reach the place you knew my book and I could go.

To my proofreader, Lucia Ferrara: Thank you for your supportive professionalism and great attention to the smallest details that made the final manuscript shine.

To the designers at Damonza.com: Thank you for creating the most perfect cover I could ever have imagined, even on my best day of imagining. It is utterly beautiful.

I also owe thanks to several people for inspiring the world and the characters in *Keeper of Scales*. In particular, I must thank Merlyn Querido for teaching me much of what I know of elementals and Donald Samson for introducing me to Brother Hugh.

To those who traded stories with me and pointed the way out of the sticky spots: Your guidance has never steered me wrong, and I am grateful for it. And, of course, I must thank the story itself for choosing me as its writer, and the characters for being my companions all this long time.

To my friends, family, colleagues, teachers—and sometimes complete strangers—who have given me love, support, and encouragement on this writing journey: Thank you from the bottom of my heart. You have no idea what your kindness has meant to me or how it bolstered my resolve.

Finally, to my readers: You make the journey come full

circle. Thank you for reading my words and sharing my world. I sincerely hope to hear from you all someday.

ABOUT THE AUTHOR

Anne Mollova is an author and musician living with her family in Pittsburgh, PA. Aside from writing, she loves being in nature, making music, eating chocolate, drinking tea, and creating things out of yarn and needles.

"Thank you for reading! Please consider leaving a brief review of *Keeper of Scales* on the site of your choice. Even a very brief one helps to ensure I can keep writing books for you. Please accept my gratitude in advance!"
—Anne Mollova

Connect with Anne
For books and updates visit: www.annemollova.com

Subscribe to Anne's newsletter at
www.annemollova.com/newsletter
and receive a free bonus scene.

goodreads.com/Anne_Mollova
bookbub.com/authors/anne-mollova

9 798985 760316